TWENTY-ONE NIGHTS IN PARIS

LEONIE MACK

First published in Great Britain in 2022 by Boldwood Books Ltd.

Copyright © Leonie Mack, 2022

Cover Design: Alice Moore Design

Cover Photography: Shutterstock

A CIP catalogue record for this book is available from the British Library.

Paperback ISBN 978-1-80415-835-7

Large Print ISBN 978-1-80415-831-9

Hardback ISBN 978-1-80415-830-2

Ebook ISBN 978-1-80415-828-9

Kindle ISBN 978-1-80415-829-6

Audio CD ISBN 978-1-80415-836-4

MP3 CD ISBN 978-1-80415-833-3

Digital audio download ISBN 978-1-80415-827-2

Boldwood Books Ltd
23 Bowerdean Street
London SW6 3TN
www.boldwoodbooks.com

*For my dear friend Sarah R – so many good times (including in Paris)
and many more to come*

1

'Why is he holding his own severed head?' Ren grimaced at the chipped stone sculpture propped up on her friend Malou's desk. It wasn't the usual beaux-art or haute couture found at a fine art auction, but the grisly sculpture was certainly antique.

When Malou didn't answer, Ren glanced around the cluttered office, tucked up under the slate roof of the stately stone building. If she pressed her face to the glass of the dormer window, Ren could make out the dreamy, slender pyramid of the Eiffel Tower past the chimneys and rooftops. On the floors below her were the extensive Paris galleries of Asquith-Lewis, the renowned auction house and fine art dealer. The tree-lined Avenue des Champs-Élysées paraded by around the corner, the grand axis of an illustrious city.

'He carried his head from Montmartre to the monastery in Saint-Denis,' Malou finally explained, carefully turning the statue and making notes as she examined it. Ren waited for her to elaborate, but she didn't.

'You'd think he'd put it in a bag or something,' Ren muttered, but Malou was deep in her work and Ren was only distracting her.

As she was now technically her best friend's employer, she probably shouldn't do that. 'Anyway, I'm not sure he'd look good on my mantlepiece,' she commented.

'I know, your precious Instagram aesthetic, courtesy of the Asquith-Lewis social media experts. But this one comes from the estate of Pierre Leclercq. That alone is enough to sell it.'

Ah, yes, the important work of winning estate auctions, which her grandmother excelled at, while joking that it must be because she was close to the grave herself. Not that Ren believed her. Grandmama was too tenacious to ever fall off her perch.

She caught sight of a fragment of stained glass in a wooden frame, propped up on the desk behind the ghastly statue. It showed three men with crowns and coloured robes on a vibrant blue background, surrounded by thick, irregular leading.

'This is perfect for an auction just before Christmas. Is that the Leclercq estate, too?'

'He was something of a collector of historic artefacts, it seems,' said Malou. 'Since *Game of Thrones* was such a hit, this stuff is sure to fit *someone's* aesthetic.'

'Are you going to have dinner with me tonight?' Ren asked. 'I'm heading home on Sunday. If I have to do without you in London these days, you can at least let me buy you dinner at the Ritz once.'

'Wouldn't it be awkward, though? I think Charlie's still mad at me for quitting.'

'Charlie... didn't come with me this trip.'

'Oh? He always comes with you.'

'There's a first time for everything,' Ren mumbled around the lump in her throat.

'Okay, I'll come if I get to return the favour next time,' Malou said with a grin. 'There's this fabulous Ivorian street food café around the corner from my apartment.'

'What... kind of hygiene certificate does a street food café need?'

'You are such a snob!' Malou said fondly. 'I have no idea why you're my friend.'

Ren mustered a smile. She knew Malou was joking, but friend-ships were a sore point since she'd been forced to realise how few she truly had. She hated to think how lonely she would feel, now, if Malou hadn't decided to befriend Ren five years ago simply because she *liked* her. 'You know very well why you're my friend,' Ren said defensively.

'Because you needed to make appointments to see your fiancé and I used to organise his diary!' Malou laughed. 'I was worried when I got this job and moved back to Paris that his new assistant would replace me.'

'No one will ever replace you,' Ren said earnestly. These days, she was dealing with Charlie's new assistant so she *didn't* have to see the man himself. 'If I wasn't so happy for you that you got this job, I would be annoyed that you left me.'

'I left Charlie. Never you.' Leaving Charlie might turn out to be another thing they had in common, Ren thought bitterly.

'But okay, let's go for dinner. Anywhere but the Ritz,' Malou insisted.

'What's wrong with the Ritz?'

'You never leave the Ritz. I'm not suggesting you suddenly get your hair braided or a tattoo, but there are nineteen other arrondissements of Paris you've never visited – or eighteen, since you obviously come here to the eighth occasionally.'

'I've been to the seventh, too.'

'Ah, of course. To visit the Tour Eiffel, I assume?'

'No, the Musée d'Orsay. I've never been up the Eiffel Tower.' Ren glanced at the window and stifled a sigh. 'I should leave you to it. Text me when you're done for the day and meet me at the Ritz.'

'I said *not* the Ritz!'

'Just meet me there.'

'You're hoping to lure me into l'Espadon!' Malou accused, not without grounds. L'Espadon *was* Ren's favourite of the restaurants at the Ritz.

'Just think: scallops, or pork medallions in jus – or lobster salad!'

'And I'm thinking you're afraid of change,' Malou replied. Her friend had no idea.

Ren's phone buzzed and she fetched it out of her pristine white leather handbag. When she saw the short message, her breath deserted her. Her throat seized up. *No...* Not now. Not like this. She hadn't finished preparing the company, her grandmother – the world – for this.

Oh, God, she'd held it all together for nothing. *Shit!*

'Are you okay?'

She fumbled to shut down her screen before Malou saw. Not that it mattered. Those four words in the text message meant even Malou would find out – probably before the day was out.

Shit! Just before Christmas, before year-end. The investors would have a meltdown, after everything her grandmother had done to build up the business.

As if on cue, her phone rang, Grandmama's face flashing up on the screen. She quickly silenced the call. *Sorry, I've been lying to you for six months while I tried to work out how to save our image after Charlie dumped me* didn't feel like something she could blurt out over the phone.

'Ren? Seriously, you're scaring me. You look white as a sheet!'

'I have to go – now.'

'Go?'

'Back to London. I'm sorry about dinner.'

'Is your family all right? Charlie?'

'Yes, everyone's okay.' At least until her grandmother had a heart attack at the news. She twisted the marquise-cut diamond ring on her finger in agitation. She'd been wearing the four carats of vintage Cartier on her left hand for over a year, but now it felt like it was burning.

Ren wanted to flee back to the Ritz, dive under the embroidered silk duvet and forget who she was. Unfortunately, the world would always remind her that she was Irena Asquith-Lewis, and by the end of the day, she knew her name would be splashed all over the news.

Without stopping to kiss Malou on the cheek, she stumbled out of her friend's office and clutched the banister of the grand marble staircase as she made her way through the galleries to street level. She dismissed the photographer and the social media assistant who were waiting for her in the lobby. She had to get back to London and formulate a new plan, even if it meant talking to Charlie.

Ren burst out of the double doors and fumbled for her phone to call her Paris driver. The message was still there.

Everyone knows. I'm sorry.

She swiped it away and made the phone call.

Bilel was much too diplomatic to comment on the fact that Ren was quietly hyperventilating in his Mercedes. He took her to the Ritz and waited while she threw her things into a suitcase and hastily settled her bill. Less than half an hour later, her assistants had sent a ticket to her phone and she was on her way to the Gare du Nord for a five o'clock train.

She might have been nervous about travelling alone in the gathering dusk, but she was too worried about Grandmama, and about how they would fix this mess, to care. She'd had six months to find a solution of her own and had failed.

The boulevards of Paris were a blur as she stared out of the window without seeing. It felt as if everything had fallen apart at once. Six months, she'd held onto her sanity, her despair, keeping the secret, and now it was all for nothing.

Charlie Routledge didn't want to marry her. What that meant for the proposed merger of their family businesses – the eminently sensible union of a real estate empire and a centuries-old auction house – was unclear, but Ren was sure it wouldn't be good.

And what it meant for Ren herself? She was an heiress and a socialite, the personification of the Asquith-Lewis brand that traded on exclusivity and mixing in elite social circles. But she was also thirty and now single, with a lifestyle that made it almost impossible to meet people.

Charlie had been perfect. He was an old family friend, good-natured and attractive, and they had a lot in common, she'd thought. He'd shared Ren's commitment to her aspirational social media feeds and the expectations of the family business. Apparently that just hadn't been enough for him.

The black car slowed in traffic and Ren roused herself to some kind of attention. The red lights of the car in front were out of focus. The windscreen wipers were on full. The boulevard shone in the dim light of the waning December afternoon as the car rolled to a slow stop.

'I'm so sorry, Mademoiselle Ren,' Bilel said. They inched along the road another few feet. Ren peered out of the window and checked the map on her phone.

'I'll just get out here. The station's not far.'

'But it's raining!' Bilel protested.

The weather might suit my mood. 'It'll be all right,' she said faintly, thinking of more than just the rain. She glanced at the sky, willing the light to hold out. If darkness fell before she got to her train, she'd have a whole host of new problems.

'What about your suitcase?'

Ren pictured the buckled, monogrammed monstrosity in the boot of the car with another dart of panic. 'I'll manage,' she murmured. 'I'll have to. Thank you again for all your help, Bilel.' She felt unexpectedly sad to be leaving Paris. Her phone was still buzzing non-stop in her pocket, but at least in Paris nobody took a moment's notice of the heiress who had been dumped and struggled to get herself to the train station on her own.

'Let me park by the trottoir.' Bilel swerved and the front wheel jumped the kerb as he attempted to drop her off more safely.

Her mind a jumble, she shoved open the door – and snatched her hand back with a shriek. She heard a piercing cry of, 'Putain!' and then a metallic crunch.

Ren cowered on the seat with her hands over her head as the window shattered. There was a heavy thud and a long groan. With the bang of Bilel's door and shouts of alarm in Arabic, the world came suddenly back into focus.

So much for 'it'll be all right'.

A cyclist lay prone on the tarmac, his feet tangled in his ruined bicycle, and he wasn't moving. Ren sprang into action despite her pounding heart and when Bilel tried to hold her back, she wouldn't let him.

She heard a clatter that sounded like her phone as she rushed to tend to her victim, but she ignored it. Kneeling beside him and positioning his arm carefully, she grasped his leather jacket at the shoulder and the waist and managed to haul him into the recovery position. Her fingers groped for the snap of his helmet and she supported his head while she unwound her cashmere scarf and settled it underneath as a pillow. She took deep, even breaths to keep the panic at bay as she searched for injuries.

The man's hair was black and curly and tumbled over his face. He had an inch of unkempt beard. She ran her hands over his head, searching for any indication of injury, and she spied a line of cursive script that was tattooed on his neck. Ren couldn't help worrying it might be needed to identify his body, but she couldn't see any blood.

She cursed, realising she should have checked his airway first. She dropped her ear to his mouth and to her relief, his breath tickled her ear. Before she could draw away and check the rest of his body, he opened his eyes – wide open – and stared at her.

He had fine, dark eyes, framed with thick lashes. He drew in a deep breath and she felt him exhale on her cheek. His eyes were too dark for her to check the pupils for signs of concussion, but she tried anyway.

He was breathing evenly. She drew back a little, not quite trusting the good signs enough to remove her hand from his head – or tear her gaze from him. His face was oval, with high cheekbones, and his brow was thick and lopsided. His was an undeniably interesting face.

As the rain flowed in freezing droplets down the back of her neck and turned her hair into a frizzy orange mess and her cardigan to a sodden lump of cashmere, she held his cheek and stared into his eyes until she could barely believe he was a stranger.

Suddenly the man frowned with a deep twist of his brow and looked away, glancing at his legs and shifting experimentally.

'Careful,' she said softly, hoping he understood English. 'You might be hurt.'

He met her gaze again and raised a hand in front of her face, tugging up his sleeve and presenting his wrist. A pattern of tattoos in bold, geometric lines peeked out of the cuff.

'Do I have a pulse?' he asked. He mispronounced the 'u' and Ren was so distracted by his earnest frown that she didn't realise he'd made a joke until it was too late and she was already reaching for his hand.

She took his wrist hesitantly, pressing on the warm skin. His pulse fluttered under her fingertips.

'I think you'll live,' she murmured, breaking eye contact. 'This was entirely my fault. I shouldn't have tried to get out of the car onto the bike path – especially without looking. Whatever you need, I'll pay—'

'C'est bon, ça va. It's fine. I'm fine.' He pushed himself up with a grunt.

'Stay still! Bilel, call an ambulance!'

'Vraiment... really. Can I check my vélo, uh, my bicycle?'

Ren glanced at the mess of his bike, lying twisted and pathetic on the kerb. Behind it was a single-wheeled trailer which had tipped over and spilled a few boxes onto the bus lane. Not only had she possibly injured the poor man, but it looked as if she'd taken away his livelihood too, at least until he could repair his bike.

She grasped his arm and carefully helped him to his feet. 'Don't worry about anything. I will compensate you, if this means you can't work until the bike is fixed. We'll take you to the hospital and... Let me know how much it is and I can... Here, take the money I have on me.'

Ren dived to the footwell for her handbag and produced a wad of Euro notes. The man took a long look at the cash, but didn't accept it, even when she shook it at him in agitation.

He stooped to gather up her scarf and handed it to her. Why wasn't he taking the money? Was he planning to sue? It was certainly his right.

'Let me take care of this,' she pleaded. 'I can pay my driver to deliver the rest of these packages for you today. If your employer—'

He gave an unexpected laugh, short and sharp. 'I'm not a courier.' He ran a hand through his unruly hair. The way he said 'courier' danced off his tongue and Ren noticed that his accent was much stronger than those of the employees at Asquith-Lewis. She spent several heartbeats marvelling at how lovely it was to listen to him talk, before his words sank in, along with her confusion.

'Oh. What?'

2

Sacha stepped gingerly forward, testing his legs. There didn't seem to be any broken bones. His shoulder throbbed, but even that pain was subsiding now.

He inspected the wreck of his bike with an enormous sigh, propping his hands on his hips. The stranger – the woman with the warm hands and expensive shoes – followed him, but he threw out his good arm to stop her. The area was littered with glass shards – not many, because of the high-quality safety glass, but enough for him to realise his helmet had saved him a serious injury.

He glanced back to see her still clutching the bundle of notes. 'Put the money away,' he said through his teeth, trying not to laugh at the ridiculousness of the situation.

One moment, he'd been pedalling furiously along the Boulevard de Magenta and the next, he'd bounced off his own handlebars and was headed for the concrete – after smashing the woman's window with his head.

If that wasn't surreal enough, he'd then opened his eyes to find this woman – blurred and soft around the edges – filling his vision.

Her voice, speaking the plum sort of English that was easy to understand, had soothed his adrenaline-induced shock.

With the weak sun behind her and his thoughts scattered, he'd had to ask himself if he was imagining her. His mind was clear, now, but she still looked dreamlike, with her red hair – the kind that wasn't really red, but bright orange – her pale face and subdued features, not to mention her stiff posture and tailored clothing.

Then there were her eyes... brown eyes, the colour of caramel syrup, bright and clear.

'Stay back, Mademoiselle Ren,' the driver called, hurrying over. Had the man said 'reine'? A queen? Sacha was quite confused, which he sincerely hoped wasn't because of the knock to his head.

But that was enough daydreaming. He had somewhere to be and no way to get there, now his bike had been reduced to twisted metal.

Sacha turned to the driver. 'Pourriez-vous m'aider?' he asked, gesturing to the boxes that were blocking the cycle path and spilling into the bus lane.

'Je m'en occupe.' The driver assured him he would take care of it and reached for a package. But, instead of piling them up on the footpath, as Sacha had intended, he opened the luggage compartment of the car and dropped the first ones in.

'Non, non, non!' Sacha cried, grasping his shoulder when the pain shot down his arm again.

'You're hurt!' With a gentle grip on his arm, the woman turned him back to her. 'We need to get this treated. Let Bilel drive you wherever you need to go – after we've taken you to the hospital.'

'I can call a friend,' he insisted. 'You don't need to worry.' He needed to get in touch with Joseph anyway, even though his friend would likely fuss just as much as this stranger.

'You can't tell me not to worry when I've just caused an accident! Come and sit in the car.' She tugged on his good arm.

'I can take him to the hospital, mademoiselle,' the driver spoke up. 'You might still catch your train.'

'No, I'm not leaving until I know he's going to be okay.' Her words brought a tingle to the back of Sacha's neck, but he ignored it. It was probably nerve damage from the wrench to his shoulder.

'I will take him,' the driver insisted. 'What would your grandmother say?'

'Go catch your train,' Sacha urged. 'I'll let your driver take me to hospital. Je vous promets.' Those eyes... The way she looked at him with her heart in her eyes prompted so many questions he'd never know the answer to. 'Je vous en prie. Allez-y.'

'I am coming to the hospital with you.'

The driver Bilel clucked his tongue, but he didn't protest any more, he simply snagged another box. Before he got to the car, the sodden flaps underneath gave way, sending the contents onto the road with a clang.

Sacha lurched to catch what he could, narrowly avoiding a collision with the woman as she did the same. She retrieved a silver snuff box and a bronze coffee pot, inspecting the objects with interest and glancing doubtfully at him. He ignored her look and plucked the items out of her grip, not daring to check for damage. It was none of her business why he was transporting small antiques. She'd already misjudged him once. Another time wouldn't make any difference.

Sacha picked up another box himself, willing away the pain in his shoulder. He didn't have time for it, not with Joseph's Christmas nonsense next weekend, on top of the usual pressures of life and work.

He got as far as the tail-light of the Mercedes before Bilel took the box from him. The luggage compartment was full, with his boxes and a large patterned suitcase that matched the woman's expensive shoes and even more expensive manners.

Next Sacha fetched his bike, grimacing at the damage as he hauled it off the cycle path. The trailer was a piece of shit he never bothered to lock and no one bothered to steal. He chained up the bike with a fleeting worry that it would be taken it away as rubbish, but this was Paris, after all, and the council would never be so efficient. He'd need a new front wheel, but he could probably repair the rest himself. The damage to her car door was more serious.

Bilel produced a brush and cleared the shards of glass from the back seat of the car, right where the woman must have been sitting. Sacha frowned and turned to her.

'Et vous alors, ça va? Are *you* all right... madame?'

'Ren,' she corrected him quickly. 'Irena, really, but call me Ren. Not madame.' So, not 'reine' after all. 'But I'm fine.' As though only now realising his meaning, she glanced at her hands and patted her damp head.

A fragment of glass was trapped in her hair, winking in the light of the streetlamp. 'Here,' he said, gently retrieving the shard. It wasn't sharp, but it snagged in her hair, making her chignon even more of a mess.

She smiled at him in thanks. 'And you are?' ...staring at the pretty woman like a tongue-tied imbecile.

He looked away quickly, clearing his throat. 'Sacha,' he said curtly. He noticed something on the road near the front wheel and bent to retrieve it, grimacing when he saw it was a phone. The screen was smashed and there was a large crack in the casing.

He held it out. 'Yours?'

She grabbed for it. 'Crap!' she muttered when it wouldn't turn on.

'I'm sorry,' he said.

'It's just... been a bad day.'

'You must sit in the front, mademoiselle. I will tape the window for now. The hospital is not far,' Bilel interrupted.

'If Sacha is injured, he should take the front seat,' she insisted. Bilel clucked his disapproval once more, but didn't argue. He merely gave Sacha a long look and ushered Ren protectively around the car to the other side.

The driver's wariness made Sacha try one more time. 'Why don't we go to the Gare du Nord first and then to the hospital? The station is not far.'

'What if you have a head injury? The symptoms don't always appear right away. I can take a later train, but I won't forgive myself if...' She gestured helplessly and Sacha nodded with a sigh. So much for a busy evening in Joseph's workshop.

* * *

The hospital was the usual mix of endless corridors and confusing signage, even more overwhelming in French, but Ren had a surprisingly clear head. There was nothing she could do to stop the fallout from her suddenly public break-up with Charlie, but she could make up for her stupidity in injuring a stranger.

A stranger called Sacha. If she'd thought the name Sacha was feminine before, she never would again. It was difficult not to notice his broad shoulders and tough body language. He was wiry, rather than muscular, and not particularly tall. There was a competence about his movements – an efficiency and lack of elegance that appealed to her. And her eyes continually strayed to the tattoo on his neck.

'Do you have a headache?' she asked as they took their seats in the waiting area.

'No,' he replied. She helped him tug his jacket gingerly over his shoulder. His rough woollen pullover was thankfully dry, unlike her cardigan, lying in a sodden heap in the back of the car. She'd shrugged into another one before rushing into the hospital, but her hair was still damp. Perhaps she should have taken the time to find her coat.

'I think you were unconscious for a few minutes, but I didn't watch the time,' she said.

'It will be okay.'

She glanced up, realising she'd been clasping her hands into tight fists, and he spoke with a gentle tone, as though she was the patient. 'My bad day seems to have spread to you.'

'Un malheur n'arrive jamais seul,' he said softly. Ren repeated the words back under her breath, trying to translate what he'd said. 'A bad luck doesn't never arrive alone,' he supplied.

His poor translation, combined with the utter earnestness of his expression, made her smile. She wanted to write it down to remember it later, but that would seem strange. '"When it rains, it pours," we say in English.'

'Ah, we say that, too. A more appropriate saying for the weather today.' He fell silent again and they both stared blindly at the public health posters about hand hygiene and alcohol consumption. 'You are going to London?' he asked.

She nodded, trying not to think of everything she had to face when she got home. 'I was only in Paris for a few days on business.' She hoped he wouldn't ask what business. It would be difficult to explain that visiting the boutiques on the Place Vendôme was part of her job.

'I'm sorry Paris could not solve your problems.'

She laughed bitterly. 'I didn't realise Paris was a therapist.'

'A therapist, a poet, an artist and a clown – that's Paris. Which do you need?'

'All of them,' she said. 'Most of all, I need a miracle worker.'

'Ah, well, perhaps you are in the right place after all,' he said lightly. 'You've heard of the cour des miracles? *Les Misérables*? Or *The Hunchback of Notre Dame*?'

'The gypsy hideout? I only know the Disney version.'

He couldn't quite conceal his grimace. 'It's... not quite the intention of Victor Hugo's tragedy.' He pronounced it 'Victor Oo-go', which Ren found utterly charming.

'No? Well, I don't like tragedies, so I apologise to your friend Monsieur "Oo-go" if I give his book a miss.'

'You don't appreciate the romance of the hunchback dying out of love?'

'Is that what happens?' She shuddered. 'How awful.'

'But he is the best of men, Quasimodo.'

'Good for him,' she muttered. 'It doesn't sound very romantic.' Although what did she know about romance? The warm, thick hospital air suddenly choked her. What was Charlie doing right now? Celebrating that he could now go out in public with his new love?

The bloody ring felt wrong on her finger. The elongated diamond only reminded her that it had been impossible to find a wedding band to match. She should have taken that as a warning.

On a sudden impulse, she gave the ring a tug to remove it. She didn't need to pretend any more. She was officially un-engaged. She should at least get some satisfaction out of that fact. The ring was tight over her knuckle, but she just pulled harder.

'Oww!' she groaned.

'Ren.' Her name sounded strange in his strong accent that pronounced the 'R' far back in the throat. 'Ren!' A pair of rough hands closed over hers.

She looked up. Sacha's face was close – the deep, furrowed brow and his big, soulful eyes – and his lips were pursed, which made her realise she was staring at his mouth. He gently loosened her fingers.

With Charlie's ring stuck on her knuckle, her phone dead, the world ready to celebrate her scandal with schadenfreude and the moment lit by harsh white hospital lights, Ren stared at Sacha and wondered what it would be like to kiss him.

3

'Sacha Mourad?'

Sacha snatched his hands back from Ren's, leaving the ring still stuck on her knuckle. She tried to shove it back into place, but it wouldn't budge in either direction. The voice summoned him again and heat rose to her cheeks.

She inwardly shook herself. Tattoos and work boots were a strange fetish to be suddenly developing. *Pull yourself together, Ren!*

Only when they were halfway down the corridor did she realise she probably should have left him alone to see the doctor, but she found herself in the consultation room, standing in the corner clutching his jacket as he and the nurse held a conversation in rapid French.

Before Ren could decide whether to sit or stand, Sacha had hopped up onto the examination table and was stripping off his shirt and it was somehow too late to tear her eyes off him. He had a full sleeve of tattoos, with another – two crossed swords – on his left biceps.

The hospital lighting showed up all the grooves of lean muscle.

She couldn't help thinking that Charlie, for all his hours in the gym and bulking diet, didn't have definition like that.

Sacha exchanged more words with the nurse, a tight smile sometimes touching his lips. His front teeth were a little crooked – not much, but in Ren's circle they would have been corrected. She quite liked them.

The nurse checked his eyes and performed a series of tests for balance and, Ren guessed, memory and concentration. While Ren stood in the corner, trying not to watch Sacha and definitely not to appreciate his expressive looks and incomprehensible words, the next Eurostar from the Gare du Nord pulled out of the station.

Sacha lifted his gaze and caught Ren staring. She took an instinctive step back, hitting the wall. What kind of idiot checked out the man she'd just knocked down?

An hour later, Sacha had been cleared of a concussion and they wandered out of the double doors of the Emergency department, his arm in a sling. Night had fallen and the rain had turned to misty drizzle that gathered around the streetlamps in hazy brightness.

Ren shivered at the sudden change in temperature and the encroaching darkness. A moment later, Sacha's fleece-lined coat landed on her shoulders and she grasped the collar reflexively.

'Shouldn't you stay—'

He shook his head to cut her off. 'Your hair is still wet.'

'I'm sure Bilel isn't far,' she said, shrugging into the jacket. 'Ow,' she muttered, realising how much her finger ached from the ring wedged onto her knuckle.

'Let me see,' Sacha said, taking her hand. 'Aïe, your finger is purple.'

'It's not...' Sacha held her hand up to the light and Ren grimaced when she saw the mottling on her fingertip. She tugged once more ineffectually at the blasted thing, her breath hitching.

Ren took a slow breath in and out. 'You know what else we say in English about bad luck? It comes in threes.'

'Also in French: jamais deux, sans trois. Never two without three.'

'As long as we do without four, I can keep it together,' she muttered for her own benefit.

'Do you have cream for the hands?'

'In the car,' she said. 'Where is Bilel?'

'Perhaps he called?'

She muttered another curse, remembering her dead phone, but on the other hand, she reflected ruefully, no one could call her if her phone was dead. No notifications, no urgent demands that she turn up and face the scandal.

Ren tried the smashed device one more time, but it definitely wouldn't turn on. With a sudden laugh that was probably bordering on hysterical, she tossed it into a nearby bin, feeling liberated. Until, that is, she realised she was out at night with no phone – alone, without Charlie or an assistant. Had it suddenly got darker?

'Do you have Bilel's number? I could call him.'

She glanced at her companion. The warmth of his coat around her shoulders attested to the fact that she wasn't quite alone. After another rummage in her bag, she handed Sacha a business card with Bilel's number on it.

There followed a quick conversation in French, where all she caught was, 'En fait?' and, 'Jusque-là,' although she couldn't remember what they meant anyway. After he ended the call, Sacha explained, 'Bilel has had trouble changing the car for a new one and he'll be at least half an hour. He is profoundly sorry.'

Ren glanced around and then wished she hadn't. She was somewhere deep in the tenth arrondissement. There was a Turkish snack bar across the road and a handful of shops with their shutters down. A concrete wall ran around the hospital, covered in posters and graffiti.

So much for the city of light. Outside Ren's beloved first arrondissement, it was a city of dark corners. She shuddered, taking a deep breath.

'I'm sorry you're not at home resting,' she said, although it wasn't quite true. If it weren't for those mysterious boxes of antiques held hostage in Bilel's car, he would have left her all alone with her irrational fears.

He shook his head, sending little points of light off his curls from the drizzle. 'I have an idea,' he said abruptly, 'to fix both of your problems.' He thought she only had two problems? 'On y va!' Gesturing for her to follow, he took off into the dark evening in the depths of a Paris she didn't know. She should be wary of following. But being in Paris with a handsome stranger was a hundred times better than facing Grandmama's wrath in London.

On y va, she thought to herself. Let's go.

* * *

Sacha phoned Joseph as they walked, glossing over the reasons for his delay. He couldn't explain to the old man that he'd been to the hospital, but he was fine, and he was now taking a strange woman to a bar, but not for the usual reasons. Although he couldn't remember the last time he'd taken a woman to a bar for any reason.

Within ten minutes, they had made it to the twentieth arrondissement, and paused at a crossing. The intersection wasn't anything special. Sacha didn't even need to look any more to picture the graffitied shutters of the Chinese supermarket, covered in profanities in six languages. The building had been repurposed from a theatre and the chunky lettering still remained, the concrete awning in need of a clean.

It was a typical Parisian crossroad, with cobbled streets, a mix of golden stone buildings from the nineteenth century, contemporary apartment blocks, and everything in between. Scooters and bikes and rushing pedestrians swept past them and shivering smokers sat at tables outside the café across the street, still busy at this time of night. It was Belleville – home – but Ren stared as though he'd taken her to Disneyland.

'Welcome to Paris,' he said drily.

'This is not the Paris I know,' she replied.

'It's not quite the court of miracles – the slums were demolished 150 years ago – but perhaps we will find here what you need to solve at least one of your problems.'

She followed him with a wide-eyed smile. He had noticed she smiled a lot.

As he paused across the street from their destination, she took it all in as though this was her first trip to the Louvre, not a bar. He kept hold of her hand when she nearly tripped on the uneven kerb. 'This place is... interesting,' she said, peering down the neighbouring alley, where the patrons of the bar spilled out, huddled under heaters.

'First time in Paris?'

'No, I visit all the time, I just... don't know it well, apparently.'

Once inside, Ren stared at the red neon lettering above the bar, the bottles of spirits in rows and the clusters of young patrons. A tourne-disque in the corner played a mixture of cabaret, chansons and rhythmic Congolese soukous. A couple of white women with dreadlocks and lip piercings grooved in the middle of the room after setting their drinks on a decoupaged table.

Ren would have looked out of place, except her thoroughly

dishevelled state disguised her chic outfit. She was pale and her make-up had worn off. Freckles had come out on her cheeks like stars. No one would even notice her tailored trousers, black-and-white designer boots and the earrings that matched her ring. Well, perhaps someone would notice the earrings. The diamonds were enormous.

'Une margarita glacée et un thé à la menthe,' he ordered when the barman approached.

'Oh,' she said and reached into her bag. 'Do we pay now? Or later?' She placed a 100-euro note hurriedly onto the bar.

Sacha slapped his hand over it and swiped it back in her direction. 'Don't you have anything smaller?'

'Why? Are there pickpockets around?'

'I've only seen a handful of 100-euro notes in my life. You don't need to be extravagant. Most places in Paris do take credit card these days.'

'I'm not being extravagant,' she mumbled. 'Surely there won't be too much change from 100?'

He was speechless for long enough that the barman returned with their drinks and casually took the note, holding it up to the light to check it was genuine. Ren sniffed at the slight, before glancing down at her rumpled clothing with a sigh of dismay.

'Thank you for the drink,' he muttered, clearing his throat.

She didn't reply, but turned her perplexed gaze to her glass. 'Is that a frozen margarita?'

'It's for your finger.'

'My... what?'

He picked up her hand and lifted it above her head. She stared at him, her mouth ajar. 'We elevate the hand and then you hold your finger on the glass. The cold makes your finger contract and we take the ring off.'

'O-oh,' she stammered. 'Good. I don't want to... damage it. The ring, I mean, not my finger.'

'Your finger, also. The ring is important to you?'

Her eyes clouded and he wasn't sure if he wanted to know or not, but his hand curled around hers instinctively. 'No,' she said. 'It's not important at all. Perhaps it never was. Perhaps *I* never was – to him.' He was close enough to notice her lip trembling. He opened his mouth to say something – he had no idea what – but she spoke instead. 'But it is vintage Cartier.'

He released a slow breath. She was from a different world, after all. 'Cartier makes it important?'

'Of course!' She glanced up at their joined hands – her *elevated* hand. 'Have we held it enough, yet? My arm is going numb.' And her face was too close.

He cleared his throat. 'I hope it's not the gangrène.'

'It's not gangrene. That's a bad joke.'

'Sorry. I have the habitude.'

'The habit,' she corrected gently. 'It starts with an "h".'

'So does "habitude". But I am French. We don't breathe on each other when we talk.'

She spluttered for long enough that he almost felt bad for teasing her. 'Well, you gargle my name like mouthwash.'

'Ren?' he repeated, stifling another unexpected smile. 'It does not sound like mouthwash.' He repeated her name a few times. 'It sounds like reine, the French word for queen.'

'Queen?'

'It suits you, no?'

'No!' she said, her tone defensive. 'Now, can I lower my hand?'

He nodded, letting her hand go and nudging the glass in her direction. He picked up his own tea, left-handed because of the sling, and took a sip. Ren closed her fingers around her tumbler and held it there, wincing at the cold.

'Why "Ren"? Why don't people call you Irena?'

She leaned heavily on the bar, as though she'd already had a few margaritas. Seeing the look on her face, he wished he hadn't asked what he'd thought was a simple question. 'My mother was Russian – hence the name.'

'I'm sorry.'

'That she was Russian?'

'No, that she... *was*.'

'Oh,' she said, her voice trailing off. 'I don't remember much about her. She... My grandmother disapproved of her humble origins and refuses to call me Irena to this day. Since my parents died when I was a child, there isn't anyone else to call me anything except Ren,' she explained with false brightness.

'What does it mean, do you know?' That seemed safer than all of the other follow-up questions that sprang into his mind.

'My name? I have no idea.'

'You never looked up the meaning?' She shook her head. 'Here, let's look.' He pulled out his phone.

'You're not into some weird astrology with names, are you?'

'Astrology is about stars.'

'You know what I mean.'

'If you mean do I think there is... destiny in a name, then... no. But...' She was staring at him with an unexpected focus that made heat rush to his cheeks. 'But words have meaning and... power, in their own way.'

'So what does my name mean then?' she asked with sudden eagerness.

He unlocked his phone as quickly as he could and opened a browser to search. 'It means peace. It comes from the ancient Greek goddess of peace.'

'Hmm. I suppose that figures. I hate conflict.'

'And tragedies.'

'Exactly.'

He leaned on the bar and studied her. He'd met her at a low

point, it appeared, but her low point was full of grace. He'd rarely reached for that word: la grâce. It sounded old-fashioned and almost reverent. He was probably just awed by her million-dollar manners.

'What does your name mean, then?'

The tables turned, it felt strangely personal to share the meaning of his own name – a name his parents had chosen with care. But she'd answered him. 'As a masculine name it derives from Alexander, which means... defender of people. It is also a feminine name of Arabic origin. In that case, it means helper or supporter.'

'That's... a lot to live up to,' she said softly. He met her curious gaze and immediately wished he hadn't. He didn't need to set his heart pounding because a wealthy stranger looked at him like that.

She released a slow breath through pursed lips. Then she lifted her glass and took a sip of her margarita – a big sip.

'Oooh,' she said, cocking her head to inspect the cocktail.

'Here,' he said, spreading salt around the edge of her glass from a little bowl the barman had placed next to them. 'And take a pincée and throw it over your shoulder.'

'Does that make it taste better?'

'No. It sends away the bad luck.'

'This margarita and I were meant to meet tonight,' she said with a smile. She reached for a pinch of salt and began to toss it over her shoulder, but he lurched to stop her, grasping her wrist.

'Not that shoulder. The left.'

She grimaced. 'I already let it go.' He groaned. 'Does that mean more bad luck? What do I do about that?'

'I think the best thing you can do is drink the margarita.' She laughed more heartily than the poor joke deserved and he laughed, too – slightly bewildered and reluctantly charmed. 'You've never had a margarita before?' he asked.

'No,' she admitted. She took another long sip. 'Mmmmm, it's

good with the salt. I'll have to see if they have these in the bar at the Ritz.'

'I'm sure they do,' he said. *The Ritz*... it figured. 'Why haven't you ever drunk a margarita?'

'Oh, there are so many things you'd think I would have done and I... haven't.' She propped her chin on her other hand and looked around the bar again. 'I've never been to a bar like this.'

'I've never been to the Ritz.'

'Oh, you must! There's nowhere quite like the Ritz.'

'I believe you,' he said drily.

'Ha,' she responded. 'Do you live around here, then? Not that you need to give me an address. I'm just making small talk! I'm not going to follow you home and steal your things.'

He didn't need the reminder that they were strangers who didn't know each other's surnames. 'I'm more worried about you following me home and posting cash into my letter box. Yes, I live some streets away. The quartier is called Belleville.'

'You have a quartier and I have Cartier,' she said with a chuckle. 'Were you going home from work when I... hit you?'

'No, I was going the other way. My friend restores antiques. I was going to his stock room in Saint-Ouen.'

'Oh, okay.'

'You won't report me to the police?' She froze and opened her mouth, but no sound emerged. Her eyes were huge and alarmed. 'It was a joke,' he said with a frown.

'Ohhhhh,' she said. 'Your "habitude" strikes again.' He inclined his head, staring into his tea. 'If you smile when you joke, I won't be so confused. So, why were you transporting stolen goods to wherever it was?'

'They're not—'

'I know, I know. My turn to joke.'

'Oh, I am helping to prepare for a grotte du Père Noël – you know?'

'Père Noël? You're playing Father Christmas?'

'Non, my friend is the Père Noël.'

'You're one of his elves?'

'Elves? Yes, you could say that.'

'You don't look like an elf.'

'No? I look like a bicycle courier who steals antiques, non?' Her tongue-tied apology tempted him into a smile, but she still didn't pick up that he was joking. 'Don't worry. *You* look like the Queen of England to me.'

'I hope I don't look ninety years old,' she said glancing at her rumpled outfit. 'I look quite unkempt.'

'My fault. Thank you for ruining your clothes for me. Those pantalons are probably by Louis Versace.'

'Louis Vers— oh, you're joking again. Actually, they're Givenchy. But you're lucky your head is worth more to me, because these are ruined.'

He imagined his definition of 'ruined' differed from hers. 'I am lucky tonight,' he agreed lightly. 'Shall we try to take the ring off? You don't have much ice left.'

'Oh, it must have stopped hurting,' she said, squinting at her finger. 'Right, here goes!' she said.

4

She pulled hard. Too hard, as it turned out. The ring slipped off easily, but she lost her grip and it went sailing through the air.

The music stopped at that moment, as though every pair of eyes in the bar were on the glinting white gold band with the enormous diamond. Ren watched with wry detachment. There went the five years of her life she'd spent with Charlie, hurtling towards the sticky floor of a dodgy bar.

With an audible tinkle, the ring landed somewhere near a curved velvet sofa the colour of vomit. Sacha leaped to his feet and went after it. Despite the sling, he dropped to his knees and started searching one-handed. Ren knew she should join him. She should *feel* something.

Charlie had known she loved Cartier from the Art Deco period. He'd hunted down the perfect ring and commissioned a matching set of earrings. No one knew her better than Charlie. But Charlie wouldn't recognise her now, sitting in a bar, in a graffitied corner of Paris, in the company of a tattooed Christmas elf, staring after her precious ring as though it wouldn't matter if she lost it forever.

Strangest of all, she liked the idea of surprising Charlie, surprising everyone. Now the worst had actually happened, a host of possibilities unfolded in her imagination, all of them preferable to pretending that she was still with Charlie.

Despite the bad luck and the accident, this had been the best evening she'd had for a long time. In the morning, she'd be Irena Asquith-Lewis again, and decide how best to mitigate the damage she'd caused to her family's legacy, but not now.

She lifted the melting cocktail and tossed the rest of it back in one gulp. The salt and the citrus made her grimace – or perhaps that was the tequila. When she stood to help Sacha, she had a pleasant buzz to go with her dizzying uncertainty.

He was peering under the ugly sofa, near the ugly lamp. The view of him searching on the floor improved the ugly sofa somewhat. She shouldn't ogle her victim, but she'd had such a shitty day that she couldn't stop herself.

He fumbled under the sofa with his left arm, but his injured shoulder gave out and he crumpled, face-first, onto the polished concrete floor. She rushed over as he hauled himself back up, hitting his head on a barstool with a yelp.

She dropped to her knees and grasped his thick pullover at the shoulders. 'Are you okay?'

He smiled faintly at her, his brow bunched over his soft eyes. A sweetheart. That's what he was. 'I didn't find it yet. But thanks for saving me – again.'

'I only seem to save you after making you fall.'

'Getting up again is more important than how many times you fall.'

Ren stilled, staring into his eyes. She had the impression he spoke from experience, but she'd never know and she was surprised how sad she felt when she realised that. 'I think my family's motto is "don't ever fall" – or maybe "don't let anyone see you fall".'

'Is that why you've never had a margarita?'

'Exactly.'

'Are we going to find this ring?'

'I don't know,' she smiled ruefully. 'But I suppose I have to look.' He gave her a curious glance.

They searched the back of the sofa, along the skirting board, in the rug and even in the filth under the bar, but the blasted thing was nowhere to be found.

Sacha sighed and propped one hand on his hip. 'I didn't think a diamond that size would be so easy to miss.'

'Are you suggesting my engagement ring was showy?'

His gaze snapped up to hers. 'I – euh.'

'Don't worry. I won't take it personally, coming from you.'

'I... thank you.' His look was full of curiosity. 'Your engagement ring,' he repeated.

'Yes,' she said flatly. 'I suppose I should give it back, if we can find it.'

'We'll find it.' He sounded as though he'd search until sunrise and come back tomorrow with a metal detector if she let him.

They returned wordlessly to the hunt. When the patrons standing nearby heard they were looking for an engagement ring, they crouched down to help, as did the two girls with dreads and piercings and, a few minutes later, the barman – after handing Ren a tequila shot on the house that made her gag and then sneeze.

Half an hour later, Ren felt guilty and told everyone to stop looking. She'd also realised the time, mainly because her stomach was rumbling. It was dinner time in Paris – 9.30 p.m. – and the last Eurostar had just pulled out of the Gare du Nord. Was it wrong of her to experience a little fizz of excitement at the realisation?

'I'm sorry we didn't find it,' Sacha said earnestly. She waved him off with as few words as possible. If she seemed to grieve for the ring too much, she'd give him the wrong idea, but if she pretended it didn't matter, she was behaving like an incredible snob – the incredible snob she was. She was just wondering if she could manoeuvre him into joining her for dinner at l'Espadon when he broke the spell. 'Bilel has probably been waiting some time. And I should go.'

Unfortunately, Sacha didn't exist simply for her amusement. They called Bilel, who was parked at the hospital and only five minutes away. Ren wrote her name down and told the barman to contact her at the Ritz in case anyone found the ring in their mojito. She fetched Sacha's jacket, but he refused it when she held it out to him, so she draped it over her own shoulders again. It was heavy and thick, so different to the fine lines and elegant fabrics she was used to, but she was glad of the warm layer when they stepped outside and the temperature had dropped, turning the puddles to almost freezing.

A single lamp illuminated the alley next to the bar. There were plenty of people about, but no one was lingering. It should have been dark and terrifying; she should have felt vulnerable. But she was wrapped in a thick coat and she'd just spent the evening with a man who believed in the meaning of words and not money. She didn't need to be afraid in this parallel universe.

Ren took a few steps along the alley and peered at the loud and colourful wall of graffiti. She picked out the word 'fuck' in English, a vandalised French flag and a stylised Mona Lisa with bare breasts. Grandmama would have hated it all with a passion, but Ren was struck, that night, with the confidence of the artists who thumbed their noses at convention, who set out to disturb, rather than please their audience.

'Belleville is known for poor artists and working class... révolte, you know?' Sacha said after a long silence. 'They say Édith Piaf was born on the footpath just over there. And this way,' he gestured to the alley, 'leads to the Rue Ramponeau, the last barricade of the Paris Communards before they were defeated.'

The simple facts came alive somehow as she stared at the graffiti and soaked in the liveliness of Belleville at night, to the soundtrack of an impassioned French chanson playing in the bar.

'You... are a communist?' she asked, half-joking and mainly to keep him talking.

'No!' he said with a fine Parisian pout. 'And the Communards were defeated in 1871. It's just... conversation.'

'A casual conversation about revolutions. I suppose I *am* in Paris. What is your job, then? That's a better topic of conversation.'

'I'm a—'

'Mademoiselle! Here!' Bilel beckoned to her from a car that had pulled up across the street. 'I am very sorry.'

Bilel held the door for her and she beckoned Sacha into the back after her, ignoring Bilel's disapproving look. There was some confusion between the two men about who would close the door. But it wasn't long before the car was cruising through the dark streets of Paris, in the warm glow of the twinkling fairy lights.

Ren remained quiet in the car, feeling off-balance at the strong impression that she'd just made a friend – even though she'd never see him again.

When the avenues of elegant stone apartment buildings began sloping upwards on the hillside of Montmartre, Sacha said suddenly, 'Turn here, you can take Ren back to the Ritz first.'

'I've inconvenienced Sacha enough. We'll take him first,' Ren insisted. Bilel met her gaze in the mirror with a wary one of his own.

'The destination is outside the boulevard périphérique, made-moiselle – the Paris ring road. Are you certain?'

Ren resisted a smile. His statement had the opposite effect from the one he intended. Tomorrow she would worry, but her night of adventures wasn't over yet. 'I'm sure, Bilel. Thank you.'

5

She was a lot less sure when the car pulled up on a narrow street with squat garages on one side, next to a driveway blocked off with a flimsy wooden gate stencilled with the words 'Auto Reparation'. She wouldn't have been surprised to see Parisian tumbleweeds blow past.

Sacha jumped out and knocked on the roller door of one of the garages, near a haphazard depiction of wonky male genitalia – the favourite motif of the most unimaginative graffiti artists.

Bilel got out to help unload Sacha's things. Ren opened her door and ventured one Chanel boot onto the asphalt, but Bilel appeared immediately, shaking his head.

'There is no need to get out of the car. Please. It's not safe for you.'

Ren frowned, watching Sacha greet another man with a back-slapping hug. It was safe enough for Sacha, but then Sacha had a sleeve of tattoos and the look of someone who had lived close to the edge – at least, closer than Ren. She didn't even know where the edge was.

She peered out at the shadows and harsh light. She was a long way from the Place Vendôme, with its enormous Christmas trees and twinkling garlands illuminating the stately baroque square. If this were London, she wouldn't risk setting foot outside the car.

But in Paris, her curiosity got the better of her fear, and surely she'd already had her portion of bad luck for the day.

'I'm sure it's all right,' she insisted, and stepped out of the car.

Sacha was unloading the boxes with his good arm while holding an animated conversation in French with an older Black man. Was he the friend who would play Father Christmas? His white beard certainly fit the part. She picked up a box to help, but nearly dropped it again in surprise. What was in there? Iron ingots?

'Bonsoir,' she said tentatively as Sacha's friend approached to greet her, walking with a limp. He wore a leg brace.

'Bonsoir, madame,' he replied with a smile.

'I'm the one who hit him and wrecked his bike,' she explained, juggling the heavy box and holding out her hand. 'Ren.'

'Joseph,' he responded warmly. 'Welcome to our magical workshop.'

Like Santa's workshop? She stepped over the threshold with interest. Inside, it looked less like a workshop and more like the place where furniture went to die. Bits of wood and metal were strewn haphazardly on a work bench. Cabinet doors stood in a row to one side, some missing panels.

Sacha tried to take the box from her. 'It's too heavy,' she said, holding tight, but the tug was enough for the box to tear. He lurched to catch the underside with his good hand and they were locked awkwardly together, arms intwined around the box and faces suddenly close. She could have stared into his eyes for a lot longer than the few seconds it lasted before the box breathed its last and gave up its contents to the floor with loud metallic clanging. Sacha sprang back with a groan as something landed on his foot.

Joseph stepped forward to help, but Sacha raised his hand forcefully and said something in harsh French that nonetheless made the older man smile. Ren dropped to her haunches to help Sacha, and her hand closed around a rustic piece of blackened metal.

'A horseshoe,' she said in surprise. 'Why do you have a box of old horseshoes?'

'Joseph can never refuse a load of rubbish from a farm.'

'For l'upcycling!' Joseph explained. 'These will become useful and beautiful objects for the home. And a charming gift for this time of year, no? For the good the luck.' She shared an amused glance with Sacha. 'We are celebrating the season of the fêtes next weekend at the market. It is bad timing that my knee surrendered and Sacha must be my helper.'

'If there's another way to get you to rest, let me know,' Sacha grumbled.

'I thought he was going to be your elf,' Ren said with a smile.

Joseph clapped his hands and grinned. 'That is exactly right. That is why I prepared him a costume and made him grow that poor excuse for a beard.'

They dumped the pile of horseshoes onto the bench and Bilel stacked the last box next to them.

'We should go, mademoiselle.'

Ren knew it must be late by now and a wary glance confirmed the night was very dark. She took a step in the direction of the street, annoyed that the familiar stab of panic returned at the prospect of a few steps back to the car.

'Attendez! Just a minute.' She turned back far too eagerly at the sound of Sacha's voice. 'Perhaps you need this.' He pressed a horseshoe into her hand.

The metal was cool, heavy and a little rusty. She hated to think of how dirty it was making her hand and then she noticed another problem too late.

She hurriedly righted the horseshoe in her hand, the open end facing up. 'Phew,' she said.

'What?'

'It was upside down,' she explained.

'Hmm?'

'That's not bad luck in France?'

'A horseshoe always has good luck,' he assured her.

'I hope you're right. It is a French horseshoe, after all.'

'Perhaps it will bring you luck only in France.'

Then maybe I shouldn't leave... He stepped closer and gestured her forward with his good arm.

'Oh!' she said with a start, clutching the soft leather of his coat before shrugging out of it. She handed it to him with mumbled thanks. 'Make sure you look after your shoulder.'

'I will. Don't get cold!' he said gesturing to the car. 'And don't worry about me.'

Something in his tone made her think he said that a lot. She wondered if he had family – and, belatedly, a wife or girlfriend, and it was concerning how suddenly she was jealous of someone who was hypothetical. Perhaps she should get back – to the Ritz, to normal life. She hadn't been mugged, but crossing the Paris périphérique appeared to have stolen her good sense.

'I'm so sorry – again.'

'C'est oublié,' he responded. That much she understood: it's forgotten. She hoped she never forgot anything about tonight, even the bad luck.

Sacha stood near enough that she could take a single step and press her mouth to his. His kind eyes would close and they would exchange the softest kisses, eager and... imaginary. The best she could do was gather her courage and press her lips to his cheek.

'Thanks for the margarita,' she said.

His expression turned serious, with that now-familiar furrow, and he dipped his head to look her in the eye. He gestured to her left hand. 'C'est vrai, you are too good for him. You know that?'

She nodded, once. 'C'est vrai.' *That's right.* One day, she might believe it.

* * *

Sacha draped his coat around himself and watched her go. His shoulder ached in the cold, but he wouldn't go inside until the black Mercedes pulled away.

You should have kissed her... He didn't kiss women he'd just met, but the inner voice was insistent, as though there was something about her he should have understood, like the first reading of a poem where the meaning was little more than a half-formed impression.

But what difference would a kiss have made?

Every difference.

Apparently, these were the strange thoughts one had after being knocked off one's bike by a woman who insisted on removing her valuable engagement ring in public and thought a margarita cost fifty Euros. She didn't know how to pay at a bar and he didn't know how to get into a Mercedes with a private driver. Fate had put him in her path as a twisted social experiment. She didn't even realise the extent to which the world considered them unequal.

The headlights of the Mercedes blinked on and he lifted a hand in farewell. He should go in, but his feet wouldn't take him. Instead he stood there, squinting in the harsh light that picked up the droplets of rain, and stared after her.

At the last moment, just before the car accelerated into the night, she pressed her face to the glass and his heart thumped wildly. It was nothing. The whole evening had been nothing. But *she'd looked back* and that was enough to suggest possibilities, a chance for... something.

He exhaled slowly and turned away and Joseph looked at him strangely when he came back inside. But instead of volunteering any further information, Sacha started stacking the boxes.

'I hope I'll be better by Sunday at least,' he said. 'We've got a lot to do. I've got Raphaël this weekend, so he can help, but we don't have much time.'

'Don't worry,' Joseph assured him. 'Whatever we have, we sell. I dare say you spent your evening in a more pleasant way than with this old man and a soldering iron. I only regret not getting out the mistletoe.'

Sacha scowled at him. 'I'm never going to see her again.'

'Jamais, c'est long! Who knows, Sacha? Who knows?' He pulled out a Middle Eastern coffee pot and set it on the bench, inspecting it in the light. 'This polished up well. Did you give it a rub, too? Make some wishes?'

Sacha resisted rolling his eyes – and he definitely resisted thinking about wishes. 'It's not a lamp. I'm only sorry I was so late.'

'It's all right. We'll get started on the horseshoes tomorrow. For now, let me take you home,' Joseph offered.

'*I'll* drive *you* back to Saint-Denis and make my own way home.'

'The doctor has cleared me for driving,' Joseph said indignantly.

'Only yesterday! I'm not going to let you take me home when you could be resting. Now go and get into the passenger seat.'

'I allow you to be my lutin de Noël, my "elf" as she called it, and the power goes to your head.'

Sacha kept his reply to a grumpy snort. At least he had far too much on his plate to continue thinking about beautiful eyes and a bright smile. He tugged on his coat, cursing the sling.

'What's that?' Joseph asked, squinting at him. Something was catching the light on his pullover. He brushed his hand over the hem, dislodging the object, and it fell to the floor with a tinkle.

There on the concrete, the enormous diamond winking in the light, was Ren's engagement ring.

6

'Fuck Charlie!' Malou had already said those two words several times, interspersed with, 'How many macarons did you *eat*?'

'I'm inexperienced at bingeing,' Ren mumbled around another lemon-flavoured meringue. 'At first, I thought I should order a burger and fries, but then I thought, what if they really are as awful as Grandmama says and I thought of... these.'

'Only you would binge eat *macarons*! On behalf of French people everywhere, I take grave offence. And can we turn the TV off for a minute? I can't hear myself think.'

'We're just getting to the good bit. They escape the palace and fly through the sky on a magic carpet and she sees that the outside world is beautiful and it's absolute crap that she has to marry a prince. What's so crash hot about princes, anyway? Some men society thinks are princes are actually toads.'

'I couldn't agree more. But how many of these films have you watched this weekend?'

'Hmm, I started with *The Hunchback of Notre Dame* yesterday, and then *Mulan* and then... five, I think? Wait, what time is it?'

Malou took the opportunity to switch off the discreet TV screen hidden in a baroque mirror. 'It's nearly ten o'clock.'

'Oh, shit!' Ren said, scrambling off the bed in a cloud of sugary almond-flour crumbs. But she lost steam halfway to the bathroom. 'I've missed it anyway. My train home.' Had that been on purpose? 'Missing trains has become a... habitude.' She turned away to hide her slightly manic smile. All her emotions had been flooding out of her since Friday afternoon, including the enormous crush on the stranger who'd crashed into her life for one night.

'Ha,' said Malou, thankfully not understanding the full context of the joke. She clutched a hand in her black curls and glanced around the room in dismay. 'What would Grandma Asquith-Lewis say if she could see you now? Or Charlie?'

'Don't even suggest that they might see me like this!' The grand matriarch would lock her up for eternity if she saw her only descendant a whiffling mess. And Charlie? He'd probably congratulate himself on his narrow escape. 'Please don't tell anyone about the macarons! I'd be in such trouble with Ziggy.'

Just thinking of Grandmama's right-hand woman Ziggy made Ren swallow her tongue. *It's called haute couture, not chubby couture, my darling. Monsieur Givenchy does not want your thighs.* She'd nearly retorted that Hubert de Givenchy didn't want anyone's thighs, now he'd passed on, but Ziggy didn't have a sense of humour – unless you included facetious laughter.

Malou hefted the server of macarons and put it on the table out of reach, then her gaze snagged on the horseshoe sitting humbly on the gilt-edged marble tabletop. She ran her finger over the rusting iron with a grimace, but the chunky piece of metal had a different effect on Ren. *It will bring you luck only in France...*

More than luck, it was holding open a channel to her memories of Friday night. *Sacha.* Even thinking the name added giddy wonder to her mess of emotions.

'We need coffee, yes? And fresh air,' Malou said, clapping her hands together.

'I can't go out looking like this!'

'I will wait while you get dressed.'

'I mean... like *this*.' She gestured vaguely to her face. 'And if I call someone to do my make-up, it'll get back to Ziggy that I ate macarons and Grandmama will hear that I have no pride!'

'So... don't do your make-up? Or do it yourself?'

'But the *pictures*! Have you seen my skin?' She knew how she looked: pitiful under a layer of rust-coloured freckles. Her mother's complexion. The bad genes.

'Ren, your social media entourage has gone back to London. The doorman will chase away any photographers, if they are about. I can take you to any number of cafés where no one will recognise you.'

'No one will...' It sounded like Ziggy's idea of pointless. *You're the heart of the company*, she always said, meaning 'image' rather than 'heart'. She wasn't sure Ziggy knew anything about hearts. A slow smile stretched on Ren's face. 'You mean we could just... go out?' To anyone else, she would have sounded like a madwoman, but Malou knew what her life was like, between the demands of her Instagram feed and the clutches of her grandmother.

'You're not in London,' Malou said with a smile. 'You're in Paris.'

* * *

'Oh, my, I'm in *Paris*.' Ren had the odd feeling that she'd never seen the city before, despite the number of times she'd stayed at the Ritz. They were strolling under the arcade along the Rue de Rivoli, past cafés and brasseries from the Belle Époque with their ornate wood panelling and murals. The Jardin des Tuileries was on the other side of the road, noisy with laughter from the Christmas market. The sloping iron roof and stone chimneys of the Richelieu wing of the Louvre rose ahead, the leaded windows glinting in the weak winter sunlight.

'Don't worry, we haven't left the first arrondissement.'

Malou led her to a small café on a side street that combined historic stucco cornicing with contemporary lines and metallic accents in the furniture. The patrons were a mix of tourists in bumbags and locals in carelessly stylish outfits.

'Oh, there are nineteen other arrondissements in Paris, you know,' Ren quipped with a smile. 'I even went to the twentieth on Friday night.'

'What?'

'Keep your hat on. I survived to tell the tale and didn't post about it on Instagram. In fact, I can't post anything at the moment. My phone died and I don't know my logins, anyway. I'm sure Ziggy would think that's for the best.'

'Don't you think it might be best for you, too? You could just... be.'

Ren froze, glancing around as though Malou's utterance had been treasonous. She could just... be... *what*? Ever since Ziggy had transformed her from a lonely teenager into an Insta-worthy socialite whose handbags were the envy of the Internet, Ren had never 'just' been anything.

She tried to relax back into her seat, observing the way the people around her were sitting. She'd taken her earrings out, at least, but her tailored outfit was recognisably 'Louis Versace'.

After ordering them both coffee, Malou studied her. 'I was upset you didn't tell me about Charlie, but I'm more upset that I couldn't be there for you through all of this. They're saying he's been cheating on you for months and you don't look surprised.'

That had been the wrong moment to take her first sip of hot coffee. Ren fumbled for the tiny glass of water and tried to open up her throat again. 'You're right, I knew he had a new girlfriend. We've been broken up for months, so why shouldn't he? I wanted time to work out what to do about Grandmama and the business and he said his girlfriend was fine with keeping it a secret. I assume Charlie let it slip.'

'Not quite,' Malou said. 'It seems the girlfriend wasn't really fine with it. She announced it on her social media.'

Ren focused on breathing – in through her nose, out through pursed lips and repeat. But although she knew she was technically breathing, everything inside her curled up tight.

'It hurts.' The two words escaped unpremeditated. She hated to admit it. Whether it was her pride or her heart, she didn't know, but the honesty felt good, felt *real*. Like Friday night... 'I don't know how much is my fault, but...'

Malou grasped her hands and squeezed. 'He's a crétin, Ren. You can't defend him to me. I worked for him for four years. I know what he can be like and he has been nothing but a *fuckwit*. And then his maîtresse tells the whole world and you are the one who has to clean it up. No, it's not fair, Ren, and I can believe it fucking hurts, but he never deserved you!'

'Who deserves me, then?' she asked bitterly, wishing she had her friend's potty-mouthed nonchalance, but feeling empty inside.

'Someone who loves you.'

'Can I have a unicorn instead?'

Malou laughed ruefully, but her phone rang, interrupting their conversation. Her friend glanced at the screen, perplexed, and connected the call with a cautious, 'Allô?' Then she froze, with an expression of horror, and her hand gripped the table as though for balance. 'It's your grandmother,' she whispered through clenched teeth.

Ren snorted coffee again, this time sending droplets over Malou. 'Shit!' Ren cried, searching for a serviette. 'Serviette, s'il vous plait!' she called to the barista, but Malou shushed her and reached for the little metal dispenser of paper serviettes. Ren blushed, realising she'd been looking for a thick, fine cotton cloth.

Malou held the phone like a hot potato and dabbed at her blouse. 'Are you going to take the call?' she mouthed.

Ren had been able to block all calls at the Ritz. How had Grandmama known to phone Malou? That was a stupid question. Livia Asquith-Lewis knew *everything*. 'Tell her I'm not here. I mean, pretend you haven't seen me today!' The alarm in Malou's gaze suggested Ren's stage whisper hadn't been quiet enough.

'Ren! She's the owner of the company I work for!'

'Damn it! I should have just kept you as a friend!' But wasn't that typical? Everyone made sacrifices for her. She took the phone, telling herself it was just Grandmama. Why was she so worried? *Because she might make you come home...* She swallowed. 'Hello, Grandmama,' she said too brightly.

'Thank goodness! First I heard you didn't catch the train this morning and then the receptionist at the Ritz told me you'd gone out and I panicked!' As usual, there was no trace of panic in her tone – no trace of any emotion at all.

'I'm fine.'

'You're not, darling. You're in shock. You need to come home. The newspapers, thank God, think you've just been keeping the secret and that we all knew, but we can't fix this without you.'

'I'm okay. There's nothing to fix,' Ren lied. When was the last time she'd been okay?

'I mean the merger, the company. If you hide away in Paris, how can we convince the world that this doesn't affect us, that you're so much more than this fitness fashion woman with too many teeth that Charlie found goodness knows where? We need to tell your side of the story.'

What *was* her side of the story? And Charlie obviously thought that too many teeth was better than freckles. She didn't blame him. She'd knocked a man off his bike, lost her valuable engagement ring and spat coffee all over her best friend and in between she'd watched children's films, binged on the most ridiculous food imaginable and avoided reality. Yeah, she was such a catch.

'I... don't think I'm ready to leave Paris. I need some time to recover.' *Heal* from the past six months of playing a role she hated – after nearly fifteen years of playing the socialite role she had never quite mastered.

'Darling, you're worrying me. How about you come home to the country estate and—'

'No!' Ren blurted out before she could stop herself. The country house held too many memories of disappointment and helplessness from other times she'd failed her grandmother. 'I just meant Paris is lovely at Christmas time,' she said weakly. 'I'd like to stay a little longer.'

'But it gets *dark* so early! And you're alone.'

'I'm not alone,' she insisted.

'I don't count Malou. She doesn't understand what it's like for us.' Ren was sick of being a lonely 'us' with only her steel-spined grandmother and Ziggy the tyrant.

'That's not what I mean,' she said, struggling for the words to convince her grandmother to give her some space without admitting that she was falling apart. Emotional outbursts were up there with burgers and fries in her grandmother's book. 'Charlie and I have both moved on,' she blurted out in desperation. Malou stared at her as though she'd lost her marbles along with her engagement ring. 'I've met someone, too. A man. Here, in Paris. That's why I don't want to come home.'

Malou raised both hands and flapped them about, shaking her head furiously. Grandmama was completely silent, except for the whistle of her furious breathing.

'A... man?' Of course it was preposterous. Ren only hoped her grandmother was so shocked she would believe her.

'I should go,' she said. 'I'm having coffee with Malou and then I... I should get back to my boyfriend. We... enjoy spending time together.' Her grandmother burbled inarticulately in response. 'He's wonderful, Grandmama. Truly. Handsome and fit and he has some amazing tattoos. Not my usual aesthetic, but you can't choose who you fall in love with, can you?' Ren forced her mouth shut before she blabbered anything further.

She ended the call and handed Malou's phone back apologetically. Was it okay that she felt so good about the lie she'd just told?

Ren could almost see the mushroom cloud above her friend's head. 'What have you done?' Malou said. 'If that wasn't the quickest way to get her to rush to Paris to collect you, I don't know what would be!'

With a start, Ren realised she might have made another mistake.

7

'I'm losing it, aren't I?' Ren murmured when, five minutes later, her grandmother's assistant called to inform her that Mrs Asquith-Lewis required her presence for Afternoon Tea in the Salon Proust at the Ritz at four o'clock that afternoon. She glanced at her watch. 'Gosh, I'd better go if I'm going to make myself presentable in time!'

'Perhaps you should remind her how you really look.'

'She's going to be disappointed enough as it is.'

'You horrified her so much with the prospect of a new tattooed boyfriend who's "fit" that she'll be relieved he doesn't exist!'

Ren forced a laugh. 'He does exist,' she muttered.

'What?'

'I did meet someone – on Friday night. I was lying when I said he was my boyfriend, of course. Not that I... I don't mean "met someone", like hooked up. We just... met. That's all. And then I stayed in Paris.'

'Because of a guy?'

Ren thought of the horseshoe. 'No – well, yes. I missed my train. And then I missed the last train. And on Saturday morning... everything looked different.'

'I think you'd better start from the beginning.'

Ren recounted the chance meeting and Malou's eyes grew wide as Ren recounted the visit to the hospital and the frozen margarita and, finally, 'Santa's' workshop and... by some miracle she managed not to blurt out how badly she'd wanted to kiss him.

When she'd finished, Ren clutched her hands in her lap, grateful for the proof that that night had truly happened, in the absence of her engagement ring. Malou was speechless.

'Usually, I'm all for you stepping out of your comfort zone, but... that was a *bad* idea!'

'I seem to be full of bad ideas.'

'Why do you sound happy about that?'

Ren smiled helplessly at her friend. 'I am... kind of happy about it. That's why I'm sure there's something wrong with me. I don't know. It was fun to *not* be me for a little while.'

Malou's smile faded. 'Ren, it's okay to be you. Charlie is the one with the problem, not you.'

'I'm not so sure.'

Malou insisted they stay for another coffee and a sandwich that Ren only picked at. For once, she had no desire to return to the hotel, even though she knew she should select an outfit and at least try to do something about her face. They dawdled back through the grand streets around the Place Vendôme.

When they were finally standing outside the Ritz, Ren felt the full-on effects of two cups of coffee and nothing in her stomach except a few crumbs of bread and about a thousand macarons.

She grasped Malou's hand. 'Can you come in with me for a minute? To brainstorm. I have to work out what to tell her to let me stay here for a bit longer.'

'For you, I'll even condescend to enter the Hôtel Ritz.' Malou tucked Ren's arm under her own. 'But please don't expect me to show up to afternoon tea. I love you, but... not that much.'

Ren was glad of her friend's presence as they entered the marble foyer with its enormous, twinkling Christmas tree. A blue-clad porter tipped his hat in their direction. She was about to take the steps up to the next floor, when a figure, sitting stiffly in a gilded baroque-style chair by the reception desk, struck her as familiar. She peered more closely. Even if she'd doubted the distinctiveness of the messy curls and the dark beard, that woollen pullover and beaten-up jacket were surely one-of-a-kind fashion items.

The receptionist called him to the desk and he stood, brushing off his jeans. She couldn't do anything but stare as he leaned on the reception desk, listening and nodding earnestly. Her eyes flickered over him. He said something to the receptionist, but she was too busy watching his lips to attempt to understand.

'What's the matter?' Malou prompted.

Ren shushed her without taking her eyes off Sacha. Why else would he be here but for her? Had she made as much of an impression on him as he had on her?

'What is it?' Malou hissed.

Ren opened her mouth to explain, but it was several long moments before any words came out. 'It's him, the guy from Friday night,' was all she managed at first.

Malou's gaze whipped around. '*That's* the guy? Putain de merde,' she whispered. She looked him up and down with a thoroughness that Ren felt wasn't quite warranted. 'Wow. Just. Wow. What's he doing here?'

'How should I know?'

'He really isn't your... type.'

'I know.'

'Well?'

'Well what?'

'Are you going to talk to him?'

Ren completely froze. Part of her wanted to rush forward for the kiss she'd been too afraid to give him on Friday night. How often did a missed opportunity present itself again? But her brain hadn't completely clocked off. She was in a nervous state and had had one too many shocks this weekend. Her impulses were not to be trusted.

Sacha frowned as the receptionist spoke. He fetched something out of his pocket and held it out, speaking in rapid French.

'Je dois retourner ça,' Ren heard him say as he clutched the small object in his fingers. And, with a shudder of awareness that was as cool as it was unfortunate, Ren understood.

'He found the ring,' she said flatly. 'That's why he's here.' She laughed, one small huff that would have to suffice to release all her stupid disappointment. So much for destiny and Disney endings. She started forward.

Malou stilled her after a few steps. 'Ren, if you're thinking what I'm afraid you're thinking, please be careful. You don't want another broken heart right now and he... God, he's probably got heartbreak tattooed on his neck!'

'It's not what you think,' Ren insisted.

'Oh, thank God. I thought you were going to invite him to afternoon tea with your grandmother and then it will all go to hell, you can believe me.'

'Invite him to afternoon tea?' she repeated slowly.

'Ohhh, no, no, no!'

Sacha's head turned at Malou's sudden exclamation, but he was still listening to the receptionist and didn't take much note of them. 'That is a terrible idea,' Ren agreed, a smile forming on her lips. 'And that's what makes it so perfect.' The more she thought about it, the happier she was.

'No. Seriously. She will never believe you're in love with him.'

'He's not my type,' Ren repeated thoughtfully. 'Which is the perfect excuse to stay out of the limelight. And then, when the "love affair" ends after a few short weeks, they'll all be relieved. Because he's the last man in Paris I could ever be with,' she marvelled.

That was the moment Sacha turned and looked up. Ren froze. Something in his eyes made her wonder if he'd heard every word she'd just said.

* * *

The last man in Paris I could ever be with.

It was clear enough, and better to hear that now than to agonise about whether to ask if she'd like to go for a drink. As if she'd be interested. He'd surprised himself that he'd considered it. He had enough on his plate without adding a complicated stranger who should have left Paris already.

Sacha met her gaze as she tentatively approached. She was wearing a different pair of boots, this time with buckles everywhere and dainty toes. The conspicuous diamond earrings were missing, but even in simple gold studs she looked elegant and expensive.

She'd put herself back together since Friday night, much to Sacha's unexpected disappointment. But she lost a little composure the closer she came, until she was standing in front of him, biting her lip in uncertainty.

The last man in Paris, he reminded himself, trying to match her reserve. He would give her the ring and go. No matter what Joseph had said, finding the ring was not a sign of anything except the tensile properties of wool.

But as she peered up at him, obviously bursting with something to say that she didn't know how to begin, his resolve slowly crumbled.

'You found the ring! Where was it? Did you go back to the bar?'

'It was trapped in my pullover.' He tugged on the hem for emphasis and her smile grew.

'I don't believe it.'

'Neither did I. It must have got caught when I was searching for it under the sofa. I found it soon after you left. I'm sorry I didn't have time to give it to you yesterday. I thought you had already left Paris.'

'No, I... I keep missing the train,' she said. 'Listen, I...' She glanced at her watch.

He held up a hand to stop her. 'I should go.' He made a helpless gesture at the grand surroundings, then took a step back and tripped on a rug. He caught himself on the reception desk and winced when his shoulder twinged. She lunged for his other forearm to steady him.

'I need to carry that horseshoe with me everywhere I go,' she murmured. He noticed she didn't let go of his arm. 'How is your shoulder? Where's the sling?'

'It's fine. I wore the sling yesterday, but it was much better this morning. Not much damage. Don't worry. I rested it.'

'Hm, I hope so. But I'm glad you're here.'

'You are?'

'You have to let me pay for your bike.'

'No,' he said immediately. 'I don't want your money – thank you.'

'I'm not a crime lord or anything.'

'I know,' he said. 'You're Irena Asquith-Lewis.' Heiress, socialite, and very easy to find on the Internet. The pause between them was eloquent. 'I was going to bring the ring to your Paris offices tomorrow, but I saw an article that said you were hiding in Paris, so I thought I'd try here first.' He didn't miss her slight flinch at the comment that she was hiding.

'Who are you in real life, then? Not a Christmas elf, I'm assuming.'

He considered his answer. He could easily put her mind at ease by admitting his day job, but a glance at those boots that probably cost as much as he earned in a month made his pride flare up. 'I'm the last man in Paris.'

She blushed. 'I didn't quite mean it like that.'

'It's okay,' he said gently. 'Given your recent luck and the way I seem to hurt myself whenever you're around, you're probably the last woman in Paris I should spend time with.'

To his surprise, she smiled. 'Good,' she said. 'Now we've established that, I have to ask you a favour.'

'Of course,' he said automatically.

'God, you are so perfect,' she murmured. 'So sweet and so serious.'

'Ren, no,' her friend interjected. 'I mean it. Bad idea. Let the poor man go.'

'I'm not poor!'

'It's a figure of speech,' Ren said.

'It's the same in French,' her friend pointed out, eyeing Sacha. His only response was an inarticulate cough. He wasn't going to admit he was oversensitive after finding out exactly who he'd wanted to kiss on Friday night, especially as she still had no idea of his history and humble origins.

Sacha leaned against the reception desk and crossed his arms. 'I think you should tell me what favour you need and the poor man can decide for himself.'

'Great. Malou has to go, don't you?'

Her friend narrowed her eyes. 'Just remember I reserve the right to say "I told you so" when this gets you into trouble.'

'Trouble? Moi?' With kisses on the cheek and one last wary look, her friend Malou left them alone. Sacha shoved his hands into his back pockets and rocked on his heels, waiting for Ren to say something, but she was inspecting him with a thoroughness that made him uneasy.

He returned the favour, but it wasn't particularly satisfying. 'What is it today, Pradior?' He waved his hand at her outfit.

'You know very well what the real brands are.'

He gave a non-committal shrug. 'What help do you need?'

She squared her shoulders and looked him in the eye. Her voice didn't waver as she said, 'I need you to have a wild affair with me.'

He choked on his own breath. His vision of her went hazy at the edges, but he'd misunderstood, surely. She hadn't just asked him to have an affair with her. Had she?

8

Sacha was staring at her as though she'd said she wanted to join him on Santa's sleigh, dressed in green with a pointy red hat. Although, now she thought about it, seeing him dressed up as an elf sounded fun, especially if it was a tight-fitting costume. Maybe he'd be a naughty Christmas elf with no shirt. That worked.

But the mental image wasn't helping her determine why he was gawking at her. When his gaze dropped to her mouth, lingering barely a second before he wrenched it back up again, she remembered what she'd just said.

'I don't mean really!' Ren rushed to explain.

'What do you mean? "Really"?'

'I mean pretend. I mean I... that is, if you don't mind – if you don't have any plans. I need you to pretend to be my... like a boyfriend, just for afternoon tea.'

'Pretend? What do you mean "like a boyfriend"? I don't understand. Perhaps it's my English.'

A blush bloomed on her cheeks. 'It's not your English,' she mumbled. 'It's a long story and I don't have much time,' she said. 'Will you come with me for now and hear me out?'

'Uhm... sure,' he said with a little tip of his head. 'I assume,' he said, once they'd rounded the landing of the first flight of marble stairs, 'that it has something to do with this?' He held out her engagement ring.

She took the ring, flinging it carelessly into her handbag. She nodded in response, but she couldn't work out where to start without making herself sound like the spoilt idiot she was.

'I'm sorry about Friday,' she said. 'It was the shock. You know I'm... really already over the break-up. It happened more than six months ago, now. You read about that too, did you? I knew about his girlfriend and it was my idea to keep it a secret. I don't know why I cracked up.' His expression was wary. 'Truly,' she insisted. 'That's what I have to convince my grandmother. She's on her way to Paris, to make me go back and fix everything.'

'You don't want to go back to your family? For support?'

Support? Her grandmother's attempt at sympathy would probably be a mortified pat on the shoulder. She allowed herself to imagine for a moment that Grandmama was a hugger and... nope. She couldn't.

'My grandmother is...' She snapped her mouth shut. How could she succinctly describe the force of nature that was Grandmama and the symbiotic relationship she had with Asquith-Lewis? 'You'll see, anyway. If you agree to help, that is. She doesn't do... feelings and if she thinks I'm struggling, she'll take charge of everything and make it worse. But... I also can't go back to face all the media attention just yet.' Ren swallowed. She needed another lifetime. 'And the best way to convince her to leave me alone right now is...' She gestured wildly between the two of them.

'To tell her you're sleeping with me?'

She stopped so suddenly that he ran into her and tripped. If she hadn't grabbed handfuls of his thick pullover, he would have found himself sprawled at the bottom of the steps. Sacha righted himself against the polished wood banister, tugging on his collar.

'Thank you,' he murmured.

'Somehow I'm not sure I deserve your thanks.'

'I surprised you,' he said. 'Was that not the purpose of your request? Did I misunderstand?'

'I... wouldn't have put it so baldly, but you didn't misunderstand. Yes. You would be doing me a favour if you would pretend that we are having a... steamy rebound affair.' She rubbed her suddenly clammy hands down her twill trousers.

'A steamy—'

'Yes, that,' she said, cutting him off. 'I mean, not completely without feelings. It has to be believable.'

He made a choking noise. 'That might be a problem. Who would believe I'm your... lover?'

'It won't take much,' she assured him. 'I was never demonstrative with Charlie, so I'm not expecting you to ravish me in front of my own grandmother.' Her words petered out when she caught the alarm in his expression.

'I didn't mean... Ren, I'm happy to help you, but perhaps you should think again. You said it yourself: I'm the last man in Paris. This idea is doomed from the start.'

Happy to help you... think again... doomed. With a gulp, she dismissed the latter phrases and focused on the former. She smiled and squeezed his hand. 'Thank you. I appreciate you... your help – so much. I've got it all worked out. You don't have to pretend to be an appropriate boyfriend. An inappropriate one is even better.'

'An inappropriate... wait, they won't let me in looking like this!' He ran an agitated hand through his hair.

'Oh, don't worry about your outfit,' she said. 'No one will say anything if you're with me.'

* * *

It was lucky Nadia didn't know where he was. Although, Sacha thought to himself as they descended the stairs back to the ground floor, she would probably think it was hilarious. He almost wished he could send Raphaël a picture of himself on the grand staircase of the Ritz with Irena Asquith-Lewis on his arm.

It had taken two hours and three different employees to get her ready, during which time he'd twiddled his thumbs and stared at the gilt mirrors and antique clock in her room. He looked like a ruffian, but partly because she truly looked like a queen now. She was barely recognisable as the woman who'd got her knees dirty giving him first aid.

She wore a silk dress and a slightly ridiculous tweed cardigan that knotted at her throat. A pair of emeralds surrounded by diamonds winked in her ears. Their reflection in the numerous gold mirrors made him uneasy, as though someone would take him discreetly aside and escort him out for bothering an esteemed guest.

As they approached the doorway to the salon, he ran a hand through his hair in a vain attempt to tame it. 'Here,' she said, tucking it behind his ear with cool fingers. There was so much wrong with this moment, but, as he studied her face, trying to find the woman beneath the make-up, all he could think of was that he should have kissed her on Friday, before it all got so complicated.

'You have a very deep line, right here,' she said lightly, gesturing to her own forehead.

'I have a very bad feeling, right here.' He tapped his chest.

'How do the French get rid of bad feelings? Toss herbes de Provence over your right shoulder?' He could only respond with a flummoxed laugh.

He turned to the mirror, nudging her shoulder as they regarded their reflection as a fake couple. 'Do we pass?'

'We fail... miserably,' she said, 'but we look good doing it.'

'*You* look good. I look inappropriate, as requested.'

'I like inappropriate,' she said with a smile. 'Is it okay if we hold hands?'

'I think we must.'

She wiped her hand on her cardigan and thrust it at him. He grasped it, hesitating a moment before threading his fingers through hers. She swallowed, staring at their hands. At least they were both nervous.

'Sorry. We shouldn't need to display any more affection than this.'

'T'inquiète – don't worry. I don't mind holding your hand.'

The maître d' approached as soon as they stepped into the opulent salon. His disdain for Sacha was evident, as was his distaste as he took Sacha's worn coat and threadbare rucksack, but he greeted Ren by name and led them through the tables.

Sacha tried to play it cool, but it was difficult when he was suddenly transported to the turn of the previous century, surrounded by wood panelling, gold edging and an imposing marble fireplace. Gold beads and baubles the colour of a fine Bordeaux were arranged artfully on the mantlepiece. But what truly struck him dumb and made him drop Ren's hand to look were the bookcases, built into the arches and enclosed in glass. Every tome was leather-bound, many first editions – fiction in French, poetry in English, philosophy in German and classics in Italian.

He caught sight of the portrait of Marcel Proust, hung in pride of place above the fireplace and wearing sprigs of holly for the season. 'The Salon Proust,' he murmured with a huff of disbelief. 'Papa would have loved this. So many books.'

'Hmm?'

'This room, it's named after the French author who wrote about the lives of the beau monde at the time the hotel opened. Can you imagine it? The wealthy families patronising the artists and writers, marrying off their children and suffering in their own unhappy marriages while celebrating wealth and progress. And outside the Ritz, the real world. Proust described the lives of the rich and educated, but most of France was poor – and not welcome in the dining rooms of the Ritz.'

He snapped his mouth shut when he noticed her gaping at him.

'I'm not sure my grandmother would appreciate that. What did your father do?'

'He was a taxi driver.' It was a simple description for a complex man, but he doubted Ren wanted the long story.

'And he loved books,' she repeated softly. Sacha stared at her, searching for a trace of derision, waiting for her to dismiss the memory of his father, but she simply took his hand and squeezed.

'Mrs Asquith-Lewis is here, now,' the maître d' informed them, and Ren's smile vanished. Her other hand closed around the sleeve of his pullover. There was a light floral scent in her hair that made him take note of the spicy-sweet smell of the hotel. Her nerves troubled him. It was all a touch overwhelming.

'Don't leave me alone with her,' she said under her breath.

'I won't go anywhere.'

'There you are, darling!' A tall woman, spindly and rigid like a piece of wire, approached. She wore a loose-fitting beige outfit with flowing lines and perfect folds and her knuckles winked with several rings. She looked agelessly chic, but also older than he'd imagined. She must be approaching eighty, if she wasn't already there.

Sacha loosened his fingers, but Ren held tight, not letting go even when her grandmother placed a kiss on her cheek and clasped her shoulders. Sacha had to shake Ren off forcibly to hold out his hand to her grandmother.

'Madame Asquith-Lewis,' he said. He felt Ren's gaze and glanced down to find her staring at his wrist, where his tattoo peeked out.

'This is my grandmother, Livia,' she said. 'Grandmama, this is my boyfriend, Sacha.'

'Sacha,' the woman repeated, her tone flat.

'Sacha Mourad,' he introduced himself more formally. Would Madame Asquith-Lewis – there was no way Sacha would call her 'Livia' – notice what he suspected Ren hadn't? Would she recognise the Arabic surname and make assumptions about his humble origins – assumptions that wouldn't be far from the truth?

'And... Ziggy?' Ren was pale as she submitted to a hug from another woman who appeared at her grandmother's side. 'Ziggy is the chief strategy adviser for Asquith-Lewis,' she explained, not that it was clear to Sacha what that meant.

'How lovely to meet you, Sacha,' Ziggy said in a tone that made it clear she meant the opposite. 'We have planning to do to get us out of this pickle,' she said to Ren, and Sacha had the distinct impression he'd just been included in whatever she meant by a 'pickle'.

'Enchanté, Madame... Ziggy,' he said.

'Very... French, isn't he?' Ziggy commented across him.

'His English is very good,' Ren insisted.

'I wasn't sure if you'd bring your... Mr Mourad to afternoon tea,' Livia said gruffly. Oui, she had probably guessed that Sacha was a mixed-race kid from an apartment tower in the neuf trois, the notorious Paris suburbs. It was usually something he took pride in, especially at work, but he didn't think he'd do Ren any favours by drawing attention to it right now.

Sacha hesitated to plonk his backside on one of the upholstered museum pieces that passed for chairs in the Salon Proust, but Ren grasped his hand and tugged him down next to her on the gold velvet sofa.

A waiter immediately poured champagne, as though he could sense the misery at their table. Ren took a long sip that reminded him of the margarita on Friday night. He squeezed her hand under the table and she squeezed back twice.

'Un café, s'il vous plait,' he murmured to the waiter. He suspected he was going to need it.

9

'I don't understand all this,' Livia began, but she was interrupted by the arrival of a tower of cakes and biscuits, along with four bowls, each with a single madeleine in cold milk.

Sacha couldn't help but smile at the ingenious menu item, but, given the pinched expression on Livia's face, he didn't imagine she would be interested in an explanation of Proust's evocation of childhood memories.

She touched the spoon as little as possible, as though suspecting it could be dirty. Her lips pursed as she chewed. 'Quite... simple.'

'That's the intention,' he responded, but no one appeared to be listening.

Ren reached for a biscuit, but Ziggy's hand shot out and stilled her. 'The madeleine will do. I can't imagine you've had much exercise in the past few days.'

Sacha froze, watching this exchange with consternation.

'No, but...' Ren sighed heavily and didn't bother finishing the sentence. He couldn't let it stand. He didn't want to cause trouble, but wasn't he supposed to be an inappropriate boyfriend anyway?

He took a viennois biscuit, dipped it in Ren's tea and held it out to her, ignoring the disapproving look that Livia delivered with such vigour. 'Mon chou, have one.' When Ren just stared at him, he lifted the biscuit to her mouth, holding his hand underneath. She blinked in shock and Ziggy tittered with disbelief. 'Open,' he demanded. With a whisper of breath, she opened her mouth and took a bite of the pâtisserie.

'Oh, my God...' she groaned, quickly covering her mouth when Livia and Ziggy – and a stiff-looking couple at the next table – eyed her. 'Give me some more,' she murmured. The shortbread biscuit dipped in dark chocolate was the handiwork of one of the finest pâtissiers in France, so Sacha should have expected this reaction.

When Ziggy pointedly took a biscuit with the silver tongs, rather than her fingers, he realised the full extent of his faux pas. But he straightened his shoulders, dunked the biscuit again and offered her another bite.

Her eyes lit with amusement as she chewed slowly and appreciatively. She took the remains of the biscuit from him, her hand lingering on his. 'Thank you... darling.' He just managed to swallow a snort of laughter.

'I can't imagine how the two of you met,' Ziggy said as she failed spectacularly to eat any of her marble cake with chocolate glaze. 'Was it at the office? Are you a porter?'

'I'm not a porter.'

'How *did* you meet?' Livia demanded.

Ren had a terrible poker face as she chewed and tried to think of what to say. 'It's quite funny, actually,' she said. 'I knocked him off his bike.'

'You ride a motorbike?' Livia cried.

'No, no,' Sacha reassured her. 'It's a bicycle.'

'A... bicycle,' she repeated, as though she'd never heard the word before.

'Oui. I don't own a car.'

'You don't...'

Rather than allow her grandmother to dumbly repeat everything Sacha said, Ren rushed on with the explanation. 'I was opening the car door and... Sacha crashed into it – into my life.' He groaned inwardly at her attempt to make it sound romantic.

'After that, she took me to the hospital to check... and then... we had a drink together and she took me... home.'

Livia choked. 'She took you home?'

'I mean, I—' Ren gave him an urgent look and it slowly dawned on him that he'd implied something very different to what he'd intended.

'She *drove* me home. To my home,' he explained.

Livia's pallor looked increasingly alarming. 'You stayed at his *home*? A stranger you'd just met?'

'Um,' Ren said helplessly.

'No, Bilel drove me home and then Ren left again, without staying.' He held his breath, waiting for Livia's reaction.

'And then what?'

'Sacha found something of mine that I'd dropped and returned it here the next day. That was when we decided to...'

'Date,' he said, his voice clipped. 'We decided to date. We had dinner together.'

'Here, at the Ritz?'

That didn't sound plausible. 'Euh, no. There is a bistro I know – a nice place – in the Marais, near the Place des Vosges.' Every word he said seemed to take Ren's grandmother's blood pressure up a notch.

'Ren, your *safety*! Was this at night? What do I always say?'

'Safety is non-negotiable,' she mumbled, as though she'd said the words many times. 'I was safe with Sacha. I *am* safe with Sacha.' He bit his tongue before mentioning that she was just as likely to be mugged around the Place Vendôme as anywhere else. Where there were rich pickings... 'I never expected to meet someone... like this. It all happened very quickly, by chance. You know, like it was meant to be.' That sounded a little far-fetched. He tapped her foot with his in warning, but she eyed him. 'What? Do you want them to think our relationship is just casual?'

He coughed, glad he hadn't touched the champagne, or he would have spat it across the room. 'Dating,' he ground out. 'Casual *dating*.'

'We're very happy, anyway,' Ren said, patting his hand. 'And I couldn't possibly be parted from Sacha right now.' He unclenched his jaw with difficulty. If he'd known she was such a terrible actress, he might not have agreed to this, but he suspected saying 'no' to Ren would be a challenge.

'What did you find?' Livia asked with a narrow gaze. 'What did Ren lose that you found?'

'One of my earrings,' Ren saved him. 'The diamond ones.'

'What were you doing wearing the earrings Charlie gave you in an unsavoury part of Paris?'

'It wasn't an unsavoury part!'

'You expect me to believe *he* was loitering in the Place Vendôme? Come to think of it, are you sure that's not what he was doing?'

'The important thing is, she's all right, now,' Ziggy said calmly. 'We can work out what there is to be done to sort out this mess.' She produced a tablet as though it were an extra limb. 'We've created a schedule of posts and events that send the subtle message that life goes on without a Routledge-Asquith-Lewis marriage—'

'But what about—' Livia gestured curtly between Sacha and Ren.

Ziggy cleared her throat and eyeballed Livia meaningfully.

'Could we discuss something briefly? In private? Do excuse us,' she said to the two supposed lovebirds.

'Oh, God, I'm so sorry,' Ren said in a rush after Ziggy and her grandmother had disappeared out of the doorway. 'They don't believe us.'

'They do believe us. They just believe we're having casual sex,' he muttered.

'Why didn't you back me up when I tried to make it a love story?'

'Because nobody would believe *that*. There's no "meant to be", at least not for us!'

'Someone's not a romantic. And now she believes I'm using you for sex.'

'She thinks *I'm* using *you* – for something worse.' He rubbed a hand over his face. When he opened his eyes, she had a strange look on her face. 'And you find this funny,' he accused her.

'It is kind of like *Pretty Woman* in reverse.'

'Except I'm not a prostitute,' he muttered, lifting the tiny glass of water to his lips.

'No, but you are a pretty man.'

He nearly spat the water. Swallowing with difficulty, he coughed and eyed her dubiously.

'It's a compliment,' she said with one of her smiles.

'Is it? I'm wearing jeans in the Ritz. How can I believe you're serious?'

'Sorry. I'm teasing you because it makes you smile and it's cute.' He eyed her. 'It wouldn't kill you to smile more.'

She should know how perilous smiles could be. Hers had landed him in this absurd situation. 'I don't think smiling would make your grandmother believe we're in love. That's what you need me for, right?'

'Right,' she agreed. 'And I don't think casual lovers will cut it. It's so out of character for me, she'll be even more convinced I'm upset about Charlie and need saving from myself.'

'What do you suggest we do? We aren't very good actors.'

'I'll think of something. We've got all of afternoon tea to get through.' He groaned. 'I'm surprised you haven't run away screaming. My life is... complicated.'

'I promised I would not go anywhere. But this plan might not work, and you'll have to tell her the truth anyway.'

'The truth? Which part? That I'm a disappointing granddaughter who can't step up when the company needs her? To be honest, I think Grandmama knows that already.'

'Surely, if you explain you are too fragile to come out in public, now, she will respect that.'

'Ohhhh, no,' Ren said, her eyes wide. 'One whiff of weakness and Grandmama doubles down. Our company... we trade on image. That's my job. I post photos of myself on the Internet wearing Louis Versace to make it look like the company is more than just a glorified version of eBay.' She grimaced. 'Eek, don't tell anyone I said that!'

'No one cares what I think of Asquith-Lewis.' She looked for a moment as though she would disagree.

'I don't know why I dragged you into this. They're being rude and I... I should have expected that. I didn't think it through. You can go if you want. I won't blame you. I might envy you!'

'One afternoon is not going to hurt me.' Sacha took Ren's hands, brushing his finger over her left ring finger.

'I bet we look like a real couple, now,' she commented, turning her hands over to grasp his.

'Try not to worry. Logically, she would never suspect that we're pretending.'

'This *is* the stupidest idea ever,' she agreed with a sigh. A sound made her look over her shoulder. 'They're coming back,' she whispered in sudden panic. 'Quick!' Before he realised what she intended, she planted her lips on his.

It was a terrible kiss: stiff and jerky and clumsy. It must have been obvious they'd never kissed before. He pulled away, ignoring her look of dismay.

'We should at least do it right,' he whispered, grasping her face with both hands. Swallowing his final reservations, he tilted his head and swept her mouth into a real kiss.

Then he promptly forgot where he was.

10

Ren needed something to hold onto. What she'd intended to be a quick smack of lips to drive her point home to her grandmother had turned into the most divine kiss of her life. It was firm, but gentle, and with his lips slightly parted, his mouth fit hers in a way that scrubbed every thought from her mind.

The Ren of two days ago would have pushed him away in shock – if she'd ever found herself kissing a relative stranger. But today's Ren, developing a thirst for chaos, returned the kiss, opening her lips against his. He was the one to draw away, sucking in an enormous breath.

She stifled a smile, watching him turn pink and rub his hand over his mouth. He was perfectly sweet.

'Sorry,' she mouthed just before her grandmother cleared her throat loudly from where she was standing by her chair.

'Are we intruding?'

'Non, madame,' Sacha said, his voice gravelly. Ren would never have guessed that an inappropriate boyfriend was just what she needed.

'Grandmama, no matter what you say, I'm not coming back to London yet.' Yes, finally she'd actually said it straight!

'Because of *him*?'

'Yes.' She wasn't quite lying.

'Darling,' her grandmother said, and Ren steeled herself. 'You were still engaged only a few days ago. You're grieving.'

'I haven't been engaged for six months. You can't expect I'd just... tread water, hanging onto Charlie all that time?' Ren knew she might be lying, now, but there was too much at stake to admit it, even to herself. 'I knew he'd moved on. Why shouldn't I?'

'I expected you to come to me when the problem first arose! You don't fold at the first challenge. An Asquith-Lewis stays and fights!' Which was exactly why Ren sometimes had trouble believing she really was an Asquith-Lewis.

'What do you think I should have fought for?' God knew Charlie wasn't worth it.

'We had the contracts for the merger drawn up, hundreds of hours of discussions with the lawyers, and Charlie had no intention of honouring it? Honouring you?'

'This isn't about the merger.'

'Two family firms with a lot of history don't just merge without some kind of insurance.'

So much for a grand romance. 'What about feelings? What about love?' Ren choked on the word.

'You and Charlie were together for years. You wouldn't have got this far if you didn't love each other. He'll take you back, if he knows what's good for him. You're meant for each other, Ren. You've known that since you were teenagers.'

Ren's stomach turned and she almost regretted eating the biscuit. How could Grandmama on the one hand suggest her relationship had been about the business and then claim they were meant for each other? But what more had she expected? For

Grandmama, 'destiny' and 'business' were practically the same thing.

Ren knew she had a duty to her family, to the business that was more precarious than anyone realised, but she just wanted some time to recover without anyone watching. She wanted more time in Paris.

She had no phone, no social media logins. This was the perfect opportunity to run away and hide – just this once. Grandmama couldn't be any more disappointed in her than she already was. Where was the harm?

Ren took Sacha's hand, pushing away the guilt for dragging him into this. She slowly linked her fingers with his. '"Meant for each other" is supposed to describe a great love that is destined to be,' she said. 'That's not what I had with Charlie.'

'You think you've found love with *this*...?' Livia waved her hand at Sacha, unable to find a word or simply too British to insult him to his face.

Ren reached for him protectively. 'I'm willing to take the chance.'

'I will not approve of this. I can't sit back and let you get hurt!'

'You can't protect me from everything!' she exclaimed, realising a moment too late that her comment was like poking the beast. Even a hint of a reminder of what had happened twenty years ago was enough to bring out the dragon.

'You are my granddaughter and I will protect you from *everything* that threatens you!' Ren gritted her teeth. Livia's statement might have had more power a week ago, but that day she could only think, with some bitterness, that Livia had never been able to protect her from the things that hurt her most. 'Come back home and forget all this nonsense.'

'I'm staying,' Ren insisted.

Ziggy placed a hand on Grandmama's arm and she calmed immediately. 'If Ren is truly set on this, we can only... *support* her.'

'I will not—'

'We will all be in Val d'Isère for the ski weekend with the investors in two weeks,' Ziggy continued, ignoring Livia's outburst. 'I'm sure by then this will all... *blow over* and Ren will be by *your* side again to entertain the investors at the chalet. Two weeks in Paris will be a relaxing holiday for her to rediscover her place in the world.'

Ziggy's support surprised Ren, but she wasn't going to question it, despite the uneasiness that crept up her spine at the purposeful emphasis in those sentences. 'I don't want to spoil your afternoon tea, so Sacha and I will go,' she said hurriedly, wanting to leave before her free pass was revoked. 'I'll see you in Val d'Isère.'

'Wait!' Ziggy said. 'Where's your phone?'

'It broke. I threw it in the bin.'

'That's fortuitous. If you're going to walk away from your family for two weeks,' she continued, her tone sending shivers down Ren's spine, 'then no social media. No media of any kind. No photos. No paparazzi. No one knows about... him. Is that agreed?'

Ziggy had no idea her words were received by Ren as a blissful get-out-of-jail-free card, although she hadn't realised granting her wish could sound like a veiled threat. 'All right.'

Her hand was horribly damp, but Sacha hung on regardless. He was a saint for what she'd put him through – and she'd better get him out of there before he became a headless one at her grandmother's hands.

'You know this is a mistake,' Livia declared as they rose from the table.

'Yes,' she agreed – another sliver of truth in this farce. 'Mistake, opportunity – it's difficult to tell the difference until you've made them.'

* * *

It was only when she'd stumbled out from under the awning and onto the pavement of the Place Vendôme that Ren breathed again. She managed to take a few steps away, so the doorman wouldn't pay too much attention, before doubling over, propping herself up against her knees and trying not to suck too much frigid air into her lungs all at once.

'Oula,' she heard Sacha's voice somewhere close, 'tu vas être malade? You're not going to vomit?'

His words made her laugh – a loud laugh from deep in her stomach that echoed around the elegant square. The darkness of evening had fallen and the mist of a light rain brought a hush to the stone buildings and slate roofs, enhanced by the cobweb of warm fairy lights above and the two solemn Christmas trees.

A sense of freedom swept through her, with the prick of goose bumps on her skin. Her cardigan didn't provide much protection from the cold, but she didn't care. She wanted to feel each molecule of damp Paris air. If this was how it felt to embrace mistakes, to run into the unknown, then she should have done it a long time ago.

Ren hauled herself upright and leaned a hand on Sacha's shoulder. 'After everything I've put you through, I really hope I don't vomit as well,' she said. 'But I'm glad you're calling me "tu", now.'

He coughed, regarding her with a reluctant smile. 'I think we're a bit past "vous". And vomiting would be a waste of a very fine biscuit.'

'That biscuit *was* divine!' she said, whirling on her heels. She'd barely had one glass of champagne, but she was drunk on relief. 'I'm sorry I kissed you.'

'You didn't,' he insisted.

'What? Were we in the same reality? Have you forgotten the lip-locking that totally sealed the deal for my grandmother – or for Ziggy, at least?'

'I haven't forgotten,' he said. He bit his lip – it was for less than a second, but it gave Ren a tingle of something very pleasant over her skin. 'But *I* kissed *you*.'

'Ah, semantics,' she said with a dismissive wave.

His frown was particularly deep. 'It's not semantics. Semantics is about the relative meaning of words. You mean interpretation.'

'Ah, *interpretation*,' she repeated with another wave and a smile. His lips twitched and she wasn't sure what she wanted more: for him to smile fully or to say more of those long sentences in his charming accent. 'Whatever it was, I'm sorry if you were uncomfortable. It wasn't agreed and I just panicked.'

'C'est bon. Kissing was not a problem,' he said. 'Now I have met your grandmother...' He couldn't find the words and finished his sentence with a shrug. 'I played my part willingly. *You* were magnificent.'

'I *was*!' she giggled, stepping across the road and doing another twirl under a chandelier made of fairy lights. Sacha raced after her and caught her when she tripped. 'Stupid heels,' mumbled Ren. 'Why do women have to wear heels anyway?'

'They don't have to.'

'You're right. Perhaps I'll decide to never wear them again. I wouldn't want to part with my Chanel boots, but four-inch heels can fuck off!' The 'f' passing her lips with emphasis gave her immense satisfaction.

An icy gust blew through the empty square, and she shivered. A moment later, a familiar fleece-lined leather coat was placed onto her shoulders.

'You need it more than me.'

'Thank you,' she said, taking another peek at that gorgeous

face. Then she opened her mouth without premeditation. 'Let's get out of here! There's so much of Paris I want to see.'

'And I have seen enough of the Hôtel Ritz.'

'So, take me somewhere. Take me... to the Sacré-Cœur! I've never been there and I'm suddenly dying to go.'

'Now? Are you... serious?'

'Why? Is it unsafe at night?'

Sacha huffed at her in a laugh that wasn't quite a laugh. 'No, it's safe – well, usually, for normal people who aren't wearing diamonds and evening dresses.'

She tugged out her earrings and stuffed them into her purse. 'This isn't an evening dress. It's a cocktail dress, so we're good to go.' She grabbed his hand and tugged him into motion, only to stop a moment later, realising she had no idea where she was going.

'Don't you have to call your driver?'

'I thought you were going to take me?' She realised he hadn't actually agreed, but she didn't want to give him the chance to turn her down.

'You know I don't have a car.'

'How did you get here, then? Are we taking the métro?'

'Why are you so excited about the métro?'

'I've never taken it before!'

'It doesn't taste as good as a margarita.'

'I wasn't planning to lick it.'

He coughed again. 'Well, if you insist I must take you...'

'I absolutely insist,' she said.

'Alors,' he said, 'this way.'

She followed him to the north end of the square in the light of the wrought-iron lamp posts with three lanterns each. His hands were shoved into the pockets of his jeans, probably against the cold, and she tucked her hand into one elbow, making him glance at her doubtfully.

As they walked quickly north, Sacha jerked his head in the direction of a bicycle chained to a traffic sign. 'That's how I got here.'

'You got it fixed!'

He nodded. 'Don't offer me money.'

'I wouldn't dream of it. I know about your fierce pride, now.' She studied the bike as they walked past. 'You could take me on the frame.' She could wrap her arms around him and let him pedal her through the night. It wasn't quite a magic carpet, but it would do.

But he snorted in response. 'I'm not cycling up the butte Montmartre with you on the back.'

'Are you saying I'm heavy?'

He turned to her with a sharp look that made her stand up straight. It reminded her of something – or someone – but she couldn't place who or what. 'Are you worried about your weight? Because you shouldn't be. I can't believe that woman told you not to eat the biscuits of a famous French pâtissier!'

'I thought you were defending me, when you were merely offended on the part of some French pâtissier.'

'I *was* defending you!' he insisted. The pâtissier could have concocted a masterpiece from her warm, gloopy, sugary feelings.

She gave him a cheeky smile. '"That woman" remembers when I was a chubby teenager with an aversion to the gym. Honestly, I think I would hate myself more if I was on social media every day with even bigger thighs.'

'Bordel de merde, can you hear what you say?'

'Why do you care so much?'

'I... this attitude causes problems – for others as well.' Her steps slowed as his words struck her. 'I see it in my work.'

'You haven't said what your work is yet.'

'No.'

She waited for him to say something else, but he didn't. 'Are you a… doctor?'

'No, but good effort.'

'I might have been born wealthy, but I do know not to judge a book by its cover. Do you say that in French?'

'We say the dress doesn't make the monk. But I like the English better. Any other guesses?'

'You're going to make me guess your job?'

'Yes.'

'Well, then, lawyer? Lawyers know about semantics and interpretation.'

'No.'

'Hermit?'

'Hmm?'

'You've grown rather monosyllabic, so I thought you might be a recovering hermit.'

'Ah, you mean ermite.' He didn't dignify her joke with a laugh. 'No. I don't think that would pay my rent. Some of us require a salary.'

'Ha. I earn a salary. But, to be honest, I'd rather like to be a hermit, if it means I don't have to face my grandmother ever again.'

The sidelong look he gave her, out from behind thick lashes, held an unexpected spark of amusement. 'I'm not sure you'd be a good hermit. And I mean that like a compliment.'

They arrived at the Place de l'Opéra and Ren paused, pulling Sacha to a stop. 'Look,' she said. Her breath caught at the play of light projected onto the stone buildings on the square. The stately façades glowed red and blue, Christmas lights twinkled gold while the shadows of the wrought-iron balconies traced their own lines. Watching over the glimmering square was the Palais Garnier itself, the grand Paris opera house, imposing and ornate with sculpted figures and grand arches and touches of gold.

'If you want to go to the opera, you can go without me.'

'I don't want to go to the opera,' she said, nudging him with her shoulder. 'I'm looking at the lights. They're beautiful.'

He looked as though he was going to contradict her at first, as he studied the lights critically, but then his expression softened and he inclined his head. 'Très beau,' he agreed quietly.

She stared at him, his words echoing in her mind. She had enough poor French to understand that he'd said, 'Very beautiful,' and she had enough hope to imagine that instead, he might have looked at her and said, 'Très belle,' not meaning the lights at all.

It was such a romantic cliché and she knew she'd watched too many films with happy endings. But she couldn't help peering at him and thinking the words, 'Très beau,' so fiercely she was concerned he would hear them.

'Is something wrong? You look...' His gesture to his own face wasn't flattering. Ren got the message. Pining wasn't a good look.

'I'm fine. Let's go!'

He ushered her along the pedestrian crossing and down the stairs to the métro, with a grand view of the Palais Garnier in front. Underground, the lighting was suddenly harsh and the tiled walls and concrete made the station feel like the entrance to a giant underground public toilet.

Ignoring the décor – or lack of it – she followed the stream of passengers to the barriers, where she was quickly defeated by the LED crosses and arrows and the strange silver turnstiles.

'You need a ticket!' Sacha called out.

'I know I need a ticket. I'm not entirely stupid. Where do I put the money?'

He managed to look fiercely disapproving and reluctantly amused at the same time. 'You're not stupid at all. I just... have you taken the London Underground? It's similar, except that this is Paris, so we never quite managed to get rid of the paper tickets.'

'Of course I haven't taken the Underground!' she said with mock horror. 'Can you imagine what Ziggy would say if I tried?'

He released a long breath. 'D'accord. This way to the ticket machines.'

'Are you a bus driver?' she asked abruptly.

He smiled, flashing his slightly crooked teeth and crinkling up the corners of his eyes. 'Non,' he said. 'Why would a bus driver care about his passengers' body image?'

'Well, *you* would be a caring bus driver,' she said with a shrug.

'I don't know which way to look! It's all so beautiful!'

Sacha wasn't sure which way to look either – for a different reason. Ren had raced up the stairs to the lane outside the glowing white basilica and stood precariously close to the edge in her impractical heels. The pavement glittered a warning of ice and he could barely feel his hands.

Yet Ren's smile and the audible exclamation points in her sentences made him look up and out. The city was laid out before them, a lattice of shadows and glowing light. Beyond the glittering carousel halfway down the hill, the buildings at the bottom were illuminated in the warm yellow of the streetlamps. Rows of slate roofs and clay chimneys spread out into the distance, interspersed with the spires and cupolas of parish churches. Clusters of squat tower-blocks, further south, reminded the world that Paris was just a city, after all, and people needed to live somewhere.

Just a city... That description wasn't quite right, not for Paris. Sacha gazed outwards, feeling the touch of the past behind him and the prickle of possibility in the air. He'd expected to be eating at Nadia's tonight – bickering and laughing and slumping on the sofa. Instead, he was standing at the top of the hill of martyrs, with a person at his side who didn't feel at all like a stranger, as the world rolled out before him. 'The world' was a better way to describe Paris – with some hyperbole, perhaps, but he appreciated it.

'I've so rarely been... outside... in the dark,' she admitted. 'In a car, yes, or at an event, but never just "out".' He could believe it, the way she gazed around her in wonder. She glanced at the two other couples nearby, one in an amorous embrace. She stared until it would have been rude, if they hadn't been oblivious. 'No one's watching and it's like I could be anyone, do anything. It probably sounds crazy to you.'

'I began to understand a little when I met your grandmother,' he replied.

'You probably think I'm an idiot for letting them have any say in my life. I'm thirty years old, but sometimes I feel like I'm still ten. Grandmama and I... we're all the family each other has got. And the business *is* family.'

Sacha considered his words carefully. 'I don't think you're an idiot. But worrying about what a stranger thinks of you is... not ideal.'

She turned to him suddenly, studying his face with too much intensity so that it brought warmth to his cold cheeks. 'Are you a psychologist?' she guessed.

'Wrong again.'

'Well,' she said thoughtfully, 'I'm not used to being a problem, anyway.'

'You're not a problem.'

'I've been nothing but a problem to *you* since we met. Are you a used car salesman, since that was such a good lie?'

'No. And perhaps what I meant was... you're welcome to be a problem.'

She mumbled something like, 'You don't know what you're in for,' but she didn't seem to expect a response. Instead, she turned back to the view of the winking lights, linking her arm with his.

He stood stiffly, feeling her arm looped through his. 'I suppose it's the right of every human being to be a problem.'

'Are you an activist? A yellow vest or whatever it's called? Or was it a blue collar?' she mused.

'I don't think that's what you meant by "job". I wouldn't be Parisian if I hadn't attended a protest or two, but I'm not a member of the gilets jaunes.'

'A gang?' She looked unexpectedly cheerful at the prospect.

'No!'

'An undercover police officer?' He shook his head again. 'I bet it's something obscure that I'll never guess.'

'Perhaps,' he said, stifling a smile.

'A chimney sweep?' she asked with a grin, but he didn't dignify her joking suggestion with a response. Her gaze wandered the rooftops. 'Paris in December certainly is la Ville Lumière – the city of light.'

'Paris,' he said with a thoughtful huff. *Pa-ri*, emphasising the silent final consonant. 'Where I grew up, we had a few different nicknames for it.'

'Oh?'

'Paname, Bériz, Soixante-quinze, or Ripa – as I am sometimes called Chassa.'

'Are you speaking another language?'

'Paname is from a scandal long ago about the construction of the Panama Canal and corruption in the Paris élite. Soixante-quinze you can perhaps translate?'

'I think you overestimate my French,' she said with a laugh.

'It is a number – seventy-five, the number of the département of Paris, and the beginning of the post code.'

'Ahh,' she said. 'I caught "soixante" and got confused because of your wacky numbers. Sixty-fifteen, right?'

'Our numbers are not "wacky",' he said in mock affront. 'I understand it is difficult for English speakers.'

'It's difficult for everyone! Don't tell me little kids don't struggle to say four-twenty-ten instead of ninety? You need a degree in maths just to count!' She turned to him suddenly. 'Do you have a degree in maths?'

'No,' he said. 'But you're supposed to guess, not ask me twenty questions.'

'Is that called "vingt questions" in French?'

'Yes, but you don't pronounce the "s".'

'Why do you bother with all these letters nobody says?'

'You should write to the Académie Française and complain.'

'I might just do that. Are you going to explain Chassa and Ripa?'

'It's called "verlan", from "l'envers", you say reverse in English? It's French word play. Sa-cha becomes Cha-sa. Paris is Ri-pa. Irena is... Aneri or perhaps Na-ire.'

'I like Naire. I could be Naire the night nymph, whose powers emerge with the setting of the sun. I'll have to swear you to secrecy!'

'We are already held together by a secret.' It couldn't be a good thing that they'd just deceived her grandmother, but the idea of sharing a secret with Ren wasn't as unpalatable as it should have been.

'Well, Ripa is ly-love in the ning-eve. Why can't I see the Eiffel Tower, by the way?'

'You can probably see it from the top of the belltower, but those trees are in the way, here,' said Sacha. 'Why? Don't you believe it's Paris without the tower?'

'Have you been up?' she asked.

'No.'

'Really? Why not? You live here.'

'Do you expect I climb up the stairs twice a week for exercise? It would be cheaper to join a gym.'

'There's no need to be all sniffy and Parisian about it. You might have gone up once,' she said defensively.

He hesitated. 'I never think of the Eiffel Tower as... *my* Paris. It's for the clients of an expensive restaurant and middle-class tourists. I'm neither and it's not cheap to go up.' There was no way she'd understand, even though she watched him as though she wanted to try.

'I haven't been up, either.'

'Sérieux? Never?'

'It's stupid, really.' He didn't like how often she used that word, always in reference to herself. 'Paris was the first city I visited after... well, I had a difficult few years as a teenager with, you know, anxieties and things. When I saw the tower, I thought to myself that I wanted someone to propose to me at the top.' She laughed humourlessly.

'Did you tell Charlie?'

'Maybe. I'm not sure. But he didn't get the message. His proposal wasn't very romantic, anyway. It was all planned and photographed and pretty much live-streamed. And then, I thought to myself that I'd save the Eiffel Tower for our tenth wedding anniversary. I'm such a chump. Gargh, forget it. I don't want to go on about this stuff. I'm trying to... live a little and you're too serious as it is.'

'Too serious?' He'd thought he'd made a lot more jokes than usual that evening.

She tucked her arm through his again. 'You have a perma-frown.'

'A perma – ahhh, I understand. Perhaps this is the result of your company,' he said lightly.

'I'm your bad luck charm.'

'It must be true that I'm not good at making jokes, because that was one – a joke. I didn't mean *you*. I meant... everything that has happened since we met, this comédie.'

'A comedy of errors,' she murmured. 'That sounds right. At least you'll be rid of me after tonight.' She sighed, shrinking into his coat, her gaze growing distant.

'What will you do? With your freedom?'

'Freedom! Gosh, I don't even know. I've wasted my time so far, watching Disney films and barely feeding myself. But I hope... Paris might be good for me. It has been so far.'

'There are many more views to discover,' he said. She looked earnestly up into his face. He cleared his suddenly thick throat. 'Are we going into the basilique?'

'What basilique? Oh, you mean this one?' She twirled to gesture wildly at the edifice in mock surprise, but her smile faded as she regarded the white stone church that looked ghostly in the crisp winter darkness. 'It's not like other churches, is it?' she said softly. 'It almost looks like it's made of clouds.'

Sacha shuffled closer, ducking his head in a vain attempt to see the basilica exactly as she did. 'You are right, it's unique. This church is not old – not by Parisian standards. It was only finished about a hundred years ago, but the architects rejected many of the fashions of the time. This church was to be a connection to a past that was lost.'

Her surprised look suggested he'd explained with a little too much flourish. But when she said, 'Go on,' he couldn't refuse her.

'The arches, they are the Roman type. And the cupola is in the Byzantine style – from the east. But the statues are uniquely French: Jeanne d'Arc and Saint Louis – or King Louis neuf, as he was first. This is the dream of French Catholicism. But it was built to carry the nation's grief, too.'

'Grief?'

'All history is change and grief,' he said with a shrug. Ren still stared at him, as though she was soaking in his words with her eyes. He cleared his throat and continued in a measured tone. 'This church was a memorial for a terrible siege that saw people eating cats and dogs and even flowers in desperation. And when the siege was lifted and the people could eat, there was fighting again – this time between the French army and the Parisian Communards who took over the city, starting on this hill and ending as martyrs or traitors, depending on your point of view.'

'You're ruining the grand church.'

'You'd rather keep your head in the clouds?'

'Wouldn't it be simpler to forget?'

'And have to learn the lessons of the past over and over again? No, it's not simpler. The world looks black and white when you regard the Sacré-Cœur against the night sky, but it's not. Just think, by the time they completed this church, only forty years later, there was another war, this time with a different winner, but a terrible loss of life. And it is the indirect reason my father spoke French. Do you think we should forget this, too?'

'Of course not,' said Ren. 'You've made your point. Are you sure you aren't a politician?'

'Definitely not!'

'Maybe you should be.'

'I would not want to be examined so closely,' he explained, lightening his tone.

'*That*, I understand,' she said emphatically. 'What war were you talking about, when the church was finished? World War I? What does that have to do with your father?'

'The Ottoman Empire was defeated and the part where my

ancestors lived was taken by France to govern. My father was born in the new independent state of al-jumhūrīyah al-Lubnānīyah in 1946. The République libanaise.'

'Lebanon.'

'Correct.'

'So we're standing on a bit of your history.'

'We're always standing on a bit of our history. The past is set out like the streets of Paris, interconnected, sometimes forgotten and covered up. Where you are standing is an intersection – the sacred hill of Paris, where Saint Denis was beheaded more than a thousand years ago and we still remember.'

'Ah, yes, I remember that guy. He took his head for a little walk, right?'

'It wasn't a little walk. He gave a sermon and went to the place where his followers would establish the city of Saint-Denis – while holding his head.'

'Good for him. Are you a historian, then?'

'No.' He should just put an end to her suffering and tell her, but he had to admit he was enjoying her guesses. She followed when he strode up the steps to the grand portal of the basilica. He made sure she didn't see him smile.

12

Ren sneaked a glance at Sacha, her night-time guide, as he grimly regarded the prayer candles flickering in the hushed ambience of the church. Who was he, this man who weaved history with threads of meaning and wielded words so powerful they made her heart beat wildly?

Whatever his job was, she was certain he held a position of authority – that he used for the powers of good. He didn't hesitate to tell her difficult truths. He'd stood up to Ziggy. But he'd been... gentle in the face of her outrageous requests and tolerant of her teasing him.

'Gentle' was the right word. He was a gentle man – a gentle-man. He wasn't the picture of a gentleman she would have conjured three days ago, with his neck tattoo in looping script, unruly long hair and creased forehead.

The light in the church was extraordinary. With no sunlight to brighten the stained glass, only the interior lamps illuminated the vivid colours of the mosaics, giving them a brushed quality, with extremes of light and dark.

Above the choir was an enormous mosaic, so stunning she

could barely believe it was made of pieces of coloured stone. On a background of vivid blue, the figure of Christ looked as though he were about to leap out of the mosaic and give her a hug. The figures on either side were rendered flat in comparison: bishops and knights, women in robes and rows of saints with matching halos.

One saint caught her eye and she tiptoed closer to Sacha, leaning on his arm to point out the figure in the mosaic who'd caught her eye. 'That's Saint Denis!' she whispered.

'They are all the important saints of France,' he whispered in reply.

'Were you born in France, then?' she asked. He nodded in reply. 'In Paris? Around here?'

'No, I didn't grow up in the seventy-five,' he said with a small smile.

'You're enjoying being mysterious,' she accused, 'you dork,' she finished with a nudge to his arm. 'Are you a tour guide?'

'No, but I am mysterious and I don't know what a dork is.'

'You're definitely one of those. Look it up.' He pulled out his phone and chuckled to himself a moment later, tilting his head in agreement.

Contentment settled over Ren as she wandered over the marble flagstones. She wasn't measuring every word; she felt no pressure to be anything more than herself. She was *teasing* him – a stranger. No, not a stranger, but not quite a friend, either. In her other life, she would have been desperate to label this unexpected relationship, to compartmentalise it and make it safe.

But whatever it was, she was fairly certain it wasn't safe.

They stopped in front of the elaborate nativity, the 'crèche', sculpted of fired clay, with real moss on the roof of the stable. Sacha pointed out the three wise men.

'This is Paris, come to honour the baby,' he said with a smile.

Ren didn't understand the joke at first. 'This one, he's Congolese. This one could be Algerian and this one – well, that's obvious.'

'It is a bit,' she agreed, studying the figure with the pointed hat – a clumsy stereotype of a person from east Asia.

Her stomach growled all of a sudden, filling the apse of the church. She clutched herself around her middle guiltily. She might be filled with happiness and freedom, but her metabolism was running on empty.

'Is there a restaurant around here? A cheap, dodgy one?'

'Of course there are restaurants nearby, all of them "dodgy" in comparison to the Ritz.'

'As long as it's not a "Siege of Paris"-themed restaurant, I'll be okay.'

'You don't feel like cat or dog tonight? What about rat?'

'No flowers, either. That sounded weird. What about a Lebanese restaurant?'

'There are flowers in Lebanese cuisine – capers. But do you think a Lebanese restaurant would be dodgy?'

'No! Someone's touchy. I didn't mean that at all.' She still blushed. Her suggestion had been only 10 per cent prejudice and 90 per cent curiosity about him. It didn't seem fair, when he had the Internet to find out about her. Sometimes it felt like her life was lived more in packets of data sent and received, rather than breaths or heartbeats.

He'd drawn her in, with his descriptions of a past neither of them had lived. For a second, she'd felt part of this great web of history, rather than simply the web of absurdity that was social media. She'd bet Sacha wasn't even on Facebook.

'You like shawarma, then?'

'I don't know what that is,' she admitted. 'But it sounds good.'

'Let's see what we find. On y va.'

She followed him out onto the cobbled street, where the drizzle misted into frost. The streets on the hill were narrow and the houses small and gabled, with leaded windows and coloured shutters. They peered at a tiny walled vineyard with its gnarled, dormant vines, and wandered through little squares and past art and antique shops. She could almost forget she was out in the dark, where every danger could be lurking. The bare trees were strung with garlands of lights in white or blue and gold stars hung from the iron lamp posts.

'Ooh!' she exclaimed as they reached a cobbled square surrounded by quaint cafés with bare vines that would be verdant in the summer. Some hardy patrons sat under the heaters, braving the elements for the sake of their friends and their rituals. A stand selling crêpes and mulled wine perched on the cobblestones at one end, steam emerging from the hatch along with the smell of cinnamon and cloves.

She grasped Sacha's arm. 'Vin chaud! I know what that means.'

'I thought you were hungry.'

'Wine first, food later,' she said, tugging on his arm. He eyed her sharply, his brow low, and she dropped his arm. 'You're right. Food first.'

'This restaurant is nice... enough, I hope.'

She followed him into a sweet, low-set building with green shutters and a string of multicoloured lights over the door. A taller man would have had to stoop, but Ren had decided Sacha was the perfect height. She could raise her face to his without stretching too much.

Inside the small restaurant, she was too pleased by the inviting smells of garlic and rosemary to notice the rustic brown tiles and plain wooden tables. Their table was charmingly set with a pillar candle surrounded by pinecones and looked out a window into the luminous Montmartre evening. Ren sat with a sigh.

The backs of her heels hurt and had probably been rubbed raw.

Her cheeks were stinging and she'd taken none of her usual precautions for safety, but she refused to dwell on any of it. She wanted to be part of life tonight. Grandmama could keep her triggers and Ziggy could shove her rules.

Ren ordered something Sacha called a pot of fire and described as a peasant dish which she gathered was a hunk of pork with braised vegetables. Taking a sip of wine, she knocked over her handbag on the windowsill and as though it had been plotting its escape all afternoon, the blasted engagement ring tumbled out.

Sacha grabbed it and stuffed it back into her bag, treating the Fendi leather far too roughly. 'You didn't think to leave it in your room?'

'I was kind of distracted this afternoon. Is someone going to mug me?' She asked the question lightly so he wouldn't realise she was serious.

'Probably not. It... worries you?' he asked.

Her gaze flickered to the window, feeling the horizons closing in again. She picked up her wine and took another cautious sip. It was a more complicated question than he could have realised.

'Isn't everyone worried about someone attacking them?' She was dismayed at her own words.

'I don't think about it. And I have seen some... incidents.'

She studied him, wondering what he'd seen and where. 'But you probably weren't the target,' she said before she realised what she was giving away. 'But I realise a mugging is statistically unlikely and no one will recognise me here.' She changed the subject before he could ask anything further. 'So, Mister Mysterious, if you weren't born in Paris, but you still insist you're Parisian, what's going on there?'

'I am Parisian. But I grew up in grand Paris – outside the périph, the ring road. It is no longer soixante-quinze, it is the neuf trois, the nine-three. It is the suburbs, the département Seine-Saint-Denis, named after your headless saint. I grew up in the HLM, a... housing project, you know what I mean?'

Her gaze dropped to his tattoo before she could stop herself. She kept her mouth carefully shut.

'Now, you say nothing?'

'I'm worried I'll say the wrong thing.'

'You weren't worried about that with me before. I have judged you. You can judge me. That's fair, non?'

'That's the problem, Sacha,' she said. His eyes locked on hers when she said his name and she wished she'd said it more often. 'I don't want to judge you. I want to understand.'

'No, you don't,' he countered immediately.

'Why? Was it such a bad place to grow up?'

He regarded her curiously. 'No, there is a... richesse from my childhood that I carry with me always. But it is a perspective that I had to fight for.'

'What richness?'

'Community, language – mine and others. No one speaks the language of my heart, except perhaps my sister, but neighbours can come close. Cosmopolitan, you understand? The world lives in my old neighbourhood, and so does art and music and literature. But... I moved into Paris itself when I could, so...'

'Why did you move?'

'My father dreamed of Paris,' he began, but he ran out of steam and his expression drew taut. 'I told you he loved literature – poetry en particulier. He always told me there was power in words, although I didn't understand until later. My father had many, many words in several languages, but, where I grew up, he had no power – we had no power to change.'

'I'm sorry you lost him,' she said when she could no longer remain silent. 'Has it been long?'

'Yes, nearly twenty years.'

'Oh, God, you lost him at a young age, at an important time.'

He nodded once. 'I was fifteen. You're right, it was an important time and very sudden.' Ren stilled. She wished she didn't understand the way past events could cling on in the darkest parts of the psyche. 'You also... you have lost both parents, non?'

'Yes,' she said softly. 'A helicopter crash. But I was even younger than you – only five years old. I barely remember them.'

'That is another loss you live with. I at least carry memories.' He glanced at her when she didn't say anything. *Loss* was a powerful word, like grief, but Sacha was brave enough to say them out loud. 'Did I say something wrong? Sometimes I am taking the French word and... feeling for the English. I have read a lot in English, but speaking? Not much.'

'You didn't make a mistake. I was just... trying not to cry.' She waved a limp hand in front of her face.

'Ouille, Ren. I'm sorry. You have enough troubles of your own.' He raised her chin and wiped her cheeks with his thumb.

She grasped his wrist. 'I'm okay,' she insisted as another tear fell.

'You... need the tears.'

She nodded wordlessly. 'I'm sorry,' she said with a hiccough.

He shook his head. 'You must feel the things you feel. It must be allowed.'

'Oh, God,' she said, seeing sparks behind her eyes when she closed them. How her grandmother would *hate* that attitude, like she hated Ren's fears and Ren's uselessness. The world wasn't ready for the things she felt. 'I need another drink.'

13

'I thought I didn't exist, you know,' she said, her voice as slurred as her steps were wobbly. He kept a firm hand on her coat – *his* coat – to steady her. She made a little frame with her thumbs and forefingers and held it up to capture the façade of the Ritz. 'My life is just a series of photos and videos designed to make people want what they can't have. None of it is real. Grandmama is so afraid of something happening to me. But I really think the world is... beautiful and... terrifying and... I didn't even know how to buy a fucking ticket on the métro!'

'You have your carnet of ten tickets now,' Sacha said through gritted teeth. 'You can go anywhere you like.' She was growing heavy, propped up against him as they stumbled back to the Place Vendôme.

'Thank you for giving me a ticket to Paris,' she mumbled into his shoulder.

'Shh, you will want to be quiet, now.' He paused a few metres from the doors of the Ritz.

The fairy lights twinkled in the row of Christmas trees between every window and the doorman tipped his blue hat. Sacha sighed, knowing the outwardly polite action hid keen vigilance. Anyone would look suspicious dragging a drunken heiress back to her hotel room, even without the ancient jeans and visible tattoo. He hadn't felt it was his right to stop her enthusiastically refilling her wineglass over dinner, but now he wished he had.

'Bonjour, Monsieur Schilling,' Ren said to the doorman with a bright smile.

'Bonsoir, Madame Asquith-Lewis,' he responded. It somehow didn't surprise Sacha that she knew the man's name.

The smell – that *Ritz* smell – struck him as he entered the lobby, a warm spice with a hint of vanilla and hauteur. It held an overtone of cinnamon, too, in honour of the season. An enormous fir filled the lobby, tucked into the curving marble staircase and extending all the way to the high ceiling. He couldn't help shooting a glance along the gallery to the doors of the Salon Proust, the scene of so much trouble that afternoon.

'Je suis revenu ici pourquoi?' he muttered to himself.

'Why what?' she asked.

'Why am I here?' he translated with an irritable sigh.

'I've got it. You're a philosopher.'

'We're all philosophers.'

'Exactly what a real philosopher would say!' she said, pointing a wobbly finger at him. 'Maybe you can tell me if I really exist outside of Instagram.' She hobbled a few steps on her own, but it pained him to watch her haphazard progress and he took her arm again to help her up the stairs.

'If I am a philosopher,' he said, 'then I don't get paid for it. But I'm pretty sure you exist, Ren, although there might be just as much alcohol in your veins as blood right now.'

Her room wasn't far and they thankfully didn't meet anyone in the corridor. She managed to extract an ornate key with a little crown on top from her handbag, but he had to fit it into the gold lock and open the door. He hesitated on the threshold as she stumbled in. Would she be all right?

'Wait, your coat,' she said, unzipping it. The phone in the room shrilled into the silence and they both froze. It was nearly midnight. Ren stumbled to answer, still wearing his coat. 'Hello?'

After listening for the answer, her eyes squeezed shut. She thumped her forehead against the white-and-gold wood panelling, paused, and then did it again. Sacha sighed heavily and entered the room, closing the door carefully behind him.

'I'm fine,' she said, but it came out like a sob. 'How many times did you call? No, Charlie, it's fine. Just... don't worry about me. I know Grandmama's upset. If she gets in touch, just say I'm fine.' She set the handset back in the cradle with too much force and it clattered away. She had to try two more times before she managed to hang up.

'God, why did I answer the phone? I'm such a mess,' she moaned. She looked it, too, her eye make-up smeared and her hair askew. 'I was always a mess, but at least before, I hid it. The only thing I ever did right in Grandmama's eyes was get engaged to him, and now... she'd probably rather have him than me.' She beat the wood panel behind her with her palm, still spitting expletives. 'Why is it so satisfying to say fuck?'

'It is not your fault that your grandmother doesn't know how to choose friends. If she wasn't your only family...'

Her miserable look returned and Sacha grimaced, biting back any further words. His perspective as the inappropriate fake boyfriend was obviously unhelpful. 'But she is your only family,' he said grimly. 'Perhaps you will face it better tomorrow.'

'You think I'm facing it badly?'

'No,' he insisted.

'I can't stop swearing. And every time I think about Charlie, I want to be sick.'

'That might be the alcohol,' he suggested. 'You need to go to sleep and I have work in the morning.'

She sat heavily on the bed, her face worryingly devoid of expression. She tugged her shoes off with a groan and Sacha cursed when he saw blood on her heels, but he hastily turned away when she tugged up her skirt to peel off the tights.

'Let me find a bandage,' he muttered and headed for the enormous bathroom. Although he rummaged in every drawer, he couldn't find one. Did the hotel expect rich people to heal themselves?

When he emerged empty-handed, she'd tucked herself into bed and was moving restlessly with her eyes closed. He called down to reception for plasters and sat gingerly on the bed while he waited for someone to bring them. Ren barely stirred when he dabbed at her heels with a compress and applied the dressing. But when he stood to go, her hand shot out and grabbed his wrist.

'Please don't go. Just stay until I'm properly asleep. I don't want you to go, Sacha. It will be dark without you.'

His skin prickled. A deep part of him didn't want to go either and it had nothing to do with the opulent bedroom that reminded him he wasn't good enough. 'Shhh, I'll stay,' he murmured before he'd given it enough thought. The strength ebbed from her grip immediately and her hand fell to the blanket.

Sacha toed off his boots and peeled off the pullover that was too warm in the hotel heating. His phone battery was dead, but the ancient handset rarely lasted a day, so he had his charger with him and plugged it in, hoping the few minutes before he left would get him home. He was wary of the sudden exhaustion that gripped him, but Ren's restlessness and the tears on her cheeks kept him where he was. He sat heavily on the other side of the bed. He would go soon.

* * *

The supposedly calming tune of his alarm had Sacha leaping out of bed with an immediate sense of unease. It was dark, but a faint glow from the bathroom illuminated the gilt cornicing and reminded him where he was.

Merde, he must have fallen asleep. He fumbled to turn off the alarm and took several deep breaths. An antique clock on the mantlepiece goaded him with its ticking and his own dim reflection in the mirror above the fireplace was terrifying. He was still wearing the T-shirt from yesterday; his hair was wild; he hadn't tidied up his beard all weekend and shadows fell at odd angles over his face in the darkness.

He had to get out of here, for a multitude of reasons.

Daring a glance behind him, he saw the dark form of Ren still tucked under the blanket. He tiptoed around the bed, setting his phone on the side-table and retrieving his backpack. He sealed himself into the bathroom and, feeling rotten, he decided a quick shower would save him time at home.

He'd just stepped out of the luxurious spray of hot water, when a sound from behind the door made him freeze. With a curse, he recognised his ring tone. A phone call at antisocial o'clock could only be something important. He grabbed a towel from the pile and slung it around his hips.

He burst out of the bathroom and froze. Ren stood in the middle of the room, her eyes glazed with sleep and her jaw hanging open. She held his phone to her ear.

'I'm – I'm sorry. Je parle un petit peu français seulement. Do you speak English?' She jumped when she caught sight of him. Her eyes widened. 'H-h-here is Sacha,' she stammered and thrust the phone at him.

He nearly dropped it, but it was better than dropping his towel.

'Allô?' he asked, turning his back on Ren. Not that it helped, as he could still feel her gaze.

'Sachou?'

For once, he let her get away with the teasing endearment, a combination of his name and 'mon chou', my little pastry. 'Nadia? Qu'est-ce qu'il se passe?'

She answered him with a rush of words in her usual harried inflection, but he quickly caught on to the problem.

'Don't worry, Nadi. You're right. His game console is probably at my place. He had it with him on Saturday night. I'll check as soon as I get home and let you know, but don't immediately assume—'

'If you're not at your place, where are you? And who answered the phone?'

He opened his mouth to speak, but none of the words he considered would do. 'Euh,' he said stupidly.

'Did you cancel on me because of a *rendez-vous*?'

'No, it wasn't like that.'

A choking noise reached his ear and it took him a moment to realise she was laughing. 'Have you... joined Tinder?'

'Non!' he insisted. 'I'm not on Tinder. I'm not... looking. You know that.'

'I know we don't usually leave you much time for relationships,' she said softly. 'Good for you, Sachou.'

'No, it's not a... she's not... I don't know what the devil she is. A friend, maybe, who needed my help.'

Nadia groaned. 'Are you collecting strays again?'

'Not exactly.'

'Well, wherever you are, I hope you're not far from home. I need to know if the console is at yours. He was out yesterday afternoon and if he's sold it again...'

'We solve that problem when it comes, Nadi. I'll let you know.'

'Is everything okay?' Ren asked tentatively after he'd hung up.

'Yes, but I don't have much time.' Perhaps he hadn't schooled his expression enough. She was staring at him in dismay. 'Ça va bien? Did you sleep? Do you have... mal de tête, ehm, headache?' She shook her head so fiercely that he had to believe her. 'Then... is something wrong?'

She stifled a cough. 'No, just... go and put some clothes on.' Heat swept up his chest to the back of his neck and he hoped it was just embarrassment.

When he emerged from the bathroom again, dressed in his own clothes, Ren had gone back to bed, lying on her side facing him, her eyes closed. He tiptoed to the nightstand and set down the glass of water he'd filled for her.

'Thank you,' she murmured, her tone miserable. 'For everything.'

He studied her for a long moment, rubbing a hand over his mouth in indecision. 'D'accord,' he whispered to himself. He couldn't go without leaving the door to the future open a tiny crack. He rummaged in his backpack for a pen and a ripped a scrap of paper out of his notebook. He scribbled hurriedly, placed the note on the nightstand and then whispered, 'Sleep again. It's early.'

14

Sacha took a deep breath of frigid air as he stepped out of the Ritz after greeting the new doorman. He'd offered to let the man check inside his backpack, but had been politely refused with a few clipped words and a quickly smothered look of puzzlement – at his offer or his scruffy appearance, Sacha couldn't be certain.

It was still dark, the same fairy lights in the shape of chandeliers illuminating the square, but there were fewer people about than when they'd arrived late the night before. He left the elegant Place Vendôme with quick steps, but when he arrived at the lamp post where he'd left his bike, he cursed.

It was gone. His helmet lay, discarded, to one side and the lock had been chopped through with bolt-cutters. Whether it had been stolen or impounded, he'd have to discover later. He picked up the ruined lock and tossed it into a nearby bin with too much force. Swiping up his damp helmet, he rubbed his fingers absently over the scratches on the top as he headed for the métro – scratches from the moment he'd met *her*. What strange luck.

The day continued downhill from there. The console wasn't at his apartment and he had to spend twenty minutes talking Nadia down. It might still be at the workshop. He couldn't remember any more if Raph had had it with him there on Sunday. And, although he understood Nadia's worry, he didn't want to believe the boy had sold another one. Sacha had been certain Raph was making progress standing up to his older, so-called friends who kept asking him to buy pot for them. 'Asking' was too gentle a word.

But the looming start of his work day was a more immediate concern as he sat fidgeting on the métro on his way to the eighteenth. Despite the glut of electric scooters usually littering the footpaths in the centre of Paris, he only found one and it wouldn't work, so he set off on foot. The other choice was a further two changes on the métro and walking was quicker.

The walk became a run for the last stretch and he arrived with two minutes to spare, to the expected ribbing from his 'colleagues'. It was a rowdy day at the office – nothing he wasn't used to, but his patience wore thin by the end of the day, especially when one of them boisterously suggested his poor mood was because he hadn't got laid this century.

Sometimes he addressed those comments seriously, which quickly put a stop to them, but he ignored it that day. He didn't have time. Cursing his missing bike again, he hurried to the main road, scrolling through public transport options to get him up to Joseph's apartment in Saint-Denis.

The bus was more direct than a circuitous route on the métro, but he got stuck in evening traffic and nearly missed the grocery delivery he'd ordered for Joseph. He hauled the bags up the six flights of stairs, horrified at the idea of Joseph doing this himself only two months after his surgery.

'You didn't tell me the lift was broken!'

'Salut to you too,' Joseph said drily as he opened the door wide for Sacha and the grocery delivery.

'How are you getting down the stairs?'

'Very slowly.' Sacha scowled at him. 'I'm taking care. And the physiotherapist is happy with my progress. If you can convince Nadia of that, I'd appreciate it, because she doesn't seem to believe me.'

'We'll believe you're better when you're running marathons.'

'I didn't run marathons before the knee replacement!' Joseph laughed.

'Would you prefer we left you to ruin your new knee?'

Joseph chuckled and patted him on the shoulder. To his annoyance, it still gave the slightest twinge. 'You're kind to this old man, but I'd rather see you busy with your own... life.'

'Are you suggesting I don't have a life?' Sacha quipped. His smile faded and he groaned when Joseph gave him a pointed look. 'Don't start.'

Joseph held up his hands in surrender. 'Did you give the ring back?'

'Oui,' he said in a clipped tone and stalked into the kitchen to put away the groceries.

'And?'

'And what? I gave it back. Fin de l'histoire.' End of story. That was a happy lie. 'You're getting older all alone in this apartment and you're worried about me?'

'Pfft, I'm only getting older in my body and I've got this brand-new knee. Besides, I'm not alone. I am surrounded by neighbours. You, on the other hand...'

'How can I be alone when I have you and Nadia and Raph?'

'What about Rita?'

'What do you mean? You know we broke up months ago.'

'Then... perhaps it's time to let someone else into your heart.'

Sacha huffed his inarticulate disagreement and wrenched open the fridge door. He'd tried with Rita, but he hadn't been able to give her enough.

'You see Rita at work?'

'Of course, but it's fine.' Except when she looked at him as though she regretted giving up on him.

After doing a few more chores for Joseph, Sacha grabbed the key to the workshop and raced down the stairs of the tower block, trying in vain to work out an efficient way to get to Nadia's place via Joseph's workshop that didn't involve a thousand buses.

When he finally arrived at the workshop and heaved up the roller door, the console was sitting innocently on the bench. He slumped against the wall with an enormous sigh, pinching the bridge of his nose.

He pulled out his phone. 'Nadi, j'ai trouvé la console.'

'Merde!' was her only response at first – not the one Sacha had been expecting. 'I forbade him to see his friends this afternoon and he's furious with me.'

Sacha leaned his head back and braced himself for a conversation he'd had many times. 'Trust goes two ways, Nadi. He screwed up once. It doesn't mean he'll do it again. And it's better if he feels like he can talk to you.'

'Like he talks to you?'

'No, like he talks to his mother. He knows you love him. You're doing great.'

'I'm sorry,' she sighed. 'I put too much of this onto you.'

'You know I'm here for you. I'm... just sorry I missed dinner last night. Écoute, I'm on my way, but it will take me a little while to get there. Raph will be fine on his own for half an hour if you have to leave for work. I'll see you later.'

But Nadia wouldn't let him end the conversation. 'Are you going to tell me who she is?'

'Nobody,' he said firmly. 'She is nobody.' He could almost hear her eye roll.

His mind wandered as he waited for the bus and then sat on

the RER, the suburban train. He pulled the old notebook out of his backpack and found the stub of a pencil.

As usual, he read a few pages from the front before the tip of his pencil ever touched the page. He scribbled a few lines – observations, connections, individual words. Then he found the page with the bottom ripped off. He brushed his thumb over the rough edge, and all the wondering he'd been trying not to do rushed back. Would she call?

By the time he reached Nadia's apartment in a back corner in Aubervilliers, it was past nine – late enough that he felt sixty-four instead of thirty-four, but not so late that Raphaël would already be in bed. He let himself into the building with his key and rapped on the apartment door.

After a few muffled thumps, Nadia opened it and threw her arms around him. He enclosed her in a tight embrace, always able to feel her moods and vulnerabilities. She was older – thirty-six, now, with a few strands of grey in her hair from the years of completing her studies while juggling motherhood. Sacha had stepped up to be there for her, but he'd been a student, too, only twenty-three when Raph had been born.

He held her tight, and all of the rushing around was worth it. 'Sorry I'm late.'

* * *

Ren's day had begun in a much more luxurious manner, with a late breakfast delivered to her room. She sat at the table with her feet up on the upholstered dining chair, running a finger absently over the plasters on her heels and staring at the scrap of paper with its looping handwriting.

Who was he really, this man who told her compelling stories and opened up the world for her? Not to mention, he was an excellent kisser. It had only been for show and, after the mysterious phone call that morning, she couldn't even be sure he was single, but wow, it had been one for her lonely imaginings in future years.

A knock on the door burst her fragile bubble. She snatched the piece of paper and stuffed it in her pocket. Steeling herself, Ren opened it to admit Ziggy and her grandmother. She wondered if she should fake a terrible lurgy to scare them off. They seemed a little taken aback at her appearance already.

Ziggy sighed pointedly and took a seat at the table, setting her tablet in front of her. 'Livia and I have a plan.'

Bordel de merde. The curse sounded deliciously filthy. 'If it involves me coming back to London...'

'You've made your position on that clear,' Ziggy said evenly. 'And reception informs me that at least *he* had the sense to leave early in the morning.' Grandmama harrumphed as though it was taking all of her energy not to speak. 'You can take leave until the chalet weekend, as you requested.' Ren tried not to snort at the idea of taking leave from her life. 'But, Ren, I'm sorry, you can't stay here at the Ritz. For one, think of the expense. And secondly, the chances of you being seen with him are simply too high.'

Ren wondered if her sudden stomach cramps were from nerves or lingering after-effects of the wine. 'Where do you want me to stay?'

'Didn't you want to be free to choose? I got the impression your... new boyfriend would love to have you stay with him.'

Was it really necessary to save the money or did Ziggy suspect the fake relationship and was trying to smoke her out? Whatever her motives, Ziggy had succeeded in making Ren feel like a helpless dependent again.

'Of course,' continued Ziggy, 'you could stay here for a few more days for some careful sightseeing. I can hire Aleksy to take the photos and it won't be a problem to organise a new phone. You could have your break from London, without going completely off the radar. But, of course, Sacha could *not* be seen with you – at least not the way he looked yesterday. It would send entirely the wrong message. You are not desperate or sad. You were not dumped. Do you know that Charlie has been posting from the ski slopes already?'

Ren gritted her teeth. Had Ziggy always manipulated her like this? Or had she simply taken the dictates so meekly that she'd never had to be 'managed'? Ren hated the implication that she'd enjoyed her time with Sacha because she was desperate and sad. Those words described her life in London more accurately than the two evenings she'd spent exploring the dark corners of Paris.

Ziggy's attempt to manipulate her was so obvious that it had the opposite effect. She didn't want to be the clueless socialite who didn't know how to look after herself and was afraid of the dark.

'Fine,' she said curtly. 'I'll ask Sacha if I can stay with him.' She'd ask Malou, but they didn't have to know that.

'Fine?' Grandmama cried, clutching the arms of her chair. 'You'll stay with him? But we've said you don't have to come home right away. Wasn't that what you wanted?'

'I want to stay with Sacha.'

Grandmama gave Ziggy an outraged look, but the inscrutable Ziggy shook her head subtly. 'It sounds like her mind is made up,' Ziggy said lightly. 'As long as you will be *very careful* about photos, we will try to cover your absence for two weeks. And after the ski trip, we'll travel back to London together for Christmas, the *three* of us, hmm?'

Ziggy stood and Grandmama followed, muttering, 'This is not what you assured me would happen. The Ritz is the only place she knows. We can't let her really stay with some Parisian...'

'Street rat?' Ren suggested with a smile that quickly faded when she realised that either Ziggy and Grandmama had never seen

Aladdin or they didn't remember that part. 'He's not a street rat,' she mumbled. 'I was joking.' Grandmama looked ready to breathe fire.

'We discussed this,' Ziggy continued. 'There are paparazzi on every corner of the Place Vendôme and there is already speculation about why you haven't been posting to Instagram. And besides, would a man like that appreciate such a lovely room?'

'Not at all!' Ren agreed. She was nervous about leaving the Ritz, but Grandmama hadn't quite been right when she'd said it was the only place in Paris she knew. Ziggy eyed her, so she erased the satisfaction from her expression as best she could.

Ren ushered them out quickly and took a deep, cleansing breath. She'd bitten off more than she could chew, but it was still her victory. She had two weeks to pull herself together and... perhaps see more of Paris.

'Oh, just a moment!' she called, rushing back to the door. 'There's something I need you to give back to Charlie.' She rummaged in her handbag, experiencing a moment of panic that the stupid thing would hide again and she'd be stuck with it for the rest of her life. With a sigh of relief, she produced the engagement ring and pressed it into Ziggy's hand. 'You'll see him before I will,' she explained.

With one last critical look, Ziggy and Livia left her alone to enjoy the growing feeling of lightness. No more pretending she was still with Charlie. It was over. And she was in *Paris*.

She retrieved the crumpled scrap of paper from her pocket and smoothed her fingertip over his neat lettering. *Sacha Mourad*, followed by a mobile number with the French country code. Was it strange that what she most wanted to see in Paris was his face?

15

Ren packed her suitcase and went to find Malou. She felt guilty about calling Bilel to take her to Asquith-Lewis, when Ziggy had stressed the importance of saving money, but she remembered all the steps at the entrance to the métro and she had no idea what Bilel did all day when he wasn't ferrying her between traffic jams.

Malou agreed to meet at a bistro a few streets from the Champs-Élysées for lunch, as Ren thought it best to avoid the galleries themselves in case her grandmother or Ziggy was there.

'Tell me *everything*!' her friend demanded instead of a greeting. Ren couldn't help wondering what Malou would have said if she'd brought her suitcase instead of leaving it in the car. 'I am torn between relief that you're safe and wondering if you had sex with that hot guy!' She took her seat opposite Ren in the wooden booth with its Art Nouveau detailing.

'He's not a hot guy,' Ren said defensively. 'He's a lovely guy.' When Malou said nothing, she continued, 'I need to stay with you. Is that going to be okay?'

'Putain de bordel de merde.'

'Why does everyone give their swear words an upgrade every time I say something?'

'What's happened? She didn't disown you, did she?'

'Don't be ridiculous. Why would Grandmama do that?' Although, when Malou put it like that, Ziggy's veiled threats had felt like a step in that direction.

'Oh, I don't know. I was worried you told her you were going to marry this guy or something.'

'No, Grandmama mainly got the impression that we were having a raging hot affair.'

'I don't want to know why she got that impression.'

'The result is the same: I got what I wanted. I have two weeks away from the Irena Asquith-Lewis production, but I had to agree to check out of the Ritz. So, can I stay with you? They think I'm staying with him, so the expense of another hotel would be difficult to explain. I promise I won't judge your flat. And I know how to catch the métro, now.'

'I'm not sure I believe you about not judging, but of course you can stay with me. I'll give you a key right now. But wait. What exactly happened yesterday afternoon?'

Ren explained as briefly as possible, leaving out the part where she'd kissed Sacha – or he'd kissed her, or goodness knows what it had been. When she came to the bit about Montmartre, she hesitated again.

'Ren, did you... sleep with the guy?'

'No! Well, technically, yes, but it wasn't – it's not – shit!' She hid her face in her hands, but the words spilled out. 'I really like him, okay?'

The flummoxed expression on Malou's face was comical, but Ren groaned. If her friend looked at her like that when she admitted the truth, what would everyone else think?

'I can't decide if it's great you're discovering you're human, too, or worrying, because you're buying into this fake boyfriend thing a bit too much and that guy looked scary.'

'He's not scary.'

'I assumed *you* would think so. Is he a tattoo artist or something?'

'Why didn't I think of that?' she muttered to herself. 'I have no idea. He won't tell me what his job is. Why are you looking at me like that? I didn't pick you for the prejudiced type.'

'Neither would I, usually, but, Ren, you may as well have a target on your forehead at the moment. He found your ring.'

'Charlie's ring.'

'I mean he knows you've just broken up with your fiancé. He knows how rich you are. It's a reasonable assumption that he might get something out of this, even if it's just a few free dinners.'

Ren straightened so suddenly that she banged her head on the wood panelling behind her. 'Ow! I think I let him pay for dinner!'

'You think?'

'I was... quite drunk. I mean I remember everything. I went to the loo and when I came back, we just left. I didn't even think about it, but he must have paid. But there, that proves he's not out to fleece me.' Malou's expression still looked doubtful. 'I'm serious. He's turned down money every time I've offered.'

'You offered him money?'

'Only when I knocked him off his bike. Seriously, he's not the kind of person you think. He's playing a Christmas elf at some market.' If that wasn't the most trustworthy thing a person could do, she didn't know what was.

Malou coughed. 'He didn't look like a... Christmas elf.'

'Well, it's for his friend who has some kind of business in the nine-three...'

Malou choked again and Ren sighed. Everything she said seemed to make things worse, instead of putting her friend's mind at ease. 'The nine-three? Who are you? Renny from the block?'

'Do I look like Renny from the block?' Ren giggled.

'No more than that guy looked like a Christmas elf.'

'Sacha,' Ren said.

'Hmm?'

'His name is Sacha.'

Malou eyed Ren, making her wonder what her friend had detected in her tone. 'And my name is Malou, your best friend, and I'm warning you not to get hurt. You said it: he's the last man in Paris you should be with.'

Ren sighed. 'I know I said that and... you're right. I'm not... imagining a sweeping love affair, here. Maybe I shouldn't call him. I know it's fake, and not just what I'm doing with Sacha. I'm faking being a normal person for two weeks too.'

'You are a normal person,' Malou insisted. 'I'm sorry, Ren. If you say he's a nice guy, then... I'll believe you.'

'But if you're honest, you don't think I'm a good judge of character?'

'No,' Malou said too quickly.

'I'm a terrible judge of character. I admit it. I'll be careful. I promise.' Then, just because Malou hadn't spat any of her coffee in shock for five minutes, she asked the next important question: 'Now, tell me where you buy your clothes. If I'm going to be a normal person for two weeks, I need new threads.'

* * *

Ren had seen some fantastic things in her life: Natalia Osipova on stage with the Royal Ballet; Marcus Wareing preparing a private meal in his own kitchen; she could even look at her very own Matisse in the foyer of her apartment. But when she stepped under the steel-and-glass dome of the Galeries Lafayette, where an enormous Christmas tree dressed in red and silver baubles hung suspended, she froze in awe.

A shower of lights dangled around the Christmas tree. The galleries beneath the dome glowed gold, adorned with wrought-iron railings, curving in graceful counterpoint. The grand Art Nouveau staircase invited her to climb to the next floor with the rest of the public.

Everywhere she looked, she saw racks of beautiful clothes, piles of perfumes and the bounty of too much choice. Shoppers bustled and meandered and everything in between, as though the whole world had come to shop this afternoon. If Sacha were here with her, no one would bat an eyelid.

Ren had met the founder of the conglomerate that owned the extravagant department store at a gala, once, but she'd never stepped foot in the glorious building itself. Prêt-à-porter was not usually in her vocabulary and she'd grown accustomed to shopping in small boutiques in private, where Ziggy could control what photos emerged and Grandmama could be assured of her safety.

That afternoon, the Christmas crowds under the vaunted dome were not a source of worry. Without her photographer and assistants, with her hair in a simple ponytail and her jewellery stowed at Malou's flat, Ren was satisfyingly anonymous. She searched out her friend's favourite brands, ate pastries while perched on a stool and watched the light fade in the dome and the festive glow intensify.

Weighed down with bags, she waited her turn for the glasswalk on the top floor, arriving just in time to see the last of the sunlight passing through the decorative stained-glass elements in the dome. The colours were strikingly different to the glimpses she'd had of the mediaeval fragment at Asquith-Lewis. The blue was gentler, the orange less searing. There were no pictures to educate the illiterate masses about the mysteries of the church, only elegant, dynamic patterns with no function other than to please the eye.

She wondered what Sacha would have had to say about it, if he'd been there. For all she knew, he was there, now, doing his Christmas shopping, given the thread of luck – good and bad – that had run through their relationship

She decided to find out if the horseshoe was working.

Setting her shopping bags down, she leaned against the wrought-iron railing and fetched the pre-paid phone she'd bought that had luckily had enough charge to set itself up. Then she rummaged for the slip of paper she had held so often it was now wrinkled and the ink smudged. Who used fountain pens these days anyway?

She typed the +33 at the beginning of the phone number, then frowned, remembering that her own number was French, too. Deciding to delete the numbers and start again, she fumbled with the wide phone. She grabbed at it with her other hand before it could tumble over the railing and smash spectacularly on the marble tiles.

She released an enormous sigh of relief when she held the phone secure in her hands, but a flash of white caught her eye. Over the heads of the oblivious shoppers, the precious slip of paper floated downwards through the atrium, making whimsical twists and turns as the warm air from the heating system buffeted it.

Staring after it in dismay, she leaned over the railing in a desperate attempt to keep it in sight. At first, she thought it would land right on top of the Chanel make-up store, but it changed its mind and swerved to the right, sailing over Dior and disappearing by the watches. Frantically memorising the last place she saw it, she grabbed her bags and raced for the lifts.

Seeing a queue at the gates of the lift, Ren ran for the stairs. No longer interested in the beauty of the Art Nouveau curves, she focused on keeping her balance and not knocking anyone else over as she took the stairs two at a time, immensely glad she'd told four-inch heels to fuck off.

She wasted several precious seconds orienting herself when she arrived on the ground floor, but then she was retracing those last few seconds of the slip of paper's descent. When she reached the watch stands where she'd seen it disappear, she dropped to her knees and searched, her bags hanging off her wrists like wings.

'No!' she muttered as the seconds ticked by and she still hadn't found it. Something fluttered tantalisingly in the dust beneath the Seiko display. She shook off her bags and thrust her hand underneath, but could only sigh – and then sneeze – when she came away with an old receipt.

Ren was just about to roll out her new favourite word beginning with 'F', when a voice came from behind her. 'Pardon, mademoiselle, puis-je vous aider?'

Her face burning, she slowly got to her feet. Grandmama would be horrified by her public display. Even if she could forget that, she wasn't sure how to explain herself to the security guard. *No, thank you. I'm just looking for a piece of paper with the phone number of my fake boyfriend on it.*

She cursed herself for the flair for the dramatic that had led her to hold onto the paper instead of saving it in her phone the instant she turned it on – or was it a flair for the romantic? Judging by the result, she had a flair for the idiotic.

She mumbled, 'Non, merci,' and forced herself to collect her shopping and walk away with dignity. Her mind was picturing breaking in at midnight to have another look. As she stepped out of the store, bleakness overwhelmed her. Despite the golden shooting stars and clusters of lights along the Boulevard Haussmann, it was the deepening of the sky that caught her attention. What was she supposed to do now?

She pulled out her phone to call Bilel to take her back to Malou's flat, but she shook her head and opened a browser instead. But she wasn't surprised to find that none of the 'Sacha Mourads' on social media were *her* Sacha Mourad. There was one in Paris, but he was far too young. Several were female and most of the others lived in the Middle East.

If she wanted to find him, she would have to pay someone to dig deeper, the thought of which made her nauseous. No, having him investigated was exactly what her grandmother would do.

She slumped, allowing the wash of disappointment to weigh her down like the shopping bags. It started to rain, tiny droplets glistening in the glow of the twinkling lights strung up on the grand old department store. This wasn't supposed to be the ending. If she'd known she'd never see him again, she would have...

'Kissed him' wasn't right, because she had kissed him, and it had been wonderful. She would have told him she'd meant that kiss. She might have told him all her secrets. She could imagine being that brave.

A cyclist whooshed past and she stepped back in alarm, before gazing at the retreating figure on the bicycle, wishing he was wearing a familiar fleece-lined leather jacket instead of the high-tech rain gear she saw. This was the part where some stroke of fate brought them together again. He would frown in disbelief to see her in front of him, until his frown gradually transformed into that rare smile. But Sacha didn't appear and there was no genie acting behind the scenes. With a grimace, Ren turned to take the stairs down to the métro. She would try to do without Bilel.

16

'You look more like the Grinch than a Christmas elf.'

'Hmm?' Sacha said absentmindedly. 'You were the one who suggested I grow a beard.'

Joseph's smile was wide as he clapped Sacha on the shoulder. 'I'm not talking about your beard, although it is rather pitiful, given how many weeks it's been. I'm talking about your face. Where's your Christmas spirit?'

Sacha glanced critically around the stand which he and Joseph had transformed during the week. Everywhere he looked were candles, colourful fabrics, pine boughs and the vintage decorations Joseph had collected over the years. To one side stood the street organ that had cost them hours of work and, at the back, after the forest of lights and textures, was the Belle Époque centrepiece that was admittedly impressive, but probably still not worth the effort Joseph had put into restoring it.

'Not enough Christmas spirit?'

'You know what I mean. Something's bothering you.'

He waved away Joseph's concern. 'It's going to be a busy day.'

It had already been a busy day, hanging pine and holly and

working out how to string up all the lights without overloading the precarious wiring in the old arcade. The market was an eclectic mix of retro and antiques, books, clothes, furniture and bric-a-brac, the prices varying wildly. It was an environment that filled him with nostalgia, especially when the older traders spoke to him as though he was still the teenager that Joseph had first brought here.

'Oula! C'est magnifique! Vraiment!'

'Bonjour, Mireille!' Joseph turned with a smile to greet their neighbour from the next stand with kisses on the cheek.

'Bonjour, Joseph. Sacha! So lovely to see you, chéri.'

A gust of wind rushed through the arcade, bringing a hint of moisture suggesting sleet – typical. Joseph pulled up his red hood, lined with fur that might have been real.

'And where is your costume, Sacha?' Mireille asked.

'I'll put it on, soon,' he mumbled.

'I know what you two need!' Mireille said suddenly and disappeared back to her own stand. 'I went to the Bois de Vincennes on Thursday and collected lots,' she continued, as she bustled in. 'Hang it right here!'

Sacha took the little bunch of narrow leaves and pale berries before he realised what it was. Le gui. No, mistletoe was definitely not what he needed.

'Oho! The Grinch disapproves of mistletoe,' said Joseph. 'Or is it the thought of kissing that's making you frown? Or *not* kissing?'

Sacha's gaze shot up. 'Why would you think that?' he blurted out. He cleared his throat. 'It's nothing.'

'You saw her again on Sunday, didn't you? Your eyes were too shifty when I asked you what happened.'

'My eyes were not shifty.' If he had said something, Sacha could only imagine how much his friend would have talked about her during their evenings spent in the workshop, ruining Sacha's efforts *not* to think about her.

He blamed the necessity of public transport that week for the amount of time he'd spent trying not to think about her. Between trips to the workshop, Nadia's place and his own apartment, it was a lot of wondering. And now he was wondering what the Asquith-Lewis heiress would have made of all this. She was familiar with the world of antiques trading, but not like this.

But wondering didn't matter. He'd never see her again, and it wouldn't bother him. Perhaps he'd think of her when he caught glimpses of the Sacré-Cœur as he cycled past – if he ever found his bike – but nothing more.

Sacha hung the mistletoe begrudgingly and pulled on his costume just before the market opened, doing up the row of brass buttons. He wore an embroidered green waistcoat and a pointed felt hat, borrowed from a friend with a vintage clothing stand in the Marché Dauphine. The waistcoat wasn't a genuine antique; it had been used for a film, which made it valuable, but not too valuable to borrow for a weekend. The felt hat was misshapen and could have been genuinely old.

With the combination of the richly embroidered waistcoat and the gnome hat, all he needed was a pair of spectacles and to lose a few inches and then he could be mistaken for a festive Henri de Toulouse-Lautrec. He only hoped no one mistook him for the Père Fouettard, Saint Nick's evil sidekick. With his hair and beard, it was a distinct possibility.

Why had Joseph had his knee surgery just before Christmas?

Thoughts of Ren even followed him on his lunchtime pilgrimage to the second-hand books in the Marché Dauphine. Although he picked up his usual – something in Arabic – he also walked out with an old canvas-bound tome called *English Romantic Poetry*. As soon as he'd picked it up, the book had fallen open to a dog-eared page and the words had pounced on him:

> *And all that's best of dark and bright*
> *Meet in her aspect and her eyes*

With all the references to the 'tender light' of night, of smiles and innocence, Byron could have written it for Ren, so now he had the stupid book to remind him of her even more – and to hide from Joseph in case his friend asked questions.

* * *

'Don't freak out, okay? I did warn you.'

'You did,' Ren agreed faintly, clutching Malou's arm. 'And I'm trying not to.'

'Look, it'll be okay as long as we don't get separated. If we do, stay where you are and call me. Don't leave any of the markets without me. And repeat after me: casse-toi!'

'Casse-toi,' Ren repeated carefully.

'No, with more… punch. *Casse-toi!*'

'Casse-toi!' she tried again, drawing looks from the passing crowds in the market. It was Saturday morning and Malou had dragged her to the legendary Paris flea market. Despite the overwhelming chaos of the crowds and the piles of stuff, Ren was glad of the distraction.

Her week hadn't improved from the moment she'd dropped the piece of paper. She'd made the mistake of giving Grandmama her new mobile number and, before she knew it, she was ignoring several messages a day, each more agitated than the last. The worst one had come through last night: tickets to a matinée performance of *The Nutcracker* tomorrow – *three* tickets, along with instructions to make sure her *boyfriend* wore a suit. She'd been trying not to panic ever since.

'Bien,' Malou said, approving Ren's rude French.

'What does it mean?' she asked.

'Oh, it's kind of like "go away". You might need it for some of the more persistent sellers on the fringes. And if that doesn't work, there's always "va te faire foutre".'

'Va te faire foutre!' Ren practised, with plenty of punch this time. More heads turned. 'What, is that one "fuck off"?'

'C'est ça – that's it,' her friend said. 'But I think *I* might freak out if I lose you in the crowds, so hopefully you won't need them.'

'I am capable of finding my way out of a market.' Malou gave her a doubtful look. 'Okay,' Ren admitted, 'this is way more than a market and I'm lost already even though the métro is only back there somewhere. Wait. Or was it that way?'

She gazed at the milling crowds, the squat shops with tin roofs, announcing their wares with simple signs in dated lettering. The Marché aux Puces de Saint-Ouen, the Paris flea market – or markets, more correctly – was a wild place where everyone mixed and customers could buy anything from cigarette machines from the 1950s to upholstered Louis XVI chairs, as though Ren had passed under the nearby boulevard périphérique into this upside-down version of Asquith-Lewis, where the quality over quantity rule was inverted and every punter was welcome.

'Grandmama would hate this place,' she murmured.

'I'm pretty sure she does hate it. Despite the humble location, some of these traders have pieces that are just as stunning as the things I see in your auction house, but they can often sell them more cheaply. Some even sell to Asquith-Lewis on occasion. They're professionals, too.'

'Of course. And you're the only professional here. I just... know what I like.'

'You're a connoisseur,' Malou said fondly. 'Meaning everyone will want to sell you stuff.'

'Va te faire foutre!'

'That's only for the streets around the market! *Do not* break that one out in the Marché Biron, je t'en prie!'

'Is the Marché Biron the fancy one? You don't have to go there for my sake. We're off-duty. What about this one? It looks interesting.' Ren steered Malou under a dated blue sign, draped with tinsel and baubles, that read 'Marché Vernaison', and into a warren of lanes.

The Christmas decorations, the stalls piled high with every object imaginable – and a few she would never in her life have imagined – made her think of Sacha's friend Joseph's workshop. Sacha had said Joseph ran a market stall. Could it be here? Surely that would be too much luck even for the old horseshoe, but Ren was struck by the possibility.

Ignoring Malou's curious look at the sudden spring in her step, Ren headed for the first stand. Outside was a pile of carved wooden boxes and a ceramic tea pot shaped like a savoy cabbage.

By lunchtime, she'd bought a top hat, a handwoven Malian cloth from the 1950s, which she draped around her shoulders, and an ugly gnome who she'd felt sorry for, all the while holding on to the naïve hope of seeing Sacha somewhere in the crowd.

'You are a terrible businessperson,' Malou murmured.

'That's what Grandmama always says. But you never know. Maybe this little guy is Sèvres porcelain and worth a fortune.'

'He's not,' Malou assured her drily.

Ren enjoyed the most delicious hamburger at a stand under a gas heater – not that she'd eaten enough hamburgers to judge. But it came with a glass of wine, which made the experience suitably French – that, and the fresh brioche bun and truffle cream on the burger. She could certainly get into fast food if it was cooked by the French.

In the afternoon, Ren's eyes had started to ache from constantly sifting through the mountains of jumbled wares and the faces in the crowd. Then, of course, the worst happened. She was inspecting an impressive display of antique clocks and candelabras, thinking of Cogsworth and Lumière from *Beauty and the Beast*, when she looked up to find Malou nowhere to be seen.

She took a deep breath and closed her eyes until she was certain she could hide her panic. 'Va te faire foutre,' she repeated under her breath to make sure she still remembered.

'Quoi?' replied the horrified trader of the antique clocks.

'Non... pas de... rien, merci. Excusez-moi,' she rattled off and backed away hurriedly. After a minute of frantic walking to and fro, she, her top hat, her Malian rug and her ugly gnome were all lost.

17

Ren's teeth were chattering and her fingers ached, even inside her gloves. In the crush of the market, she'd kept warm enough not to have felt the hours passing in the winter cold. But now she found herself out on the street, the wind whipped at her hair and the sleet was getting in her eyes. She fumbled for her phone, but her hands wouldn't work. She wrapped the Malian rug more tightly around her and put on the top hat, although the stupid thing did nothing for her ears. Monsieur Gnome (with an audible 'g', according to Malou) was safe in her handbag.

Looking around desperately for shelter, she noticed shafts of warm light emerging from the gates of another market, painted a lurid yellow that was somewhat softened by the pine boughs hanging below the sign. Praise the Lord, the market had a roof. Ren hurried in that direction, sighing when she reached shelter and the sleet no longer stabbed her nose.

There was a thick warmth radiating from further inside and she followed the sensation as though drawn by a magnet. When she reached the source of the warmth, she could almost believe flea market Christmas magic did exist.

The warmth came from a wonderland of Christmas past. At the front stood a white carousel horse with a grey mane, finely sculpted, with a golden bridle and a glittering saddle. Carved wood panelling and antique mirrors adorned the walls, along with embroidered curtains with twisted rope tie-backs. A beautiful mahogany escritoire was off to one side, covered in letters addressed to 'Père Noël'. Two fragrant Christmas trees stood in opposite corners of the space, glowing with lights. The moulded ornaments were plump and nostalgic – shiny pinecones, stars, baubles and Father Christmas. Some showed enough wear for Ren to guess that they were all vintage.

Opposite the escritoire, Ren found the source of the glorious warmth: an iron stove, with elegant scrollwork and glazed patterned tiles. She tugged off her gloves and stepped forwards to warm her hands with blissful relief.

At the back of the stall, on a small platform covered by a Persian rug, stood the most extraordinary thing of all: Santa's sleigh. It was curved like a shell, with a space on the side to get in and out. The two benches were plush red velvet and the outside was decorated in the effusive, joyful golden ornamentation of the Belle Époque, with leaves and plump swirls and a giant fake jewel. She guessed it had originally come from a carousel, but it was perfect for its new role.

Two small children sat in the sleigh talking to the man himself, gazing with wide eyes at his bearded face and the red fur-lined robe. They were admiring their gifts: two rustic horseshoes that they clanged together, making a satisfying tone in the hushed market stand. Ren stared at the horseshoes, her skin prickling.

When she slowly raised her gaze to take in 'Père Noël', she couldn't believe her luck. 'Joseph?'

'Ah! Ren! Quelle surprise! Welcome to my shop.' He emerged gingerly from his sleigh to shake her hand vigorously, then he clasped her shoulders to give her two fond 'bisous' on her cheeks. 'So lovely to see you again.'

'Wow, your costume is perfect,' she said.

'You know what they say: Père Noël is really Black.' He tapped the side of his nose and grinned.

'You've convinced me,' she said with a smile. 'Is... is Sacha here?'

'Ah, non,' Joseph said, his smile fading.

'It's okay,' she murmured, although it really wasn't. The disappointment at her near miss was momentarily crippling. What difference would it have made anyway, seeing him one more time?

'I don't know where he's gone. He helped Mireille with a client half an hour ago and he never came back.'

Her head whipped up. 'Oh, he was here? He is here – somewhere?'

'Yes. He's my... elf for the day, ho, ho.'

'Well,' she said breathlessly, 'perhaps I could... wait for him here?'

'Bien sûr, I insist.'

The shot of adrenaline at the possibility of finding him again rushed back through her veins and she gushed, 'This is really the most beautiful Christmas display. I hope you've been overrun with visitors.'

'Ah, not quite. The Christmas display at the Marché Paul Bert is better known. But I don't complain. It makes everyone happy.'

She studied him thoughtfully. 'Joseph, do you have Instagram?'

* * *

He was an idiot. How long had he spent rushing around the Marché Serpette after someone he wasn't even sure was there?

Cold, wet and annoyed, Sacha swiped at his hair as he stepped under the shelter of the familiar yellow arcade. How long had he left Joseph alone? And all because he thought he'd caught a glimpse of Ren's friend. The stupidity of hope.

He fished the crumpled hat out of his coat pocket and shoved it back on. It could have kept him warm and dry, but he hadn't wanted to go running after Ren looking like a festive imbecile.

He shrugged out of his coat as he approached Joseph's stand, transformation to Christmas elf complete, but as the stand came into sight, he froze in shock.

It was packed. Families huddled together outside, smiling and pointing. A queue had formed and someone in a top hat and a strange cloak was busy selling ornaments out the front. He blinked, wondering if the sleet had damaged his eyes.

Sacha came closer, hearing the cheery, but slightly creepy rendition of 'Minuit, Chrétien' on the barrel organ – played a little too fast by the enthusiastic hands of a child on the crank. A group of customers was singing along with the English words, 'O Holy Night', and not quite reaching the high notes.

When the song came to an end, the elf in the top hat stopped to cheer and clap, turning in Sacha's direction to smile at the carollers. Sacha shook his head to clear it. He must be imagining things. For a moment, he'd thought he'd seen *that* smile. *Just great.* Trying not to think about her appeared to be the same thing as thinking about her.

She caught sight of him, and her face brightened even more.

'Sacha!' she called out. He was rooted to the spot, unwilling to accept she was really there because it made him so damn happy. Nom de Dieu, her eyes. He'd forgotten how his heart raced when she looked at him like that.

Her voice propelled him forward, but, when he finally stood next to her, by the display of decorative items he'd helped Joseph solder together from more old horseshoes, he couldn't think of a thing to say.

'I'm sorry... to surprise you here. Would you believe I dropped the slip of paper from the top floor of the Galeries Lafayette and I lost your number?'

'What?'

'I was going to call you.'

'You didn't have to...' No more words came. He just stared dumbly at her, remembering their conversations and completely charmed by her strange appearance.

'I... my friend brought me here. It's... educational, I suppose. And then I saw Joseph and...'

'Voilà,' he finished for her.

'Voilà!' she repeated. 'Look, I'm wearing *jeans* from Zara and no expensive jewellery. I'm so glad I could help Joseph, too. This is amazing!'

She looked amazing. The freckles on her cheeks were bright, which only seemed to emphasise those clear eyes. She didn't look like the miserable granddaughter of Livia Asquith-Lewis. She looked... herself... in a top hat.

'Um, is it okay that I'm here? I don't mean to intrude. You were probably happy to be rid of me on Monday morning.'

'No!' he spluttered, finally throwing himself into gear. 'Juste... ah...' He scratched the back of his head. 'I was... disappointed you didn't call and now...' Merde, had he really admitted that?

'Sacha! Where have you been?' Joseph called out in greeting. 'Ren made me an Instagram account and performed some magic with a hashtag and now everyone's pouring in! Every génie needs the Internet, these days, il paraît.'

Sacha turned back to Ren in surprise. Her smile had turned wry. 'I thought I could use my powers for good.'

'Thanks,' he said, still struggling with multiple syllables. 'I'm glad you found us,' he blurted out.

'Me too.'

With the newfound popularity of Joseph's Christmas wonderland, the next hour passed in a blur. Despite her boundless enthusiasm, Ren's French was terrible and her ability to count change similarly so. Sacha took over the sales and she worked on Joseph's new Instagram account, posting photos of the small details of the stand, taking a video of the barrel organ and visiting the other traders.

Sacha felt adrift, in limbo between his expectations and reality. She must have seen thousands of high-quality antiques in her life – she probably had a house furnished with them. But she admired Soufiane's rugs with enthusiasm and listened raptly to Mireille gushing about her boho peacock armchair. After a few minutes of conversation, they appeared to be best friends and each trader had their own Instagram account, too.

'You look like someone, but I can't think who,' Mireille said, making Sacha look up sharply. He shared Ren's look of alarm. Announcing her identity would probably take 'using her powers for good' a step too far. He knew what a name like Asquith-Lewis meant in this market. 'That's it!' Mireille snapped her fingers and studied Ren's face with interest. 'You really look remarkably like... What did you say your name was, chérie?'

'Oh, gosh, didn't I introduce myself? I'm...'

Sacha hurdled a wooden chest and hopped through a forest of limestone statues to land at her side, taking a deep breath. He wrapped an arm around her shoulder and squeezed. 'This is Ren, my girlfriend.'

Mireille clapped her hands together. 'Pourquoi tu ne me l'as pas dit? C'est super! I knew you'd find the right one, one day. She's lovely, just lovely. I don't know why I thought... perhaps all red-headed English look the same! What did you say your name was? Renne? Like the animals of Père Noël?'

'What?'

'Renne is the French word for reindeer,' Sacha explained.

'I had no idea my name was so difficult. Erm... no, my name is... Wren, w-with a "w". It's actually a bird in English,' she said, the lie falling with some hesitation from her lips.

Sacha shepherded Ren back to Joseph's stand and adjusted her top hat. 'Thanks,' she said softly, peering at him from under the brim. 'I didn't want to lie to her, but Ziggy would kill me if word got out that I'd visited the Marché aux Puces.'

He rather felt like murdering Ziggy himself. 'What did you say about a bird?'

She grimaced. 'I was worried "Ren" would be too easily connected to Irena,' she murmured. 'But there is a name in English, "Wren" with a w. It's a kind of bird.' She looked it up in her phone and showed him the French translation.

'Roitelet huppé?' he said with a laugh. 'Yes, this is a bird, but in French we call it a little king – or queen in your case. And huppé can also mean... upper class.'

'The perfect name for me, then,' she said drily.

'No,' he said softly. 'The perfect fake name. I begin to suspect that you are not... huppé at all.'

'Despite my collection of Chamani boots?' She gave him a wobbly smile.

'Là! Regardez! Le gui!' Mireille called out behind them. 'Here, give me the phone. We need a picture of you kissing under the mistletoe!'

'Mireille,' he began, not certain how to protest without arousing suspicion. 'History has moved on from forcing women to kiss.'

'I wouldn't mention it if she was a stranger! But you can indulge an old friend who's never seen you look at a woman the way you did just now,' Mireille replied softly in French. 'It warms my heart, Sacha.'

The effect on Sacha's heart was quite different. It seemed to beat too fast, one moment in panic and the next in anticipation. But he couldn't contradict his old friend, and not only for the sake of the ruse. Mireille was right. He didn't think anyone had ever had this effect on him. But he was far from a handsome prince and had no intention of complicating her life any further.

He shouldn't kiss her, but he wanted to.

'It's okay,' Ren said. 'I think the tradition these days is to give couples an excuse to smooch in public!' Mireille grinned and held up her phone. Ren tugged off both of their hats and looped her hands around his neck.

They'd kissed before, so this was no big deal. Except it was.

18

Ren was a little too eager for the kiss. She tried to cool it, but then she made the mistake of looking at Sacha. His expression was so grave and utterly gorgeous. She lifted her face, a kiss now more important to her than the mistletoe, or the necessity of protecting her identity. He bent his head and her eyes fluttered closed.

The touch of his mouth was everything she remembered and she sank into the kiss, her hands sliding to his face, appreciating the faint, peppery scent of him. God, it was good – the tension in his shoulders, the heave of his chest.

She was just wondering whether the French also called it French kissing, when he eased away. A cheer rang out under the roof of the market and the families clapped and laughed. Ren was glad her thoughts about French kissing hadn't progressed past thoughts, as she suddenly remembered all of the underage eyes on them. But it was a damn shame.

Mireille showed them the picture she'd taken. Although it was backlit and on an angle, Ren still had to stifle a gasp. Their eyes were closed. His brow was low and his hand splayed on the back of her neck, while Ren was clutching at Sacha as though she would drown if he stopped.

Joseph appeared and clapped them on the back. 'Bon, vous deux. I suspected already last Friday that you would get to that. Now, do you want some time alone? I can manage here.'

'No, you can't,' Sacha contradicted him, looking pointedly at Joseph's conspicuously unfestive knee brace. 'That's why I'm here.'

'You aren't a professional antiques trader, then?' Ren asked him.

'No. I would have told you already. Conflict of interest or something.'

'I could believe you're a professional garden gnome, the way you're dressed,' she said, tugging his hat back down over his ears. 'Here, I think I bought this for you without knowing it.' She retrieved Monsieur Gnome out of her handbag and pressed the ugly thing into his palm. Sacha gave her a dry smile, but his fingers closed around the small gift more graciously than it deserved.

'And you are Charlie Chaplin de Noël,' he said as he tweaked her top hat in return.

She grinned at him and retrieved her phone to take a selfie. He raised his eyebrows at her. 'I don't have any social media accounts on here, thank God. This is just for me,' she explained. 'And maybe I'll send it to M— shit! Malou!' She saw she had ten missed calls.

She called her friend with a torrent of apologies and ten minutes later, Malou strode into the little market, her eyes wild. She clutched Ren's wrists. 'You escaped! You're going to give me a heart attack!'

'I didn't *escape*! I just got lost and then... caught up. You sound like Grandmama and Ziggy.'

Malou blanched. 'I always thought they were just controlling, but... you're a menace, Ren.' She pulled her friend into a tight hug. 'What have you got yourself int—' Ren turned to see what had stopped Malou in her tracks. She was regarding Sacha with deep mistrust. 'I thought I saw him.'

'And you didn't tell me?'

'We should go. I've been looking for you for two hours.'

'But I'm helping Sacha's friend Joseph.'

'His friend, an antiques trader who wants a contact at Asquith-Lewis?'

'Of course not!' Ren hissed. 'They don't know who I am – except Sacha.'

'Pute borgne de bordel de merde!'

'I didn't quite catch that? What kind of prostitute of shit?'

'A prostitute with one eye,' Malou explained with a grumble.

'I like that one. Can we just stay a bit longer?' Ren asked hopefully. 'You could go tell Père Noël what you want for Christmas!' She settled the top hat onto Malou's head and held up her camera to snap a selfie of the two of them. Malou gave the camera a dry, Parisian glare at first, but Ren draped an arm around her and smiled such a goofy grin that she gave in with a sigh. 'Just a heads-up,' Ren continued as she tugged Malou into the crowded stand. 'Sacha and I are pretending to be a couple so that no one suspects who I am.'

Malou gaped.

'Have you run out of swear words? Do I win a prize?'

* * *

The market shut at six, ejecting streams of contented faces out into a light fall of snow. Ren ignored Malou's hints that they should get going and helped pack away the stock on the tables while Sacha moved the carousel horse. One table wouldn't fit, and Ren volunteered to help Sacha take it out to Joseph's van.

The table was heavy and she had to stop every few feet. Outside in the dark, the old-fashioned mural on the wall of the market glowed and the shops with their shutters down showed off their full range of graffiti. Snippets of jazz and passionate chansons drifted out of the few restaurants and bars.

Ren expected to feel a ghost of fear, but this darkness was different, when she was just Sacha's girlfriend Wren. She didn't feel threatening eyes on her or imagine every car door opening, masked men spilling out to grab her.

By the time they reached Joseph's van, she was ready to keel over with exertion. She staggered the last few steps, but her aching fingers lost grip.

'Ouf,' Sacha grunted and gasped in pain. He managed to wrench his foot out from underneath the table leg despite Ren's clumsy attempts to help. He waved off her apologies.

After he'd stowed the unwieldy table in the van, his new injury was a good excuse to take his arm as they wandered back, the light snow glinting in the glow of the streetlamps.

'Tell me about the market,' she said. 'When did it start? I bet you know its entire history.'

He glanced at her with an almost smile. 'It started with these, actually, la poubelle.' He pointed to the overflowing bin. 'Imagine we are in the time of the Belle Époque. The Sacré-Cœur is a construction site. A new Paris has been built and destroyed and rebuilt after the Franco-Prussian war and the city is looking out at the world – and taking over large parts of Africa.

'Art and literature and science all flourish with no war and Paris is at the centre of these movements. The prefect of the city is a man called Monsieur Poubelle who introduced Paris to the concept of rubbish collection, stopping the previous practice of leaving rubbish out on the street.

'All of this is progress. But at this time, the rich people had all the money and most people were not rich. The majority had no part in science or literature, except sometimes as objects of pity, and their stories are not told. Except here at the Marché aux Puces.'

Except by you, Ren thought to herself. She felt a tingle of understanding, a conviction about her own life that it would be so much easier to keep ignoring.

'The chiffonniers, the ones who used to look through the rubbish for things of value, their lives changed. They could no longer operate in the city, so they came to this place, just outside the old defences.

'And now you can buy the beautiful furniture of the bourgeois houses of the Belle Époque here. It is a mixing place, a democracy of objects and a warehouse of history.'

'A democracy of objects,' she repeated under her breath. 'How do you keep doing that?'

'What?'

'Ever since I arrived at the market this morning, I've been feeling something and you just... you just explained myself to me.' Her eyes were hot and her nose was aching with cold.

'You're thinking about Asquith-Lewis.'

'Yes. I've never seen anything like this and that's just the way my grandmother wants it. I hate to think that... my whole life has been curated to remove important things. She wants to protect me, but this is... wrong. There is so much... honour in this trade. And passion. And history. You can hear it when Mireille talks about the objects she's found and sold. My grandmother would prefer I didn't know that we're actually just the same.'

'I doubt she shares your opinion,' said Sacha. 'Rather than honour, I imagine she thinks about dishonesty. You're... not like her, you know. You're not... like anyone else.'

He meant it as a compliment, but did he realise how lonely it was to be unlike anyone else? She leaned her head against his shoulder for a few steps. 'What about you? How are you connected to the market? Joseph is an old friend?'

Sacha nodded and his steps slowed. She wondered whether he would dodge the question. 'He used to do some restoration work at the museum in Saint-Denis, many years ago. He offered to show me his work and... I caught the fever.'

'You work for a museum? That's it!'

He shook his head. 'Wrong again. And in any case, I was only sixteen at the time. I was doing general service work.'

She wondered at his tight tone. 'General service work? Is that like an internship?'

'No,' he said with a cough. 'It's... alternative to prison, you know?'

Prison... The word echoed in her thoughts, and unconsciously she stopped walking altogether.

He wouldn't meet her gaze. She could understand that, given she had no idea what expression was on her face.

'It's the only time...' he began stiltedly, but his voice trailed off. 'And it was for theft. Not a violent crime.'

She nodded vigorously. For all her vague anxieties about crime, she would never have believed him capable of violence. Her grandmother would assume, on the other hand... But Grandmama didn't have to know.

Ren couldn't decide what to say. She had no right to ask and no confidence that he'd answer a well-meaning question, which, from her, would doubtless come across as naïve at best. But she had to say something so he'd understand it didn't change anything for her – it didn't change what she felt, what she wasn't supposed to be feeling anyway.

'If you were sixteen, your record must have been expunged.' He nodded. His expression was matter-of-fact, accepting, and even that broke her heart a little. 'I suppose you can't expunge something from your memory, though.'

He glanced at her sharply, but said nothing. The streetlamp threw dark shadows over his features as tiny flakes of snow whirled between them. She lifted a hesitant hand and traced the deep groove on his forehead. He blinked, his soft eyes clouding under thick lashes. In a delayed reaction, he caught her wrist and gently removed her hand and she let it drop with a sigh.

'Thank you for explaining why you're spending your evenings and weekends setting up Santa's Belle Époque Wonderland and dressing up as an elf.'

He shoved his hands into his pockets as they turned back to the arcade. 'You were an excellent co-elf.'

'They're lovely people, Mireille and Joseph and Soufiane and the others.'

'This market is home for Joseph – and for me, too, in a way.'

'Huh,' she said, her smile fading. 'No one would say that about Asquith-Lewis, and yet we've worked so hard to preserve it.'

'Don't take too much on yourself. You employ many, many people – including your friend, I heard. You have history, like this market.'

'Yes,' she said thoughtfully, 'a long history of hobnobbing with aristocrats. I'm not sure it's a history I want to repeat.'

'History doesn't repeat. We are always writing it.'

'Can you tell me what the ending is? I always need to know the ending!'

He laughed, then, with a wide smile that was crooked and utterly infectious. He lifted a hand and brushed the backs of his fingers along her hairline and she nearly stumbled at the hesitant tenderness. His smile faded. 'Malou will be wondering where you are.'

'Hopefully Joseph has distracted her with more bickering about his stock.'

'I wonder what he would be doing if he knew who you really are.'

'Nothing, I'm sure. He's too good a man – like you. But I'll tell him tomorrow when we finish up.'

'Tomorrow?'

'The market is open tomorrow, right? I promise I won't break anything or undercharge too many people.'

'If you can find your way back here, you're welcome to come.' He took off towards the slanting light from the door of the market.

She scrunched her nose at his retreating form. 'You think I'll get lost again.'

'I have faith in you,' he called over his shoulder.

'That makes one of us,' she said with a sigh. As he disappeared into the arcade, Ren suddenly remembered where she was supposed to be tomorrow afternoon and who she was supposed to be bringing. But she didn't want to ruin the night by mentioning it.

19

Ren rounded the corner of the stand the next morning with a bright smile and a cocktail dress in a suit bag. But her smile quickly faded and she froze.

Sacha was grinning, warm and wide, full of affection and ease. It would have made her knees weak, if she wasn't so taken aback by the rest of the scene. Next to him stood a young boy, she guessed somewhere around ten years old, and it was impossible not to see the striking resemblance he bore to Sacha.

Ren nearly turned and ran away. She'd thought of him as her night-time guide, soul-searching through Paris. She'd felt as though he'd been there for *her*. What selfish nonsense was that? They'd only shared two fake kisses and a few deep conversations.

He wasn't her Prince Charming. He was a stranger who didn't need her butting into his life. Prince Charmings were for suckers. She'd been naïve and a little bit stupid. Sacha had a family and she definitely wasn't in it. And now, would he have to pretend to be her boyfriend in front of his own son?

He looked up and saw her before she could do a runner. The best she could do was stuff her dress down behind a chest of drawers before he could ask and be guilted into coming with her to the opera. Grandmama had probably only invited him to rub his nose in their lifestyle anyway.

'Ren!' he said with a smile that she stupidly noted was not as wide or natural as the one she'd witnessed a moment ago. He hesitated before brushing light kisses to her cheeks. 'This is Raphaël. Raph, this is Ren,' was Sacha's only introduction. Did he think he'd mentioned his son before?

'Erm, hi,' she said with a smile she feared was toothy with awkwardness.

'Hi,' was the only reply.

'I explained to him,' Sacha said quietly, 'about… us.'

'I'm so sorry,' she whispered back. 'Does he speak English?'

'I learn English,' Raphaël responded himself, with a grump he must have inherited from Sacha.

As the market opened to fresh crowds, no matter how she tried to distract herself, Ren kept watching the pair of them talk and laugh until she felt thoroughly miserable. She escaped to check on the rest of the traders and their new social media accounts, pleased to feel useful. On her return to Joseph's stand, she studied the beautiful antique carousel horse with its jewelled harness and colourful saddle. 'Is Raphaël too big to fit on the carousel horse? I wanted to get a photo of it. It's so beautiful.'

'You go on the horse,' Raphaël suggested.

'Could I? I thought it was just for children.'

'You don't want your photo on the Internet,' Sacha reminded her reasonably, damn him. Her disappointment must have shown, because he continued, 'But… if you want to, vas-y, please.' He gestured at the horse.

She grasped at the elegant mane enthusiastically and placed one Chanel boot onto the metal bar beneath. 'I've never been on a carousel before,' she whispered as she hauled herself up.

She clutched the pole and imagined the horse lifting gently up and down to creepy music like the version of 'O Holy Night' that Joseph's barrel organ wheezed out. It would be evening, with warm lights and a dark sky, and she realised that night-time in Paris was now full of dreams, rather than the nightmares she'd always associated with darkness.

'The carousel just goes around,' Raphaël said. 'It's not the 6G.'

'What's the 6G?' she asked.

Sacha rolled his eyes. 'A manége, an attraction at the fairs in the Tuileries. Raphaël has wanted to go since the marché de Noël opened. It also "just goes around", tu sais.'

'Oh, God, one of those horrid ones that throws you down so you feel like you're going to fall to pieces – or leave your stomach behind? Urgh.'

'It's excellent,' Raphaël insisted. 'Very fast! But Sacha will stay on the carousel, I think,' he said with a smirk at Sacha. Wait, he called his father by his first name? Perhaps French kids did that.

'How old are you?'

'Eleven.'

'That's a good age for those rides,' she said, patting his shoulder. 'Broken bones still heal well.'

'Oh, vous trois! Look at the three of you!' came the sound of Mireille's voice. 'Let me take a picture.'

Ren shared an alarmed look with Sacha. He came around behind the horse and leaned close and at the last minute, he tipped her top hat forward. She wasn't sure whether he'd been intending to obscure her face, but it didn't work. Instead she caught the falling hat and turned to him with a surprised smile. His face was close.

'Adorable!' Mireille exclaimed and showed them the photo. Ren barely recognised her own smile. She and Sacha certainly looked oblivious to everything else around them in the photo – especially to Raphaël, who was looking heavenward as though their behaviour was terribly embarrassing.

Raphaël knew they weren't really together, but nothing about that picture looked fake.

In a brief lull just before lunch, Sacha took Raphaël to grab some more stock and Ren attempted to serve customers, while Joseph played Father Christmas with his booming voice.

A dark-haired woman approached, glancing around. 'Can I... help you? Puis-je vous aider?' Ren asked.

Instead of a polite smile, the woman stared. 'Vous êtes quivous?' Ren's mind hummed into gear for a translation. Qui: who. *Who are you?* 'Et où est Sacha?'

'Um...' she began dumbly. 'He'll be... right back.'

'Ahhh, "Sorry, do you speak English?" It's *you*.'

The woman was pretty and down-to-earth, with bright brown eyes and a frank smile. Her curly dark hair gave her an everyday glamour that Ren wanted to like. But to like this woman, she had to master the sting of jealousy she wasn't naïve enough to ignore.

This was 'Nadia', the woman on the phone. She must be Sacha's ex.

'I'm Ren. I'm... er... a friend of Sacha's.'

'Nadi!' Sacha appeared, but it did nothing to stem Ren's blush. How did she keep putting him in these ludicrous situations? He kissed both of Nadia's cheeks affectionately. Raphaël joined them, submitting to hugs and kisses from Nadia.

Animated conversation in French erupted around her. Nadia grasped Ren's hand warmly and switched to English. 'It's nice to meet a... *friend* of Sacha's,' she said with a wink. A muscle in Sacha's jaw twitched.

'Ohhhh, we're not, like... you know, *special* friends. I didn't even know about—' Ren said, gesturing helplessly at Nadia and the boy. 'You guys,' she finished. She looked helplessly at Sacha. 'I'm sorry,' she mouthed. 'I didn't mean to get you in trouble—' He started to shake his head in reassurance, but she stupidly finished her sentence without taking the hint, '—with your ex.'

A sudden silence descended and they all stared at her. 'My... what?' he asked in confusion. Ren gestured wildly.

Nadia burst out laughing, looking between them. 'Typical Sacha. He hasn't told you anything. And don't worry. Sacha is always single – except for a few months when he pretended he wasn't dating a colleague.'

'Well, he's only pretending to date me, so that's all right, then.' Ren clapped a hand over her mouth.

'Quoi?' Nadia asked, her smile stretching. After glancing back to make sure none of the other traders were listening, Sacha launched into an explanation in French, full of hand gestures and eye rolls, his shoulders inching towards his ears.

Then, to Ren's surprise, Nadia approached and squeezed her shoulder. 'I like you,' she declared. She held out her hand again and Ren shook it, mystified. 'I'm Nadia, this idiot's sister. That's my son Raphaël.'

A rush of heat travelled up Ren's chest and stung her cheeks, but it wasn't only embarrassment, even though she'd shoved her foot firmly into her mouth with her stupid assumption. It was also vindication. She'd been *right* about Sacha. He was her diamond in the rough. He was kind and trustworthy and had wisdom and strength and a family who obviously adored him – a family she felt privileged to meet.

The relationship she'd found touching when she'd thought they were father and son was even more moving now she knew Sacha was his uncle. They were so close. She remembered him talking about his own father with a soft, reverent tone. Someone who could love like that...

* * *

Sacha was itchy from all of his sister's meaningful looks by the time Nadia finally said she and Raph were going. He knew he had to explain about Ren – in some way that would make sense – before Nadia developed... ideas.

Sacha walked them back to their car. 'I'll see you at the Tuileries later.'

'Are you sure you still want to come with us?' Nadia asked.

'Of course. Why wouldn't I?'

She patted his arm and laughed. 'Frérot, you are a disaster. You say you are pretending to date, but you have a woman there who likes you – a lot.'

'I've only known her a *week*! And you don't know who she really is.'

'You complicate everything.'

'I don't complicate things. They are complicated when they arrive,' he insisted as they made their way down the bustling street.

'Imbécile! Relationships don't "arrive". You *make* them – or you don't.'

'Like we "make" mistakes!'

'Exactement.' She glanced at Raphaël. 'Sometimes what others call a mistake is the best thing in your life.'

Lines of poetry rose in his mind, as though the collection of old books growing up the walls of his flat were opening themselves all at once. *The bird of time has but a little way to fly* from Omar Khayyam's 800-year-old Persian quatrain. And then there was the bleak war-touched love poetry of Louis Aragon. *There is no love that does not live on tears...*

And a line from the notebook lying at the bottom of his backpack: Who you are and where you come from – these are written for you; love is your blank page.

'You think too much, like Papa. But even Papa managed to fall in love with Maman.'

Trust his older sister to bring out the heavy artillery. 'You think mentioning Papa will convince me to ask a girl out?'

Nadia had never read Papa's notebook, the lines of bleakness and struggle amidst the occasional moments of happiness. What had love brought him, in the end? And why was Sacha even thinking about this, when it was clear Ren would be in a very difficult position if she did have the misfortune of falling in love with him?

'What did he used to say? "The indifferent have only one soul."'

'"But when you love, you have two,"' he finished the couplet from Mademoiselle de Scudéry with a grumble. 'But you don't understand. This is not a fairytale. Ren is an heiress. Her world is Cartier, Chanel and Place Vendôme!'

That shut Nadia up, if only for a moment. 'What's she doing *here*?' She could have added 'with you'.

'Damned if I know.' He sighed as Nadia gave him one more long look before unlocking her little Citroën that was as old as Raph.

'Perhaps you need to stop looking at her like that, then,' she said with a frown as they kissed each other's cheeks.

'You're telling me,' he muttered.

He wandered slowly back through the stands overflowing with past eras, with the fingerprints of generations on them, but for once he didn't see the history. All he could see was the moments when he and Ren had looked at each other and it had meant something to him.

But what could he do about it?

20

'Ren is an unusual name. Is it short for something?'

She glanced up from the coat hooks made of horseshoes that she'd been admiring. She'd been waiting for this chance. 'Actually, it's short for Irena.' She dropped her voice low. 'I thought it was best if we didn't make a big deal of it, but my name is actually Irena Asquith-Lewis, from the auction house.'

'The granddaughter of Livia Asquith-Lewis? At my stand? I would roll out the red carpet if I hadn't sold it last week.'

Ren was secretly relieved that Joseph didn't seem to share Sacha's problem with her wealth – or the difference between their finances. 'Thank you, Joseph, but there's really no need.'

'My shop is so far below your... standard,' he declared.

'I love it,' Ren insisted. 'It's... a labour of love.' She hated to think what her grandmother's opinion of this place would be, knowing that Livia could never acknowledge that these traders were colleagues, equals in every way that counted. And they had more grace about it.

'I understand why you wish to keep quiet about your visit,' Joseph said.

'I'm sure it's all right. My grandmother is just... overprotective and... to be honest, I'm enjoying being incognito for a little while.'

'I won't put you in my new Instagram,' he said with a smile. 'Although I might tell the grandchildren I don't have that Irena Asquith-Lewis from the famous auction house visited my shop.'

'Go right ahead,' she said with a laugh at his tone. 'How many children do you have?'

'None,' he said drily. 'Adoption for gay couples has only been legal for ten years in France and, by then, my partner had unfortunately passed away. But I've known Sacha nearly twenty years and Nadia almost as long. Raphaël is everyone's blessing, when he's not getting into trouble.'

'It's wonderful that you have each other.'

'Oui, oui, c'est vrai. Sacha was the most unusual boy when I met him.' Ren pricked up her ears, thinking of Sacha's confession the night before. 'His father had died not long before and my husband, too. He didn't say anything about himself for months, but every time I struggled with memories, Sacha quoted poetry.' Joseph's laugh was halting, as though the story still amazed him. 'I wish I could have met Karim, his father.'

'The taxi driver who loved books,' Ren murmured.

Sacha arrived back, blowing on his hands against the chill, with a dusting of snow in his hair. He immediately admonished Joseph for being up on his feet and they bickered good-naturedly.

A bell rang somewhere in the distance. The constant clang of bells and the rumble of wheels over cobbles were the unmistakable soundtrack of the city – but it gave Ren a start to realise what time it was.

'I have to go,' she said, straightening. 'I'm so sorry.' She rummaged for the suit bag. That morning, she hadn't cared that the dress would be crushed and her make-up would be a disaster, but now she felt a shot of panic. Could Grandmama take her dishevelled appearance as a reason to drag her back to England? She pulled out her phone to call Bilel, not able to meet either gaze.

'Ren.' She heard Sacha's voice through her haze of misery and realised he must have said it several times. 'What's the matter? Where do you have to go?'

She made the mistake of looking at him and it all came flooding out – Grandmama's phone call, her fear of being made to leave, the expectation that Sacha would be with her. She ended with, 'I probably made a mistake... ever pretending that we... I should just get a grip and talk to her.' *Like an adult.* Her relationship with Grandmama had never progressed to that of two mature adults, as though time truly had stopped when Ren was ten and their lives had changed.

The brush of his finger under her chin made her realise she'd squeezed her eyes shut. 'Give me ten minutes?'

She gave a huff of surprise and a dazed smile. When was the last time someone had dropped everything and come running when she needed them? She bit her nails waiting for him, grimacing at the state of her manicure, but Joseph's jolly assurances helped. True to his word, Sacha arrived back ten minutes later, clutching a vintage suit on a wire hanger.

'Bilel is out the front,' he said. He took her hand as they raced for the doors of the arcade, as though he'd forgotten that they didn't have to pretend yet, but Ren wasn't about to point it out to him.

Bilel hurried to turn off the radio when they'd opened the doors, but Ren insisted he leave it on, wondering why she'd always travelled in silence in the past. They crossed the eighteenth arrondissement to a soundtrack of Ed Sheeran and David Guetta, with the odd interruption for Mariah Carey and Michael Bublé with their Christmas crooning. Bilel hummed in tune and Ren pestered him until he sang along with the lyrics he knew, his deep voice making her smile.

As they swung past the Moulin Rouge, looking faded and strangely unhappy in daylight, a hip-hop track came on. Sacha was looking out of the window, but his fingers tapped to the beat. Bilel bobbed his head and they shared a smile.

'Do you like hip-hop?' she asked. 'Do you call it 'ip-'op?'

'Hhhhip-hhhhop,' Sacha said carefully. The 'o' was still delicately formed in his French accent. 'Growing to like hip-hop is a danger of the job.'

'Oh? Do you work in radio? Are you a journalist?'

'No,' he said emphatically.

'Go on,' she prompted as his fingers continued to tap. 'Don't you know the words?'

He inclined his head and cleared his throat, joining in when the second verse began. As she'd suspected, he knew every line. It felt strangely like a serenade as he punctuated the lyrics with his hands and the words flowed off his tongue in rhythm, too fast for her to have any idea what he was saying.

When the verse ended and the chorus cut back in, she applauded raucously. He laughed with her, their shoulders shaking against the seats.

'Impressive!' she said.

He held up a dismissive hand. 'I like that song. And rap can be like poetry, especially in French.'

'I doubt my grandmother would agree,' she said with a chuckle, but her amusement kept her nerves at bay.

The contrast was stark when they slunk into the opera house to a dramatic soundtrack of Verdi's *Don Carlo*. From the warren of chaos that was the Marché aux Puces, they entered the marble grandeur of the Opéra Garnier, hurrying through the ornate rotunda with its mosaic floor and continuing to the imposing staircase. The staircase broke off into three directions at the top, like something from Hogwarts – if Hogwarts had been built under Napoleon III. Sacha was so busy gaping at the gold leaf and the stucco and the floating chandeliers bathing the foyer in light that he tripped and fumbled for the marble banister. She had to admit the enormous atrium was intimidating, seven storeys high, with its painted ceiling and opulent décor.

Ren was tempted to laugh at the absurdity of taking Sacha from the neuf trois, with his beard and tattoos and his taste for hip-hop, to the ballet with Grandmama, but she knew her grandmother would not be laughing.

They found the bathrooms and disappeared inside to change. Something had certainly changed by the time they emerged again and warily inspected their reflections in the floor-length mirror in the corridor.

Sacha tugged at his collar and grimaced at the patterned silk bow tie. 'Your reaction doesn't fill me with confidence.' The suit was a little tight across his shoulders and too long in the trousers. Grandmama would notice.

'You look good.' That was part of the problem. She liked how unpolished he still looked, stuffed into the suit. But that wasn't a good enough reason to make him uncomfortable. 'Ten out of ten,' she said to lighten the moment. 'Although it's a low three for the tie.' She untied the twisted mess he'd managed himself, looping the silk smoothly and retying the knot.

'You used to do that for Charlie,' he said bluntly.

She fumbled the knot and had to start again. She nodded, taken aback by how seldom she thought of Charlie, now. Certainly, she'd never felt such tangled desires while tying Charlie's tie. Sacha's jaw was tight, and his Adam's apple bobbed as the backs of her fingers brushed his throat.

Suit or not, he made her weak-kneed, and she was afraid that

Grandmama would see how he affected her. But wasn't that the idea? She was so confused.

He frowned at his reflection. 'C'est terrifiant,' he said under his breath.

'You do look pretty terrific.'

'I said terrifying, not terrific. I don't think Signor Armani will be signing me for his next campaign.'

'I don't know...' she said. 'I'd buy anything Armani wanted to sell, if you're modelling it.' She turned to go before she said anything else stupid.

'Am I—' He ran an agitated hand through his hair. 'Do you still want me to be an... inappropriate boyfriend? Or should I try to... fit in?'

'Let's just aim to get out unscathed,' she said. Ren held out her hand and he took it and they walked, shoulders bumping, back down the steps to meet Grandmama.

The matriarch's greeting was exactly what Ren had expected. 'Good, you didn't linger in the foyer. I asked Bilel to check for photographers, but, for the matinée, they were thankfully scarce.'

'Hello to you, too.'

Livia blinked. 'Did you expect a warm welcome when I had to blackmail you into meeting me and allow you to bring your... *lover*? And you are so late, I started to suspect you weren't coming.'

'I'm sorry about that, I... we got caught up.' Ren blushed at the images that vague suggestion produced in her mind, especially after last week's misunderstandings at afternoon tea.

'We need to take our seats,' Livia said flatly and took off to promenade up the grand staircase, wielding a cane that Ren had never seen before and she hoped was just for effect.

Ren had the distinct impression that they walked in a circle to reach their seats, Grandmama striding nonchalantly ahead through the gilded Salon du Glacier with its painted ceiling and glowing Christmas tree. Sacha was slack-jawed, gazing at his surroundings, and Ren couldn't help wondering if that had been Grandmama's intention.

Their seats were in a private box, with champagne on ice that neither Ren nor Sacha dared to touch first. He folded himself into a seat and tugged at his ill-fitting jacket. Livia eyed him pointedly as she took her own seat, but of course she was too well-bred to mention to his face that he should have waited until she'd sat down.

'Are you a connoisseur of the ballet, Mr Mourad?' she asked in a barbed tone.

'I... No, I would not say that.'

'You mean you have never attended the ballet before, am I right?' She continued without waiting for him to answer. 'They say the first time you experience the ballet, it can feel like love at first sight.' Ren stared, wondering what Grandmama knew about love at first sight. 'I trust you will enjoy the performance.'

Sacha managed a vague grunt in response. Ren had no better idea what he should have said. If *she* felt out of her depth, she couldn't imagine how he felt. Grandmama finally settled back in her seat and Ren took a breath.

'Will the chandelier fall, tonight?' Sacha whispered to her, a wry glint in his eye.

'What?' Livia asked down her nose, although his comment hadn't been directed at her.

'*Le Fantôme de l'Opéra*,' he explained with a twitch of a smile. 'Is he here tonight? Or still down in his underground house?'

'I don't know what you're talking about, but I do hope you will hold your tongue during the performance.'

Ren flushed with embarrassment at her grandmother's rudeness. 'Is that something about the history of the theatre?' she whispered.

He nodded. 'Some real events during the construction of the Palais Garnier inspired Gaston Leroux's novel, which Mr Lloyd Webber adapted with such success.'

'The chandelier really fell?'

A twitch of his lips suggested her expression was comically wide-eyed. 'A man was killed.'

'The phantom?'

Livia looked daggers at them as the lights went down but Sacha calmly ignored her, leaning over to whisper in her ear, 'You know the Phantom of the Opera dies at the end, don't you? In the novel, he dies of love.'

She turned to reply, finding their faces close. She licked her lips and brought them to his ear to whisper, 'These French romantic heroes can be so useless – just quietly expiring instead of standing up for themselves and their feelings. I think I suspected it ended tragically, but thank you for confirming that I *never* want to see it.'

Was his amused gaze tinged with affection? Ren moved reluctantly back against her own seat and waited for the curtain to ascend on a ballet she must have seen at least ten times. But this time, everything felt different.

21

It started well enough. It wasn't difficult to hold off on applause until he was certain the time was right. But Livia was watching him like a hawk. The first time he slipped up, shifting in his seat and lifting his hands when the movement was not, in fact, over, attracted a scowl that made him question all of his life choices.

During a dramatic pause, his phone beeped. He hauled it out of his pocket like a hot potato, muttering an apology to no one in particular as he turned the sound off. Livia must have had laser eyes because he swore he could feel her glare, even though he didn't dare look at her. He settled back to watch, but the velvet seat was bouncy and uncomfortable, and all the frolicking and music looked and sounded the same to him.

Other patrons had concert programmes and, at the twenty-minute mark, he was wishing he had one, too. If he knew what on earth was going on, between the men in tights and military uniforms and the women in pastel tutus, he might have been able to concentrate – and at least with a programme, he would have had something to do with his hands.

He gathered there was some sort of battle taking place on stage partway through the first act, but it baffled him more than ever. All the arms and legs and swirls of colour acted on him like hypnotism. He snapped upright with a gasp, realising he'd almost fallen asleep. He risked a glance at Ren, to find her grinning ruefully at him.

He leaned on the armrest to whisper in her ear. 'Kick me if it happens again.'

'Shh,' hissed Livia from Ren's other side.

He settled back in his seat, rubbing his eyes and blinking to try to stay awake. The interval seemed to arrive all of a sudden and he squinted as the lights came up. Before his eyes had adjusted, Livia was whisking Ren away and he had no idea if he was supposed to follow. The soothing music had dulled his other senses somehow – either that, or this whole scenario was designed to make him feel stupid. A bit of both, he suspected.

When they'd been gone ten minutes, he decided he should stretch his legs, too, and stood to leave the box, but he paused when he heard muttered voices on the other side of the door.

'You are so much more than this, Ren – than *him*. You are an Asquith-Lewis. I know Charlie hurt you, but it's time to hold your head up and take responsibility for your next steps. This *man* is only getting in the way.'

'Listen to yourself, Grandmama,' came Ren's voice. 'I'm not "more" than anyone. There is no "us" and "them". There's so much out in the world to experience—'

'And you are going to get hurt experiencing it! I had hoped by now that you'd be ready to end this farce and return to London.'

'Farce' was a suspiciously apt term, Sacha thought.

'You gave me until next Friday and I want to spend that time with him.'

'I can't imagine why. You know full well that there is no way I will *ever* approve of him as a partner for you.'

Swallowing a lump in his throat, Sacha turned away and headed back to his seat. There was a lot in that conversation he shouldn't have overheard, but that last part would be the most difficult to forget, especially because he was struggling to remember that Ren had been playing the role and not telling the truth when she'd said she wanted to spend time with him.

He slumped down in his seat, taking deep breaths and not caring if Livia made snide comments about his posture. He glanced at Ren as she strode back to her place, her expression troubled. He refused to move his legs when she tried to get through.

'I have bad manners,' he murmured so only she could hear him. He took her hand to help her climb over him. 'I'm the last man in Paris you would want to sit next to at the ballet.'

She took his hand and leaned close to whisper in his ear, 'You can take me to a hip-hop concert next time.' He snorted in surprise and Livia glared at him again, but he it didn't bother him so much with Ren's hand still clutched in his. She settled back, her eyes on the stage, but her fingers still looped through his.

One more act to go. He could do this.

An hour later, he'd survived the experience and applauded the end with genuine enthusiasm. He'd resisted the temptation to hum along with the 'Dance of the Sugar Plum Fairy', when he recognised it and managed to stay awake by fiddling with Ren's hand.

When they emerged from the palais, the last rays of weak sunlight streaked the sky and the Christmas lights were blinking on in the square. If it had been his family, they would have raucously critiqued the show as they wandered around looking for somewhere to have a drink, but Livia rushed to her waiting car as though it was about to turn into a pumpkin.

'Darling, I must hurry to the Gare du Nord.'

'You're going back tonight?' Was Ren... relieved?

Livia merely nodded, once, in reply. 'There is important work to be done in London this week. I will see you in Val d'Isère on Friday night.' She gave Ren a lipless peck on the cheek. 'All of... this will be behind us.'

'Goodbye, Grandmama,' Ren called as they waved Livia off.

When she'd disappeared from view, a stillness settled over them and he realised he was still clutching her hand. 'That went... well,' he said haltingly. And then she burst into laughter.

'Oh, God.' She clapped her hand over her mouth as her shoulders shook. 'I've never... standing up to Grandmama is not something I usually *do*, but...'

'You did it.'

'I did! And so did you! If you hadn't been there, she would have been finding all of *my* faults instead.'

'I'm happy I was of service,' he muttered.

'I'm sor—' He cut her off with a sharp look. 'Okay, I won't apologise, but... I know you don't deserve to be treated the way she and I have treated you.'

'*She* I accept, but not you. You were kind to my family today. Your grandmother evidently doesn't understand or appreciate you.'

Ren opened her mouth to say something – to defend her grandmother, he suspected – but she closed it again, her expression pensive. 'She's the only family I have.'

He squeezed her hand and then, with a gruff sigh, wrapped his arm around her. 'I understand.' He was lucky the day hadn't gone worse for her. He would be gone from her life soon and that was for the best.

'And I wasn't *kind* to your family. I liked them,' she insisted, resting her head on his shoulder. '*You* were kind to *my* grandmother when she didn't deserve it.'

'They liked you, too,' he blurted out before he could stop himself. 'You're not... what I expected, Ren. I think I... wanted you to misunderstand me, to judge me and my family. But you didn't,' he admitted.

She smiled up at him, her eyes so warm he needed to blink so he could breathe. 'Remember I thought you were a bicycle courier the first time I saw you. Is that why you won't tell me your job? Because I judged you on that first day?'

His brow rose. 'Yes, perhaps. Shall I tell you? Now I know you?'

Now I know you... When had that happened? 'Is it something that requires a university degree?' she asked. He gave her a slight nod. 'Are you a writer? A poet?'

Only in his head. 'No, I'm a—'

'Shhhh!' Ren said, pressing her fingers to his lips. 'I want to guess. I have a bit more time.'

But they didn't have any more time, with no actual plans to see each other again. If he asked her to dinner with no pretext, would she come? And then what would they be? At least as a fake couple, the expectations were clear.

Love is your blank page... It felt as though someone had tattooed those words on his chest without his permission. Ren had to take her place in her illustrious family, while his family took up all of his time and space. He could fill the page with some kind of love story, but it wouldn't have an ending she would care for.

He should let her go... 'Will you... would you like to come to the marché de Noël with us?' was what emerged instead. 'I am meeting Nadia and Raphaël at the Tuileries.'

Her face lit up and he was struck by the thought that he would make many more bad decisions for that smile. 'I'd love to. That sounds a thousand times better than an afternoon at the ballet with my grandmother.'

* * *

If she'd thought the city of light was magic at night, then the Christmas market in the Jardin des Tuileries was a full-on fantasy world. The outline of the Ferris wheel glowed against the night sky. The gabled roofs of the stands selling food and artisanal products made a cosy zigzag of light, softened by lush pine boughs and shiny baubles. Wooden nutcracker dolls the size of humans stood guard next to Christmas trees, decked with rustic straw stars and ribbons and glass teardrops. The scents of cinnamon and honey and herbs tickled her nose and teased her tastebuds.

Ren's newfound passion for 'le streetfood' was indulged as they stood at a wooden barrel and ate grilled ham and cheese sandwiches, made in a stall nearby in a cast-iron skillet dripping with butter. She was certain it tasted better simply because it was called a 'croque monsieur' instead of a cheese toastie, and the side serving of fresh oysters and champagne didn't hurt, either.

When she was tempted to try a giant gingerbread heart, Nadia steered her towards the loaves of pain d'épices instead, the dense honey and ginger cake that went a little too well with vin chaud. Ren was pleasantly tipsy in no time, which helped the stilted conversation she was determined to have with Raphaël. She discovered he and Nadia still lived in Aubervilliers, where Sacha had grown up, and that Nadia was a nurse. Raph looked at Sacha a lot when he answered her questions about school, and she gathered he was a strict homework monitor.

The only time she saw any enthusiasm from the boy was when they reached the 6G, a horrible, whirly nightmare of a ride. Nadia grumbled as she paid for his ticket and then stood biting her nails as he took his turn. Ren was too anxious to watch, but Raph returned miraculously intact.

After wandering past stalls piled high with fragrant natural soaps, glassware, ceramics and woodcraft, they reached the vintage carousel, glittering with mirrors and glass jewels, playing jaunty pipe music as the horses slowly rose and fell. Ren studied it in wonder, thinking of all of the smiling faces the ride had seen over the decades, the changing faces of Paris it had witnessed. Before she realised what he'd done, Sacha pressed a token into her hand and gestured towards the gate with a smile.

'I can't go on my own!'

'Do I have to supervise you?' he teased.

'No! I mean, we're two adults. Won't it look silly?'

'Not with that smile. You look... very childlike.' She scrunched up her nose, but his warm smile suggested he'd meant it as a compliment. 'You've never been on a carousel before. You must.'

Raphaël appeared beside them with a bored sigh. 'I can go, also,' he said impatiently. She whooped with excitement and he looked even less impressed. But Ren clutched his arm and dragged him in with her.

'Choose your horse carefully!' Sacha called after her.

Raph laughed at her as she took Sacha's advice seriously and studied the grave, horsey faces and their painted finery. She chose one with its mane whipping out behind, as though it were racing at Ascot, and the music started as she clambered on.

She yelped as her horse rose with a slow shudder, but the old ride soon reached its stride and she clung laughingly to the swirled pole as she was gently buffeted up and down in a movement that felt nothing like real horse riding. Under the painted landscapes and old-fashioned portraits on the carousel, with fairy lights and the dark sky above, the world felt generous and full of hope.

Then a voice reached her ears dimly and intruded on her moment. 'I say! Is that...? No, what the hell am I thinking? On a carousel?'

'Hmm?' came the bored response.

'Gosh, it really looks like—'

She didn't dare to look. The ride slowed, the music growing

distorted and eerie, like a dream turning into a nightmare. She sought out Sacha, his smile fading as he studied her. He stood to one side of the gate, completely unaware of who stood on the other side, only a few feet away, and he didn't deserve what she was certain was coming.

'Ren? It *is* you!' said the voice as she exited the gate of the carousel as calmly as she could. Sacha's head whipped around to take in the blond swoosh of hair, the broad shoulders and arrogant posture to match the patrician vowels. Sacha drifted closer, his hand closing in her coat at the waist without thought.

'Putain,' he muttered.

'De bordel de merde,' she added under her breath. She lifted her chin and faced the man she'd thought she'd marry. 'Hello, Charlie.'

22

Ren was shocked at how unfamiliar Charlie's face appeared. It wasn't that he'd changed. His blue eyes were bright and affable, as always. She recognised his fine wool coat as one that had hung in their closet last winter.

But he felt like a stranger.

'Oh, hello, Charlotte,' she said, mustering a smile for the woman she usually only saw wearing Lycra in exercise videos on social media. Who the fuck actually got together with someone called Charlotte when their name was Charlie? 'Are you enjoying the marché?'

'Yes, thank you,' Charlotte managed in a halting tone, just as forced as Ren's. Charlie was inspecting Sacha pointedly. His narrowed gaze settled on Sacha's hand, still clutched in her coat.

'Charlie Routledge,' he said all of a sudden, extending his hand. The false politeness in his tone made her itch.

'Sacha Mourad.'

'Mourad, is that... Egyptian?'

'Lebanese.'

'Ah,' was Charlie's only response. He was peering at the line of cursive tattooed on Sacha's neck. A quick glance reassured Ren that Nadia and Raphaël were sensibly keeping their distance. 'Oil, then? Or shipping?'

'What?'

'Your background.'

Sacha gave a little cough. 'No, euh... books.'

'Ah,' Charlie replied with a satisfied smile. Even if he assumed Sacha owned a publishing company, it still settled the question of who had more money – the tactless question Charlie had been asking while dressing it up as interest. He eyed Sacha's outfit, the scuffed boots and ragged jeans that he'd thrown back on in the toilets of the Opéra Garnier. 'I must say I'm surprised,' he said, addressing Ren.

'Me, too. I thought you were in the Alps, taking advantage of the standing invitation to Grandmama's chalet.'

'Does she know you're here... with him?'

'Don't worry about Grandmama. She's not the one in a relationship with Sacha.'

Charlie choked, which hadn't quite been the reaction she'd expected when she made the joke. He leaned closer to speak more privately, but she couldn't stand the proximity and shifted away. 'You'll forgive me for being slightly sceptical,' he continued after he'd recovered. 'I know you took it hard six months ago and it's not as though I didn't care about you. I do care about you, which is why... I'm worried you're compensating. This...' his gaze grew disdainful, 'is all very sudden. Are you seriously going to turn up to meet the investors at the chalet with a guy like this who makes his money in "books"? If that's even true.'

Ren recoiled. Charlie had become a stranger in more than just his appearance – or had he always been like this and she'd been too afraid to acknowledge it? The shock didn't make her angry with him, she was upset with herself. Had she truly been so wary of the outside world that she'd convinced herself she was happy with him?

'You're acting out. But I know you. You'll regret it if you go too far,' Charlie continued.

'You have no right to talk to her like that,' Sacha spoke up, his tone dark.

'And you think you need to defend her from her own people?' Charlie huffed.

Something inside Ren cracked and broke. It felt like her old life. She couldn't go back to the way she'd been before. Charlie wasn't her people. 'Don't make this about you, Charlie.'

'What?'

'Listen to yourself. I've had six months to move on from you and to realise how wrong I was about our relationship. This isn't self-destructive behaviour with the wrong guy. It's finally finding the right one.'

'All right, Ren. I'm sorry.' His bearing changed, suddenly, as though either his previous concern or current acquiescence was faked. Neither possibility put Ren's mind at ease. 'I'm happy to hear that. I really am. In fact, it's great that we ran into each other. We'll see each other at the chalet on Friday and everything will be simpler. We could have dinner together through the week, shall we? Friends again?'

Her throat closed. 'Y-you'll be there this weekend?'

'Yes. After everything that happened with the merger, Ziggy thought it would be a good idea. My parents are flying out, too.'

She felt walls closing in around her again and panic rising. What did Ziggy hope to achieve by inviting Charlie? She felt like a pawn in a game she didn't want to play, and the feeling of powerlessness was concerningly familiar. If she didn't take Sacha to the chalet weekend, she'd have to face Charlie's false concern. But if she did take him, her grandmother would burst a vein – to say nothing of the thinly veiled abuse he would suffer for her sake.

A light switched off behind her, obscuring Charlie's face. She gripped Sacha's coat as the sudden darkness shot panic through her. Her eyes pricked with tears that she willed away in desperation.

'Look, they're shutting down for the evening,' Charlie said, still infuriatingly affable. 'Where is your car? Shall we walk out together?'

'No, we'll call a taxi,' she said firmly.

'A taxi? My driver can take you. It's no trouble at all. What would I say to Livia if she heard I left you alone here to take a public taxi? What happened to your driver?'

'I gave him a holiday,' she said tightly. Charlie was only growing more suspicious and she didn't know what was the best course of action. The mention of her grandmother made her uneasy. Grandmama had already used him to get in touch with her last weekend.

'We can take a taxi,' Sacha maintained.

'Oh, I insist.'

Ren suddenly remembered that Ziggy thought she was staying with Sacha. Perhaps if Charlie took them home, at least that information could be corroborated. She could take the métro from there back to Malou's apartment. Her head was starting to ache from the threads of truth and lies.

'Thank you, Charlie. It might be a little out of your way. Sacha lives in the twentieth arrondissement.'

Charlie's eyebrows rose, but he didn't say anything.

'Let's go and say goodbye to Nadia and Raph,' she said, hoping Sacha picked up the apology in her expression.

* * *

All the breath drained from him as the black Mercedes rumbled away over the cobblestones. The car was so similar to the one he'd crashed into just over a week ago, but its occupants vastly different. Ren slumped in slow motion, clutching the collar of his coat in her fist for balance.

He tugged lightly, encouragement to come closer if she wanted to, and her forehead fell to his chest. He wrapped an arm around her and smoothed her hair with the other hand. 'C'est bien, tout est fini,' he whispered. 'It's over.'

'I'm so sorry. And to Nadia and Raph. You guys didn't deserve that. Charlie was rude and I can't believe I...' She shivered violently.

'We'd better get you inside.'

'I don't want to intrude. I can get the métro back to Malou's flat – even though I'm in her bad books, now, too.'

'You can't take the métro tonight. I can take you in a taxi?' She looked ready to resist, but the adrenaline was leaching from her almost visibly and he suspected a crash was imminent. 'You're welcome to stay here. It's not a problem. It might make up for my free night at the Ritz.'

She peered up at him. 'I am a problem.'

'Alors, you can be my problem for the night.'

'Thank you,' she said softly, her tone too raw to allow him to dismiss her thanks.

She peered at the tall double doors of scratched and pock-marked wood and up at the stone apartment building with its assortment of graffiti tags at ground level and swirls of wrought iron on the floors above. He wouldn't have been surprised if she could feel how important this building was to him, how hard he'd worked to reach a place his father had dreamed of – *Paris*, the étage nobile, the second floor of a building from the Haussmann transformation, in Belleville, which wasn't quite Montmartre, but it had its own history.

'I wondered what your home would be like,' she said. 'It's real. I wonder sometimes if I'm imagining you. I've never known anyone like you. You're kind to the people who hurt you. You're a son to a man who saw you at your lowest point. You're a father to your nephew and a rock for your sister.'

He paused at the sudden pressure on his lungs. She should be drowning in her own emotions, but she picked up on his, instead. He pulled his key out of his pocket, but she didn't move away. She stayed tucked against his side, making him do everything one-handed.

'And you keep picking me up off the ground as though you still believe I can walk on my own.'

'You can,' he said. 'You've learned to take the métro. You can find your way through the labyrinth of the Marché aux Puces. You just faced the man who hurt you. You can do anything.'

'Because I'm leaning on you, my darling fake boyfriend.'

'There's a song in there somewhere,' he muttered before continuing. 'You might need someone to lean on at the moment, but you're still the one walking through it.'

Her palm brushed his cheek, followed a moment later by her lips. A smile formed on his mouth of its own accord. Her hand closed in his coat and she urged them forward, arms still wrapped around each other. He switched on the light in the stairwell, which made her blink and hide her face in his neck.

'My eyes adjusted,' she murmured, as though that fact surprised her. With a sigh, she lifted her head, but paused again before she'd drawn more than a couple of inches away. She was staring at his tattoo, cocking her head to study the words. 'I told myself that I was allowed to ask when I'd been close enough to read it myself.' With hesitant fingers, she traced the line of cursive on his neck.

He held still with some difficulty as her fingertip moved on his skin, over the words that sometimes felt like a benediction and sometimes a curse. He could probably have explained glibly if she'd asked a week ago, but it was difficult to bear, that she'd known she needed to wait if she were to truly understand.

'It's hard to read,' she said. 'The script is... very particular.'

Another arrow through the heart. How did she *know*? How did she see him so clearly when few people did? She was supposed to be wrapped up in her own chaos, but instead of shutting down in fear, she'd opened and blossomed and made herself – and him – vulnerable. Did she realise how powerful she was?

'The handwriting is my father's,' he said, swallowing.

Her gaze flew to his and, as though it had been planned, the timer for the stairwell light ran out and it blinked off. His hands closed in her coat. 'What does it say?' she asked in a whisper.

The words came more easily, in the darkness. 'It says, "La lumière va et vient." The light goes and comes. It's a line from a poem he left me in a notebook.'

'What did he mean?'

'The next line is...' He paused to translate from French to English, feeling the echoes of his father, switching fluidly between Arabic and French. Each time the words were uttered, the meaning was new. His father had understood that. Sacha had never spoken the words in English. 'I learn to breathe in darkness.'

She was perfectly still in his arms, except for the quiver of her breaths. A sniff and a hasty wipe of her cheeks gave her away.

'I didn't want to make you cry,' he said, his hands clutching her coat more tightly.

'You didn't,' she insisted with a cough. 'Your father did. It's beautiful. It's like he knew me. Like I feel about you.' Her fingers found his cheek. 'I'm such a mess.'

'No,' he contradicted her gently. 'It's just a... time.'

'The light will come again,' she said softly. 'Sacha.' Hearing his name spoken in her soft, aching tone made everything seem possible. He curled his hand around the back of her neck, his thumb in her hair. Without thought, he dipped his head, close enough to feel the warmth of her on his skin. But even the darkness wasn't enough to erase the memory of Charlie's superior smile, her grandmother's dire warnings. What good were these feelings if they only complicated everything for her?

'Let's get inside,' he murmured, drawing back, hoping she was oblivious to how close he'd come to kissing her for real.

23

'Tea?' he said as he switched on the light in the hallway.

She stepped gingerly over the threshold into his space. 'Thank you.' She needed something to do with her hands, which were suddenly damp. She couldn't stop thinking about what would have happened if she'd planted her lips on his as she'd wanted to a moment ago.

She wasn't sure of the rules of dating these days, but she was fairly certain you weren't supposed to share your first kiss with a guy after a confrontation with your ex. A normal person would have kept it together enough to kiss him properly. But no, Ren had nearly lost it over his beautiful tattoo.

Sacha probably thought she was grieving for Charlie. She wished she could set him straight, but that would involve telling him everything. *The light goes and comes...* It was a weird sign. What would he say if he understood the true extent of her limitations?

'Come and sit.' He opened the door to what was presumably the living room and that feeling of magic swept over her again as she stepped inside.

'You weren't kidding about the books,' she murmured, gaping at the shelves and shelves, from floor to ceiling, that lined two walls of the room, and more between the windows. It was a small room in the corner of the building, with wooden floorboards and a thread-bare Persian rug. The dark wood shelves were stuffed with paper-backs and hardbacks; most of them looked older than she was. The tall shelves wouldn't have fit in her own apartment. He needed the high ceilings of the second floor of a Parisian Haussmann building.

While he disappeared again to boil the kettle, she ran her fingers along one shelf, seeing books in English and French, Arabic and even Latin and Ancient Greek. Some of the spines were worn and nearly unreadable, whereas others looked pristine. She pulled out one tattered book, a slim volume of poetry called *Romances sans paroles* with a black-and-white photograph of a man on the front – the poet, Paul Verlaine, she guessed.

A book in hardcover, with coloured flags all along the top, poked out of the shelf just below eye level. It was called *Narcisse et Goldmund* and, when she flicked through the pages, she saw exten-sive annotations in pencil, in careful handwriting.

She clutched the book and gazed at the top shelves, too high for her to reach. The bookcases themselves were solid and looked old and she realised she was looking at two generations of his family at least. Her family had kept a safe full of jewellery and a couple of pieces of show furniture as heirlooms. Sacha had inherited books and poetry.

Ren knew which of them was richer.

She ran her fingers over a dog-eared book that lay abandoned on the scratched antique coffee table. She couldn't read the script and the spine appeared to be on the opposite side of what she expected. 'You're reading this?' she asked as he returned with two cups of mint tea.

'I found it at the market yesterday. It's the collected works of Ibn Sina,' he translated. 'It's a habit. I buy books in Arabic whenever I find them. When I was growing up, they were much harder to find, and my father forced Nadia and me to read everything. He was unusual like that. Most Lebanese prefer French or English, and Arabic is the language of the market, but... not my father. He made sure we could both speak and write standard Arabic.'

'That's useful, though. For your job? You use Arabic?'

He gave an eloquent shrug that answered yes and no. 'I'm not a translator or an interpreter, but Arabic has been useful in my job, yes.'

'Hmmm,' she said with a calculating smile, tapping her lips in thought. 'I'll work it out one day.'

'Sit.' He beckoned to the sofa, handing her the steaming mug and draping a blanket around her shoulders. 'Look, Monsieur Gnome guards the plant.'

'Honestly, I thought you would throw him out.'

He sat next to her and gave her a hesitant look. 'One doesn't throw away gifts,' he said softly.

'Are you... going to ask why I got upset?' She stared into her tea. Surely he was wondering what was wrong with her. Then again, maybe he didn't care and all of this was in her head – including the almost-kiss.

'I saw how Charlie treated you, Ren,' he said with an abortive attempt to take her hand. 'I have some idea of what upset you.'

'No, you don't,' she said with a sharp laugh and a disturbingly reckless swell of emotion. 'No one does. Except Grandmama. And that's the way she wants it to stay. Her and me against the world.' A dark and shrinking world, with danger lurking around every corner.

She heard her name again and the tea was plucked from her limp hands. Only when her head settled on his chest and his arms closed around her did she realise her cheeks were burning with fresh tears. The comfort was physical, but it was also more, reaching into the darkness she feared most because it lived inside her.

The thought of letting it out made her panic, but she also felt something new and unexpected: faith. If anyone could accept her, it would be Sacha.

'Talk,' he said, and the brusque order acted on her like a key in a lock.

Her jaw wobbling, she rested her head against his collar bone and spoke the words she hadn't said to anyone since her therapy more than ten years ago. 'When I was ten, I was kidnapped.' The urge to stop there was strong, but the warmth of his body lulled her into an alluring sense of security. 'They incapacitated my driver and grabbed me outside school. I was held in a garage while they contacted Asquith-Lewis for ransom. There was... no window.' Her breath started to come more easily. 'I don't remember many details. I was told it was six days that I was in there. It was forever and it was no time at all.'

Sacha's breath left him in a hiss. His chest rose and fell under her cheek.

'It was a bad time for Grandmama. The company had a lot of debts. It was before Ziggy arrived and started turning things around. We always looked so rich, but... at that time we weren't, not below the surface. She struggled to raise the money for the ransom. But she hired investigators and the police did what they could, even though there had been a threat on my life if the police got involved.'

Sacha's hand fisted in her sweater. He was rigid next to her.

'The ransom was paid, and the investigators came to get me. I can remember more from that point. Everything hurt when they picked me up and I could barely open my eyes. I had been given food and water, but... nothing made sense in that place and I hadn't eaten or drunk in... I don't know how long. I had been too scared to move. I'd... given up, like I was already gone, like I *was* the darkness.'

'You survived,' he murmured, in a tone that made her wonder whether he'd spoken for his own benefit.

'My special skill,' she joked, but it fell flat. Lightening the mood didn't make the memories go away. 'They took me home, these other strange men, and... Grandmama was horrified. I must have peed myself over and over. I remember her cleaning me up without a single hint of emotion. It killed something inside her. She'd already lost her only child. All she had was me and I was... damaged.'

'You're not damaged.'

'I was then. I didn't recover immediately. I couldn't leave the house at all for over a year and the rest of my schooling was... fraught. We were all afraid it would happen again. By the time I had therapy and recovered some independence, I struggled so much I failed every subject in my first term at university. Because of Ziggy's strategy, I at least have a place in the company.'

'And Charlie doesn't know any of this?'

She shook her head. 'Grandmama was terrified – still is. The police never caught the kidnappers. She was worried that people would find out how vulnerable we really were. She was mortified that she'd been forced into paying the ransom at all. She's been... holding everything together all alone for a long time.'

'She made you act as though it hadn't happened.'

'Everything is an act, my whole family, my whole life. We're pretending it's safe, when all the money in the world won't make us truly safe.' Her brain sluggishly caught up with her words. Grandmama relied on wealth and power to make her feel safe. Ren had always understood that wouldn't work. Why had she allowed herself to be trapped by her grandmother's fears and misapprehensions? And how could she make Grandmama see that the world didn't have to be full of darkness? 'I feel safe with you,' she murmured before she lost the courage to say it.

'I'm not sure you should,' he replied, but his soft hand on her face told her something different. 'I'm angry at everyone who's ever hurt you – including your grandmother.'

Her breath caught at the passion in his words. 'She never expected to raise a child at her age and... she loves me in her way.'

'I understand. And I see your courage – perhaps better than you do. There's courage in every one of your smiles.'

'You thought I smiled too much,' she accused gently.

'No, I feel... something when you smile.'

'Your frowns are beautiful, too.' *I love you.* She wondered if he could hear the words. It was ridiculous. She'd known him just over a week.

'You are stronger than you think,' he murmured.

'I hope you're right.' She felt stronger, as though keeping the secret had been a dressing over a festering wound, when what it needed was water, fresh air, and rest. Life was such a wonderful, complicated, messy thing outside of the walls she was accustomed to.

Her eyes drooped, exhaustion swift-acting and powerful. She sighed deeply and turned her face into his neck. He never moved, lending her his warmth and his body, the poignant words on his neck and his quiet dignity, as she drifted to sleep.

24

No matter how much Sacha wished he could hold it off, morning crept over Paris. It was still dark outside, but the muted sounds of the church bells made their way through the windowpanes and into his bedroom.

His eyes were scratchy. He'd struggled to close them all night. At some point, he'd settled her in his bed, taken a shower and perched next to her, but he'd awoken regularly from his doze, checking for her even breathing.

He turned his head on the pillow, terrified of disturbing her, of breaking the spell that he imagined was keeping her safe from everything that haunted her. But, while he was rigid and stiff from a long night, she was soft and peaceful beside him. How she slept at all, he didn't know.

He ached from more than lack of sleep. Every word she'd said last night was still reverberating in his blood – as well as a few she hadn't said. He saw the past two weekends in a new light. He understood why the tentative steps outside of her familiar environment had meant so much to her. But he was angrier than ever with her grandmother. The incident itself was shocking, but she'd forced Ren to recover alone, withdrawing the emotional support Ren needed because of her own cowardice. He hoped it was only cowardice.

Six days... It struck him as far too long. He hoped his suspicions were wrong. It would break her heart all over again. One more reason he could only give her more trouble and not the happy ending she longed for. If only he could stop thinking of their relationship as an epic, unfulfilled romance, like the old stories from the Middle East, full of yearning and adversity.

He slipped out of bed as quietly as he could and dressed for work. The desire to stay was strong, but he understood it would be for his own benefit. She was more than capable of looking after herself. But he couldn't leave until he'd hurried across the road for fresh croissants and poured a coffee into an insulated mug.

He hesitated with a pencil over a piece of notepaper. What could he write? The only words that came were ones he *couldn't* write down.

I'll call you later. S

It would have to do.

When he emerged from the door of the building for the second time, he was greeted by three photographers waiting on the pavement, lenses at the ready. After a moment of mutual surprise, a flash blazed in his eyes, and he cowered behind his arm.

'Is she in there?'

'Are you her new boyfriend?'

'Allez vous faire foutre!' he said through gritted teeth and pushed past them. With an uneasy glance at the window of his apartment, he headed for the métro. He tried to tell himself they couldn't know who he was or which apartment Ren was in, but it was difficult to restrain his anger. He would have to warn her when she woke up.

* * *

Ren met the new day marvelling at the lightness in her entire body after the upset of the evening before and the hours and hours of sleep – lightness, and a pleasant ache of memory that was triggered every time she found some small sign of Sacha's recent presence: a stack of books on his bedside table; a recipe on the fridge; and the delicious breakfast he'd taken the time to prepare for her before he left.

She suspected he had not felt as cosy and well-rested when he'd left for work early that morning. What she remembered from the evening before were only the brief periods of lighter sleep, where she'd groped for him and he'd been there. She vaguely remembered his damp hair after he'd showered and a soft cotton T-shirt covering his chest.

She took a seat at the tiny table by the window in the kitchen niche and tucked into her fresh croissant with two hunks of cheese. A slip of paper was tucked under the insulated cup and she snapped it up eagerly.

I'll call you later. S

It was only a few words, but somehow enough. She brushed her thumb over the 'S', enjoying the familiarity in the shortening of his name.

Her phone rang and she stood to fetch it out of her handbag, grimacing when she saw it was a UK number. Her heart sank when she connected the call and it was exactly who she'd feared it would be.

'I'm so sorry to disturb your time off,' Ziggy began, 'but I'm afraid the situation has changed. Our media team is working to counteract the story, but I'll need you to work *with* me on this.'

'What story?'

'There's no need to read the ridiculous headlines yourself, but... let's just say your boyfriend is one of the most wanted men in Paris right now.'

Ren's stomach flipped, thinking of Sacha's admission that he'd committed a crime when he was a teenager. It couldn't be what Ziggy meant, but she was suddenly afraid of what would happen to him if her life invaded his. 'Do they know who he is?'

'Not yet, but they know where he lives, and I can imagine they'll scour that flea market this weekend. I don't know what you were thinking going *there*. I've contacted the police to ask them to move the photographers on, but you need to stay put until it's safe.' Ren gave the window a startled glance. 'The mystery is unfortunately feeding speculation. Livia has been working much too hard to reassure all the investors that the merger will still go ahead and given all of the medication she's on... well, you need to play your part, now.'

Knowing that Ziggy was using guilt as a tool didn't stop Ren from feeling it. 'What do you need me to do?'

'Mr Mourad needs to come to the chalet this weekend. No fanfare, no announcements, just showing our investors that everything is normal and that your relationship status no longer influences the future of the company.'

'That's a message I can get behind,' she mumbled.

'But... please clean him up.'

Ren bit her lip to stay silent. The uncoupling of her personal life from the company only went so far. 'I'll do my best.'

'Your best it will need to be,' Ziggy continued in that warning tone that gave Ren goosebumps. 'We need the investors on side. These kinds of headlines aren't good for business.'

Ren ended the call as quickly as she could and dialled Sacha before she could second-guess herself. He had every right to refuse her and part of her wanted to protect him from what would surely be an unpleasant weekend. She'd always loved to ski, but it was the veiled posturing, the negotiations disguised as friendly chats that she'd never coped with.

Sacha didn't pick up the call and her stomach twisted with worry. Had the photographers bothered him this morning? She was tempted to look at the headlines, but experience had taught her that was disastrous for her already fragile confidence.

What she really wanted was to believe his words from the night before. Was she stronger than she thought?

The phone rang once more, and Sacha's name flashed up. She connected the call with a sigh of relief.

'Are you okay? Did the reporters bother you?' she asked.

'No, I wanted to ask you the same. Did you leave already? I wanted to warn you, but it's my first break—'

'Ziggy warned me. I'm still... here.'

'Good,' he said. There was a long pause where she tried not to read too much into his emphatic tone. 'How are you feeling?'

'Kind of... better, actually, except for the encampment of paparazzi. I'm sorry for crashing into your life. You really didn't need this.'

'The reporters didn't know who I was.'

'Actually... they did. Not who you are, exactly, but between Instagram and Charlie, they've been tipped off about... us.' The silence was ominous, but she ploughed on. 'Z-ziggy thinks the mystery is feeding the media interest and she wants to... bring you out into the open. I know you probably can't take the time away from your family the weekend before Christmas and I don't want to ask you because I can't ever seem to give you anything in return and you know what you're in for now, so I can't imagine you'd—'

'What do you need me to do?' Something in his tone reminded her of that simple 'S' on his note.

'Will you come to Val d'Isère with me this weekend? To ski? With my grandmother and Ziggy, and Charlie and a whole lot of stuffy investors?'

'I can't ski,' was all he said at first. She tried to formulate an understanding response, but she was choking on her disappointment. 'But if you think it will help, I'll come.'

Her happiness revved up again and she'd never been so glad of one of Ziggy's dictates before. 'It'll help. I owe you—'

'You don't owe me anything,' he said gruffly.

'Isn't there something I could help you with in return?' She experienced a little twinge of guilt, knowing full well her question was just an excuse to see him again during the week.

'I suppose there is something.'

Yes! 'Anything!'

'It's for my work,' he said. 'You'd have to let me tell you.'

'No, just tell me where to meet you and I'll guess before you give it away. I'm definitely going to guess.'

'You want to win,' he said drily. 'D'accord. It's on Wednesday. You'd have to come early. Is that okay?'

'I'll be there.'

'You don't even know what you have to do.'

'I don't care. If you'll be there, I'm looking forward to it.' His splutter in response suggested she'd laid it on too thick, but she was too happy to care.

'I've got to go. I'll text you the address. I – I'll see you on Wednesday.'

25

Early on Wednesday, Sacha hurried along the dark street, the buildings the same grey as the early morning sky. One day soon, he'd have the time to phone the police about his bike, but until that day, he had to rush from the métro, past a Hindu temple, a youth hostel and two schools where he *didn't* work. This involved getting up in the full dark and this morning, the darkness was amplifying his crowded thoughts.

He reached the corner where he'd agreed to meet her. He should have sent her the exact location of his workplace and given away the game completely, but she'd been determined to guess. He glanced around for her, wondering how she was.

He was so absorbed in his own concerns that he jumped when she appeared from around the corner. She beamed when she saw him, clasping her hands behind her back and straightening her shoulders.

'I took the métro!' she blurted out instead of a greeting. 'All on my own! In the dark! I lost my ticket and had to pay a fine at the gates, but I made it.' She was brimming with energy, which was not what he'd expected, after his two days of hurting for her.

He studied her with growing amusement. Taking her arm, he mimed pressing a stamp to the back of her hand. 'Well done. B plus, with an A for effort.'

'Are you going to give me a quiz?'

'Maybe at the end of the day.'

'Wait!' she said suddenly. She took hold of the front of his coat and nudged him a couple of steps backwards. He blinked as the light of the streetlamp streamed straight down on him. She tilted her head, her eyes roving all over his face.

'Something wrong?'

'No,' she said faintly, her gaze now travelling down his trousers to his neat loafers. She looked up at him again and blinked. 'You cut your hair.'

'And the beard. I don't normally look like a gnome. It was Joseph's idea.'

'You looked like a handsome gnome,' she said with a teasing smile. 'But you left some fluff on your chin.' He ran his fingers self-consciously over the trimmed bristles on his jaw. 'I'm glad you didn't get rid of it all. It looks good.'

He coughed and rubbed at his hot cheek. 'Shall we go?'

She glanced around the intersection with narrowed eyes until her gaze settled on their destination. He smiled faintly, waiting for her to finally guess correctly. It was a plain building with a single tree in the courtyard and nothing else to soften the blunt lines of concrete that bore the name of the collège and the obligatory, 'Liberté, égalité, fraternité', the motto of freedom, equality and brotherhood that had been formed in protest and was now so ubiquitous it symbolised little more than the French state itself.

'Are the chinos and loafers an unofficial teacher uniform?'

He took off across the street, fishing his keys out of his pocket. 'Is Louis Versace the unofficial uniform of heiresses?' he called over his shoulder, but he straightened his trousers self-consciously.

'I suppose I deserved that,' she said cheerfully, skipping to catch up with him.

This early in the morning, there was only one moped chained up on the corner, where there was usually a haphazard pile. It reminded him of the grumbling when he'd told the class they needed to bring a métro ticket today. Since most of them had only just passed their traffic exam, driving a moped was the pinnacle of their lives.

Sacha was used to the numerous digs about how he must have failed the exam himself, since he still rode a bicycle. He was surprised none of them had noticed he'd been rushing in on foot for over a week. His explanation would be a mess of stammering and blushes that would make them hoot with laughter.

He'd told the class that a friend was accompanying them on their excursion, and the rest of the day had been mostly catcalls of, 'Oooh, Prof has a girlfriend!' and implausible conjecture about where they'd met, making him glad he hadn't told them until the final class of the day. When he'd found himself groaning that no, he hadn't used Leila's aunt's match-making service, he'd been more than ready to hear the school bell.

Now he was experiencing a flutter of anticipation that did not usually accompany his arrival at school. He took classes on excursions without help every year. They weren't nursery school children. But Ren added a certain excitement, and such a good opportunity to practise their English was very rare.

That was what he told himself, anyway.

'What subjects do you teach?' she asked as he unlocked the gate and gestured her through.

'That, I think, you should guess.'

'I suppose that's fair. Do you teach literature? French?'

'No. French literature is not my passion.'

'Your passion,' she repeated thoughtfully. 'History,' she said confidently. 'You're a history teacher.'

'Correct. And I have a principal class of kids in the troisième, the fourth year of collège. I think you say year ten?'

'If it's the fourth year, why is it called the third?'

'It's the third last, before the Bac. We count down.'

'That's crazy. Are teachers in France allowed to... have tattoos, then?'

'Probably not in Catholic schools, but I don't offend the state too much.'

'It all makes sense now. I should have guessed, but you didn't look like a teacher until you cut your hair and put on those loafers!'

'This is how I usually look.'

She lifted a hesitant hand to tug on one of his longer curls on top. 'Well, it's nice to meet you, Monsieur Mourad. But I kind of miss my Christmas elf.'

He opened his mouth to say something, but she turned and hopped up the steps to the doors of the building.

'Don't you even have a Christmas tree?' she asked as he led her through the warren of linoleum corridors.

'It's a school, not the Galeries Lafayette.'

'The kids don't deserve a bit of festive spirit?'

'Their festive spirit comes from anticipation of the end of term. They can go and see the Christmas lights in their own time. What?' he asked, catching sight of her poor attempt to stifle an amused smile.

'These poor kids. You are such a grump.'

'First Joseph, now you. I am not the Grinch. I have no problem with Christmas.'

'The Grinch?' she snorted a laugh. 'That's perfect.'

'I assume it comes from the word grincheux in French. It just means grumpy.'

'That only makes it more appropriate! It's funny that we stole the French word to describe a grumpy person who doesn't like others having fun,' she said with a smile and nudged him.

'I like to see others having fun. Just not during school hours,' he added. 'This is my classroom,' he said when they'd reached a door with chipped paint and an iron handle. He had to admit, a few decorations would make a nice change.

The sound of the front door opening and then rapid footsteps made them look up and Rita appeared around the corner. Sacha rushed to unlock his classroom, giving her a wave and a mumbled, 'Bonjour.' It might have worked on another morning, but Ren was not easily ignored.

'Bonjour,' Rita echoed, coming to a stop and studying Ren with unconcealed curiosity. At least she was wearing her off-the-rack disguise, although, as she'd said, she hadn't been able to part with the expensive boots. 'Tu es bien matinal. Est-ce que tu as trouvé ton vélo?' Rita asked after his bike as he gave her perfunctory kisses on both cheeks.

'Non,' he said and explained about the class excursion in clipped sentences, his hands shoved into his pockets. Rita was still shooting glances at Ren. 'This is Ren, uhm, a friend from England,' he introduced, switching to English for Ren's benefit. 'My colleague, Rita.'

Ren threaded her arm through his and held on and Sacha blinked, resisting a laugh at her less-than-subtle proprietary body language. Rita gave him a long look that ended in a nod, and wished them both a good day in impeccable English. He watched her go, wondering if the farce hadn't been the kindest hint he could give.

He still turned on Ren when he'd shut the door of his classroom behind them. 'Why did you do that?'

Her smile vanished. 'Ouch, did I get it wrong? Did I just screw up your chances with her?'

'No, no. You got it right. It's just... You didn't have to.'

'Like you don't have to help me? She is your ex, then? What happened?'

'It's not very interesting,' he said, hanging his coat.

'Unlike my break-up, which made headlines,' she said darkly. 'I take it you broke up with her.'

'No...'

'No?' Her open-mouthed disbelief made the heat rush to his face again. Merde, he hoped he wouldn't spend the day blushing in front of the kids.

'You don't really think I'm a... bon parti, Ren? A good... catch, you say?' He gave her a pointed look. 'I have not much to offer – not time, not commitment. Rita deserved more and I couldn't give it to her when she asked. It was the right thing that she broke with me.'

He wanted to turn away from Ren's thoughtful gaze, but he liked the soft look on her face too much. He tried to think about the kids, about the tour he had planned to bring to life a unique and little-known period of the city's history, but Ren ruined all of his efforts by reaching up to press a kiss to his cheek and his mind went blank again. 'Well, you are "très bon" to me and... she shouldn't have asked for something you couldn't give.'

The door banged open and he sprang away from Ren. 'Ohé, bonjour! C'est ta meuf? Ta fatma, Prof?' Hamoud grinned at him with his usual cheeky bravado as he sauntered into the classroom followed by his best friend Felix.

'Votre,' he corrected first, pinning Hamoud with a look. 'This is...' Would the kids know or care who she was?

'I'm Ren,' she said, 'or should you call me Miss... Lewis?'

He cleared his throat. 'You need to practise your English and your politesse, les gars.' And *he* needed to stop imagining what it would be like if Wren Lewis really existed.

26

'Oh, my God, what the fuck? Qu'est-ce que c'est ça?'

For most of the day, the kids' vocabulary had been limited to, 'Can you repeat, please?' or 'You comprend?' and she'd been told numerous times that she was 'gentle' and 'too jolly for Prof', which sounded about right, even though she was fairly certain it didn't mean what she thought it did.

But show them a cabinet full of mediaeval phalluses and some colourful English phrases emerged.

'Prof! C'est une bite!'

Sacha stood calmly at the back of the group, his arms crossed, and let them get through their gleeful exclamations and sniggers. When they grew too rowdy for a museum – even one with a collection of objects shaped like penises – Sacha lifted his chin and spoke, his voice sharp, but not loud. The class guffawed, but the chatter died down.

'What did you say to them?'

'I just asked if they thought people didn't have penises in the Middle Ages. This is why historical context is so important. You see the artefacts on display in the Louvre and you think you see history, but what you really see is your own suppositions – and the curation of history by a small group of people in our time, as well as a process of selection through centuries of conservation.' Ren wondered if he knew how much he gesticulated when he talked about this stuff. It was gorgeous.

'I've seen a bazillion depictions of saints in my life, but I've never seen a mediaeval pin in the shape of a cock until today.'

He raised his eyebrows at her choice of words, but agreed. 'C'est ça. Exactly.'

'Do you really think that's the lesson they'll learn from today?'

'No, they'll go home and tell their parents they went to the Museum of Cocks, but it's better than repeating the dates of the Troisième République and the events of the revolution. This, at least, makes them think.'

'Maybe historians through the centuries have been missing a trick.'

'You haven't read the Greek and Roman historians.'

'No, but it sounds like I should.'

The kids fidgeted from room to room and Sacha mostly let them explore according to their own interests. Occasionally, he'd point out an object or two: a jewelled box that integrated carvings from ancient Egypt; an engraved Italian sword, for which his enthusiasm was obvious; and a fragment of fabric, one thousand years old, woven in Muslim Spain. He shared jokes with the kids as he spoke and kept order, while sometimes tolerating interruptions. And he listened as much as he spoke, meaning Ren couldn't linger at the back and keep him to herself as she was tempted to.

She'd admired the Impressionist masterpieces in the Musée d'Orsay countless times, but she'd never had any idea that mediaeval art could be so fascinating – a glimpse into another world. In the room dedicated to stained glass, artificial light shone through the displays, bringing out colours more vivid than the textiles or the polychrome sculptures. Up close, she could see the detail of the faces, the sorrow and pain, or awe and adoration.

'We have something like this in our current auction,' she said, when Sacha came up beside her. 'It's so beautiful, with the light shining through it.'

'You have vitraux? Stained glass like this?' She nodded. 'Provenance?' he asked.

'We don't know exactly. It's been in private hands for a long time.'

He frowned at her answer, making her stomach drop. It felt awkward, contemplating historical artefacts that would be hidden away in private collections, rather than in museums for the public good.

'These are more beautiful,' she added, hearing her own defensiveness and wishing that distance didn't exist between them.

'Prof?' One of the girls called him into the next room. Ren heard the word 'amour' – love – and leaned over the display case to see what they were looking at.

'C'est latin, pas de français,' Sacha was explaining. She caught that much: it was Latin, not French. She saw the enamelled rectangle they were referring to, part of a fourteenth-century belt. It bore the word 'amor' in wobbly ancient script.

'Mais ça veut dire amour?' the student – Ren thought her name was Alicia – asked, a smile forming on her face.

'Oui, oui,' Sacha confirmed earnestly. Alicia glanced with a smile between her teacher and Ren, and her friend giggled as they hurried after the other kids.

'They think we're going to sneak back to the naughty section on our own later,' Ren whispered.

Sacha choked on a laugh. 'They're fifteen. They still have simple notions about human relationships.'

'I don't know that my notions are any better developed.' And if the kids thought she and Sacha were attracted to each other, they weren't wrong – at least not on her part.

'You have a point, là.'

The final room of the museum was dedicated to the incredibly well-preserved mille-fleurs tapestries, known as *The Lady and the Unicorn*. Although there were one or two sniggers at the symbolism of the horn, the works themselves, the intricate weaving in dyed wool and silk, more than 500 years old, were enough to maintain a hush among the students.

When they left the museum, too quickly for Ren's liking, the streets were slick and shiny with drizzle. Sacha led the group past the imposing stone buildings of the Sorbonne and pointed out the glimpses of the façade and the dome of the Pantheon, columns flanked by vibrant green Christmas trees.

He painted a picture, first for the students in French, and then translated afterwards for Ren, of the Quartier Latin as it had been centuries ago, when it received its nickname because of the dominance of Latin at the universities. He described long-destroyed abbeys and colleges, bringing them to life while pointing out the few vestiges of the time, like a trail of clues: a bell tower now built into a school, the late Gothic-Renaissance façade of the church of St-Étienne-du-Mont, with its rose window, and a fragment of the mediaeval city wall, now attached to a grand apartment building from the nineteenth century.

'So, why history?' she asked, as they headed towards the deli where they would stop for lunch. 'Because of Joseph and his antiques?'

'Partly. When my father died, I felt... disconnected.' She held her breath, waiting for the rest of the story. 'And powerless.

Restoring antiques with Joseph... there was meaning in it. I started reading, to find the stories of the objects. The stories... There is a power in understanding where you come from and how societies change. People use these stories, bits of history, to make decisions that form the future. If you don't understand what happened in the past, you can't be part of that. That's what some teachers wanted – in earlier generations. Especially in France, in *Paris*, you know what can happen when the students have power.'

She didn't, not really, but she could guess from his tone. 'You were their age when you lost your father,' she realised with a stab of sympathy.

He nodded. 'I want them to place themselves in the story – in history.'

'You make it mean something to them,' she murmured.

'Yes. Just think about their families and what they have seen and done, in comparison to *your* family. They have just as much history – their families' stories and the city, their home. It's just more difficult to find – like mediaeval Paris is lost among the grandeur of the nineteenth century.'

His words struck a chord inside her. She was the same as everyone else, deep down. Grandmama couldn't allow that to be true, or the principle on which their business rested would be exposed as a lie. But for Ren, it was a revelation.

A flicker of unease rippled through her at the realisation that she couldn't return to her previous complicity. Something would have to change, as difficult as that was to contemplate.

* * *

There was barely room in the little Lebanese deli for all of the students, but they found perches and spoke loudly to each other as they ate. Ren was watching Sacha closely enough to see him slip some money to the man behind the counter for a couple of students who didn't have their own.

Sacha leaned on the counter and spoke to the owner as the man prepared flatbreads stuffed with shawarma, kofta, or falafel, hummus and vegetables. It took a moment for Ren to realise he wasn't speaking French.

'Arabe, miss,' Felix, one of the boys at the table with her explained.

'Very bad!' said another boy, who'd introduced himself as Hamoud.

Sacha eyed them. 'Not very bad. You need to improve your arabe standard moderne.'

'Why? No one on the street speaks that!' Hamoud insisted. 'You must learn arabe maghrébin!'

'Hadi lmekla bnina!' Sacha responded with a wink, making Hamoud laugh.

'Stop! Very bad! Felix speaks better! You keep the arabe standard and the arabe du Liban!'

'What did you say?' Ren asked Sacha.

'I said the food is delicious. But he's right. My spoken Arabic isn't good.'

'How many of these kids speak it?'

'About ten, most of them maghrébin, the dialect from North Africa. If they don't want me to understand, then I don't understand. It's different to what I learned. But it's useful to shock them sometimes and I do better with the Syrian dialect.' He flashed his teeth in a quick smile. He looked relaxed, leaning on the counter, his legs crossed at the ankles.

He passed her a rolled-up flatbread with a flourish, just when she'd been about to say something heartfelt and approving and probably very embarrassing. It was for the best. 'Your first shawarma sandwich, non?'

The aromas of the marinated meat, fresh herb sauce, olive oil and green peppers filled her palate and she took an eager bite. 'Mmm, what did you say? Hadi mekla something? The food *is* delicious,' she said, wiping a drip of sauce off her hand with a serviette.

'It's not swordfish with salsa au citron.'

'Ha. Do you know every Lebanese restaurant in Paris, then?'

'No. Do you know how many there are?' he said with a huff. 'But I've been here a few times. The Syriac Catholic church is not far. I was baptised there.'

'Your history,' she commented lightly. 'And the history of the city, your home.'

'You are my best student, today,' he said with another wink. He had to stop doing that. With the teacher voice, the meaningful tattoos and his habit of spouting poetry and history, her insides were already mush.

After their late lunch, Sacha led the march further along the boulevards of the Latin Quarter in the direction of the Seine, pausing briefly to point out the Grand Mosque of Paris. Ren trailed at the back with Felix and Hamoud, letting them laugh at her ignorance of Stormzy and Paris Saint-Germain and computer games.

They finally stopped in a paved courtyard in front of a contemporary building of glass and steel. Ren was eager to hear what Sacha's next surprise would be while the kids rolled their eyes and took the brilliance of their teacher completely for granted, calling her 'fayot' behind their hands, which she guessed meant she was the teacher's pet and she didn't mind a bit.

His introduction in French was surprisingly short, punctuated by his crisp hand gestures and clear sentences that she was frustrated she still couldn't understand. He finished with, 'On y va,' and gestured to the doors of the building.

'This is the Institut du monde arabe, but we're not going into the exhibition,' he explained as they passed through the building, peering out of the metal apertures that decorated the façade in geometric shapes, and took the lift up to a rooftop terrace.

Ren grinned. 'Am I finally going to get a glimpse of the Eiffel Tower?'

'No,' Sacha said with a laugh. 'The Seine bends and you can't see it from here.' He strode to the railing and gestured expansively. 'But you can see...' He paused for effect. 'Notre-Dame-de-Paris.'

She stepped up next to him, gazing along the pale blue-green river, to the two islands, the Île-Saint-Louis and the Île-de-la-Cité, the ancient heart of Paris. The towers of the formidable cathedral stood, almost forlorn next to a crane and metal scaffolding, the roof covered with white canvas. The elegant buttresses looked fragile and vulnerable from above.

'It took them more than two years after the fire just to make sure the vault didn't cave in and that the towers were secure,' Sacha explained quietly. 'For 800 years, the vaults and buttresses supported the structure. And after less than two hours of burning, the spire came down. Over 500 people fought the fire. And now the cathedral makes more history.'

He caught the students' attention and repeated himself in French – with more drama, Ren suspected, if his gestures were anything to go by. Ren's mind was full – as full as her heart – as she gazed over the rooftops of Paris under the slate sky. It was a unique view – a view for history, with the poor cathedral dressed for surgery, while the fairy lights in the bare trees across the Seine blinked on.

She felt the gift that Sacha was giving his students – their own history, as well as his. She remembered that morning, seeing his ex-girlfriend. He gave so much to his family, his students. She could understand why he'd felt as though he had nothing more to give. Remembering how they'd met and everything that had happened since, Ren couldn't help worrying that she was yet another burden he was bearing.

What would it take to give him some of the lightness of spirit that she'd found with him? He'd turned his own history into something that gave his life meaning. But did he ever share the dark bits?

27

'Can I... see you to Malou's flat?'

She turned back from the classroom door, where she'd just waved off Felix and Hamoud, who'd looked ready to invite her to dinner themselves. 'I think,' she began, 'I should see *you* home, now I am a pro on the métro.'

'It's not on your way.'

'Taking me back wouldn't be on *your* way, then,' she countered. 'Oh, you probably have your bike, though.'

'No, my bike... got stolen.'

'Oh, no, really? When?'

He adjusted the pens under the whiteboard unnecessarily. 'You don't want to know.'

'Shit, it got stolen from the Place Vendôme? Oh, Sacha, I really am your bad luck charm!'

He didn't think she was, but when he looked at her, he did start thinking about the word 'chance'. It meant luck in French, but with a touch of fortune or fate.

'It's fine,' he insisted.

'I really should see you home, then. Actually,' she began thoughtfully. 'I have an idea. Do you trust me?'

'Yes,' he said curiously.

She blinked. 'Okay. I hope that was the right answer. Let's go. You showed me mediaeval Paris today, so let me show you something.'

He felt a twinge of unease. He did trust her. He trusted that her heart was always in the right place and that she was capable of more than she thought she was. But he didn't share her staunch commitment to optimism.

His unease grew when they emerged up the stone steps under the Art Nouveau sign at the Franklin D. Roosevelt métro station, right in front of the Gucci store.

'Please tell me you're not taking me shopping.' He was mostly joking, but the strain in his voice was real. He wasn't sure what she could have to show him here that wouldn't remind him of all the reasons she shouldn't be opening up to him like this.

'Don't look so worried.'

She hurried around the large intersection, the epitome of Haussmann's eighth arrondissement, past skeletal plane trees and fountains trying valiantly not to freeze as the evening temperature dropped and the moisture in the air became crystalline. Behind them, the iron-and-glass roof of the Grand Palais was visible over the treetops. If Sacha's quartier was the rebellious heartland of working Paris, this intersection was the grandiose veneer of the elegant city.

She hurried down a grand avenue and hesitated, gazing at a building across the street. With a sigh, he followed her gaze and wasn't surprised to see the name 'Asquith-Lewis' in elegant grey lettering above the ground-floor windows. He tried not to visibly flinch.

'The current sale is an interesting mix of historical objects from a collector. I only wish I could have invited Joseph and the others from the market,' she said softly. 'They welcomed me into their businesses.'

'And you think this is the same?' He'd spoken too harshly, but the words were out, now.

'I wanted to think so,' she said, her voice barely more than a murmur. 'You brought me into your life and I... stupidly hoped you might want to see mine.' She started across the street, but he caught her wrist to stop her.

'Forget what I said.'

'I can't,' she responded with a sombre look. 'Besides, I'd rather know what you really think. If you think I'm a princess in a tower with no clue about the real world... maybe you're right.'

He curled his fingers through hers, searching for the right words. 'I'll come and see your gallery. This isn't about what I think of *you*. It's about what the rest of the world thinks.'

She swallowed, glancing across the road at the doorman guarding her domain. 'They *shouldn't* think that way. It wasn't my intention to make you feel... unwelcome or in any way less than what you are: an amazing teacher and an incredible human being. Exclusivity is a double-edged sword.'

'I know that wasn't your intention,' he said gently, brushing his fingers against hers. Words were still inadequate. 'You... know why I invited you today, don't you?'

'I was afraid to ask. I loved it and I loved meeting the kids, but you obviously didn't need my help and... it doesn't really make up for what I've asked you to do for me.'

He shook his head, dismissing her concern. 'You...' He sifted through the flashes of thoughts and feelings that filled him. 'You are open, listening. And my students... not many people listen to them. I thought... you might be good for each other.'

'They were definitely good for me,' she said with a faint smile, her gaze averted. She tilted her head and leaned close to mumble, 'I'm not good for you.'

His hand tightened around hers. 'Sometimes I think you are.'

She shook her head and raised her gaze haltingly to his. 'I've brought you nothing but problems since the moment we met.'

His thoughts scattered as he studied the forlorn line of her brow and remembered the moment they'd met and everything that had happened since. He wasn't thinking about the problems. He raised his other hand to touch her face, but snatched it into a fist at the last moment.

What the hell were they doing?

He turned his gaze ominously across the road at her esteemed family legacy. 'We should go in before they close.'

* * *

The doorman peered sceptically at Sacha's jacket. Ren marched past him with a frown, clinging to Sacha's hand, but she feared she'd only proven the opposite of her point: the screwed-up world did not view them as equals and bringing him into her life would only hurt him.

But it wasn't Sacha that was wrong. He'd set aside his wariness and, when they handed over their coats and stepped into the illuminated gallery, he stopped and stared and she hoped she might make some kind of point after all. The gallery was an opulent function room with gilded baroque furniture teamed with lighting in subtle colours. Tonight, fairy lights twinkled in the ornate cornicing, ribbons and silver stars and brushed gold baubles creating a festive ambience for a Christmas auction.

Sacha let go of her hand and moved from piece to piece, his focus intense. He took in the baroque chest of drawers with marble inlay and the glinting neoclassical chandelier in the grand Russian style. He reached out to run his fingertips over the polished wood of an Art Deco dining chair. He studied the display case of mediaeval jewellery and ornaments, much of it shaped like skulls, and some pieces carved from ivory.

'This is mostly the collection of Pierre Leclercq, you know the—'

'I think everyone knows who Pierre Leclercq was,' Sacha cut her off, his expression grim with fascination. 'And he... just had this stuff in his house?'

'Something like that.'

'Do you...?' He shook his head and swallowed. 'Don't answer.' He moved to the next display before she would work out how to respond. The truth would be: yes, her sideboard was probably worth as much as everything he owned. But she wished it didn't matter.

They came to the mediaeval sword, next, and he stepped back in awe, tilting his head to inspect the lines of fine metalwork. Ren came up next to him.

'Al-Iskandandariyya,' he read, pointing to an inscription on the blade in Arabic script. 'This is one of the swords from the arsenal d'Alexandrie? Incredible.'

'What do you know about it?' she asked, wanting to keep him talking so he wouldn't feel uncomfortable. She thought of the crossed swords she'd glimpsed tattooed on his biceps.

'These old swords... They're fascinating. I held a replica once at the Marché aux Puces. It's very heavy, not like sword sport, tu sais? You don't wave it. You kill someone with one touch, or they kill you. And if you can't get a good touch, you cut off his hand.'

'Urgh.'

'It is brutal. Is it authentic?'

'Yes, of course,' came a voice behind them.

Ren whirled. 'Malou! You're still here?'

'The doorman thought you were coming to see me and I was confused when you didn't appear. I was just leaving for the day.'

'You remember Sacha.'

'Of course.' She greeted him with the lightest kisses on his cheek. 'Bonsoir. Your interest in antiques extends to mediaeval weapons?'

'I wanted to show him – bring him...' Ren said, her words a defensive tangle. 'Sacha is a history teacher and his knowledge is... immense.'

'I'm glad you're interested in his immense... knowledge,' Malou said with a straight face. 'I heard what you said about this piece. Not quite Ren's usual cup of tea.'

'It's certainly not Disney,' he murmured, drawing a curious look from Malou. 'Even the handle can kill someone. This was a valuable object 600 years ago, which is probably why this Italian sword was taken to Egypt – as tribute after a battle. But the winners become the losers again and the Mamluk dynasty was defeated by the Ottomans. Centuries later, that empire falls, too, and the sword comes back to Europe.'

His words rendered the ghastly blade a little less sinister. 'At least it's not killing anyone any more,' Ren said softly.

'Ren is too sheltered,' Malou commented.

Sacha met Malou's gaze with his usual grim look and Ren had the odd inkling that they understood each other. 'Come and see the stained glass,' she said.

His brow shot up when he caught sight of the framed fragment. It was a stunning piece, bringing distant history to life in colour with the painted faces of the three kings and the deep, shocking blue. Sacha read the label with a frown.

'You really don't know where this came from?' he asked Malou.

She shook her head. 'The adoration of the magi is a very common theme for stained glass. The owner inherited it with no further information and it was difficult to get an appointment with someone from the museums we often work with at this time of year.'

'And the French Ministry of Culture?'

'Remains silent,' Malou finished his sentence for him. 'We send them a catalogue for each sale so if they thought it was of national significance, I assume they would have contacted us by now. Why? Do you know something about this?'

'No,' he said immediately. 'It just reminds me... this part here looks like a medallion form, a feature of early Gothic windows. I did the travail d'intérêt général at the museum in Saint-Denis and we worked with the conservation of the cathedral windows.'

Malou blinked at what Ren assumed was Sacha's bald admission of his criminal history, but her friend thankfully made no comment. Ren's chest was tight with something like pride. Far from her family's obsession with appearances, Sacha was more interested in the truth, even when that was difficult to face. He'd never looked more attractive to her than he did then, wearing his background as proudly as he wore his tattoos.

'You think it could be from Saint-Denis?' Malou asked.

'Very few of the panels survived the revolution and some have been found in unexpected places, but I'm not an expert. And surely... it would be unlikely.'

'What's so special about the cathedral in Saint-Denis?' Ren asked.

'It's the earliest example of French Gothic architecture. The windows are some of the oldest in the world. This was twelfth century, there was no electricity. To the people, these colours, the enormous windows, the light looked like the power of God. And, of course, these windows opened the way for the grandest achievements of mediaeval stained glass, including the rose windows of Notre-Dame-de-Paris.'

'It really looks like some of the fragments we saw today,' Ren commented. She turned to Malou. 'We went to the Museum of Cocks – I mean the Musée de Cluny.'

Malou snorted. 'He really is showing you a whole new world.' She pulled Ren to one side as Sacha studied the pieces. 'The gallery is closing in a minute. Want to come home with me or he is whisking you away on his magic carpet?'

'Thanks for not being weird about this,' Ren said softly.

'I don't think you have a happy ending in your near future, but it's obvious he's twice the man Charlie is, so I don't want to stop you... broadening your horizons.'

'He's good for me,' she agreed. 'I only wish I could say it was true the other way around.'

'Just make sure he doesn't break a leg skiing.'

'Don't even suggest it!' Ren groaned.

Her stomach dropped when they left the gallery half an hour later to be greeted by a cluster of cameras shoved in her face. She cursed inwardly, berating herself for coming here, where she was too recognisable.

'Who's your new lover? Does this mean you won't take Charles Routledge back? Give us your name, monsieur! How did you meet?'

Malou stepped in front of them with colourful curses and hand gestures to match, but Ren felt bad for her, getting angry on Ren's behalf. She groped for Sacha's hand.

'We're going to make a run for it,' she whispered into her friend's ear.

'Allez-y!' her friend whispered back urgently. Ren met Sacha's gaze and he nodded. A moment later, they tore off in the direction of the métro. She clung to his hand as he weaved between the pedestrians and by the time they hurtled down the stairs and flung themselves through the barriers, there was no sign of the photographers.

Ren grinned, struggling to get her breath back. He'd invited her into his life today and survived the visit in hers. She'd never felt so free, loping through Paris in the evening with her hand tucked into his.

'This way,' she said, tugging him in the direction of line nine. 'There's one more place I want to go tonight.'

28

'Shut your eyes,' Ren said at the bottom of the concrete stairs.

'I know where we are,' Sacha said drily, but he complied, closing his fingers around her hand when she took his again.

'Indulge me,' she said and guided him up the stairs to the exit. The sound of heavy traffic and scuffling pedestrians reached his ears. He could picture the cobbled intersection, the grand museum buildings to his left.

He tripped on the kerb and caught a glimpse of the hazy light from the streetlamps before he shut his eyes again. Perhaps this wasn't such a sensible idea.

'Oops, sorry.' She slipped an arm around his waist to lead him more securely.

He imagined their progress, past the illuminated columns and gold statues of the Palais de Chaillot. He gestured with his free arm, eyes still closed.

'These buildings were ultramoderne when they were built, but now they remind people of Hitler and Truman and the post-war period of the United Nations.'

'You can recount history with your eyes closed?'

'At one of the most iconic places in Paris? Oui, tout à fait.' They turned right, weaving through a crowd of cooing tourists. 'You see the inscription up there?'

'Are you sure you don't have your eyes open?'

'"Tout homme crée sans le savoir; Comme il respire; Mais l'artiste se sent créer; Son acte engage tout son être; Sa peine bien aimée la fortifie,"' he quoted.

'Why do you know that? And what does it mean?'

'All people create without knowing, like breathing. But the artist feels the creating, with his whole being. His dear pain – or sadness – makes him strong. Or something like that. My father loved the quote, and he admired the man who wrote it, Paul Valéry – a poet and philosopher. He wrote notebooks, too.'

He thought of the book in the bottom of his rucksack, full of scribbles, not all of them intelligible. Paul Valéry would have been horrified.

'I still think sadness is overrated,' she murmured after a long silence. His hand tightened in her coat, as he was reminded of what she'd been through as a child. Her preference for happy endings had seemed sweet before, but now he wondered if it wasn't brave. He peeked at her, but she pressed a hand over his eyes. 'Not yet. Although I'm thinking you've seen this view more often than you led me to believe.'

'Yes, I have stood here and looked at this view. But I've never been up... there.' It was what she had planned, he was sure. He told himself the gesture wasn't as symbolic as it felt. He didn't want to talk himself out of it. No matter what it would mean to him in the future, he would go up with her tonight. 'Can I open my eyes yet?'

'Nope,' she said, her fingers shifting against his forehead. She shuffled forward and he did the same blindly. He bumped into a stone barrier and clutched it to steady himself. 'This is your city,' she said. 'You've shown it to me. Now I want to show this to you. Tell me what you see.'

She removed her hand and he blinked his eyes open. The elegantly curved tower of glowing, illuminated latticework blazed before him. Tonight, with Ren beside him, it would become part of 'his' Paris. 'It looks like the tower was crocheted by generations of French grandmothers and it's still hanging off the needle by a thread,' he muttered. 'It was built after a century of troubles and deprivation. It's a folly and a symbol of ambition, but also of hope for the future, desire to achieve the best. It's naïve and a little bit rebellious...'

He cut himself off and turned to take in the other view: Ren staring at him with her big eyes that seemed to draw things out of him. 'Like you,' he said before he could stop himself.

Her face broke into a grin. 'Naïve and a little bit rebellious and just like the Eiffel Tower? I love it. Now, if you're done, we're going to eat crêpe and then I want to go up – all the way up!'

He grasped her hand to stop her. 'Why now?' *Why me?*

She glanced from their joined hands up to his face. 'I've spent most of my life waiting for other people to do things to me and for me. I want to do this for myself.'

'That's a good reason.'

'Don't worry. I don't expect you to propose up there. If you did, I'd probably fall off and take you down with me, given our track record.' He shook his head drily at her bad joke, but he was glad she'd lightened the mood. He glanced at the tower with a frisson of anticipation. He was going up. With Ren.

She dragged Sacha down the wide steps to the kiosk at the bottom of the Jardins du Trocadéro. She bought three crêpes because she couldn't decide which filling she wanted and they juggled the little cardboard plates to the park benches facing the Seine and the Eiffel Tower. A blaze of lights and a rumble of music reached them from the Christmas market at the base of the tower and a nearby busker on an accordion accompanied their frigid picnic.

'I'm going to spill Nutella all down myself, aren't I?' she mumbled.

Sacha held out a serviette. 'If you don't, it will only be half of the experience.' As it was, she was messier with powdered sugar and it looked as though it had been snowing in her lap.

She offered him bites and it didn't seem strange at all to let her do it. He was unexpectedly contented, looking at the Eiffel Tower at night. She insisted on taking a photo with the tower in the background, both of them biting into the same crêpe. It was goofy and embarrassing and he was so damn happy.

'Is it just me, or is the tower glittering?'

'It's glittering,' he confirmed. 'It doesn't do that all the time. Perhaps just for you?'

'Just for us,' she corrected. 'Isn't it illegal to take a photo of the Eiffel Tower at night? The lights have copyright?'

'I think so.' A little twinge brought him down a notch. 'But you're not going to publish that photo, right? So, it doesn't matter.'

'I'm sure Ziggy would want me to post it,' she said drily, but the pinch at the edge of her mouth suggested the thought upset her more than she let on.

'You know what I mean. They'd rather you posted a photo alone. I'm the last man in Paris.'

'I didn't really mean it like that, you know,' she said. He searched for her teasing tone, but she was gazing wistfully at the view. 'I was thinking about my grandmother and what she would think, not what I thought. You were far from the last man in my mind – even back then.' Her tone was so soft, the words crept under his skin. But she gave a little laugh so neither of them had to acknowledge the significance of her confession. 'Come on, Sacha,' she said, standing and brushing her hands off on her jeans. 'We've got a tower to climb!'

* * *

'Incredible!'

Ren was pretty sure that was meant to be her line, but she was distracted from the wonder of engineering by Sacha's unexpected enthusiasm. Enormous cogs turned and their little glass cocoon hoisted them up inside one of the elegant brown legs of the tower, but Ren's eyes kept drifting back to him.

'Do you think the tower might be "your Paris" after all?' she teased.

He gave a sheepish shrug. 'It's...' He gestured at the bolts and struts, the lattice of girders fanning out into a structure that was more than its parts. 'I admit I should have come here before. I've heard the story, the "inutile et monstrueuse Tour Eiffel" that would ruin the beauty of the monuments of Paris with its bolts and metal and its impossible height. Others said it was too artistic and ignored the requirements of engineering. But... when you look,' he said, peering at the swooping and overlapping metal above them, 'you can see they were both wrong and they were both right.'

The vast iron structure above her followed a pattern that was mathematical, but undeniably beautiful. Would she have noticed any of it if Sacha hadn't been there with his curious gaze and wide-ranging mind?

On the first-floor terrace, Paris stretched endlessly before them, a labyrinth of lights, the slate roofs with rows of chimneys almost close enough to touch. By the second floor, the wind picked up and Ren began to feel a little wobbly. The four pylons spread out below, like the tracks of a rollercoaster, giving her vertigo when she looked down. The ghostly night watchman, the Sacré-Cœur, stood guard on the distant hill of Montmartre.

The final lift scuttled up inside the ironwork, heading straight up to the stars. They didn't speak as they ascended, girders and trusses flying by as though the tower was moving and not the lift. The patterns of glowing metal changed like a kaleidoscope against the dark sky and Paris rapidly became a toy city below them.

At the top, the low shriek of the biting wind and a definite sense that she was swaying made Ren shiver with unease. The city below glowed with light, but above was nothing but darkness. Sacha could barely contain himself as he gaped at the long drop and the lights of the city.

'It's amazing! Look at the Christmas market on the Champ de Mars. It's tiny. And the wind! It feels like flying!' He was grinning with delight, his habitual frown nothing more than a faint groove. That she'd brought this smile to his face was almost as exhilarating as looking down.

She took a tentative step towards him. 'Come here, Ren. You look freezing!' He caught her hands and then wrapped his arms around her, tugging her back to his front and turning her towards the view.

Tucked against him, his cheek at her temple, listening to him describe the monuments they could discern among the pattern of boulevards, the darkness receded a little and the light came into focus.

'That tall building is the Tour Montparnasse, the only skyscraper in Paris outside of La Défense. We got used to it after fifty years and I don't think it's so bad. You can see the form of the Champ de Mars, the field. It was a place of celebration during the revolution, although some of the celebrations involved Madame Guillotine.'

'I'm glad I didn't have to study that at school.'

A beam of fierce blue light appeared suddenly above them, shooting out and breaking up the darkness. Ren stared in wonder, her heart and her senses full for a moment of utter contentment. She turned her head, slightly, to feel the rasp of his beard and the warmth of his skin against hers.

'I'm glad I've never come up here, before,' she whispered.

He tensed for a moment, but then tightened his arms around her. 'Me, too.'

'Do you... think you'll ever come up again?' Her breath wouldn't come as she awaited the answer to that question.

'I might bring Raph. You've convinced me. The tower is our Paris, after all.'

'I'm glad,' she said, although his answer didn't satisfy her hope that he would keep this memory as sacred as she would.

'Would you come up again?'

'No,' she answered immediately, and he tilted his head to peer at her in question. 'I don't know. Maybe in ten years' time.' Perhaps that would be enough to forget all the reasons they shouldn't be together. She glanced at her watch. 'The 17th of December at 9.15, in ten years' time. Would you come back to meet me?' She tried to inject some humour into her voice.

'It won't take you ten years to get over Charlie, will it?'

Charlie? God, no. It was this moment, the future that would never happen, she would need to get over. Damn, she hated when her past self was right: climbing the Eiffel Tower was a milestone, like falling in love for the first time. But she'd also been wrong to think she could predict and control how and when she'd first come here. Even though her Disney ending was far off, she couldn't muster any regret for sharing the moment with Sacha.

The future was a mess, but screw it. The present was perfect.

29

Sacha rushed for the métro when the school day finally ended on Friday. The kids were hanging around, celebrating their two weeks of freedom.

'Bonne fêtes, Prof!' Hamoud called and Sacha managed a wave in response. Felix called out something about being late for a hot date and he couldn't even make a rejoinder because the boy was right – except it wasn't a date, exactly. It felt more like going into battle.

He wasn't even sure what he would be fighting for. Respect for Ren, he hoped. A chance at a better future for her that could involve someone who truly loved her, rather than another crétin like Charlie.

Sacha's stomach twisted, thinking of the next person she'd be interested in. It brought back the sharp memory from Wednesday night, of holding her at the top of the tower as everything in the universe fell into place around them.

But, nevertheless, he'd still made the phone call on Thursday morning that could land Asquith-Lewis in trouble. Would she resent him if she found out? Her feelings of duty to the family firm were strong – and understandable. Should he just tell her and ruin the weekend? He grimaced, imagining her pretending to like him when she was actually angry.

The topic of that phone call wasn't the only suspicion he harboured. *Six days...* It caught him in the gut every time, but he couldn't know if he was right and he had no desire to make things worse for her.

Sacha rushed home to grab his beat-up rucksack, grimacing when he remembered the monogrammed suitcase in the back of Bilel's car. Since when did he worry about things like that? He was only pretending to care about Irena Asquith-Lewis, the sophisticated heiress whose absence from Instagram had caused a storm. And if he cared deeply about Wren, the woman with the heartbreaking smile, then... she didn't exist.

The journey to the Gare de Lyon was quick and he rushed to the platform only a few minutes later than he'd agreed with Ren. He stopped short. Ren was there, clutching the handle of a suitcase tightly. But there stood Charlie, as well, his arm looped casually around his new girlfriend.

'Here he is! I was starting to think you wouldn't make it!' Charlie said, his smile far too wide as he held out his hand to shake Sacha's. 'Would you believe it, we're on the same train!'

'Five hours together,' Ren said with a weak smile.

'We can share a driver at the other end,' the girlfriend pointed out, then slammed her mouth shut as though she'd forgotten that saving money was not a consideration in present company.

Sacha smothered his own discomfort and gave Ren a quick wink, wrapping an arm around her. He'd never been so glad of the excuse. He didn't quite trust himself to give her the kiss he wanted to, but he risked a quick brush of his mouth over hers, and he even managed to pull away when her lips parted and her breath escaped on a sigh.

The small smile she gave him was enough to see him through the miserable journey. Charlie shot questions at them, as though he were trying to catch them in the lie. Then, an hour from Bourg-Saint-Maurice, where the interminable train trip from hell would finally end, he casually dropped the next bombshell.

'I hope you don't mind,' Charlie began innocuously, making Sacha marvel at how well he manipulated the soft-hearted Ren, 'but I asked if Charlotte and I could have the usual room. We stayed there last week. I know you don't like to go out on the balcony in the evening, but Charlotte loves the mountain air at night and... well, I hoped you'd understand.'

'I don't care about the room,' Ren muttered. 'I suppose the chalet is so full that Grandmama will put us in the attic.'

'Uh, I think that's where she said you'd have to sleep. Something about not putting the investors out and... well...' Charlie glanced in Sacha's direction.

'I'm sure we'll be... very comfortable,' Ren said tightly. Then it struck him. They were staying in a small room. Together. It was probably too much to ask for there to be a sofa bed in the corner. He tried to school his features, but Charlie's smirk made it difficult.

After a long, strained train ride and a silent trip in a private car along the icy alpine roads, they finally arrived. The bluish light of the moon on the snow made him feel as though he'd stepped through a mirror into another world – where he was not welcome.

The chalet was as intimidatingly beautiful as he'd feared, all natural stone and solid wood. Decorative carvings adorned the doorway and the balconies, elegant and artistic and clearly very expensive. The ski slopes of the exclusive resort were a short walk away.

When Sacha stepped inside, it took all of his effort to keep his mouth from swinging open. Thick-pile rugs enriched the wooden floor. Painted landscapes hung on the walls between the large windows. Inviting flames flickered in a modern fireplace in the entryway. Every item of designer furniture was harmoniously placed and spotlessly clean. It floored him to think that this was what Ren was used to.

And it angered him that she was also used to that disapproving look from Livia, but it was late and they could thankfully retire without facing an interrogation. After climbing four flights of steps to their room, tucked under the wooden eaves of the enormous chalet, he finally closed the door on the prickly welcome and then let his head fall back against the wood.

The room was huge – of course it was – with an enormous bed covered in plush blankets, solid wooden farmhouse furniture and an iron chandelier. But no sofa bed.

Ren approached him, lifting a hand to brush her fingertips over his forehead. 'You're the only person I know who can smile and frown at the same time.'

'You're the only person I know who can make that sound like a good thing.'

'I'm glad you're here,' she said. He'd put himself through this a thousand times to hear her say those words.

But he tempered her enthusiasm. 'You may not feel that way in the morning. I told you I can't ski. I've never even imagined a place like this, let alone seen it. Charlie is trying to demask us and...' He gestured helplessly and stared at the bed.

'I do remember another night where we shared a bed. The sky didn't fall on our heads that time, so I think we'll be okay for two more nights. We're kind of friends, right?'

'We are friends,' he said peevishly.

'You sound thrilled about that.'

He took a deep breath, but it wasn't enough to stop the snap of emotion. His hands landed heavily on her shoulders. 'I was annoyed you said we were "kind of" friends. And I'm not worried about what *you* do. I'm worried about what *I*...' His thumb lifted, as though of its own accord, to brush her jaw. He grimaced and turned away, but it didn't help. He could hear her swallow. The silence was heavy, as though the entire world was insulated with foam and it was almost enough to make him panic, it was so foreign. 'I don't... know how to act. I think differently. I don't want to make things worse for you.' That was probably better than admitting how much he wanted to kiss her.

'I like the way you think,' she said softly. 'Your stories, your words and your poetry.'

He blinked at her, losing his train of thought. If she kept forgetting she had to choose between her beloved grandmother and him, he would soon be in trouble. 'Do we at least have our own bathroom here?' he asked, looking around with sudden interest.

'Monsieur is not satisfied with the room?' Her smile slugged him in the chest.

'Next I'll be demanding Valensace shoes.'

'Speaking of which, you need ski gear. We can grab some tomorrow morning.'

'I have the clothing.' He poked around the room as an excuse to put some distance between them.

'Why do you have the clothing?'

'Because I thought ahead and knew I would need it. The rest of the stuff... I will rent, because I don't know anything about the equipment. But I have the... salopette and the coat.'

'You bought them? How much did it cost? I'll—'

'I can afford a set of ski clothes.'

'I'm not saying you can't, but... God, I've cost you so much already.' She sank onto the bed with a sigh.

Sacha studied her grimly. He couldn't accept her money, but he hated that she felt indebted to him – almost more than the idea of taking her money. And how would she feel if he told her what he'd done about the stained-glass panel? Would she call it a betrayal? Or would she understand his commitment to the truth? The situation was impossible.

Sacha stalked to the bed and leaned down, his body rigid with purpose and his expression no doubt harsh. He propped his hands on either side of her and brought his face close. She stared at him, her eyes wide, and drew back a fraction. 'You didn't make me do anything I didn't want to do: fix my own bike, buy a *maudite salopette* or hold you while you slept.' *Kiss you under the mistletoe.* 'You are not a cost. You are a person and I am... concerned for you.'

Her gaze dropped and he suspected he'd grasped for the wrong word at that last part. He'd meant he felt something for her – cared, that would have been better. But it was safer to leave it.

'Yeah, well, I'm such a disaster area, I can understand why you're concerned.' She gave him a breezy smile. 'I'm a good skier, though.'

He reluctantly let the moment slip through his fingers. 'Livia never let you out at night, but she sent you up a mountain to risk your life on a thankless, snow-covered escarpement?' he asked with a huff.

'Pfft,' she said with a dismissive wave. 'Going out at night is so gauche. Skiing, though, is a sophisticated activity, as you will find out.'

Her smile faded as he made the mistake of meeting her gaze again. Did she still hope this would end well? Perhaps she was just better at ignoring the spark between them.

It was going to be a long night.

* * *

It might have been the smallest room in the house, but the family chalet was nothing if not luxurious to the last inch. The two nights would be completely fine. No lines had to be crossed that couldn't be un-crossed again.

Ren settled down in the big bed, covered in duvets and blankets and pillows and swimming in Egyptian cotton. She'd never even know Sacha was next to her. She would have a night of blissful sleep dreaming of soft, warm, snow-like fluff cuddling her safe – *not* any other sort of cuddling, nor strong tattooed arms, and definitely no dreams of tangled limbs that might or might not be happening in real life.

But that was the problem with trying not to think about something: it inevitably led to thinking about it. She'd proven this a moment earlier when she'd most definitely *not* thought about Sacha in the shower. She should have picked someone ugly to be her fake boyfriend. No, actually, she shouldn't have gone down this idiotic fake boyfriend route at all. But she couldn't accept that, either, if it meant she'd never got to know Sacha. Why were these thoughts consuming her, rather than worries about tomorrow, about managing investors and tiptoeing around Charlie?

When had making her family accept Sacha become more important than all of that and what was the point when he would never accept them, either? She was stupidly striving for a happily-ever-after again, imagining a world where she and Sacha could be together without sacrificing anything else – a world where he wanted her as much as she wanted him, despite the fact that every time they were together, bad things happened to him. She hadn't been enough for that idiot Charlie, so what hope did she have with someone as amazing as Sacha?

He emerged from the bathroom in a pair of loose boxer shorts and a T-shirt, his hair wet and curling, and the sight made her weak with wanting. She slammed her eyes shut as he approached the bed.

'Do you want to leave the light on?'

'The bathroom light will do,' she said stiffly, willing herself not to be touched by his concern.

His footsteps retreated and returned, and then the bedside lamp was extinguished with a click. She was hyperaware of the swish of the covers as he slipped in beside her.

'I can sleep on the floor,' he said softly.

'No,' she insisted. 'I might be your bad luck charm, but I'm not going to give you a crick in the neck when I could have done something to stop it. *I* can sleep on the floor.' She reached for the covers.

'Don't,' was all he said at first. 'Ren, it's not a punishment to sleep next to you. Last time it was...'

'Nice,' she finished for him when he hesitated for too long.

'Oui,' he said with a huff. 'Non, en fait, it was more than nice.' She froze, waiting for him to say more, but he rolled over instead. 'Allez dors,' he said, his voice trailing off. 'Sleep.'

She tried, but it was difficult with her mind drowned in conflicting thoughts. As the night lengthened, she nestled closer, facing away for the sake of tenuous deniability.

His arm flopped sleepily over her and curled tight. She settled against him and closed her eyes, feeling only the warmth of his body and the gusts of his breath on her ear.

Then suddenly the light was streaming in through the window under the eaves and Sacha stretched and sighed behind her. His hand landed possessively on her hip before he wrenched it away. A moment later, he rolled out of bed.

One night down. They had so few, Ren couldn't help but think it had been a waste of a night together.

30

Sacha clomped out of the rental shop with the gait of a posturing hip-hop artist on stage, but he still looked gorgeous enough to make Ren ache.

'I'm going to fall over before I get anywhere near the skis,' he muttered.

'You'll get used to it,' she reassured him, holding him steady as he stamped the boots into the bindings of the skis.

'Hope you both slept well!' Charlie said by way of greeting, sliding effortlessly to a stop at the bottom of the slope. Charlotte whooshed down beside him, as though they'd choreographed the move as well as their matching names. Charlie's goggles were pushed up on his forehead, sending his blond hair sticking up in a way Ren would have convinced herself was charming a year ago. But that morning, all she saw was the shit-eating grin and the disdainful look he spared for Sacha with his rented equipment and his ski clothing from a cheaper sports chain.

'We slept well,' Sacha replied evenly before Ren could find her voice. But before he could say anything else, a ski slipped, he slid backwards, poles flailing, and landed heavily on his side.

Charlie stifled a laugh. Ren had no hope of hiding her scowl, but it only made Charlie's smile wider. She popped off her skis and went to help Sacha up. He met her gaze with a grave one of his own as she clutched his arm and hauled him up. She smiled in return – not one of her desperate bright ones, but a small one, because she was touched that he was doing this for her, and for once the lure of the mountain wasn't as strong as the desire to keep looking at his face.

'Perhaps he should stay in the lodge and drink hot chocolate,' said Charlie. 'He's not going to make it to the black slopes with us in one weekend. In fact, if you don't want to break a bone, you should stay on the bunny slope.'

'I am very happy to stay on this bunny slope and learn at my own speed.'

'And I'm going to teach him,' Ren added, ignoring Sacha's attempt to deter her with a sharp shake of his head.

Charlie's smile faltered. Someone behind Ren caught his attention and he lifted his hand in a wave. 'Morning, Ziggy. I'm surprised to hear Ren will be spending the day teaching her *boyfriend* to ski. Don't you usually take her with you and chat business over lunch at one of the restaurants on the slopes? Since it appears Livia is only human after all and can't ski at her age.'

'Who said anything about my age?' Charlie nearly swallowed his tongue when Grandmama emerged from the lodge looking elegant even in silver-and-black ski clothing, with her slim frame and swept-back grey hair. 'I will meet you all for lunch. Of course my knees won't take me down the slopes any more, but there are snowmobiles. For everyone else, there is the red or the black slope.'

Everyone looked at Sacha, wobbling on his stationary skis. 'We'll meet you for lunch,' Ren blurted out. 'We can take the lift back down afterward if Sacha won't make it. Just tell me where and what time.'

'We were expecting you to join us on the slopes, Ren,' Ziggy spoke up. 'A representative of the family, since Livia can't. I'll book an instructor for him.'

'No.' For a word that was usually so difficult to say, it flowed surprisingly easily. 'I said I'd be there for lunch. No one will be discussing business while racing down the piste.' To say nothing of the fact that she was no substitute for Livia in business dealings.

Ren escaped with only a narrow-eyed stare from Ziggy that gave her the strange sensation of the walls closing in on her gradually.

'You don't need to stay with me,' Sacha said when Ziggy and the others moved off towards the lift.

'I want to.' Wow, it was all spilling out.

His brow shot up. She wanted to press a smacking kiss on his lips to make her point, but she didn't want him to interpret that as part of the act. Instead of kissing his mouth, she pressed her lips to his cheek, feeling his heavy exhale on her own skin.

'Let's go!'

Sacha had to carry his skis to the bottom of the children's area and Ren wasn't surprised to see that Charlie was acting like a small child himself and followed them out of spite. But Sacha wasn't fazed. He leaned heavily on Ren as she helped him onto the carpet lift, where he wobbled and nearly fell off. Charlie laughed behind them, but so did Sacha.

At the top of the slope, he nearly slipped over again and clung to her gloved hands, trembling, as she showed him how to set up his skis out of the fall line and dig in the edges until he could stand still.

She couldn't believe the nerve of Charlie, flying down the side of the practice slope just to intimidate a man who obviously wouldn't play that juvenile game. But it was easy to ignore her ex-boyfriend when all she wanted to do was watch the creases of concentration on Sacha's face and stay close to catch him while he learned to brake in the snow plough ski formation.

He managed a few descents of the gentle slope, but when she encouraged him to up the pace a little, he ended up at the bottom, groaning in a tangle of skis. She raced down to him, but he was laughing, and she forgot all about Charlie and his stupid pissing contest. Making Sacha laugh was her new goal in life.

Charlie eventually lost interest and the morning sped by as she skied backwards in front of Sacha, coaching him and occasionally grabbing him when he wobbled. She liked it when their faces were close, sliding slowly down the hill together.

He made it down one blue slope before lunch, only falling when he caught an edge trying to get off the lift, but Ren wasn't surprised when her phone beeped with directions for lunch and they'd chosen a restaurant that could only be reached via a red slope.

'I think that means I'm not invited,' Sacha said drily when she told him. He raised his face to the sun and gazed up at the jagged peaks. 'It must be amazing up there.'

'It is.'

'I hope you do some real skiing, too. I can practise on this slope myself, now. And if I'm not wanted at lunch, then...'

She scrunched up her face. 'I'm not really wanted either, you know. Ziggy and Grandmama just hide behind my smile when they're putting on the hard sell.'

'That sounds like an important job to do.'

She gave him a playful shove, but he slid backwards and she had to grab him again. 'I don't want to know how many bruises you've got today because of me.' *Maybe I can kiss them better, later.*

'I'll come to lunch if you want me to,' he blurted out suddenly. 'I'll get down somehow.'

'I want you there.' *Always*. Perhaps she shouldn't, but the wanting was getting too hard to ignore.

* * *

He had an audience for the awkward descent down the steep red slope. Ziggy, Charlie and his parents and the rest of the company all loomed at the bottom, ready to exult in his spectacular failure. The slope itself looked like a sheer drop from his position at the top. Sacha's knees knocked as he stared into the valley far, far below. It was stunningly beautiful – glittering ice and snow and a sky so blue it didn't look real.

He could barely believe he was here, in the crystalline cold of a landscape from a fantasy world. He couldn't help thinking it was a long, long way from the neuf trois, from anything he'd ever seen. His deep, agitated breaths puffed out in clouds and his body was so tense he had no hope of maintaining the technique that Ren had taught him.

But she was beside him. Her hair was back in a short plait down her back and her eyes lit up whenever he unlocked a new skill on the slopes. It was enough to motivate him to aim for the Winter Olympics. It was enough to get him down this hill.

'Do you trust me?' she asked over the whipping wind.

'Yes,' he replied with a smile.

'Then follow after me. I'll get you down.' She studied the terrain and then set off slowly, leading him along the flattest parts and coaching him on where to turn. Keeping his eyes on her allowed him to forget the terrifying drop, the images of falls and rescues and broken bones, as he whipped through the turns after her, crunching snow. And then they were nearly down, and he'd almost... had fun.

Only near the bottom did things go wrong. His skis slid out of control and he wobbled backwards instinctively, picking up speed. He heard her voice dimly, telling him to lean forward and curve. Leaning forward was not what his brain wanted him to do, but he forced it anyway and a second before he reached the edge of the piste, he managed to throw his weight into a turn.

He was about to shout gleefully to Ren, but one of his skis clipped the other and he ploughed right into her, rolling the last few feet to the bottom of the slope. He groaned, trying to get his breath back and wondering why nothing seemed to hurt.

'Ow,' Ren said from underneath him.

He lifted his head and rolled quickly to the side, pulling off his gloves and lifting her visor. 'Ren,' he whispered urgently, his hand on her face. He pressed a quick kiss to her lips. 'Did I hurt you?'

She kept her hand fisted in his jacket so he couldn't move too far away. 'I'm fine. The snow is soft here and... I didn't mind you landing on me.' He met her gaze and lost all perspective on what was for show and what was real.

A pointed cough made him look up. Sacha and Ren stumbled to their feet, only one ski between both of them still attached. She gripped his hand tightly and they approached the party together, the two of them against the world.

Livia had arrived on a snowmobile, her expression taut. Sacha was sick of seeing her limit Ren's potential – and he was very sick of her trivialising his relationship with Ren. Despite the ruse, she meant more to him than he'd ever imagined, and he hated to see their feelings dismissed.

He focused on Ren over lunch, wary of the rebelliousness of his feelings. She was keen to ignore Ziggy's disapproving glares and ate from the platters and fondue with gusto. She even slipped a chunk of toast dipped in cheese into his mouth with a cheeky smile and he was struck by how much had changed since afternoon tea at the Ritz.

Although her grandmother and Ziggy did bring the conversation around to business matters a few times, Ren didn't join in. The conversation with Charlie's parents, which he'd expected to be awkward, turned out to be pleasant; they were obviously relieved to see her moving on from their son and took a genuine interest in Sacha.

Livia and Ziggy were unrelenting in their disapproval, but it only gave him a sense of vindication. He could stand up to them. To see Ren be herself like this was worth it. And if she wanted him...

The mountain air and the giddy happiness of having her beside him buoyed his mood after lunch and he subdued his fear at the top of the slope with a few deep breaths. And then he flew down the mountain with her, breath tight, icy air whooshing in their faces and the surrounding peaks rising to support them.

At the bottom, she popped off her skis and threw her arms around him. 'You did it! You were incredible! I hope it wasn't too awful!'

His arms came around her and he held her silently. 'It wasn't awful,' he said after a few moments of deep, slow breaths. 'I can't believe I did it.'

Ren tugged off her helmet and dropped it carelessly into the snow. Her fingers fumbled under his chin as she did the same for him. Her breath caught and she stilled with her fingertips on his cheeks, her eyes roaming his face.

He had to kiss her. With no audience, no reason to pretend, no murky motives or second-guessing, he dipped his head and pressed his mouth to hers with a sharp passion and all of the tenderness welling up inside him. She opened her mouth and the kiss quickly escalated, frustrated desire no longer bearable. He breathed her in. She held him tight and it all came flooding out.

He kissed her from a place inside him that insisted his feelings were allowed, and held her tight to make her feel everything that had been churning inside him. She didn't pull away. Her fingers tangled in his hair and she met kiss after aching kiss with equal intensity.

He was drifting into trouble. She stirred more trouble when they paused for breath and she started speaking.

'I've wanted to kiss you like that since the night we met,' she said between gasping breaths. 'If I'd known it would be that good...' She stroked a clumsy hand around the back of his head. 'Are you going to say anything?'

Je t'aime... Those were the first words that rose in his mind – the only words he could find for a few breaths. He pulled himself together at the last moment. 'Did I hit my head, or did you really say you wanted to kiss me the night we met?'

'I don't normally kiss strangers, but...'

'I know,' he murmured, settling his forehead against hers. 'It was the same for me.'

'Maybe I'm deprived of oxygen,' she said between breaths, 'because I thought you just said it was the same for you.'

He clutched her more tightly and kissed her again, this time a little softer and a lot sweeter. His oxygen supply definitely faltered.

'I've enjoyed every moment with you,' he whispered. He hated the finality that had sneaked into those words, but they would have to do.

'A near-death experience, was it?' Charlie's voice broke into the intensity of the moment like a bucket of cold water. 'Are you going to let Ren up onto the real slopes with us, now?'

Sacha pulled away from her reluctantly. 'Ren is free to choose what she wants to do.'

'And you think she'll choose you?' Charlie was clearly no longer talking about the ski slopes. 'Over her own family? Her inheritance? She didn't even choose *me* over dear Grandmama.'

'What?' Ren exclaimed, stunned.

The crétin ignored her. 'Well, it's the purse strings, too, right? She doesn't stray too far from the hand that feeds her.'

'You know *nothing* about Ren.' The only thing tempering Sacha's words was the knowledge that Charlie was at least partly right: Ren would always do her duty to her grandmother. But not for the reasons Charlie assumed.

'And you do?' Charlie rebutted him with a laugh. 'A teacher from the hood? You think you understand her life?'

'This is unnecessary, Charlie,' Ren said before Sacha had to reply.

'I'm not allowed to be worried about you any more?'

'There's no need to worry about my choices.'

'Ever the peacemaker, Ren,' Charlie muttered. 'Always doing what's expected of you.' He glanced once more at Sacha, a warning that he would never fit into the carefully constructed life she led. Charlie didn't know that wasn't news to either of them.

'I will do the blue piste again,' Sacha said, clomping back to his skis without even a glance for Charlie.

'I'm coming with you.' When Ren's voice sounded behind him, he was touched – but worried about the future and what trouble he might cause for her.

31

Après ski drinks and dinner were a nuisance that Ren wished away with some fervour, even though the brazier flickered invitingly on the terrace as the sun dropped behind the mountain ridges. Predictably, her grandmother ushered her inside when darkness fell, but she stared after Sacha, wanting to cling to the feeling of fearlessness she'd found with him on the slopes – and in that kiss.

Grandmama and Charlie's parents got talking about the merger over the raspberry parfait, but the discussion made Ren feel numb. She'd panicked two weeks ago, worried the merger would fall through now the truth about her broken relationship with Charlie was out, but she struggled to muster any enthusiasm for the apparent reconciliation. God, Ziggy and her grandmother owed Sacha so much more than they'd ever admit for deflecting the media attention off the break-up. She couldn't let him pay too high a price for getting involved with her.

Charlotte dragged Charlie out to a bar. Ren was thankful they didn't even ask if she and Sacha wanted to join them, and she used the excuse of their departure to drift towards the stairs to their room.

Once out of sight of the others, she groped for Sacha's hand and threaded her fingers with his. On paper, she was making the biggest mistake of her life, hurtling into a rebound relationship with no future that could only cause pain with this intensity. But she knew what she wanted. She glanced at him as they reached the door. She just wasn't quite sure how to get it.

'Thank you for teaching me to ski,' he surprised her by saying once they were inside. 'It was... fun.'

'Not too many bruises?' she asked around the lump in her throat.

He shook his head. 'Bruises are a mark of honour, no?'

Oh, God, she loved his words. She drifted closer to him. 'Like tattoos?'

His lips turned up slightly. 'Some tattoos. Others are marks of youth or stupidity.'

'Did they... hurt a lot?'

'Mmhmm.'

'Which one hurt the most?'

His brow knit, and he gestured wordlessly to the sentence on his neck. She drew close, her eyelids heavy. Her thoughts fuzzy from the rush of her blood and the crash of adrenaline, she pressed her lips lightly to his skin, over the ink. His chest heaved with a sudden breath and he clutched her forearms – to fend her off or bring her closer, she couldn't be sure.

'I kissed you today,' she said softly, marvelling at the moment that still felt slightly miraculous.

'Huh,' he said, swallowing. 'I thought *I* kissed *you*.'

'It's a matter of interpretation,' she said with a smile. 'Either way, I think it was my finest moment.'

'I think... you have many fine moments still to come.' He came closer.

'I hope all of them are kissing you.'

'Some of them,' he murmured. She stared into the eyes that had fascinated her with their warmth from the first moment. There was desire there, but also confidence, trust – things that were foreign and confronting. In his eyes, she was whole, a real person – a person that Charlie and even her grandmother didn't know.

She rose on her toes and kissed him as his hand fisted in the back of her shirt and he met the kiss with all of the passion she'd felt in him at the bottom of the slope.

He lifted her against him and stumbled in the direction of the bed, his mouth sliding across her cheek to her jaw. All she could do was suck in enormous breaths as she landed on her back on the bed, the wooden beams swimming before her eyes.

'Is this okay?' he asked against her cheek.

'Mmhmm,' she said, her eyes closing as his lips brushed her ear. A tremor ran through her. No one had kissed her *ear* before. He did it again, followed by a groan and a nip with his teeth, and she wondered whether she was about to dissolve into the air.

'I always want to touch these spots,' he said, feathering his fingers over her cheek. 'You are far more beautiful in real life than in photos on the Internet.'

Real life... What had that even been before she'd discovered Paris at night? He paused, his breath heavy, and she tugged him down until his forehead was pressed to hers. How was it possible that she knew the feel of him so well, the faint scent of pepper and cold air, the smooth skin of his face and the bristles of his beard? 'Can we...? I want to... tonight?' The words caught in her throat.

'Mmm,' was all he said at first, dropping his mouth to her neck, making her shudder.

'Please,' she added.

'Anything,' he promised in a low murmur. 'Everything.'

'Everything,' she agreed, meeting his gaze and wrapping her arms around his neck to hold him close.

And, although they'd kissed thoroughly only moments ago, the next one felt like the first time, a tentative exploration of confessed wants, tense with restrained passion and wary of the enormity of what neither of them had said. Then they forged ahead, giving and taking.

Ren touched him with the delight of the messed-up woman she was learning she liked being – the woman who'd checked him out in the hospital and struggled with coherent thought when he'd burst out of her ensuite in only a towel. His fingers and mouth made her entire body feel precious. He pulled a condom from the drawer and set it on the night table firmly, a promise and an assurance that made her smile, it was so *Sacha*.

'After the kiss today, I... took precautions,' he explained.

She discovered he was ticklish at the waist and revelled in his laughter as they tumbled on the bed. But the laughter fell away when they drew together. He wasn't gentle with her, but that only proved how strong she was, bearing the passion and asserting her own.

As the tide built, she saw it, a shadow of fear that crossed his expression. He was exposed, too – more vulnerable than he was used to. Seeing him raw and uncertain was its own kind of magic, lending her a strength she hadn't realised she'd had.

'It's all right,' she whispered with all the breath she could muster. *I love you.* She twisted her fingers with his and she held on tight as they were swept away together, with a closeness and depth that was entirely new.

32

Sacha kept his eyes closed, breathing, waiting for the agony of emotion to ebb and willing Ren to keep her hands to herself until he could get his racing heart under control. To his surprise, she did. Her hand was limp in his. His shoulders began to shake with the effort of keeping his weight off her. He had no idea what came next.

He made it to the bathroom bin without risking a look at her. His steps slowed as he made his way back over the polished floorboards and thick-pile rugs of what was supposed to be the worst room in this chalet, but was bigger than his apartment. He lifted his gaze to find her watching him. She propped herself up on one elbow and there was a frankness in her gaze that he hadn't expected. She'd pulled on the shirt he'd tucked under the pillow that morning and the neckline gaped. When had the understandable attraction to her transformed into this unbearable tenderness?

His feet propelled him eagerly back to bed, where he tugged on his boxers and slipped under the covers. 'What?' he asked. 'But if it's "sorry" or "thanks", then I'll...' Her smile brightened, and his words petered out.

'I was just thinking the world would be a much better place if there were more Sacha Mourads in it,' she said.

'One wasn't enough for you?' he asked with a huff.

She laughed and her fingers wandered, up to his collarbone and down his tattooed arm. 'This is a beautiful tree,' she said, skimming the picture on his forearm and down to the bones of his wrists as she followed the roots.

'It's a cedar,' he said. 'A symbol of Lebanon. A bit... banal, you know? But I was only twenty when I got that one.'

She kept blessedly quiet after his confession, but her fingers continued on their curious path, tracing the patterns in the background of the tree. 'Is that a hand? And an eye?' He nodded, but didn't volunteer an explanation for the Middle Eastern symbols of protection. A prickle on his skin was warning him that her frankness hid her inexorable charm that had a way of making him talk. She traced the two swords on his biceps.

'I still like those,' he admitted, 'although my interest in ancient weapons did decline in my thirties.'

'Are you sure? I've seen you pretty excited about swords just this week.' It was impossible not to smile at her. 'Are you a poet or a soldier, deep inside?'

His smile faded. 'Neither.'

'Why not both?' She studied him and the hair on the back of his neck stood on end.

He couldn't hold in the question. 'What do you want, Ren? From me?' He was afraid of the answer, afraid he'd want to give her whatever she asked, no matter the consequences for his life – and hers.

She sat up slowly, her gaze fixed on him. Her back was straight. He'd sensed this in her all along, but seeing it made his breath stall. She was a powerful woman.

'That's not the right question,' she said.

'You deserve happiness. You deserve love from your grand-mother and healing and people who appreciate who you are without forcing you to be someone else. You deserve *everything*. And I don't know what you think you've found in me, but... I don't have what you deserve. My life, my family, my *history* are all I have and, Dieu seul sait, they are complicated enough. I don't have anything more to give. You should have light and sometimes... sometimes I only have shadows.'

She shook her head and grasped his chin in a firm grip. 'Then give me the shadows.'

'What?'

'If that's what you have, then it's what I want. I don't know what will happen... But if shadows are what you have, then I want them.'

He blinked at her as thoughts crowded him – flashes of memory, images, feelings, not all of them his own.

Before he realised he'd made a decision, his lips were moving and words tumbled out.

'Before he was a taxi driver... my father was a journalist.' He sat up and rubbed a hand over his face, drawing his knees up. Ren settled next to him, not quite touching, but there. 'He arrived in Paris in 1980, after reporting on the war for five years. He was about my age when he came to Paris. He never told us, of course. But... he was a man who had seen war crimes in his own country.'

Sacha was surprised that this was where he'd needed to start. He only worried where he would be at the end. 'He came here to leave it behind, but it followed him. He had periods of depression, occasional... hallucinations. He spent time in a psychiatric hospital a few years after he arrived and he couldn't work as a journalist, even though his French was excellent.'

He paused to breathe and she settled her head on his shoulder, waiting.

'As a child, all I knew was that Papa was sad sometimes and

needed to shut himself in his room, but he had some good years after he met my mother and they had Nadia and me. They were both in their forties when they met and they appreciated the good times. He would... paint his dreams for me. I think it was his way of coping. He told me about Paris, the city of his destiny, he said. And we visited everywhere we could that was free.'

'Not the Eiffel Tower,' she murmured.

'And the Louvre only once, on my birthday. He wanted to publish a book of bestselling poetry, a literary bridge between Lebanon and Paris, and support Maman and the family with not only the royalties, but the legacy of the world he wanted to create. But we lived in a small apartment in Aubervilliers – Grand Paris, but not the Paris he dreamed of. It didn't deter him. It must have hurt to see his dreams growing further and further from reach, but he held onto them. He had a much... bigger soul.'

'Sounds like someone I know,' she murmured.

'You think I inherited that from him?' He felt her nod. 'I hope so... He had an even bigger heart. If his dreams were in Paris, his heart was firmly in Aubervilliers. He knew everyone. He talked to everyone, no matter who they were. Christmas was celebrated the whole month of December for him, and he cooked and shared, and it was completely normal to me that we exchanged gifts with our Muslim neighbours, at al-Hijriya New Year, too, and we received the most decadent baskets of exotic fruits in the evening during Ramadan.

'He drove a lot of people in his taxi for free, in particular late at night. I would wake up hearing his phone ringing and he'd go and collect someone. He never asked questions. He just wanted to get people to safety. He had a collection of CDs that he would play in the taxi. He had recitations from the Qur'an for the Muslim troublemakers, hymns for the Christians. He used to laugh that they put up with his gentle reprimand because of the free trip.

'But I understood later that he was reacting to the war he'd seen, the country of his birth, which was supposed to be a safe place for Muslims and Christians of different types to take pride together in their nation.'

'A big dream,' she said under her breath.

'The biggest,' he agreed with a sigh. 'And then Maman died. I was twelve. She'd always been sick. She had heart problems and fatigue and Papa was used to looking after her. We all were. But when she died, he lost... his orientation. He looked after us as well as a single parent can, but he was restless and unhappy and he was gone more and more often, although we had less and less money.

'One night, he drove the wrong people. There had been a death. The police came to our door. They banged and shouted and the guns on their belts terrified him – and Nadia and me. They arrested him for... complice, for helping the criminals, tu sais? He was guilty of that.'

'Oh, no,' Ren sighed.

'The judge had enough pity not to send him to prison, but he had to pay. And he was so shocked that his... troubles came back and he had to go to the psychiatric hospital again and Nadia and I were... in the charge of the state, you know? Not long after he got out, he died.'

Sacha stared straight ahead, his hands limp between his knees.

'I'll never know why he died,' he said bitterly. 'Perhaps it was suicide; perhaps just a mistake with medicine. He didn't leave that information. He just left unfulfilled dreams and the best intentions.'

'And books,' Ren finished for him.

Sacha nodded slowly. 'I didn't touch his books for over a year after he died. I was angry with him for putting some local criminals ahead of us, for falling apart without Maman, as though we weren't enough to keep him on earth.'

'And that's when you got into trouble.'

'We were put in a welcome family, you know? And it was okay, but it wasn't home and it wasn't Papa. Nadia turned eighteen and moved out and I was desperate to *do* something. I stole some jewellery from a shop in the Marais. I think it was to prove that I could, to feel capable of something, even if that thing was just... screwing up. The stealing was not exactly easy, but I unfortunately could do it. But trying to sell the pieces, I fucked up. I got caught straight away and... Joseph called the police.'

He would need her to say something, soon.

'It was a first crime and Joseph spoke for me, recommended the service work at the museum, and... it felt like Papa was still there in spirit. I opened his books again. The notebook he left me, it doesn't all make sense and half of it was blank, but... he tried. "With only the little love I have, I can do more than nothing." That's on the second page. Then I saw that Joseph was grieving for his husband and... I found what I had to do.'

'You had to carry on your father's legacy of helping others,' she said, 'and thereby give his life and his death meaning.'

The breath whooshed from his lungs as she said it and his head fell into his hands.

He stared at the bed, not seeing anything. It stunned him to realise how deeply he still felt the failure, the pressure to keep the memory alive until he could accept the strengths and shortcomings of the man who'd shaped him.

The silence of the room was heavy. These mountains were so foreign, and yet he could feel them outside, the thick snow that dampened sound and amplified light. He stared at the window up under the eaves, glowing with bluish moonlight.

He stood, walking to the window and pulling it open. The sharp air burned his lungs, but a wide world opened up with each breath. His father would have loved hearing about today, when he'd conquered a mountain with the woman he loved.

Sacha knew he should stop pretending that the last part wasn't true. He should stop railing against the conflicting interests that kept them apart and start accepting that their short time together could still be worth something.

To his surprise, Ren followed him, shivering in the frigid air that floated through the window and staring up at the dark sky.

'It's beautiful out there – up there,' he said softly.

When Ren finally spoke, she didn't say at all what he'd expected. 'Joseph said your father's name was Karim?'

His throat was suddenly thick. Karim would have immediately seen past her designer clothes and socialite lifestyle to the woman beneath. Karim would have loved her like a daughter.

'Yes,' he said, his voice alarmingly rough. 'His name was Karim.' A gasp emerged from his mouth and he realised his cheeks were wet. He glanced at Ren, to find her eyes shining and her face also glistening with tears.

He took her face in his hands and kissed her – hard and deep and a little clumsy. He had no right to make her cry, or to hold her down with his past. He shouldn't kiss her like this, wanting something, but she didn't push him away. She wrapped her arms around him and drew him closer and kissed him back. She was afraid of the dark, but she held him as though his shadows were precious.

And as they made love again, this time with echoes of the conversation between them, Sacha knew they were writing a love story into the notebook of his life.

33

Everyone was in a good mood on Sunday morning – or Ren's capacity for positive thinking had revived itself overnight. She didn't want to speculate on the merger, but she suspected, given the numerous photos Ziggy snapped during the meal, that they would be formulating an announcement shortly that would take the pressure off her and Charlie.

Grandmama tried to talk to her about plans for Christmas Day, now only four days away, but she struggled to pay attention and her foot kept poking Sacha's under the table of its own accord.

'Can't we have Christmas... in Paris?' she suggested without thought. She didn't dare catch Sacha's eye. They hadn't discussed what would happen this evening when they left the ski slopes. So many times, now, she'd been on the brink of saying goodbye to Sacha. Surely she could snatch a few more days with him, extending her reprieve until Christmas.

'In Paris?' spluttered Ziggy.

'Well... we're all here,' Ren pointed out.

'And the Ritz does a lovely Christmas dinner,' her grandmother pointed out.

'You will have to come back to London at some point,' Ziggy said. 'Why not now?' *Because I've only just stopped pretending with him.*

'She'll want to meet Sacha's family, too, won't she?' Charlie's mother Gina said. That would be true, if her relationship with Sacha was normal and not a gauntlet of obstacles on both sides. 'The French celebrate Christmas on both days, don't they? Christmas Eve, too? What does your family do, Sacha?'

'I'm not sure the Mourads celebrate Christmas,' Livia commented, but Ren stared at her in confusion. Was she making assumptions about the Middle Eastern origin of his surname? Ren couldn't remember if Sacha had mentioned his father's background.

He didn't respond to Livia but turned to Gina instead. 'We celebrate on Christmas Eve overnight. Both of my parents have died, so my sister, my nephew and I celebrate with a good friend of the family.'

'Oh, I'm sorry about your parents,' Gina said. 'I always wanted to try a yule log, you know, those French Christmas cakes that look like logs. Do you bake one of those?'

'La bûche de Noël,' Sacha said with a nod. 'My sister and I prepare it together, from an old recipe from my Lebanese grandmother.'

If Ren hadn't been desperate to join him for a family Christmas before, she certainly was now. She'd never *baked* anything at Christmas. The family chef was always too much of a perfectionist to tolerate a helper who was all thumbs in the kitchen.

'That's perfect, then. Christmas Day is free for dinner at the Ritz. It sounds marvellous,' Gina said with a smile. A few seconds of spluttering from around the table were the only hint that not everyone had imagined this plan for celebrating Christmas together.

'Yes, marvellous.' Ziggy covered the awkwardness with two clipped words she definitely didn't mean.

'Christmas at the Ritz sounds lovely,' Charlotte piped up and Ren realised the trap she'd landed herself – and Sacha – in. She got more time with him, but he had to face this awful party again. She was so *bad* for him. But she didn't want to let him go – not yet.

* * *

She and Sacha tumbled into their seats on the TGV blessedly alone that evening. Ren draped her arm over him and tangled their legs, breathing an enormous sigh of relief.

'I don't think my knees will ever be the same again,' Sacha groaned. 'But it feels so good to get the boots off.'

'You were pretty good at the blue slope by the end,' she said. 'We just need to get you curving with parallel skis and it won't hurt your knees so much.'

'Thanks, coach. Somehow I don't think your grandmother will invite me back to the chalet.'

'They all give me such a headache at the moment,' she groaned. 'I don't know what's going on and the only thing that makes sense is this.' She lifted her face for a kiss and he obliged. 'It was like Grandmama was pretending she didn't disapprove of you. Charlie was pretending he wasn't threatened by you. Charlotte was pretending there was nothing at all wrong. Ziggy was pulling strings behind everyone, but I don't know to what end, and you and I...'

'We were pretending to be in a relationship, while really being in a relationship – secretly. Wait, that's absurd.' He laughed, leaning his head back against the seat.

'At least I think the merger will be back on. Then everyone can forget Charlie and I were ever together – like I want to.'

'You think you can? Forget him?'

When I look at you, I already have... 'If we're working together after the merger, I won't be able to get rid of him entirely, but I think I can forget I thought we'd get married one day.'

To her surprise, his smile faded. 'You can just... leave the past behind like that? Your desire for happy endings is that strong?'

'It's not like that,' she insisted, her skin prickling. 'I don't mean forget, forget. But I have to cross out the mistake and continue on.'

He gave a bleak laugh. 'That's exactly what I'm unable to do. Every mistake leads here, to now. Crossing things out is ignoring them and losing the thread of what makes us who we are.'

'Your father taught you that,' she said softly, and his gaze jerked back to her in surprise.

'Yes,' he confirmed. 'And you understand him. There are things you can't forget, either.'

'Don't compare what happened to me with what your father experienced.'

'Why not? They're both traumas. You can't hold it inside. It comes out.'

'What other choice do I have? Telling you... maybe I shouldn't have. You have enough burdens, right?'

'Sharing your memory is not a burden.'

Her throat was thick as she tried to work out if she could believe him. 'But sharing your father's memory is,' she remarked.

'You probably think it cost him too much, holding onto the past – it costs *me* too much.'

'That's not for me to say, but your father's life had meaning, you know,' she murmured. 'Before you took up his legacy, before you did anything in his memory, his life had meaning. I listen to you talk and it's clear. All lives have meaning and purpose. It's *you* who's not at peace, not him. You need to decide his life was complete, was worth something. Maybe you need to stop focusing on the shadows.'

Sacha sat staring blankly for so long that she wondered whether she'd gone too far. 'All lives have meaning and purpose? Including yours?' he finally asked.

He'd trapped her in her own logic and deflected her observation, but the words still struck deeply. 'I...' Had she truly wasted so much time and energy believing she was useless? 'I suppose it must,' she said in disbelief. But what exactly did that mean for her now? All she knew in that moment was that she was meant to love – earnestly and generously and perhaps unwisely.

'Are you coming back to my apartment tonight?' he asked softly.

'Yes,' she answered, enjoying the twitch of his lips at her resolute answer. 'And every night until Christmas. I've been terrible company for Malou.'

'I don't believe you were terrible company,' he said with a sceptical look.

She drew close and whispered with a smile, 'I was terrible company, because I wanted to be with you.'

A blush crept up his neck. 'Do you... do you really want to come to dinner on Christmas Eve? You don't have to.'

'Why do you think I don't want to come? I suggested Christmas in Paris because of you, Sacha, because I'm not ready to say goodbye yet. But do you still think I'm more interested in Louis Vuitton than Saint-Denis? Or do you think I'm snobby about cavorting with a flea market trader? That's who you meant, right? You celebrate Christmas with Joseph?'

'I know you better than that,' he said, but he wasn't looking at her. 'Perhaps it's us I'm worried about. They'll love you so much, I'll hear about it for years.'

'This is really petty,' she began slowly, 'but I kind of like the idea of them all comparing your next girlfriend to me.' He choked. 'I am the selfish, pampered heiress, after all!'

'I'm not sure I like the idea of your next boyfriend being compared favourably to me!'

She bolted upright and grabbed handfuls of his sweater. 'Oh, God, you don't mean that.'

'You started it.'

'I only said it because I'm a pain and you're... I've never met anyone like you.'

'I assure you, there are lots of us.'

'That's not what I mean and you know it.' She bit her lip, staring at the bland institutional carpet on the backs of the chairs in front of them. She'd never felt like this before and she wasn't sure she would again. But at least she had the sense not to say it. Sacha didn't believe there was any way they could be together – she wasn't sure she believed it herself. What was the point in burdening him with her feelings?

She definitely wasn't brave enough, and wasn't strong enough to hear him say they were a beautiful mistake, destiny off-course, a treasured memory.

'Do you own *any* books with happy endings?' she asked instead, resting her head against his shoulder. He considered the question for long enough that she had her answer. 'Well, I know what you're getting for Christmas.'

* * *

Ren was determined to make the most of the short time they had. She dragged Sacha back to the Marché aux Puces on Monday to buy Christmas presents, bickering companionably about the definition of the word 'expensive'. She revelled in every day-to-day activity, Sacha laughing indulgently when she couldn't work the scales for fruit and vegetables at the supermarket or turn on the oven. He showed her how to cook a few basic dishes and she rewarded him lavishly with kisses.

In the evenings, he sat and read a book while she draped herself over him, distracting him until he gave up and kissed her. If the days felt endless in their normality, the nights were limited and desperate, conscious of the approach of Christmas – and the end of their time together.

On Tuesday morning, the 23rd, she threw open the curtains of Sacha's bedroom to see a handful of paparazzi loitering. She tugged the curtains shut again as quickly as she could, feeling like Brian from the Monty Python film, except thankfully decent, if slightly ridiculous, in her fluffy pyjamas.

Sacha waved to the photographers with a grim smile on his way to the boulangerie and returned with croissants, which improved Ren's mood significantly, when she'd stuffed the first one in her mouth and ate the second more slowly, enjoying the delicate layers of pastry melting on her tongue.

'We just don't get them like this in London,' she said with her mouth full.

'I suppose this is why they say you should live like no one's watching.'

Ren's phone rang and she warily accepted Malou's call and drifted back into the bedroom. 'Hey,' she said with false brightness. 'I see the paparazzi are bored again.'

'Huh? The street outside the gallery is crawling with them.'

'Oh, no, not there, too!' Ren groaned. 'I just meant they must be bored if they want to get a picture of me stuffing my face with croissants.'

'You haven't seen the news, then?'

A shiver of unease rippled through her. 'What news?'

'The stained-glass panel was stolen from the gallery last night.

Not only are we crawling with paparazzi, the police are swarming the corridors as well.'

'What? Was anyone hurt? Did they take anything else?'

'Everyone's fine, and just the panel. It's odd, as though they knew something we didn't. I had a call from the French Ministry of Culture yesterday. They were supposed to come and view it today. The timing feels like too much of a coincidence and it wouldn't surprise me if the owner has something to do with the theft. But it's safe to say Asquith-Lewis is big news this morning and I don't think Ziggy is entirely unhappy about it, despite the security breach. I'm not surprised the paparazzi is back at Sacha's place, too. After the photos from the ski slopes, all of Paris wants to know who Sacha Mourad is.'

'They do not!'

'Maybe not all of Paris, but you were off the radar for long enough that the tabloids sniffed a story and now the gallery is in the news as well...'

Ren sank onto the bed, feeling the walls creep nearer. Could she really do this to Sacha, in good conscience? 'What do they know so far?'

'Pretty much everything. He's a teacher at a collège in a poor part of Paris and originally from Aubervilliers.' Ren's throat closed. She hated that news outlets were poking into his life, but that was nowhere near *everything*. 'Ziggy called the PR team back from holiday this morning to deal with both problems.'

So, she was a problem again. It had been fun at first, but now she was just upset. 'Was she planning to ask me? She's the one who told me I had to bring him skiing to show that everything was fine. Although I also suspect she wanted to scare him off.'

'That obviously didn't work,' said Malou. 'What would you say if she asked for your advice? Don't worry, it's all fake? Or yes, you haven't come back to mine since you shared a room in the mountains and had lots of rebound sex?' She sighed. 'I wish we could gossip about this like normal people.'

'I'm not normal people,' Ren moaned. 'God, I wish I was.'

'I'm sorry, Ren. You know I'm on your side, right?'

'Except that Ziggy is technically your boss.'

'I don't care. We'll find a way through it. Is it... real, now? You and Sacha? Or are you just hiding behind him.'

Hiding behind him... That sounded awful.

'He's listened to me and helped me see the world in a different way and all I've done is hurt him, and cost him money, and let my family insult him and now I'm adding an invasion of privacy on top of all of that. He's... special and he doesn't deserve this.'

Malou was silent for a long moment. 'Special?'

'Please don't ask,' Ren said with a sigh. 'I don't know. And I don't know what I'm going to do. I'm dreading Christmas. I have to let him go. Using him to avoid my problems isn't fair, so I have to find some way to say goodbye to him on Christmas Day.'

'He's coming to Christmas lunch? That shows commitment.'

She smiled faintly. It did show commitment, but not to *her*. He'd agreed to help and he took his responsibilities seriously. 'Grandmama couldn't *not* invite him, in front of everyone at the chalet. It's such a mess. Charlie and his parents, me and Grandmama and Ziggy and poor Sacha.'

'He can look after himself.'

Ren smiled faintly, remembering his expression when Charlie had tried to belittle him on the ski slopes. 'I hope you're right.'

34

Joseph's ugly apartment, decorated for Christmas Eve, was a far cry from the rich fabrics and natural colours of the Ritz, Sacha couldn't help thinking.

His friend had gone to more effort than usual. The apartment that was usually off-white and grey was silver, gold and red. Joseph's eclectic taste was evident on the Christmas tree, with its mix of patterned decorations from Africa in bright colours, his favourite vintage pieces and the traditional wooden ornaments he'd picked out years ago with his partner. He'd even tied the few remaining horseshoes onto the sturdier boughs.

But Sacha had given up expecting Ren to be anything other than thrilled with all of it. She'd even been excited, if a little taken aback, when he'd explained that they didn't eat the Christmas meal until after midnight mass. She'd grown keener on the idea after he'd promised her snacks.

His own enjoyment of Christmas Eve had a bittersweet edge; he was conscious of the memories he was making, feeling keenly the poignancy of their last night. He hadn't wanted to ask what would happen after they'd made it through lunch with her family on

Christmas Day, but he could tell by the way she spoke that tomorrow was the end. She had to return to her responsibilities, her real life. And he had to go back to how his life had been without her. That prospect grew more difficult to imagine with every moment she spent in his world.

Nadia and Ren were making chocolate reindeer with pretzel horns to fill the time. Even Raph had been drawn in, if only to laugh at the mixed results. Ren concentrated meticulously, dipping her cake into the chocolate and carefully adding the eyes, nose and antlers – until the whole thing drooped and dripped and looked like something from a horror film. At which point, she held up her phone and snapped a selfie imitating her work, before collapsing into giggles.

'Ren with renne,' she joked.

Joseph was busy in the kitchen as usual, wearing his floral apron and threatening people with his silicon oven gloves if they helped too much. Sacha had placed a chair in the corner for him to rest and goaded him into it regularly. The sponge cake for the yule log was in the oven. Joseph had announced mysteriously that dinner would arrive soon and had something to do with the enormous watermelon by the door.

After the reindeer were sloppily finished, Nadia produced paper crowns, laughing as Sacha and Raph both grumbled about them. Ren insisted they take a photo together with their matching frowns, which of course led to a grinning photo that started up the warm ache inside him again.

'I finally see the queen in her crown,' he murmured, pressing a kiss just below Ren's ear. He was painfully aware of his family gaping, but it wasn't enough for him to keep his hands to himself. She had her hair down in tangled curls the colour of autumn leaves. Every nuanced smile, every warm look made him want her more.

'Enough of that! Game time!' Joseph announced, producing four paper plates before disappearing back into the kitchen. They sat around the table, holding the plates on their heads while they attempted to draw a Christmas scene. The results produced peals of laughter, with unrecognisable zigzags and wonky flames consuming the Christmas tree instead of staying in the fireplace.

'I only hope it's not telling the future,' Nadia said with a laugh.

'Joseph doesn't have a fireplace,' Sacha commented drily, slipping his arm along the back of Ren's chair.

'It could be a figurative prediction,' Ren pointed out. 'But it's more likely a prediction for tomorrow, not tonight.'

'Are they going to flambé Christmas dinner at the Ritz?'

'Don't even mention it. With my luck, that would be a disaster!'

Sacha settled his fingertips on her back. 'With all the horseshoes in this room, your luck shouldn't be in question. And I believe *you* started this discussion about who was going to burn Christmas.'

Ren turned to Nadia. 'Has he always been this grumpy?'

'This grumpy? He is usually much grumpier! Zut, I must show you the family photos! Joseph keeps most of our lives in his spare room – what we managed to save when Papa died.'

Sacha sighed and lifted his hand again so Ren could follow Nadia to the sofa. He allowed Raph to draw him into a few rounds of *Mario Kart* so he could at least pretend he wasn't listening and blushing as Ren exclaimed over the old photo album Nadia brought out.

'It's not really fair, though,' Ren muttered at one point. 'The photos of me as a child are all chubby and freckly and full of braces, but Sacha was this adorable his entire life. Oh, here's the crooked tooth. If he'd grown up in my position, that snaggle-tooth wouldn't exist and these photos would be full of metal smiles!'

'It's the grace of God that I have bad teeth,' he muttered.

'They're not bad, they're...'

'Adorable?' he suggested with a laugh, utterly unable to affect his usual frown. 'You're adorable yourself,' he teased, slipping his thumb along her jaw. His go-kart crashed on the TV screen behind him.

'I hear a lot of joy in this room,' came Joseph's loud voice from the doorway, a potato in his hand.

'Joseph, what are you doing? I said I'd do the potatoes,' Nadia scolded him. She poured him a glass of wine and beckoned for him to sit at the table.

'I can do the potatoes,' Ren insisted, to a chorus of silence and sceptical looks. If she peeled potatoes as well as she cracked eggs, then they'd need an ambulance on hand.

'Who knew that the job of peeling potatoes was so in demand,' Joseph muttered, but allowed Sacha to lead him to the table for a rest.

'Come, we can both do it,' Nadia said, waving the bottle of wine at Ren and smiling. Sacha drifted into the kitchen after he'd lost his next race against Raph.

'Allez ouste,' Nadia said, waving him away. 'She doesn't want an audience.'

'Shit!' Ren cried. He turned to catch the blur of a semi-naked potato flying towards him. Recovering from the shock of the potato impact, he noticed her finger was bleeding and grabbed a tea-towel to apply pressure.

He cradled her arm in his. 'You push *away* from yourself with the économe!'

'Sorry,' she said with a grimace. 'But at least I didn't injure you this time.'

'The potato was very hard. Let's see how my eye looks tomorrow.'

'What?' She brushed her hand over his cheek and inspected his face.

'I'm joking. I won't appear at your Christmas dinner with a black eye, on top of everything else.'

'If I ruin your Christmas dinner, you have every right to ruin mine.'

'That's fair,' he quipped. Except she wasn't ruining his Christmas. This was the best time he'd had in years, and when he pressed another soft kiss to her lips, it was even better. He'd never grow tired of the way she expectantly lifted her face to his.

The doorbell rang twenty minutes later, when the potatoes had been tucked onto their tray, ready for roasting. 'Ah! That is Djamel,' called Joseph.

The family crammed into the hallway to greet the neighbour with kisses. 'Joyeux Noël, Joseph,' he said with a smile and handed over a plastic bag. 'Your order. I saved the best ones for you.'

'Merci beaucoup. C'est très gentil! This is for you and have a lovely evening. Say hello to Zahra for me.' Joseph handed him a pain d'épices wrapped elegantly in paper with a gold sticker. Tied to it with red ribbon was a horseshoe. 'Get the watermelon, Sacha.'

Sacha hefted the enormous melon and shared a smile with Djamel as the neighbour took it. When Djamel had left, Sacha turned to Joseph and gestured to the bag. 'If that's what I think it is, Ren should open it.'

Nadia slapped him on the arm. 'C'est méchant, mon frère! How mean.'

'Did I hear my name? Or were you talking about queens or reindeer?' Ren asked from the doorway.

Sacha took the heavy plastic bag from his friend and handed it to Ren. 'This is the dinner. Go and open it in the kitchen.'

She peered at the bag with a frown, but did as he said. Sacha grinned unrepentantly, sharing the joke with Raph while Nadia and Joseph scowled at him. 'Trois, deux, un...'

'Eeek!' Ren cried, accompanied by a rustle of plastic and a crunch as she dropped the dinner.

Nadia rushed to avert disaster – and stop the dinner from feebly crawling away.

'I touched it! Urgh. The leg moved!'

Sacha wrapped an arm around her, but she shoved him away. 'You did that on purpose. Don't expect a hug in return.' She shuddered.

'Don't you like lobster?' he asked with a twitch of a smile.

'I love lobster,' she said with a stamp of her foot.

'Alors, I thank you for... bravely subjugating our dinner.'

'Oh, shut up. And wipe that smile off your face.' She crossed her arms and regarded him critically, but her lips were wobbling with a smile already. He judged his moment and slipped his arms around her, pulling her against him until she landed with a little 'Oof,' her arms still crossed. 'You'll have to try harder than that.'

He dipped his head. 'This?' he said, giving her a light, aching kiss.

'A good start,' she murmured. He kissed her again, not surprised when she wrapped her arms around his neck and deepened the kiss.

'I'm still here, vous savez,' Nadia called out from the kitchen bench. 'I don't want to see my brother playing roll-the-galosh.'

Ren drew away with a blush. 'Roll a what?'

'A shoe, but you call it French kissing,' Nadia said.

'You don't?' Ren asked.

'Mon Dieu, non!'

The dinner prepared and awaiting the final cooking after church, Raph dragged Ren to the sofa to teach her to play *Zelda* and Sacha wandered into the spare room for his regular dose of nostalgia. He'd stayed in this room many times, often during the lowest points of his life, and now Joseph stored the bits of the past Sacha couldn't bear to keep with him – or that simply wouldn't fit in his tiny, humid cellar.

He reached behind a stack of old schoolbooks for the framed sepia photo that should be on display somewhere, but wasn't. Even the twinkle in Papa's eye, behind his aviator-style spectacles, looked different today.

Nadia peered around the doorway, but her words died on her lips when she saw what he was holding. 'I haven't looked at that photo in years.' He gave an inarticulate response and went to stow the photo behind the books again. 'Sometimes,' Nadia continued thoughtfully, stopping him in his tracks, 'I was jealous of the way you got all his spirit. He never left me any notebooks.'

'How did you know about the notebook?'

'You can't keep secrets from me. Alors, does his notebook say anything about first love?'

'Do you still think that's what's going on?' he huffed. 'And why *first* love? I've had...' He fell silent.

Nadia gave him a withering look. 'Just don't mess it up.'

'I won't have to,' he muttered. 'It came pre-messed up.'

'I was afraid of this,' she said with a sigh. 'You don't have to care about her family or who she is.'

'They want me to care. I'd never make her choose between her grandmother and me.'

'Because you're scared she'd pick her grandmother. But what if she doesn't?'

'She *should* pick her grandmother,' he grumbled, stuffing down deeper the suspicions that were plaguing him increasingly. *Six days...* He understood only too well Ren's loyalty to her only living family member, but what if he was right? What if all her family had to offer was money and grief? But then again, what more did *he* have to offer? The grief *without* the money.

'And since when do you do what people want you to do?'

'It's *family*. You don't understand how much trouble we're in because of... this. It can't continue.'

'You're right, I don't understand the trouble. All I see is my brother looking so happy he reminds me how much Papa used to love Maman. We all adore her – and you obviously do, too.'

'Loving Maman wasn't the only thing Papa felt,' he muttered.

'Perhaps not,' Nadia agreed, 'but it was one of the best things.'

One of the best things that was ripped away from him – like everything else. Life had not been fair to Karim. 'Ren deserves someone who can give her the whole world and I barely have a free evening. There's a difference between loving someone and belonging with someone. You should know that.'

'Merde, don't bring me into this! You are not young and stupid, like I was. And she's not helpless, needing "the world" from someone. I think she just wants you. You don't love easily. This is... big, Sacha.'

'What? I love you and Raph... so much. How can you say that?' But Nadia's words rang in his ears. *She just wants you...* It sounded a lot like, 'Give me your shadows.' God, he hadn't realised hope could hurt like this.

His sister clutched his shoulders. 'I know you love us more than anything. You love so deeply. I saw Maman fade away, too, you know. I lost Papa suddenly, as well. It was awful for me, too, and I understand that you never wanted to lose anyone else you loved that much. But I still say it's worth the risk. I made us both do it by accident when I got pregnant with Raph. And you know how terrifying that was, to love him so much. You can choose this time, but this is *it*, Sacha – *love*. Papa left you his poetry to *open* your heart, not to burden it. Go back and read his notebook again, with that in mind. That's what he would tell you to do.'

He stared at Nadia, his mind desperately searching for answers, because he was too scared to search his heart. Ren's words had also planted themselves in his mind. Papa was gone. It was Sacha who had to decide how to respect his legacy. 'You do have Papa's spirit,' he murmured.

She shrugged. 'How could I not?'

'You can read the notebook any time.'

She waved a hand dismissively. 'One day I will. But the important thing now is for you to forget this bullshit about trouble and tell her you love her. What better time than Christmas Eve?'

'It might not make any difference.' Christmas Eve, after all, was followed by Christmas Day, the prospect of which sat heavily in his stomach. 'And you know how soft-hearted she is. I don't want her to feel indebted to me. I don't want to hold her back.'

'You mean you're scared she'll tell you she loves you, too,' Nadia said flippantly. Before Sacha had time to react beyond a dumbfounded gape, Joseph's voice sounded in the hallway.

'Sacha? Nadi? Time to go. Messe de minuit doesn't wait for you!' He poked his head around the door and saw what they were looking at. He approached with a smile. 'Joyeux Noël, Karim,' he said conversationally. 'Don't worry. I'm taking them to mass. Oh, and Sacha is in love. Perhaps he'll tell you about it, since he won't admit it to anyone else.'

'Not you, too,' Sacha muttered, but he draped an arm around Joseph when his friend cuffed him on the back of the head as though he were still sixteen.

'Let's go.'

As his family fetched their shoes and coats, Sacha hung back. 'Just give me five minutes. I'll be down soon.' To Ren, he added a kiss and a translation into English. Then he snatched the unassuming gift, wrapped in brown paper with her name on it, from under the tree. Opening it carefully, he turned to the right page and took up a pencil.

Perhaps she wouldn't see the note tonight. He could only hope so.

35

Squashed up against Sacha in the back of Nadia's car and enjoying every moment, Ren peered out of the window and gaped at night-time in Saint-Denis. They passed blocky brutalist concrete structures with bizarre shadows, historic stone buildings reminiscent of Paris proper and contemporary edifices in glass. Murals adorned apartment blocks with myriad faces, animals and superheroes and strange allegories of city life.

When they pulled up in front of the grand stone cathedral, its arches and tracery and lopsided belltower a prototype for its damaged sister on the Île-de-la-Cité, she remembered standing beside Sacha in front of another church, listening to him talk about growing up in the nine-three, how he'd lived with the whole world as his neighbours. She was beginning to think he'd grown up with the entirety of history, too, and he bore it all with such honour and dignity.

'Is it okay? Being out so late?' he asked her softly as the others got out of the car.

She nodded. 'It's... my last night of freedom. I want to live it.' *It's my last night with you.* Her heart was twenty-four hours from breaking.

As soon as the first notes of music reached her ears, sung by deep men's voices and filling the cavernous space up to the distant vaulted ceiling, Ren couldn't stop the tears. She couldn't understand the words of the Christmas liturgy in French, but the feeling of standing among a group of people joined by goodwill, with a man she loved by her side, touched her deeply.

Sacha said nothing. He simply clutched her hand until he must have had cramps, and stayed close enough that their arms pressed together. He didn't need to say anything.

After the service, Sacha mumbled something about showing her the stained glass, but his tone was strangely reluctant.

'I'll... I need to tell you something about that stained glass in your gallery, the piece that was stolen,' he began. She didn't want to think about Asquith-Lewis or be reminded of the time she'd naïvely made him feel like a lesser human being by taking him to her gallery, so she shook her head and ushered him towards the enormous door.

'We can't see the glass properly now, anyway. At night, the light comes from within, hmm?' she said as they passed under the clusters of carved figures over the door, peering down at them in stone. His expression was conflicted, the way she felt when she thought about tomorrow.

Snow was falling with a hush, when they emerged silently from mass. Sacha's steps slowed. Words were written on his face, but he struggled to say them.

'We should get back for the meal,' was what he managed.

The same hush remained over dinner, as the snow continued to fall.

'I'm not sure I've ever been up this late,' Ren whispered to

Sacha, leaning a heavy head on his shoulder. 'But I don't want it to end.'

'I'll carry you to bed if you don't make it,' he said, but she perked up a bit for the gift-giving, grinning as Sacha's family opened her gifts. Raph had been easy – the latest title for his console. For Joseph, she'd chosen a small woven rug with a bright pattern and yellow tassels, and for Nadia she'd found a hand-painted ceramic planter – both from the streets around the Marché aux Puces.

Joseph gave Ren a polished brass oil lamp, which made her laugh, until she joked about capturing Sacha in it and taking him with her. The joke hit a little too close to home.

She opened an art print of the Seine at night from Nadia and Raph and, even though it was a print, flogged by the million in souvenir shops in this great city, she knew she would treasure it – and the memories it held – as much as her Matisse.

She and Sacha were making a study of not looking at each other. She wondered if he was also trying not to cry, but she thought not. He could relive this Christmas every year, surrounded by the love of his family. He couldn't be feeling the twinge of longing that she was.

Even the remains of the yule log on the table made her eyes sting. Ren and Raph had been a little too enthusiastic with the crumbled chocolate 'bark' and the powdered sugar, but she'd been so overcome by how he'd opened up to her while they decorated it that she would never have stopped him, even if she'd known the cake would end up so rich that no one could finish a slice.

The last two presents under the tree were almost identical. Ren retrieved the one from her and shoved it at Sacha without ceremony and he unwrapped the volume carefully.

'*Contes de Fées*,' he said with a smile. 'French fairytales? You do realise they don't all have happy endings?'

'Perhaps not, but there is some magic in them that adults need sometimes. And these were written by a woman, so I don't think they'll be quite as dreadful as Grimm.'

He opened the book and studied the contents page, brushing his fingers over the spine, and then he glanced at her with a momentary flash of melancholy that wasn't the reaction she'd intended him to have.

She tore open the brown paper of her gift, eager to see which book he'd chosen for her. She wasn't surprised it was a volume of poetry. It was a beautiful edition, blue canvas with simple gold type bearing the title: *English Romantic Poetry.* Sacha cleared his throat awkwardly as she ran her hands over the cover.

'I thought... this would be the best place for you to start.'

'Start reading poetry?'

'Start... finding... your feelings, being the formidable person you are,' he finished in a mumble.

Her fingers tightened on the cover of the book as she stared at him – she'd never expected to feel so connected to another human being.

'Ah,' he said with a groan. 'Not formidable. *Formidable*, in French. It is a good thing.'

Even that error touched her. 'I kind of liked formidable,' she murmured.

After the gift-giving, the lateness of the hour loomed inexorably. Nadia and Raph left for the short drive back to their apartment. Joseph clapped Sacha on the shoulder and said something in French, before bidding Ren goodnight and limping off to bed. Ren was dead on her feet, but she didn't want to sleep. When Sacha slid open the door to the balcony, she eagerly followed him out, shivering at the ice in the air. She held out her hand to catch the feathery flakes of snow and looked out at the view: the ghostly white forms of six identical tower-blocks and a windswept play-ground in the courtyard below.

'What did Joseph say to you?'

He chuckled. 'He told me I should start by telling you every-thing about you that I like, but... there's too much.'

'Start what?' she asked, blushing.

His smile faded and he gripped the freezing metal railing in agitation. 'I... I just want to say...' She waited, her heartbeat falter-ing. 'This... you... we... I...' He sighed. 'That's only pronouns,' he muttered. 'I don't know how to say it.'

Ren did.

'I'll never forget you, in all my life.' Her breath stalled. 'I know you like happy endings, but I... you are important to me, even without.'

Tears welled up again. She'd never liked stories where the lovers were wrenched apart, but didn't that happen to everyone, in the end? 'Even without a happy ending,' she murmured, 'I wouldn't change anything about the past few weeks.' *I love you so much*.

He pulled her tight to him, the embrace almost crushing, and kissed her with a passion that told its own story. He held onto her as they headed back inside to the spare bedroom and they clung to each other, expressing in actions what was unbearable to say in words.

36

Sacha grimaced as he stood in front of the mirror in the hallway of his apartment, wrestling with a bow tie for the second time in as many weeks. *Only for Ren...*

She emerged from the bathroom, slipping a pair of ruby earrings on, her face smooth with make-up, her hair swept up and held in place. The dark green velvet dress was festive and brought out the caramel in her eyes. But he had a pang of missing her already – *her*, the woman who had taught him to ski, found the métro exciting and stuffed her face with croissants.

'Sorry my Christmas has a slightly different dress code from yours.'

'I only hope I'm enough of a Prince Charmant for you today.'

'I'm glad your Christmas present has made such an impact already.' She tweaked his collar. 'Well, I'm your fairy godmother,' she continued, grasping his wrist and slipping a diamond-set cuff-link into place. He stared at it, and its partner, with the familiar sense of misgiving. She dropped a fine necklace to her chest and closed the clasp at her neck. It was a simple but elegant web of gold chains with rubies and enamel. 'Is that Art Nouveau?' he asked, trying to keep his voice neutral.

'I... it's more vintage Cartier.' She winced and a flash of memory reminded him of her engagement ring. What the hell were they doing? He was a poor replacement for Charlie in her grandmother's eyes and Sacha would be persona non grata when Livia found out what he'd done about the stained-glass panel, which he really should have told Ren about.

Then there was his suspicion about Livia herself that would only lead to more trouble. What good would come of destroying that relationship? It was none of his business, if he could just stop thinking about those six days.

How had he got so involved? Thank God he hadn't told her he loved her, although he'd come close in the magic early hours of that morning. It would only have put her in a more difficult position with her grandmother.

'That necklace is more valuable on its own than all of the stuff I stole.'

Her gaze flew to his and her next words suckered him. 'Do you feel better for saying that?'

'Not really.'

'You were sixteen. You had problems and you tried to solve them yourself with limited resources, which is admirable. When I was sixteen, I rarely left the *house*! I was afraid of everything, not just the dark.' He tried to say something, but she cut him off with a shake of her head. 'And Charlie wouldn't know a real problem if it bit him on the protein-shake biceps. I know who I admire most out of *everyone* who is going to be there today.'

'I don't think anyone shares your opinion.'

'I don't care,' she said, slinking her arms around his waist and pressing her cheek to the lapel of his suit.

'Yes,' he said gently, running his fingertips over her jaw, her ear. 'You do. You are a cœur tendre, a tender heart, and I wouldn't change it.' Even if it meant they couldn't be together.

'*You* have too much courage for other people and none for yourself! And, as much as I love that about you, sometimes I wish you could see yourself how I see you.' She drew back and fetched her clutch purse. She couldn't have any idea of the turmoil she'd landed him in with those words.

Did he have the courage to believe she truly saw him as an equal? And what would it mean for them if he did?

* * *

The daylight felt harsh and bare, after the magic of Ren's Paris nights. Even the quiet of Christmas Day, with fewer pedestrians on the paths and fewer cars on the cobbles, didn't bring Ren any relief from the feeling that today would ruin a lot more than her diet.

They stood on the footpath outside Sacha's apartment, holding hands as though they were about to jump off a cliff. Her mind was jumbled, angry that Sacha kept putting distance between them and confused about what her grandmother and Ziggy really wanted from her. An increasingly panicked part of her brain was trying to find a way to stay in Paris longer.

Bilel collected them, pointing out good-naturedly that his family didn't celebrate Christmas anyway, when she protested about him working on the holiday.

Before she was ready, they passed through the gap in the buildings and the Place Vendôme opened out before her. *Where it had all started* – the fake relationship, anyway. The car eased to a stop outside the Ritz and she reached for the door handle, but Bilel's voice stopped her.

'Mademoiselle,' he said quietly, 'I will be in the underground car park over there.'

'Okay,' she said in confusion. 'I hope you brought a book.'

'I wanted to let you know in case... I will be nearby. I know Monsieur Charlie will be there, and Madame Ziggy. You only need to call, and I can be here.'

Her stomach churned when she realised that even Bilel had seen how weird her life was. She squeezed his shoulder. 'Thank you, Bilel. I appreciate it – so much.' Bilel and Sacha exchanged a few words, ending with, 'Salam,' and then Ren took a deep breath and stepped out onto the smooth pavement. 'What did he say to you?' she asked when Sacha came around to her side, shivering inside his old coat.

'He said he's glad I'm with you,' he explained in a clipped tone.

'I've known him for years, but I feel like I'm only just getting to know him – like I woke up from a long sleep.'

'La belle au bois dormant? That's a fairytale, too. Sleeping Beauty, no?'

'Then if you woke me up, you must be a real prince.' Even her joke was half-hearted. They both knew he wasn't a prince.

Their colourful party was in a private room near l'Espadon, with resplendent baroque cornicing, gilded swirls and little cherubs watching them as though they were performing a play – or they were a strange, human experiment. Ren realised with a shiver that she no longer felt at home within these walls. Even the fragrant fir in the corner, tastefully decorated with hints of silver and gold and a small star on top, felt perfunctory and indifferent.

'Are you okay?' Sacha murmured in her ear.

'It feels so strange all of a sudden, like something from another life. I'm worried I'm going to argue with Grandmama and Ziggy.'

'I know what you mean,' he muttered through clenched teeth.

'Ren, darling!' Grandmama swept over to them in an elegant black gown and pressed kisses to her cheeks. But the gown made her look gaunt, and was Ren imagining it, or did her hands not have their usual superhuman strength?

'Merry Christmas, Grandmama.'

Livia's kisses for Sacha were also unexpectedly civil, but a smirk from Charlie before he pressed a kiss to Ren's cheek made her shiver with misgiving. She was reading too much into this, wasn't she? The prospect of leaving Paris was simply upsetting her and she was seeing ghosts of trouble where there weren't any.

They were seated opposite Charlie and Charlotte, and a fleet of waiters appeared with champagne to begin the festivities with toasts that were little more than empty platitudes. The waiters furnished the table with silver baskets of fresh bread and decanters of olive oil and Ren broke off a piece so she had something to do with her hands.

'You might skip the bread,' Ziggy said sharply from across the table. 'People will understand you've been enjoying the delicacies of Paris, but tolerance will only go so far.'

Sacha breathed out through his nose. His jaw was tight – his whole body was tight. 'I thought her name was valuable enough without exploiting her body, too.' Every pair of eyes averted themselves. Ren's hand flew to his thigh, her first instinct to hold him back. It brought her a thrill to realise that he wanted to say more, but was restraining himself.

'I see you know little about haute couture and a bit too much about her body,' Ziggy said. 'Waistlines are *very* small.'

'I assumed you would pay more to have them tailored to her natural shape.'

'Of course they are tailored,' Grandmama snapped.

Sacha's only response was to reach for the olive oil and set it in front of her. When the waiters arrived again bearing the entrée, he leaned down to whisper into her ear, 'I'm sorry,' his lashes fluttering against his cheeks.

She wasn't sure whether he was apologising for something he'd done or something he was going to do.

37

Sacha stared at the little collection of shells on his plate and the array of forks of varying sizes. Nom de Dieu, he was living some kind of cliché. He'd only eaten escargot once in his life and that was at a professional development seminar in an outdated conference centre in the Dordogne. He hadn't liked them. The snails were probably more tender at the Ritz, but just the thought made his stomach turn – especially as he was already on edge.

He had the feeling that something was going to happen to stuff Ren back into her box and he couldn't stand the thought. So much for his resolve not to cause trouble. The powerless feeling reminded him of the time after his father had died, which was... concerning.

First, he had to take a chance on a fork. He recognised the little set of tongs to hold the shell, but there was such an astonishing array of silver implements to his left that he could only assume the next courses would involve duelling with an assortment of other strange animals. Or perhaps the elaborate cutlery was just designed to make outsiders feel ignorant. Ren nudged him and gestured with the two-pronged fork she'd selected from her arsenal.

'You don't like escargot, Mr Mourad?' Ziggy asked. 'I'm sure we could order you some fried chicken and fries – or would you prefer lamb kofta?'

'Thank you for the offer, but I'm fine.'

'We ate fresh lobster last night,' Ren said. It wasn't the first time she'd defended him in a roundabout way. It only reminded him of how much Ren disliked conflict. 'It was still crawling when it was delivered!'

'How disgusting!' Charlotte piped up.

'It wasn't crawling when we ate it,' Sacha muttered.

'It was delicious, actually. We baked and played games and it was... a real Christmas,' Ren continued.

'You could order lobster, if that's what you'd like to eat,' Livia spoke up, her tone full of concern. He had the impression that something had aged the matriarch since the weekend. Perhaps the theft had affected the company more than she wanted to let on. He hoped not.

'I had enough last night, thanks. Would Ziggy let me eat it, anyway?' Ren asked, her voice light.

'I'm sure when... when you've got this out of your system, we can work something out with your diet. I only want you to come home and be happy,' Livia continued.

'What's this, all of a sudden?' The table fell silent. Charlie's parents' gazes were carefully averted, but Charlie himself watched with interest. Ren drew herself up. 'Why are you all tiptoeing around me?'

'What's strange about your grandmother being concerned for your wellbeing?' Livia asked. 'Especially when you've opened yourself up to all kinds of problems.'

'"Problems"?' Ren repeated. 'Everyone knows you're talking

about Sacha, but you can leave him out of this. The only one who has a problem with Sacha is you, not me.'

'Darling, you're confused and you're hurt.'

'Yes, by *you* and by *him* respectively,' she said, tossing her head in Charlie's direction.

'I knew I gave you too long to indulge yourself. He's got to you, but you'll see clearly in time. You're vulnerable on your own.'

'I'm seeing clearly right now and I'm always vulnerable. The more *you* try to keep me safe, the more vulnerable I feel!'

Sacha's nails dug into his palms. He had flashbacks to that Sunday night, when he'd stared at her in the dim light of a lamp as she'd slept the hibernation of emotional exhaustion. He wanted to stand in front of her, Alexander with his sword, but he needed to let her wield her own sword.

'You think you're safe with him?' Ziggy asked pointedly. 'Haven't you wondered what he wants from you?'

'Not everyone is like you, Ziggy. Some people value each other for themselves, because we're people who exist on the same earth. Not everyone is out to get me. I've learned that.'

'But you're not like other people,' Livia interrupted before the stony-faced Ziggy could respond more harshly. 'Your money makes you—'

'I *am* just like other people. It's a good thing. I didn't know how to catch a train or peel a potato, but I'm not so different that I can't have... friends. I'm not an asset to write on your balance sheet – and write off when I screw up your plans!'

'You know that's not what I meant.'

'Not consciously, but it's the message you're sending. I'm a liability, a crack in your impregnable empire.'

'Ren, stop this.'

'No, Grandmama, listen to me. I am that crack and I'm okay with that, whether you are or not. I'm not going to shut out the world any more. I want to be strong enough to deal with it my way, instead. No matter what you've done to protect me, you couldn't – not from the things I feared most.' Livia's face flushed red and her hands shook. Sacha wished he didn't know what she was talking about. *Six days...* He clutched his hands into fists. 'The darkness is there – everywhere. I still have to find a way to breathe.'

'What nonsense is this? Has he been giving you hashish? I swear, I will have every policeman in Paris after you—'

'It's not marijuana. It's poetry,' Ren explained.

'Poetry? Literature never fed anyone,' Livia said dismissively.

'As if we ever had to worry about being *fed*! This is exactly my point. I'm sick of being afraid because you are. I value our heritage, but not enough to give up everything just so I can be dressed in bloody haute couture!'

'You may wish you'd never opened yourself up to this, to *him*,' Livia continued, her tone oddly choked. 'Whether you like it or not, money has always stood between the two of you.'

'Isn't that right, Sacha?' Ziggy began, much more controlled than her employer. He unfortunately couldn't argue with that.

'You just bided your time, waiting for the opportunity and she handed it to you on a plate, gave you her misguided trust when she was most vulnerable.' The open hostility in Livia's voice made Sacha's skin prickle with misgiving.

He'd made everything worse for Ren. She was finally speaking her mind, paving the way for a more honest relationship with her only living family member, and his presence only weakened her position. 'I have no idea what you're talking about, but I'm happy to leave, if that's what you would prefer.'

'Stop it!' Ren cried. 'If he goes, I'm going, too.' Sacha's stomach dropped. He shouldn't have come. And he definitely shouldn't have been so close to losing control. The outcome of this many feelings could only be disaster.

Ziggy stood slowly, a sly smile on her face, and walked to the door of the room, gesturing to someone outside. 'Where he's going, you might not want to follow, Ren.'

Three police officers stalked into the room and Sacha fought the irrational urge to flee. His vision blurred and all he could think about was the firearms on their hips and the distant memory of cowering in his bedroom and watching a different group of officers drag his father from their apartment. He should be wondering what was going on, but a sense of fatalism filled him instead.

Why had he ever thought this would end differently?

Ren groped for his arm, but he disentangled her fingers and stood. 'Qu'est-ce qui se passe?' he asked the officers what was wrong.

'Sacha Mourad?' one officer asked. 'Nous avons quelques questions à vous demander concernant le vol d'un panneau de vitrail de la galerie Asquith-Lewis.'

'Quoi?' he huffed in disbelief. They thought he'd *stolen* the stained glass?

'What's going on? He hasn't done anything!'

Livia strode around the table to place a comforting hand on Ren's shoulder. 'It will be all right, darling. He stole the glass panel but please don't blame yourself. It isn't his first crime, and he must have targeted you and manipulated you to get into Asquith-Lewis. We all make mistakes. I'm sorry this is such a shock and I wish I didn't have to deliver this news to you.'

Ren stood so quickly her elegant chair tipped over. 'He didn't steal anything!' She turned to Ziggy. 'Did you convince her of this nonsense?'

'You brought him to the gallery, Ren. He is a known thief, with contacts in the antiques market,' Ziggy said.

'He was a kid who was grieving, who made a mistake, not a "known thief". And he has friends at the antiques market, not *contacts*! Did you have him investigated?' Sacha hated making Ren defend him, but if he defended himself, where would that leave her?

'Of course we had him investigated,' Livia said soothingly. 'I only wished we'd discovered what he really wanted sooner.'

'You have no idea what I really want,' he said, his voice wavering alarmingly. 'And I have taken nothing from you or from Ren.'

'He couldn't have stolen anything!' Ren insisted.

'I'm sorry I let him have such an influence on you—'

'It's not a matter of trust. It's simple logic. The panel was stolen on Monday night. *I* was with him on Monday night – the whole night! He couldn't possibly have stolen it.'

'But Charlie said—' Livia's gaze darted between Ziggy and Charlie.

'Just what did Charlie say?' The steel in Ren's tone made Sacha unbearably proud of her, but she was still one person and she couldn't change the world.

'Poor Ren,' Charlie said, making Sacha's stomach turn. 'Did you pay him for the whole day, today? I'm sure he'll issue a refund under the *circumstances*.'

'I was saddened to hear you had to resort to such desperate measures as paying someone to pose as your boyfriend,' Livia said. 'I promise, I will look after you better. But, for now, you don't need to pretend any more.'

Silence rang out in the room and Charlie's parents, at least, had the good grace to look shocked and dismayed, even if no one else did. Sacha's ears rang as he watched Ren's face fall and there wasn't a thing he could do about it. She might not have paid him, but their relationship *wasn't* real – well, not the way they'd presented it to Ren's family.

Ren looked at Sacha, biting her lip and he shook his head

gently, willing her to understand that none of this was her fault. The officers wouldn't take anything from him but a few hours of his time, because they both knew he was innocent. If she kept fighting, he would be tempted to do the same and the outcome of that wouldn't be good for anyone.

But instead of keeping her mouth shut and untangling the mess later, she spoke. 'I wasn't pretending – not at the end,' she insisted. 'And I truly was with him all night on Monday night. He never accepted any money from me. This might have started as a ruse, but... it's not, now.'

He stared at her, at the light in her eyes that made him want to whisper the words he'd almost said to her a dozen times, now.

'But you – Ziggy said—' Livia's words petered out.

'You know he reported the panel to the French Ministry of Culture?' Ziggy said evenly.

Guilt pricked him, on top of everything else. 'That's the only thing I have done,' he murmured. 'I'm sorry. I should have told you. I tried, on Christmas Eve, but...'

'You see, darling? You can't go through life trusting people.'

'Mais si, she fucking can!' Oh, no. He'd started cracking. Every eye was on him, jaws hanging open. 'She can trust who she wants, who she decides deserves her trust. Ren has a soft heart but she's not stupid!'

'And you deserve her trust?' Livia choked. 'After going behind her back to report us to the police? After stealing our property and undermining our business?'

The dismay on Ren's face struck him, but he couldn't stop now. 'Do you think Ren should take your example and only trust in money? Or do you think she should trust Ziggy, the woman who destroys her confidence and wants to turn her into someone else?'

'Ziggy *saved* this company!' Livia said.

'She saved the company and made Ren's life miserable,' Sacha huffed. 'And you made her lonely. Do you think she should trust *you?*' *Tais-toi, tais-toi, tais-toi.* He tried to stop himself, but his feelings would not be subdued. 'Six days. *Six. One* was too many.'

Livia went suddenly white. Her horrified look confirmed his worst suspicions, but he'd never been so sorry to be right. He couldn't fix this for Ren any more, not even by leaving.

He didn't have any control over his feelings. If she hated him for interfering, then so be it, but he couldn't roll over and die like a tragic romantic hero – not when she hadn't said goodbye, yet.

38

The hairs on the back of Ren's neck rose to hear that fierce tone from Sacha, the anger in his voice on her behalf. He knew about the kidnapping. Why was he throwing it back at Grandmama? And why did the indomitable matriarch look as though she could keel over at any moment?

'Get him *out* of here!' her grandmother roared, when she recovered her composure. 'Now!'

'Do you know how much she has already sacrificed for this company that you love more than life? She's not like you. You can't force her to be without hurting her.'

'I am the only family she has, and she is *everything* to me!'

One police officer gave Sacha a shove and he stumbled in the direction of the door, but he turned back to Livia, his brow low. 'When did you discover that? After two days? Or three? How long did it take before you decided to find the money after all?'

Sacha's ferocious words were like nothing Ren had ever heard from him but then she realised what he meant and a wave of nausea swept through her. Her recollections swam before her eyes, jumbled as always. But what he said made sense – horrible, unbelievable sense. Even twenty years ago, why would it have taken so long to raise the money for her ransom? The company might not have been financially fit, but someone would have loaned Grandmama the money to pay it immediately – if that's what she'd wanted to do.

But of course it was so very like Grandmama to refuse to deal with criminals. Ren groped for the table to steady herself. Her eyes wouldn't focus.

Livia had let her down at her darkest moment and had never had the courage to admit it. Ren had assumed the disappointment and overprotectiveness had been a result of Ren's weakness, but had they come from her grandmother's own feelings of guilt, instead? Ren had been held back and constantly scared because of *Grandmama's* failings, and not her own.

'Ren, I'm sorry. I knew this would hurt you and… maybe I shouldn't have said a fucking thing.' Sacha's face came into focus, a few feet away, his expression grim.

'At least you thought I deserved the truth.'

'You deserve more than the truth. You deserve *better*.'

'Better? You think you're better for her than her own family?' Livia asked hoarsely.

'No,' he said. 'But *you* need to do better. Stop making her pay for your mistakes and appreciate the person she is, despite everything you've done to her. She was hurt and upset and she still reached out to my family, to a class of strange school kids. She is *extraordinary*.' His voice broke and it felt like her heart. He stumbled another few feet, herded roughly in the opposite direction by two of the officers. 'Learn how to love her properly!'

Her breath short, Ren stared at him, at the fire in his eyes. He didn't shy away from difficult truths, and he thought she was strong enough to face them, too. She hoped he was right. And she couldn't help wondering if his feelings were the same as what she felt for him.

I love you.

With a terse sentence in French to the police officers, Sacha allowed them to escort him out, leaving Ren alone, the foundations of her existence pitching. But, like that Friday night nearly three weeks ago, landing in a situation that was worse than anything she'd imagined gave her an unexpected sense of freedom. She was still breathing. Perhaps Sacha loved her.

She stared at the familiar face of her grandmother, and for the first time, she recognised the reserve in her tight expression, the hints that Ren had always interpreted as disappointment.

'Grandmama,' she choked, belatedly realising there were tears streaming down her cheeks. She waited for the harsh words, the admonition that she shouldn't cry in public, but even Grandmama couldn't shy away from the truth, now it was out in the open.

'Perhaps we should discuss this somewhere else,' Ziggy said with a gentleness that was all pretence.

'I'm not going anywhere with you,' Ren declared through her tears. 'Ever again!'

'Because of *him*?' Ziggy gasped.

'Yes,' she said steadily. 'And no. There are some things I'm no longer willing to do for the business.' She waited for the expected stab of guilt, for the reminder of everything Grandmama had sacrificed for her and their legacy, but instead, it was a stab of pain. Had Grandmama really valued money over Ren's wellbeing? What did that say about their illustrious family?

Ren stalked from the room with just a look to compel her subdued grandmother to follow. She dialled Bilel in the foyer. The presence of paparazzi outside the Ritz was a very bad sign. Once they were safely in the car, Bilel phoned the Préfecture de Police and turned the car in the direction of the Commissariat in the eighth arrondissement, where Sacha had been taken.

Ren turned to her grandmother. 'Phone the head of PR and tell them to deny Sacha's involvement in the theft. Did Ziggy tip the press off?'

Livia nodded, looking terribly frail. It wasn't exactly that frailty that made Ren's anger slowly ebb, it was the growing pity and the power it gave her to see past her own misguided sense of duty.

'There's no one in the office on Christmas Day.'

'Then phone them at home!'

'It's true, then. He didn't steal the panel? You weren't just... protecting him?'

'I was with him. All night. And that's what I'm about to tell the detective.'

'Then who did steal it? Ziggy was so certain it was him.'

'If you ask me, the first place you should look is the heir of Pierre Leclerq, since he stands to lose the most if the piece is seized by the state. You'll have to ask Ziggy later, but you both made a terrible mistake – a mistake we need to rectify right now.'

'But Charlie said that you'd never... have an affair... with a stranger. And we knew you were staying with Malou.'

'I didn't have an affair with a stranger.' Ren paused, wondering if she was strong enough to utter the truth now it couldn't hurt him. 'I fell in love.'

'But – it's – *how*? He's—'

'Please don't finish that sentence,' Ren said with a sigh. 'I'm already getting far too many *Lady and the Tramp* vibes here.'

'Lady and the what?'

'Never mind,' she murmured. 'How did you know I was staying with Malou?'

'Ziggy suspected your story was at least partially just bravado and had you tailed back to Malou's.'

'You had your own granddaughter tailed?'

'I was worried about you!'

'But Ziggy was only worried about me getting in the way of her plans! She manipulated you. She manipulated all of us. It's to her advantage that I have no interest in the business, you know.'

Livia stared ahead. They skirted the Opéra Garnier, its gold statues dull in the grey weather. The snow refused to fall on Paris on Christmas Day, but rain was threatening, as though the weather echoed Ren's feelings and bolstered the sensation of déjà vu.

'You should have told me the truth about what happened twenty years ago.' Livia baulked, but Ren couldn't stop now. 'We should have talked about it. Those few days were... a hollowness that never left me. I felt guilty that I couldn't wish the feelings away, like you did.'

'What would you have gained to know what a selfish, weak woman your grandmother is?' Livia snapped.

'It would have been better than not knowing you at all,' Ren replied sadly. 'I never understood why you were so distant with me. I couldn't work out what I'd done wrong, except to survive my parents. After the kidnapping, I had no friends, no interests of my own. Sometimes I felt like I didn't exist, like I died in that garage.'

Tears flooded her eyes afresh, but she didn't swipe at them. She didn't resist them at all, not when they were giving her strength.

'And you are saying this now... to hurt me?'

Ren's instinct was to interpret that sentence as disapproval, but she realised now it was more of Grandmama's feelings of her own inadequacy. 'I never meant to hurt you. I never *mean* to hurt you. All I wanted was a grandmother – nothing else.'

'Which is why you were never cut out to take over the company.' The bald words should have felt like a slap on the face, but Ren was oddly proud to agree with her. 'I did the right thing, steering you into the role Ziggy made for you. The company is our past and our future – our identity and our lives. If you don't have the stomach to take over the leadership, then where do you fit? I don't know and I'm afraid for you.'

Ren stared at her grandmother, marvelling that *she* could be so fearful. 'That's one thing I'm *not* afraid of, Grandmama. I would like the company to be stable and do well and I do appreciate that its part of my history, but I can't dedicate my life to it like you did. I'll always have other priorities. Couldn't I... couldn't I find somewhere else where I fit?' Had she just asked the matriarch if she could quit? Where had the courage come from?

'You are an Asquith-Lewis!' Livia exclaimed, her voice shaking.

The old Ren would have backpedalled and worried that Grandmama had drawn even further away. It had felt pathetic to want nothing more than the woman's love but now, Ren realised how courageous it was to keep hoping that Livia was capable of love.

She clutched her grandmother's hand, smooth from a rigorous skincare regime, but the arthritic knuckles a symptom of age that money couldn't combat. 'I will always be an Asquith-Lewis, and your only living relative. And I love you.'

Silence fell. As soon as the words emerged from her lips, Ren understood the power of them. She gave an inward salute to the spirit of Karim Mourad, who she felt certain would have understood the resolve that merely thinking those words had lent her over the past few days.

'I – those are not the words I expected from you,' Livia whispered.

'I know. But... it's my antidote. You should try it.'

'You want me to tell you I love you?' Livia said with a sniff. 'What will that change?'

'My outlook,' Ren suggested. 'The way I feel about who I am.'

'You put a lot of faith in words,' Livia said, her tone clipped.

'Someone once told me that there is power in words,' she said softly. There was a power in *hearing* the words, as well as saying them.

Even her preference for happy endings wasn't out of weakness, she realised. To believe that problems could be overcome and fairness and love could prevail, that required faith. She'd lost it, for a few days. She'd tried to rationalise the consequences of her feelings and accept an outcome she hadn't wanted. But her strengths didn't lie in the ability to understand and contextualise life. Those were Sacha's strengths.

Hers was faith, an area where he was sorely lacking. Could she make Sacha see it? Could she show him she didn't need to choose between her family and love? Would he take a step of faith for her if she asked?

The car came to a stop outside a police station with a stately stone façade and Ren's hope plummeted back to her shoes. From the moment she'd met him, she'd hurt him. He was being questioned by the police because of her, and this final humiliation was enough to test the faith of the most steadfast soul.

'I have to fix things with Sacha, Grandmama.'

She heard only an inarticulate sound from her grandmother and turned to her in confusion. What she saw made her shout in alarm.

'Grandmama! What's happening? Bilel! *Bilel!* Get me the defibrillator and then go! To the hospital, right now!'

39

'I still don't understand how you met Mademoiselle Asquith-Lewis.'

That makes two of us... Sacha had been sitting in the interview room for over an hour and had already outlined everything once, including his alibi for Monday night and his tip-off to the Ministry of Culture. But he gathered his thoughts to answer the young police officer, trying to tell the story more coherently this time.

'And after the crash, you went to a bar and searched for her engagement ring? Or do I have that wrong?'

'No, no, we went to the hospital in between and she got the ring stuck on her finger.'

'She needed a doctor to get it off?'

'No, we were at the hospital for me. I was hurt in the crash.'

'And after this night, you went back to see her?'

'I found her ring in my sweater.' The officer's withering expression was eloquent. 'It's a thick, woollen sweater. It got caught...' He had to agree he sounded like Scheherazade, spinning tales to save his own skin.

'And you came to the Ritz and... asked her on a date?'

'Not quite... Ren asked me to act as her boyfriend.' A smile tugged on the corners of his mouth. What a circuitous route they'd taken, but he wouldn't change a moment.

The officer blinked. 'And you have a tax registration for this... activity?' she asked drily.

He opened his mouth to protest that Ren had never paid him a centime, but the door of the interview room burst open to reveal another young officer who seemed equally disgruntled that something had actually happened on Christmas Day.

While the second officer beckoned the first out of the room, Sacha glanced around with unexpected contentment. The appearance of the officers, firearms on their hips and arms dangling over their bullet-proof vests, had prompted unpleasant memories, but he was oddly satisfied sitting in this interview room, trying to tell his disjointed and outlandish story.

Perhaps it was because a police interrogation room was preferable to a private dining room at the Ritz with Grandmother Asquith-Lewis and her Grand Vizier, Ziggy. In all the scenarios he'd envisaged, he'd never imagined that Ren's family would tip off the police and frame him for theft.

Photographers had captured all of his progress from the door of the Ritz to the back of a police car and, to top it off, he'd been wearing an accursed bow tie. He pulled the thing off and slapped it onto the table, wrenching open the top button of his shirt.

But in the midst of what should have been a wretched moment, he was wired with unexpected energy. He'd confronted Grandmama Asquith-Lewis. Like some trigger-happy teenager in starcrossed love, he'd lost his cool, because that was just how he felt about Ren.

He felt vindicated and obstinate and far from philosophical. Inside he was screaming that, if this was the worst that could happen, then fuck it. It had already happened, and he still wanted her. Why couldn't they screw the rest of the world and their expectations and just be together? His perception of inferiority was his own problem and it was a stupid reason to push away the woman he loved. If she wanted him, he would put up with a lot more than a snobbish matriarch, a few smears in the media and assorted minor injuries.

Putain de merde, he was practically in prison for her and the only concern he had was whether she could work things out with her grandmother, as she would undoubtedly want to do – his tender-hearted Ren. Why had he ever thought she'd have to choose? Her heart was big enough for both of them.

His bag had been searched, but not taken from him when he arrived, so he rummaged in the bottom until he found the notebook, turning it over in his hands. Instead of the usual stab of loss, his thoughts drifted back to Nadia and Christmas Eve. He sensed she was right and that, when he opened the book today, he would find something different to what he'd understood before and a niggle of fear still shivered through him at the thought of what he might discover. Nadia knew about life – and love – more deeply than he did. She'd taken chances and been hurt and... let things go. Why had he lived as though he was the only one in the world who had ever lost someone?

Ren had lost her parents, her childhood and her innocence. She'd learned to smile all by herself. But his father had died and that was it? His life had to be preserved in formaldehyde so he could relive the anguish over and over again every time he looked in the mirror?

He rubbed at his neck, remembering Ren's fingers there, the way the words of his tattoo had acted on her as a key in a lock, rather than the trigger of loss and confusion they had been for him, all these years. *Go back and read the notebook in this context.*

He took a deep breath and opened it. He flipped through the

first few pages, skipping over the short, dark poems with twisted metaphors, where Karim had laid bare his episodes of depression.

He finally paused on a poem entitled 'Just a Man'.

> *Two eyes, one heart*
> *Two lungs, one spleen*
> *Two ears, one mind*
> *Two kidneys, one skin*
> *Only half a soul.*
>
> *Two nights, one day*
> *Two breaths, one fear*
> *Two words, one truth*
> *Two deaths.*
> *One life.*

He'd read it many times, feeling sadness and regret in the lines, but that day, he noticed the chronology of the poem. A few pages before came a short verse that burst with colour and emotion, Karim entirely unable to contain himself at the birth of his daughter. That poem was easier to work out, because the title was 'Hope', which was the meaning of the name Nadia.

Then came a long gap, where Karim's suffering had receded for long enough that reaching for his notebook had been less necessary. Then he'd started to write again. Sacha didn't know exactly when.

He stared at the poem. *Only half a soul...* The meaning of it transformed before his eyes as he realised the subject was not the title, but the missing part, the thing *not* mentioned. It wasn't about being a man. It was about a woman. It was about his mother.

Two deaths... That part he understood. A part of Karim had died along with his wife. Nadia had been right. Sacha was afraid of loving like that. *One life...* The life he'd committed to Maman? Or had he meant that every man had only one life, one chance to say and do the things that needed to be said and done, one life to experience that kind of love.

Despite his failures, his father had left a powerful legacy and he suddenly realised Ren was right. Nothing Sacha said or did could alter that legacy. He had been fighting a futile battle for years, trying to keep the memory alive. But he didn't have to struggle. The memory *was* alive. Sacha understood, now, what it was to be flawed, to be afraid, and to love anyway. He suspected his father would have been horrified to see how long Sacha had resisted it.

Two words, one truth.

He could think of two words that expressed true loyalty and sincerity. *Je* and *t'aime.*

Sacha silently admitted to himself why he was content to sit at the police station and await his fate. It was a reprieve. He'd been set an assignment and he'd failed. He'd almost allowed today to be the end. He would have left her, the words unsaid, the story half-written.

Until the police had dragged him off for questioning and given him the chance to see his mistake.

He couldn't control what would happen in the future, but he could focus on writing history for a little while, instead of preserving it. He could say the words and see what happened.

He closed the notebook with a deep breath. Two eyes, one look. Two hurts, one remedy. Two fates, one thread. Two words – not said.

His father didn't feel so... gone any more.

The officer returned, announcing that he was free to go, and, for a moment, Sacha didn't believe it. 'There is someone outside. A friend of yours. She says she will also provide information. We are still investigating, so please do not leave Paris, but you can go home for now.'

Sacha shoved the notebook back in his bag and shot to his feet, his heart pounding. He followed the officer out into the foyer, trying to decide what to say to her first, but when he reached the waiting area, he froze.

'Malou?'

Ren's friend stood to greet him with kisses and a grave look. 'Come on. Can I drive you home?'

'Monsieur Mourad, one more thing,' the officer said, glancing at a computer screen. 'We have a bicycle in the system registered to your name. Could that be correct? It was recovered after a presumed theft.'

He blinked at the officer. 'Yes, it was stolen from the Place Vendôme.'

'Here's the address where you can collect it,' she said, handing him a card. He took it numbly, mumbling his thanks, before following Malou out into the deepening dusk, hoping for some answers.

'Is Ren okay? Did she send you?'

'Not exactly,' Malou said, sliding behind the wheel of her tiny Renault. 'I saw the news flash. But there's something else you don't know.'

'What?'

'Livia was rushed to hospital an hour ago.'

'Is she all right? What happened?'

'I don't know anything further, just that Ren is with her.'

'Which hospital?'

'You can't go! Livia just accused you of theft. Unfairly, I know, but whatever's happened, you're not going to help.'

He groaned, propping his forehead on his hand, then he swore violently. Hesitating only a moment, he pulled out his phone, tapping his foot as it rang.

She answered with a rush of words. 'Are you okay? Will they let you go? God, I'm sorry I'm not there! Grandmama—'

'I know,' he interrupted. *I love you.* 'They let me go.'

'Thank God. I was so worried.'

'I'm sorry for everything I said. I shouldn't have—'

'What was that? Can I see her?'

'I'll... I should leave you to...'

'Sacha...' she began, an odd ache to her voice. He clenched his jaw, afraid of what she might say. 'I'll phone you later.'

He ended the call, numbness stealing through him. When would she contact him and what would she say? It was an odd anti-climax after a day of revelations. Or had his outburst changed nothing? Ren had to be by her grandmother's side, and he was not welcome there.

He knew the course of history wasn't always kind, but... he'd only just considered the possibility of a damned happy ending.

'Give it some time,' Malou said quietly.

Time was something he and Ren had never had. 'Thanks for the lift. I live in Belleville.'

'I think everyone knows where you live by now.'

40

You saved her life...

Ren was exhausted and emotionally spent, the following afternoon. Only those words, from the kind doctor, had any meaning for her.

'The merger must be announced as soon as possible and Ren's position also clarified, were... something to happen suddenly,' Livia said from her place propped up in bed. Ren gripped her grandmother's hand more tightly, but said nothing.

'I'll work on a succession plan, but the merger will take the pressure off her in terms of decision-making. I've already got the solicitors drawing up the documents today and Gina and Manny are happy to move things forward quickly. At least we have the investors on side as a result of our meetings at the chalet,' Ziggy added.

You saved her life...

Was it wrong that she was proud of that frightening moment in the car yesterday, where she'd ripped open her grandmother's Chanel gown and slapped on the electrodes with a confidence she'd rarely felt before? Was it wrong to feel vindicated that, if it had been the end, some of her last words to her grandmother would have been 'I love you'?

Her grandmother hadn't only had a heart attack. On the way to the hospital, Livia had gone into full cardiac arrest, and the defibrillator and the first aid training Ren had taken religiously since she was fifteen had kept her alive. Holding her grandmother's frail hand in hers was so much more important to her than the investors, the merger and her place in the company.

'Did you release another statement about the theft?' Ren interrupted.

'First thing this morning,' Ziggy assured her. 'But no one is asking about that any more.'

'And you made it clear that the police are still searching for the culprit? That there are no suspects?'

'Yes, exactly,' Ziggy said in a tone that filled Ren with doubt. 'Really, that story has been forgotten already. The break-up with Charlie is old news, too. We can move on. Your position in the business is a bigger issue – and Livia's health, but I think I'm speaking for your grandmother when I say that sorting out succession plans will reduce her stress.'

Ren's throat closed in fear at the thought of something happening to Grandmama. But there was another alarm bell ringing in the back of her mind, something about Ziggy's false tone that she couldn't un-hear. Ziggy was using her own guilt against her.

'I've arranged a medical plane to return Livia to the private hospital in Surrey tomorrow. You'll need to be here at eight, but, in the meantime, I suggest you go back to the Ritz and clean up.'

'Ren,' Livia said suddenly, 'you look exhausted.'

'I'm fine,' she insisted.

'You're not. You're still in your gown from yesterday!'

'I didn't want to leave you in case...' This time, when Ren met her gaze, her grandmother looked suddenly weaker.

'Ziggy, give us a moment,' Livia said, some of her usual strength returning. Ziggy left reluctantly, with a deep frown. To Ren's shock, her grandmother lifted a frail hand, stroking her fingers through Ren's tangle of ginger hair in a halting gesture of affection. 'He was right, wasn't he?' she said, her usual curtness unable to disguise the enormity of what she was saying. 'About you? God knows he was right about a lot of things.'

Ren was speechless, watching her indomitable grandmother's expression crumble. 'Don't get upset, Grandmama. I'm here and I'll stay with you.'

'Humph,' she said with her accustomed sneer. 'An Asquith-Lewis doesn't roll over so easily.'

'What?'

'I always thought it was a weakness. You cared about *everything*. I was afraid you'd go through life being hurt, over and over and I... I know I haven't expressed myself very well, but you were the reason I've kept going all of these years. I'm not... sentimental, but I love you, in my way.'

'I think I knew that, deep down.'

'And now that you know the consequences of my poor choices twenty years ago? After everything I did to you, you can still believe it?'

'I can believe it.' It wasn't even difficult.

'I should have trusted in you, and I owe you an apology and an explanation. I thought I was invulnerable and... I'm not. When they brought you home, it... destroyed me and I realised what my stubbornness had cost you. I should have reacted differently, but I was terrified of the consequences for the company, for our family.

'I want to provide a lifestyle for you that equals the luxury I've enjoyed, but not only that. I do want you to be happy. I just haven't always been certain how to do that.' She glanced away. 'I see, now, that I passed on my anxieties to you. I thought I was doing the right thing. I can only... hope to do a better job for whatever time we have left.'

Ren clutched Livia's hand, careful of the cannula still strapped in place. 'This honesty is all I ever wanted, and we'll have time. I won't lose you yet.'

'So... tender. That's the word he used, isn't it? He's... a fascinating man. I'm not surprised he fell in love with you so quickly.'

'It... we never quite got that far,' she muttered. 'But this is quite a turnaround. Ziggy convinced you he was a thief.'

'Yes, well... perhaps I need to examine Ziggy's position in the new company after the merger. You were right, I made myself far too easy to manipulate. But whatever she is planning, nothing will be agreed unless you are happy with it. And I don't mean you will be in charge of the business. I mean if you want to step back, if you want to be a silent investor, it will be done. If you want to set up a charitable foundation, I will be your first donor. I have failed you for too many years and it shouldn't have taken a heart attack for me to realise it, darling.'

Tears poured down Ren's cheeks, making Livia humph again, but the familiar reaction didn't make Ren feel chastened. It made her smile fondly at the grandmother who had been the only fixture in her life, who had made mistakes, but was willing to mend things.

'Thank you,' she said softly.

'It is only what you deserve.'

'Love isn't about what you deserve.'

'Which is fortunate for me, after everything I've done. Will it help if I... apologise to him?'

'I don't know. You got him investigated by the police and called a thief in the press.'

'If he's put off by a few inconveniences, then he doesn't deserve you, anyway.' Livia lifted her chin.

'A few inconveniences? You were quite clear that you would never approve of him for me.'

'Yes, well... we are all wrong on occasion. Now go and get some rest. I hate to see you looking so dishevelled. Oh, and I expect to take that flight tomorrow morning alone with the doctors. You have business to attend to.'

'Business?'

'Yes,' Livia said with her usual steely tone. In terse sentences, she outlined her instructions and dismissed Ren with a simple turn of her head. Then she closed her eyes – to rest or feign resting, Ren couldn't tell. Ren couldn't help watching her for a moment, basking in the power of the words they'd exchanged and the hope she held for the future of her relationship with her grandmother.

'Stop looking at me with that sappy stare,' Livia snapped, and Ren grinned and pressed a quick kiss to her cheek.

As soon as she was out in the corridor, she rummaged in her bag for her phone. She'd plugged it in occasionally, discouraged each time to find that Sacha hadn't called again, even though she had told him *she'd* call.

She was surprised the phone screen lit up without needing another quick charge. But when she peered at the device through her tired and scratchy eyes, her confusion grew. Was that a different swirl of colour in the background?

She tapped her code and it worked, but she was sure the phone was slimmer. She opened a social media app with trepidation and when her own account appeared – the account that the marketing team from Asquith-Lewis also curated – her stomach dropped. Ziggy had swapped her phone.

'I asked the team to restore it from your cloud back-up. All back to normal,' Ren heard in her ear and whirled to find the woman herself heading back into Grandmama's room. 'That cheap thing you'd bought wasn't worth the lithium in the battery, so I sent it for recycling this morning. The sooner you can get back on Instagram, the better for all of us.'

Not all of us.

'Did you at least copy my contacts?'

'Why? Which contacts could you have that weren't backed up from your old phone?'

Ren swallowed her reaction with difficulty, but Ziggy didn't matter any more. She'd only ever made decisions with herself in mind anyway. Losing Sacha's number wouldn't stop her.

An Asquith-Lewis didn't roll over so easily.

* * *

'Et alors? Her phone's been off every time I've called.'

'Wasn't she supposed to call you?' Malou's voice on the phone was infuriatingly reasonable. Just as Nadia's smile was infuriatingly amused. She'd even brought Joseph and Raph to witness his utter inability to do anything useful until he'd seen Ren.

They'd all spent St Stephen's day encamped in his living room, alternately demanding drinks, complaining of boredom and reading a few pages of the books. Aside from escaping briefly to free his bike from police custody, he'd done little but pace since he'd woken up that morning.

'It's been nearly a whole day,' he grumbled to Malou.

An amused snort sounded down the phone. '*One* day. You can wait a bit longer for her, can't you?'

'Yes, but what if she needs me?'

'Not you, too? Everyone underestimates Ren.'

'You're right,' he admitted. 'It's not her I'm worried about. It's me. What if she doesn't want to call me? I've read the news. She's expected to assume more responsibility in the company.'

'I wouldn't worry about that.'

'That's easy for you to say. I didn't tell her I love her!' he blurted out. He was an imbecile who hadn't recognised the best thing in his life until it was possibly too late and was now blabbing the truth to everyone *except* the woman in question.

Nadia guffawed into her beer and Joseph was watching him with the same glint in his eye that he'd had the first time Sacha had drunk wine with dinner at eighteen and got a little too happy.

'Écoute, I have very little doubt that she'll contact you when she can, but if you're that worked up, then I'll call my manager. He might know more.'

'Merci bien, Malou,' he said, his voice rough.

'It's no problem. But I expect to be the godmother of your children.'

He spluttered some kind of reply, pretending he wasn't imagining for the first time a future opening up before him where he and Ren could be the happiest parents on the planet. But he didn't even care if children weren't in their future, he was just fixated on turning his nose up at fate and making this the love story of a lifetime.

A gruelling half-hour later, Malou finally called back, and her tone immediately alarmed him. 'All I found out is that Livia is being transported back to the UK tomorrow morning. You're right, Ren's phone is off. I don't understand. Perhaps she'll call tonight?'

He glanced out the window at the gathering dusk. 'I can't take the risk. Is she at the hospital now?'

'Either there or at the Ritz, I think. Ziggy is staying at the Ritz and I hope Ren hasn't been losing sleep at the hospital.'

'I wouldn't be surprised.'

'You start at the Ritz and I'll try to find out which hospital Livia is in.'

Barely stopping to mumble a farewell to his family, Sacha ripped his coat off the hook and ran for the stairs. Halfway down, he remembered his helmet and bounded back up to grab it. Memories flooded him as he unlocked his bike in the courtyard and pushed it through the doors into the damp evening.

Three weeks ago, almost to the hour, he'd done exactly the same thing, never expecting he'd be knocked down on the cycle path and his life would change.

He pedalled hard, flicking his lamp on when it grew darker. He hurtled along the boulevards, weaving between delivery cyclists and commuters, pushing miserably through the sleet. He burst out onto the Place Vendôme and came to a skidding stop in front of the Ritz, to the disapproving gaze of the doorman. Sacha glanced frantically up at the windows of the grand hotel, wondering if she was in the same room.

The doorman informed him in no uncertain terms that he was not allowed to lock his bicycle in front of the hotel. He nearly did it anyway, but he caught sight of a familiar black Mercedes slowly making its way around the square on the other side. Could it be...?

He threw his leg back over the saddle and took off after it. A glimpse of a red-headed passenger in the back made his heart leap. But where was she going?

The Mercedes accelerated away, but the pattern of straight boulevards and the usual Paris traffic allowed him to keep it in sight. He had a moment of panic outside the Opéra Garnier, searching for the black roof amidst a sea of slowly moving cars while also ensuring none of those cars ran him over, but he was fairly sure he caught sight of them skirting the opera house and heading north.

Pedalling along the cycle path of the Rue La Fayette, he

suddenly realised they were headed for the Gare du Nord. She was leaving? Without saying goodbye?

He pushed himself to pedal faster, sweat breaking out on his forehead. He wasn't too late yet. The sleet caught him in the eyes and his fingers were freezing inside his gloves, but he stared desperately ahead at the car and kept going. Skidding around a frozen puddle, he nearly took out a pedestrian and had to put his feet down and apologise.

The glittering lights reflected off the footpath and the headlights of the cars blinded him. He'd followed them nearly to the end of the long street and the train station was just ahead. At the intersection with the Boulevard de Magenta, he couldn't stop himself glancing to the right, his eyes searching for the place it had all started.

That moment of inattention was all it took.

A guy on a delivery bike cut in front of him and Sacha swerved to avoid the enormous box of pizza on the back. But he lurched straight into a turning car and, with a twisted sense of déjà vu, his front wheel bounced off the door and the asphalt raced up to meet him.

41

His shoulder ached. Puddles were soaking into his jeans and the helmet had saved him for the second time. He had the fleeting thought that, if this were an American film, he might discover that he'd gone three weeks back in time and had the chance to relive it all over and over again until he got it right.

One day would have done the trick.

Concerned faces appeared in his vision and he hauled himself into a sitting position. His jeans were torn at the knee and a graze was oozing a little blood. The pain in his shoulder was throbbing, but not debilitating. There were twinges in his wrist and ankle. He was okay – but he was also screwed.

He batted away concerned hands and scrambled to his feet, searching the intersection in case fate had been kind and Bilel had seen something and stopped. But the car must be long gone. Sacha's bike was mangled once more, but he still had his legs. He took off on foot for the Gare du Nord, hobbling and grunting in pain.

The station concourse was busy – and slippery – as the milling crowd tracked in the icy sleet from outside. Sacha was disoriented by all the people and the noise, the announcements that echoed up to the vast glass-and-steel ceiling high above and the Christmas lights dazzling him. But mostly, he was dismayed by how badly he'd handled everything.

You should have told her.

He found a sign for the Eurostar and followed it, his eyes crossing as he scanned the crowd for a familiar redhead. God, he missed her! And he was only beginning to realise how much he was going to miss her if he didn't find the words – and find *her*.

He went as far as he could through the Eurostar departures zone, but he couldn't see Ren. It would be just his luck if there was a first-class queue that was invisible to the common people. He stopped at the partition, unable to follow without a ticket and a passport. He beat a fist against the glass in frustration, but clutched his hand as the action sent pain shooting down his arm.

His phone rang, startling him, but Nadia's name flashed up and he refused the call with bitter disappointment. He had nothing to report, anyway.

Ren was leaving, going back to her real life. Perhaps nothing he said could have changed that, but could he live with not knowing? Some things in his history he'd been forced to accept. Would the end of this dream be one of them?

Nadia called again and this time he answered with a grumbled snarl.

She ignored him. 'How quickly can you get home?'

'Qu'est-ce qui se passe? What's happened? Is it Joseph? He should be resting. You should take him home! Don't wait for me, if he needs to go. I'll be shitty company, anyway.'

'Nothing new, there. Joseph is fine. He's even sitting down. But—'

'Then what could you possibly need?'

'You haven't found her, have you?' Nadia said drily.

'Of course I haven't,' he muttered. 'But I don't want to give up, yet.'

'Where are you? I thought you were going to the Ritz.'

'It's a long story. I'm at the Gare du Nord. I think she's gone, but...' He glanced up at the mezzanine floor above, where passengers were hurrying in the direction of the platforms. Might she see him if he yelled at the top of his lungs? 'I can't leave until I'm sure. If there's a chance...' Nadia laughed. 'What?' he snapped.

'What are you planning? If you get arrested for real, I'm not going to bail you out.'

'I'm not going to—'

'Calme-toi, frérot,' she said with a snort. 'And bring your butt back here. You're keeping her waiting.'

'Keeping her... *quoi*?'

'Guess who arrived on your doorstep ten minutes ago?'

He reeled, and he tripped on someone's suitcase and stumbled.

'Putain de sa mère!' He froze and pulled the phone from his ear to apologise profusely to the mother of the young child staring at him in horror.

'Are you still there? Or have you seen the light and you're on your way?' Nadia continued.

He took off for the métro. 'Oui, but I wrecked my bike again, so I might be a while. Don't let her leave!'

'Give me strength, Sacha! What were you doing?'

He hobbled across the concourse, gasping at the pain in his ankle he'd ignored until that point. 'Following her! I thought she was...' He realised what had happened with a choked laugh. 'She was going to my apartment. I thought she was—'

'Leaving you without saying goodbye? I hope you've learned to have a bit of faith, brother, in time to make it up to her.'

A wild grin stretched on his face, attracting odd looks. Or perhaps they were staring at his ripped clothes, his limp – or even the fact that he was still wearing his helmet. 'Thanks, Nadi,' he said, staggering in the direction of the escalators. 'I've learned.'

* * *

Ren wrenched the door open at the first scrabble of the key in the lock, making him stumble over the threshold, stubbing his toe.

'Aïe,' he cried, flailing for balance. She grasped his shoulders to steady him, but her hands slipped, seemingly of their own accord, and then her fingers were in his damp hair. He caught himself with one hand on the wall and his other arm closed around her. How had she missed him so much when it had only been a day?

Everything was suddenly right with the world, with his face so close and his gaze locked on hers. Ren brushed her fingers over his face – the crinkles at the corners of his eyes, the grooves on his brow, his kissable lips. She breathed out for what felt like the first time since Christmas Eve.

He was smiling – as much as he could beneath a furrowed brow – but her own smile faded when she caught sight of the spots of blood pricking through a graze on his cheek.

'What happened?'

'It's not important.'

She looked him up and down, noticing the smear of mud on his other cheek, the rip in his jeans and the way he was standing to favour one leg.

'I—'

'You're soaked!' She dragged him all the way inside and slipped off his coat. The front of his sweater was wet, too, so she pulled up the hem to slip it off, but she caught him in the face with her knuckles and he stumbled back a step, biting back a groan.

'What have I done to you?' she muttered in horror.

He pulled the sweater over his head himself and Ren pretended she wasn't gazing intently at the little strip of skin at his waistband as his shirt lifted. Yep, she'd definitely missed him. A lot. Did that make up for all the injuries she'd caused him? She bloody hoped so.

'You've done a lot to me,' he murmured, taking a limping step in her direction.

'Here, sit down. Do you need a cup of tea? Or a blanket? A towel. I'll get you a towel.'

'Don't you want to hear all about what you've done to me?'

There was a catch in his voice that sent a shiver through her. 'I know what I've done,' she said with dismay. 'I've wrecked your bike – twice, it would appear. I made you late for work. I dropped a table on your toe and forced you to attend the ballet. My ex-boyfriend insulted you. I dragged you up the Eiffel Tower and down a mountain. My family was rude to you for nothing and made you eat snails. And *then*, despite knowing how much it would bring back painful memories, I let the police take you away when I knew you were innocent! Is that a complete accounting of my crimes?'

Tears stung her eyes when she'd finished. It sounded so hopeless, all rattled off at once.

He shook his head slowly. 'It's not complete.' He gazed at her, lifting a hand to her cheek and biting his lip as he took a moment to breathe. 'You made me realise all my grandiose philosophising about life and love was simply hiding my fear. You made me realise what's important to me. You made me want something for myself and fight for it. You forced me to be happy. And then you convinced me I could love someone, after all. That's what you've done to me.'

The moment she heard the 'L' word fall from his lips, she wobbled, suddenly struggling to get enough oxygen to her brain. She lifted her face and he just looked at her, his brow low and his eyes burning.

But instead of kissing her, he asked, 'Have you read the book I gave you for Christmas?'

'Not yet,' she said in confusion. 'But I have it in my bag.'

'Go and get it.' She reluctantly released him to rummage in her bag for the canvas-bound volume, eying him in question. 'Page thirty-eight. Byron.'

Intrigued, she flipped to the page and, when she saw it, she slumped against the wall. Already there, added in pencil even before Christmas, was everything she'd ever wanted to hear.

> *She walks in beauty, like the night,*
> *Of cloudless climes and starry skies,*
> *And all that's best of dark and bright,*
> *Meet in her aspect and her eyes,*
> *Thus mellow'd to that tender light,*
> *Which heaven to gaudy day denies.*

She'd read the poem before, but it came to life for her then. Sacha's pencil had underlined every reference to dark and light. He'd circled the word 'smiles' in the third verse. The last line he'd enclosed in a box that he'd traced several times, the pencil line deep:

> *A heart whose love is innocent!*

And in the margin, he'd scrawled:

> *My light, my dark, my heart. Je t'aime.*

Her breath rushed back. 'I love you, too,' she whispered. Dropping the book to the table, she reached for him and nothing stopped them, this time. He tugged her close and said it all again in that kiss – fierce and passionate and so tender she saw stars.

'I'm sorry I hid it in a book instead of telling you. I'm sorry I nearly let this end. Je t'aime. I love you.' The way he said it, he sounded almost as giddy as she felt to hear the words. 'I love you,' he said again.

'Oh, c'est merveilleux! J'en étais sûr!'

'Bien joué, mon frère. It's over, grâce à Dieu. Everyone?' Nadia clapped her hands. 'Time to go!'

Ren buried her face in Sacha's neck, but peeked out at his wonderful family with a watery smile. They were the best kind of audience and she didn't mind having shared the moment with them, since it had brought so much happiness. Sacha's hand on the back of her neck assured her he wanted her right where she was, and she peered up at him as his family gathered their coats and shoes.

Joseph grumbled a bit, lingering to press kisses to Ren's cheeks and exclaim in English and French. Nadia squashed her in a powerful embrace and even Raph came close enough for her to squeeze his shoulder and see his tentative smile that reminded her so much of his uncle.

When the door closed behind them, Ren and Sacha didn't move for a long, silent moment.

'They've left us... quite alone,' he said thoughtfully.

'Blessedly,' she agreed.

'Do we... need to work anything out?'

'Did you say you love me?'

'Several times.'

'Did I say it back?'

'Only once,' he said sternly.

'I love you,' she repeated indulgently, pressing another slow kiss to his mouth.

'Is your grandmother very angry with me?'

She shook her head. 'She's had a... change of heart. The truth about the past can do that to a person.'

'C'est vrai?'

'She ordered me to come here and work things out – as if I needed any further encouragement. Ziggy erased your number, otherwise I would have called you.'

'I was afraid... En fait, I was afraid of a lot of things.'

'I know how that feels.'

'Did you say you lost my number for a second time? We must do something about your bad luck.'

'Definitely not! My luck has been boundless these past three weeks! Despite everything, I found you.'

'There are two ways to look at everything, I suppose.'

'Exactly,' she said. He grinned at her, his arms tight around her waist. 'And you might have to get used to the idea of a happy ending,' she continued.

'I think I can watch Disney films if that's what you want.'

She laughed, joy welling up in her chest. 'That's true love. But I meant for us. A happy ending for... our story. Because I've made us one. I'm not going back to London. I love Paris in winter, but I'd like to get to know the city in spring, too – and summer, and autumn!'

EPILOGUE

'This is the best Christmas present anyone has ever given me!'

Sacha couldn't help thinking he was the one receiving the gift, when her face lit up just as brightly as the Christmas displays in the shopfronts. But he hoped his other gift, the one he was still waiting to give her, would supersede this visit to Ren's ultimate fantasyland.

'Look, it's beautiful!'

She performed a slow turn, taking in the nostalgic row of colourful shops, glimmering with lights in the early winter morning. Old-fashioned lamp posts added a warm glow. They almost looked like antiques, except they were pristine and decorated with a large dose of imagination. She stopped to gaze at the castle at the end of the street, a slender pastel confection of turrets and spires, glittering with lights. The sky behind was stained pink with the late sunrise.

'Very beautiful,' he agreed, enjoying her smile when she realised he was looking at her and not the magic kingdom around them. At unexpected moments like this one, it struck him how

LEONIE MACK

terrible it would be if he lost her. But how much more terrible if he'd never met her?

'One day you'll appreciate the land of happily-ever-afters,' she said with a teasing shake of her head. Sacha was rather hoping today would be that day. 'No headless saints, no tragic heroes and no brutal swords. Let's make this a Boxing Day tradition,' she said, slipping her arm through his.

'Surely we don't need to come every year. It is a *buffet*, after all,' came a disapproving voice from behind them. 'There isn't even a dress code.'

'All are welcome in this kingdom,' Joseph declared with a sweeping gesture. He winked at Livia. 'And you know my suit jacket doesn't close any more.' Livia harrumphed, but she took his proffered arm.

'Perhaps we can alternate, just for you, Grandmama. Next year we'll come to Cinderella's palace instead. That's ten euros more expensive and you get to see all the princesses.'

'Ten euros! What difference would that make? I could have tea with a princess of England, and you want to come and see *fake* princesses!'

'I'm not so interested in the princesses, either,' Sacha agreed gravely, threading his fingers through Ren's.

'I thought fake princesses would be right up your alley,' she quipped.

'You are confused with real heiresses.'

'At least you know I don't like princes,' she said with a grin, lifting her chin for a kiss. 'When are they going to make a Disney film where the hero is a teacher?'

'Films about teachers are usually the *comédie noire*,' Sacha said with a snicker.

'You can keep your black comedy. I'd like breakfast.'

'Me, too!' agreed Raph emphatically.

'Grâce à Dieu, someone else can provide his enormous meals today,' muttered Nadia.

They filed into the whimsical restaurant, Sacha's makeshift family and Ren's tiny one. She tugged on his hand before they reached their table, pulling him close. 'Isn't it amazing?'

'I'm glad you like it.'

She grinned at him. One year and three weeks since he'd first seen that smile, it still had the power to reorder his priorities in an instant. 'I didn't mean Disneyland, although I am up in the clouds to be here. I mean our families. I never could have expected that Joseph was just the friend Grandmama needed. He accepts her as she is. And Nadia treated me like a sister from the first day. I love them all so much.'

She blinked, her eyes suspiciously moist, and he wondered wryly if she'd peaked too soon. He wrapped his arm around her neck and drew her against him. 'Shh, mon amour. You're hungry and there are Disney characters waiting.'

Her head snapped up and he released her with a chuckle as she rushed off to take photos with the dog and the duck and the famous mouse. He could wait to say what he had to say until after she'd eaten.

She wasn't a princess in a tower any more, but he would take her to the castle and do his best to make a fairytale out of their love story.

* * *

Breakfast was divine and decidedly mouse-shaped. Like four-inch heels, Ren's tiny waistline had never been seen again after last Christmas and she didn't miss it. She couldn't quite face any delicacies from the Christmas tree of macarons, but she otherwise enjoyed every crumb of croissant and every morsel of cheese.

Disneyland Paris had woken up by the time they wandered out into the weak winter sun. Perhaps Sacha wasn't quite as enthusiastic as she was about the fantasyland of an imaginary world, but she loved that he'd thought to bring her here. And although she would enjoy her day soaking up the Disney innocence, she wouldn't mind returning to the real world that evening.

The little apartment in the twentieth, full of old books and new love, felt more like home than any of the grand houses or luxury flats she'd ever lived in. Their bicycles were locked up together in the courtyard, ready to take Sacha to school and Ren to the office each morning – the office of the Asquith-Lewis Foundation, which was tucked into the attic floor of the galleries, next to Malou's.

'Let's go in the castle,' Sacha suggested, taking her hand. He'd had a glint in his eye all morning, as though he were stifling a smile. She had been a little ridiculous in her enthusiasm, but she was so touched by his thoughtfulness.

They left the others behind and passed through the portal of the Sleeping Beauty castle. She gazed up at the vaulted gothic ceiling, supported by columns shaped like twisty trees. Sacha led her up the steps to the stained glass that told the story of the Disney film, complete with the three good fairies.

'Don't tell me these are of national cultural significance,' she joked. 'I still feel bad that fragment was lost.'

He pulled her against him, her back to his chest. 'It's part of our history.' The way he held her reminded her of the night they'd climbed the Eiffel Tower – another piece of their history, woven into the city they called home. He began speaking with a strange catch in his voice and his words revealed she wasn't the only one thinking about that night. 'I thought about taking you up the tower again, but you said we had to wait ten years and... then I thought this would be better.'

She glanced at him, the close view of his profile bringing back a flood of memories. 'You know I wasn't thinking about Charlie that night.' His soft gaze affected her just as much as it had the night they'd met. 'I never thought I'd be brave enough – or you'd want me enough – to change our lives. I was hoping things would change around us and we could try again after ten years.'

'It's strange to remember what I thought a year ago. I underestimated you.'

'You underestimated yourself, too. You should have seen the look on your face when you snarled at Grandmama.'

He grimaced. 'I gave her a heart attack.'

'You did not. I love your sense of responsibility, but you overdo it sometimes. Besides, a dose of the truth was just what we all needed. Are you going to tell me what you meant when you said this is better? Or have you written it in a book somewhere and I have to find it?'

His smile was quick and self-deprecating. 'I do have some words for you.'

'I love your words.'

He turned his face to her temple. 'I was... hoping we could write some history together, continue a tradition – scandalise your grandmother a little more.'

Her heart began a little flip-flip and her breath stalled. Was he asking what she hoped he was asking? This was already the best day of her life. Could she possibly be so happy? 'I'm in,' she said without hesitation.

'I haven't finished.'

'I don't care. Yes.'

He gave a little huff. 'Irena Asquith-Lewis, ma reine – my Ren.' He paused and lifted his closed fist in front of her with a flourish. The familiar shadows of the tattoo on his wrist peeked out, always reminding her of the night she'd checked his pulse before she'd asked his name. 'Will you marry me?' He opened his hand to reveal a stunning Art Deco ring, glowing with three rectangular sapphires.

'Yes,' she breathed, closing her hand over his. The ring was lovely, but mainly because it sat in *his* hand. 'I believe I already said yes. A thousand times, yes.' She turned to kiss him. The moment was perfect: the gothic fantasy of the Disney castle, the memories of a year ago, the kiss that promised a future she'd never known she wanted and reminded her of all the kisses they'd shared, from the very beginning. His arms tightened around her, lifting her a few inches off her feet as he tilted his head and kissed her deeply.

'A thousand and one times, perhaps?' came a deep voice behind them, just before applause erupted and Ren opened her eyes to see their family gathered by the stairs, smiles on their faces and tears in their eyes.

'What are you talking about?' Grandmama asked Joseph, dabbing at her eyes with a handkerchief as though her tears were a nuisance.

'The Arabian Nights. Sacha is Aladdin, you see?'

'I don't see at all.'

'I will take you to see the Passage Enchanté d'Aladdin and you can see scenes from the film. Sacha should have proposed there!'

'He *should* have proposed at my house, if he had any manners.'

'He loves with too much passion for manners, Livia.'

'Manners are deeply preferable to passion!'

Sacha and Ren chuckled at their fond bickering and he grasped her hand. 'Just let me get the ring on. I checked the size, so it won't get stuck.'

'It would be just my luck if it did get stuck – my good luck. I'm never taking it off.'

He brushed his thumb over one side of the ring. 'I chose this shape because it's straight here. That's where the wedding ring will go.' She couldn't doubt the earnest warmth in his eyes. 'I'm glad you knocked me off my bike that night. And I'm glad I was the last man in Paris who belonged with you.' Tears pricked her eyes. 'Because I fell in love with you despite all that. If it hadn't looked so wrong, I never would have believed it was right.'

'I think I always knew you were the one for me,' she murmured. 'From the moment I looked into your eyes after the accident. I just needed a little faith in myself.'

Ren glanced through the atrium of the fairytale castle, at the wide sky, and she thought of history and poetry, words and memories, everything she held inside her. Her story would be told with a thread of love that refused to break. It wasn't an ending, but it was certainly happy.

ACKNOWLEDGMENTS

I spent a rather overwhelmed few months in Paris in my head (sadly not in reality) while drafting this book, struggling to do that amazing city justice, deciding which places to use as settings and which to leave out (with a heavy heart). I thought back through all my visits to Paris in the past and the people I shared it with, so all of you were in my heart as I wrote. My darlings Megan Hadgraft and Sarah Radcliffe will always be in Paris with me in spirit (thanks for coming to the Museum of Cocks with me, Meg!), as well as Sue M. Sam and my boys, too – we made different sorts of memories that trip. And, going further back to my first trip, two others who were strangers before we met on the way to Paris and who became strangers again afterward. Thanks for the frankfurter sausages and baguettes!

Perhaps there is a little bit of magic in Paris for visitors, because my husband and I were both there on Valentine's Day the same year – we just hadn't met each other yet!

An especially big thanks this time go to Lotte R. James and Calli Arena for correcting my passionate, but not particularly accurate French (no matter how hard I tried with the accents!) and for your enthusiasm for this project (by which I mean Sacha, of course). And my Lucys, Keeling and Morris, you guys were lifesavers this time, listening ears, calming influences and sharers of frustration.

Every day, I am thankful for the amazing work of the team at my publisher, Boldwood Books, in getting my words out to readers. And my editor, Sarah Ritherdon, has worked her magic again, allowing me to blurble out some kind of story and she tells me what works and what doesn't! Knowing you will run your analytical eye over my book gives me the freedom to get into the story without second-guessing myself all the time.

This book made me reflect on how we are touched by creative works, from the everyday in-jokes and shared history of families to books and films and popular culture. Without the music, books and films that touched me and made their way, in little pieces, into this book, the world would be a more barren place. It's sometimes difficult or embarrassing, it takes a step of courage, but thank you to all the people out there who use words and images, technology, music and soul to create something. Be proud.

MORE FROM LEONIE MACK

We hope you enjoyed reading *Twenty-One Nights in Paris*. If you did, please leave a review.

If you'd like to gift a copy, this book is also available as an ebook, digital audio download and audiobook CD.

Sign up to Leonie Mack's mailing list for news, competitions and updates on future books.

https://bit.ly/LeonieMackNewsletter

A Match Made in Venice, another wonderful read from Leonie Mack is available to order now.

ABOUT THE AUTHOR

Leonie Mack is a bestselling romantic novelist. Having lived in London for many years her home is now in Germany with her husband and three children. Leonie loves train travel, medieval towns, hiking and happy endings!

Visit Leonie's website: <u>https://leoniemack.com/</u>

Follow Leonie on social media:

 twitter.com/LeonieMAuthor

 instagram.com/leoniejmack

 facebook.com/LeonieJMack

Boldwood

Boldwood Books is an award-winning fiction publishing company seeking out the best stories from around the world.

Find out more at www.boldwoodbooks.com

Join our reader community for brilliant books, competitions and offers!

Follow us
@BoldwoodBooks
@BookandTonic

Sign up to our weekly deals newsletter

https://bit.ly/BoldwoodBNewsletter

Lightning Source UK Ltd.
Milton Keynes UK
UKHW041009181022
410668UK00003B/22

9 781804 158357